Mermaid Magic

Gwyneth Rees is half Welsh and half English and grew up in Scotland. She went to Glasgow University and qualified as a doctor in 1990. She is a child and adolescent psychiatrist, but has now stopped practising so that she can write full-time.

She is the author of many bestselling books, including the Fairies series, the Mermaid series, the Magic Princess Dress series, the My Super Sister series and the Cosmo series, as well as several books for older readers. She lives near London with her husband, Robert, and their daughters, Eliza and Lottie.

Mermaid Magic

Gwyneth Rees

Illustrated by Annabel Hudson

MACMILLAN CHILDREN'S BOOKS

First published 2001 by Macmillan Children's Books

This edition published 2016 by Macmillan Children's Books
an imprint of Pan Macmillan
20 New Wharf Road, London N1 9RR
Associated companies throughout the world
www.panmacmillan.com

ISBN 978-1-5098-1869-3

1 3 5 7 9 8 6 4 2

A CIP catalogue record for this book is available from
the British Library.

Typeset by SX Composing DTP, Rayleigh, Essex
Printed and bound by CPI Group (UK) Ltd, Croydon CR0 4YY

For Mum and Dad, with love

Chapter One

Rani swam down through the turquoise water until her belly was flat against the sandy bottom of the seabed. Then she did a quick flip with her tail so that she somersaulted upwards again.

"*Show-off!*" she heard, as she flicked her hair out of her eyes.

She looked suspiciously at her pet sea horse, Roscoe, who had been perched on a nearby rock with his mouth shut the whole time, looking innocently in her direction. Strange things had been

1

happening to Rani recently. She kept hearing odd, whispery words when nobody near her had spoken. At first she had thought it was just Roscoe playing tricks on her but the little sea horse had denied it.

Before she could give it any more thought, the conch sounded. That meant it was time for them to go back into the school cave for more lessons. Rani swam over to where her sister, Kai, was sitting on a rock twisting her long blonde hair into a tight spiral. Rani hadn't told Kai about the strange whispers. For some reason she felt that she should keep them secret. Which was strange because she and Kai always told each other everything.

"School is boring, boring, boring,"
complained Kai loudly, letting go of her
hair so that it swished out into a gold
mass that enveloped her. She flicked
herself off the rock and kicked up a load
of sand with her tail, nearly bumping
into Marissa and Marina, the twins, who
swished their golden tresses outwards

3

proudly as they swam by.

Rani sighed. She wished she had beautiful golden hair like all the other mermaids. Her mother kept telling her that her red hair was beautiful too, but Rani didn't think so.

The conch sounded again just as a whole shoal of rainbow fish swam past, heading towards the reef at top speed.

"What's the hurry?" Kai called out after them.

"Our babies are hatching!" one of the fish called back.

"Wow!" exclaimed Kai. "I've never seen baby fish hatching before. Let's go and see!"

And before Rani had time to protest that they really should go back to school,

Kai had set off after the fish.

"I suppose we could always say we didn't hear the conch," Rani muttered doubtfully, as she followed her sister.

Rani loved Tingle Reef. The water was warm and crystal clear and the reef was full of friendly sea-creatures who all lived happily together in their colourful underwater home. It was the only home Rani could remember. She had been found as a baby by Kai's parents inside a Giant Clam-Shell at the edge of the reef. No one knew where Rani had come from and it was a mystery how she had got there. Kai's family had adopted Rani as their own. Rani felt that Murdoch and Miriam were the best parents she could wish for and that Kai was the best sister.

The only time she ever felt different was when anyone commented on her appearance.

Rani looked very different from the other mermaids. It wasn't just her hair. Her scales were a deep orange colour whereas all the other mermaids had green tails. Instead of having eyes that were sea-blue or sea-green, Rani had goldy-brown eyes. In fact, Rani's mother often joked that Rani didn't look like she came from the sea at all.

Kai suddenly stopped dead in mid tail-flip and Rani crashed right into her. She was looking at the rainbow fish, whose pink and yellow stripes made them the most colourful of all the fish in the reef.

"Look. There are the baby ones," Kai whispered to Rani, pointing at the tiny fish who had just hatched out of their eggs and were now swimming along beside their mothers. "Aren't they sweet?"

They watched happily until all the fish had swum by.

Then Rani noticed that the rock

where they had stopped to watch the fish was now far behind them. "We've drifted with the current," she said. "We're near the edge of the reef. We'd better swim back."

Kai and Rani were not allowed beyond the edge of the reef, where the sea dropped away suddenly to form the darker waters of the Deep Blue. It was easy to get lost in the strong sea currents, and fierce creatures lurked in the darkness beyond the reef. But this part of the reef was also scary for another reason. It was close to the Secret Cave.

The Secret Cave was somewhere on the edge of the Deep Blue. Long ago a strange mermaid called Morva had been banished to the cave after she had done

something terrible using bad magic.
Morva was known as the sea-witch.
None of the mermaids liked to swim too
near her cave, even though no one had
seen her in years.

No other mermaid had ever been
inside Morva's Secret Cave but Rani had
heard stories about it since she was tiny.
Its entrance was hidden by a magic bush
that would catch you in its branches if
you tried to swim through. The sea-
witch used starfish as spies, so if anyone
swam near her cave she would know
they were coming. When the water at the
edge of the reef got rough and murky,
the mermaids said that Morva must be
practising her sea-spells. Morva was said
to be capable of changing the colour of

the sea from turquoise to inky black if she lost her temper.

The more Rani thought about Morva, the more she wanted to leave quickly. "Come on," she urged her sister.

But before there was time for Kai to reply there was a terrible splashing and churning of water behind her and a crackly voice screeched, "What are you doing outside *my* cave?"

Chapter Two

Rani screamed. So did Kai.

Then came the sound of laughing and Rani saw that it was only the twins talking in cackly voices and hiding their faces behind some clumps of black seaweed.

"I am the sea-witch! I'm going to take you to my cave and turn you into a sea-frog!" Marissa hissed, as Marina rolled about in the water clutching her side from laughing so much.

"You should see your faces!"

Marina gasped.

Rani and Kai glared at the twins.

"What are *you* doing here?" Kai
snapped.

"Look who's talking!" Marissa and
Marina answered together. "What are
you doing missing school?"

"We thought we'd follow you and
see—" Marissa said.

"—what you were up to," Marina finished for her.

"You thought you'd spy on us, you mean," Kai retorted crossly. "You're worse than Morva's starfish, the way you spy on everyone!"

As the girls argued, Rani felt as though her body was filling up with pins and needles. The feeling seemed to start in her belly button and run up across her chest to her shoulders, then down her arms and into her hands. It was as though her fingers had an electric current in them as she held them out in front of her. She stared down at them but they didn't look any different. Then she was sure she heard a whispery voice calling her name. She closed her eyes tightly and shook her head.

"What's wrong with *you*?" the twins sniggered, staring at Rani.

Rani quickly opened her eyes. "Nothing," she said. "I thought I heard a strange voice, that's all."

"A *strange voice*?" Marina scoffed.

"Yes," said Kai, sounding scared. "I heard it too!"

Rani looked in amazement at her sister. "You did?"

"Of course. You don't think . . ." Kai looked frightened. "You don't think it really *could* be the sea-witch this time, do you?"

Marissa and Marina looked at each other, clearly having one of their private conversations just by thinking. Mermaid

14

twins are able to read each others' thoughts, something which Marissa and Marina used to full advantage when they wanted to play tricks on people. Without saying another word, they swam off at high speed in the direction of home.

Rani turned to her sister to suggest they do the same, but Kai no longer looked scared. Instead she was laughing.

"Good one, Rani!" she said. "They really believed us!"

"But, Kai . . ." Rani stopped, starting to get a sick feeling in her stomach as she realized that Kai had only been trying to get her own back on the twins.

Her sister hadn't really heard the strange whispery voice at all.

*

The following day there was no school. Rani was washing out shell-dishes outside their cave while Kai was inside helping their mother cook lunch. Their father had gone to a special meeting of the community leaders earlier that morning and he had been gone for a very long time.

"Ouch!" Rani complained as she accidentally grazed her hand against the rocky wall of the cave.

Roscoe was bobbing about, peering into each shell to check for plankton. Plankton gets into everything, including all your shell-dishes, if you don't watch out.

He came over and had a look at Rani's hand. "Yuck!" he said. Roscoe

16

was always squeamish at the sight of blood. Being a sea horse, he was lucky enough not to have any himself. "You've missed some sand in that one." He clanked his tail against the dish then ducked away from her and headed off in the direction of the shell-garden, which was his favourite place to relax.

"Mother, how come mermaid twins can read each others' thoughts?" Rani asked, as she carried the clean shell-dishes back into their cave. She made sure she hid her injured hand from her mother because she didn't want her to fuss.

Her mother stopped spreading plankton paste on to flat-weed cakes, turning so that her long golden hair swirled around her head. Rani's mother had the thickest, shiniest hair of all the mermaids, the most elegantly tapered tail, and her eyes were deep turquoise just like the sea out by the coral reef.

"You mean Marissa and Marina?" Rani nodded.

"Well, we don't really know. Some

identical twins are better at it than others."

"Are identical twins the only ones who can read minds?" Rani asked.

"As far as we know, yes. Except . . ." Her mother paused. "There are stories about mermaids long ago who could read the minds of all the other sea-creatures. Nobody knows if they really existed or whether people just made them up."

She reached out and smoothed down Rani's hair which had got tangled. Then she swam across the cave to check on Rani's baby sister, Pearl, who was fast asleep in her cradle, which was suspended from the ceiling. Their father had made the cradle out of one half of the Giant Clam-Shell that had brought Rani to them all those years ago.

Just then the seaweed door of their cave flapped open and their father swam in, followed by Kai. Murdoch's big powerful tail made the water in the cave churn so badly that Pearl's cradle rocked precariously.

"For goodness' sake, Murdoch! Please remember that this isn't the Deep Blue you're swimming in!" their mother said crossly.

"Sorry, Sweetheart!" Their father sat himself down on his favourite rock and wriggled until he got the end of his tail comfortably wedged into the sandy floor. Then he held out his arms for Rani and Kai to come and balance on his tail.

"Well, there haven't been any other sightings but we're going to send out a patrol this afternoon anyway," he told their mother, cheerfully.

"Sightings of *what*?" Kai asked.

"Someone *thought* they saw a Yellow-back jellyfish this morning inside the reef," he replied.

Yellow-back jellyfish lived in the Deep Blue and they were very dangerous indeed. They were so poisonous that no one had ever survived one of their stings. If anyone saw one inside the reef, the community always took it very seriously.

"It's probably a false alarm," Murdoch attempted to reassure them.

Rani frowned. "I don't think it is . . ." she said slowly.

Her mother looked at her sharply. "What do you mean?"

Rani shook her head. "I'm not sure. I just have this *feeling* . . ." She couldn't explain it any better than that. She stared down at her hands. They were starting to tingle again. And – as if by magic – the graze where she had bumped her hand against the rock had completely disappeared.

Chapter Three

"Roscoe, you've got to help me!" Rani pleaded, as she found the little sea horse sitting in the middle of the roundabout in the shell-garden. The roundabout was made out of one half of a huge cone shell with a flat surface of tight weeds netted over the top. It was balanced so that it spun on the ground on its point. Normally the mermaids would cling to the edge and be spun round together, but this afternoon the shell-garden was empty apart from the two of them.

"Push me round really fast and I'll
think about it," Roscoe said.

"Roscoe, I think something strange is
happening to me," Rani said, as she gave
the roundabout a push. "Look at this."
And she held out her healed hand for
him to see.

As Roscoe passed he had a look. He
spun round a couple more times and

then jumped off. "Hmm. Very mysterious."

"And that's not all!" She told him about the whispery voices and the strange tingling sensation in her hands.

"Even more mysterious," Roscoe said. "Come on. You'd better come with me to see Octavius. He'll know what to do."

Octavius the octopus lived next door to the school cave – in fact it had been his idea to set up a school for the mermaid children in the first place. Octavius was always saying that just because mermaids had tiny brains that didn't mean they shouldn't fill them with as much knowledge as possible.

Octavius often complained about his

huge brain and how it tired him out thinking so many clever thoughts each day. For that reason he liked to take a nap every afternoon after lunch in order to keep his brain cells refreshed. None of the mermaid children were allowed to interrupt his naps and if they ever made too much noise outside his cave and woke him up then he was always very cross indeed.

Rani hung back. "But you know how grumpy Octavius gets when you ask him things."

"He only gets grumpy if you ask him things he doesn't know," Roscoe said. "Hurry up! We need to catch him before he goes to sleep for the afternoon."

"What if he doesn't know about *this*?"

Rani asked. "And what if he's already asleep?"

But Roscoe had already bobbed off in the direction of Octavius's cave.

The entrance to Octavius's cave was covered by a beautiful yellow and red seaweed-flap with sea anemones growing round the edges of the door.

Rani paused outside the cave. She knew she had to call out and say she was there, but she was too nervous to speak. Just as she was about to change her mind and go back, Roscoe knocked his bony tail loudly against the cave wall.

"Who's that?" a deep voice grumbled, and the seaweed-flap was pushed aside

ry precious – they were made out
eaves of the book-plant which
ite rare and could only be found
Deep Blue.

tavius was clasping four of his arms
er in front of him, looking
ghtful. "Well," he said, "so you're
, are you?"

Ready?" Rani felt even more
used. What was Octavius talking
ut? She hadn't even told him yet why
was here! She started to tell him
at had been happening but he cut her
ort.

"I know all about that," he said. "It's
be expected. After all, you're not a
ingle Reef mermaid, are you? Now, the
nly person who can explain things to

by two long wriggly arms. Octavius glared at them and Rani saw that another arm held a shell-plate full of delicious-looking food. He was washing his cooking pots with another two arms and with the remaining three he was stuffing food into his mouth.

"As you can see, I'm very busy," Octavius snapped.

"This is Rani," Roscoe said, quickly. "You know . . . *Rani*. The mermaid they found in that shell."

"Ah . . . *Rani* . . ." Octavius said, and he immediately stopped eating. He pushed Roscoe out of the way with the tip of one arm and put another arm round Rani's shoulder. "Come in. Come in," he said, pulling her towards him.

"I've been wond[...]
to see me."

Rani had never be[...]
cave before. It was [...]
There was a table in [...]
floor made out of all [...]
shells, and the stone fl[...]
with a purple carpet of [...]
plants were growing ou[...]
cave walls and on one w[...]
cut into the stone on whic[...]
several books. To one side [...]
rock stove lay a large flat co[...]
the pages of which were flut[...]
with the movement of the wa[...]
Octavius had more books tha[...]
else Rani knew. Books in Tingl[...]

were ve[...]
of the [...]
was qu[...]
in the [...]
Oc[...]
togeth[...]
thoug[...]
read[...]
"[...]
con[...]
abo[...]
she[...]
wh[...]
sh[...]

t[...]

you properly is Morva."

"Morva, the *sea-witch*?" Rani gasped, open-mouthed.

"Don't tell me you believe all that mermaid nonsense! Morva is no more a sea-witch than . . ." He chuckled again. "Than *you* are!" He scratched his head and thought for a moment. "Now, you'll have to wait until I've finished my lunch. Come back in half an hour." And he started to wave Rani out of his cave.

Rani bravely stayed put. "Excuse me, Octavius, but what do you mean? Wait for *what*?"

"Why, for me to show you the way to Morva's cave of course," Octavius replied impatiently. "She's been expecting you for years!"

chapter four

Roscoe was waiting for her outside. "So?" he questioned her. "What did Mister Grumpy say, then?"

"Shush! He'll hear you," Rani hissed. "Roscoe, did you know that Octavius knows Morva?"

Roscoe looked surprised. "Does he?"

"Yes, and he *says* that she's the only one who can explain things to me."

Roscoe did a little dance. "I knew it! *You* must be a sea-witch too!"

"Don't be silly," Rani snapped. But all

the same, she could feel her heart
beating faster.

Rani swam back to the shell-garden.
She could hear Kai and the twins
playing noisily on the seaweed swings.
Kai always liked to prove that she could
swing the highest and now her long
blonde hair streamed out as she used her
tail to push herself higher and higher.

Suddenly Kai swung so high that she
was completely upside down and her
shell-haircomb flew off. It landed in a
huge bush of sea-kelp near Rani.

Rani swam over and started to
rummage amongst the big fluttery leaves.

"There it is," she gasped, reaching
down to grab at a shiny shell.

"Do you mind?" the shell said crossly,

and Rani let go of it with a gasp. It
wasn't Kai's hair-comb but a live shell
with a sea creature living inside it.

"Wow!" Kai said, joining her. "It's an
oyster!"

"An oyster!" the twins exclaimed,
hurrying over to look. "Has it got a pearl
inside?"

"Have you got a pearl inside?" Kai

asked it, excitedly.

"Don't be so nosy," the oyster snorted. "You mermaids have no manners!"

"I'm sorry," Kai said. "It's just . . . I've never seen an oyster with a pearl and – if it's not too much trouble – we'd love to see one."

"It *is* too much trouble," the oyster snapped, opening slightly and rudely releasing an air bubble.

The twins went silent. At least, it seemed like they were being silent until Rani heard Marina's voice, faint and whispery, saying, "Let's wait until Rani and Kai have gone and then come back for it."

"You can't do that!" Rani said to them, sharply.

Kai gave her a strange look and so did the twins.

"We didn't say anything," Marina said cautiously. She looked at her twin to make sure that she hadn't accidentally spoken the words. "Did we, Marissa?"

Marissa shook her head, still staring at Rani. "We didn't *say* anything, no."

Kai was trying to win the oyster round by complimenting it on the shininess of its shell.

"Flattery will get you nowhere," the oyster said. "I know what you mermaids are like. If I show you my pearl you'll run off with it!"

"No, we won't," said Kai. "We promise we won't!"

"Hmm," said the oyster, shifting

himself to a more comfortable position in the sand. "I'll tell you what . . . I'll *describe* it to you."

And he went on to describe the biggest, smoothest, most beautiful pearl any mermaid could imagine.

"Oh, *please* can we see it?" begged Kai.

"I'm afraid not," said the oyster slyly. "But I have a cousin who lives under a rock just a short distance into the Deep Blue and *he* has a pearl that he loves to show to people. I can give you directions."

He told Kai to swim one hundred of her tail-lengths straight out from the entrance to the sea-snake burrow, then turn right at a big bush of sea-kelp, then swim to the rock straight ahead that had a purple bush to one side.

"Come on," said the twins excitedly. "Let's go now."

Rani suddenly spotted Kai's shell-comb. "Here!" she cried out triumphantly, scooping it up just as Roscoe appeared with the message that

Octavius was ready now.

"Ready for what?" Kai asked, carefully replacing her hair-comb.

Rani knew she couldn't tell. Not yet anyway.

Kai looked hurt when Rani told her that it was a secret.

"Don't be upset," Rani pleaded. "I'll tell you as soon as I can."

"You don't have to," Kai replied huffily. "I'm going with the twins to find this oyster." And she swam off after the twins, in the direction of the Deep Blue.

"Kai, don't leave the reef!" Rani called after her anxiously. "If Mother and Father find out, you'll get into trouble! And besides, it might be dangerous!"

But Kai didn't stop.

"I wouldn't worry about her," Roscoe said, gruffly. "Where *you're* going is far more dangerous!" And he gave her a nudge with his bony head in the direction of Octavius's cave.

Chapter Five

"I can give you directions from here," Octavius said, stopping as they reached the edge of the reef.

"You want me to go into the Deep Blue alone?" Rani said, shocked. Octavius had already insisted that Roscoe stay behind and they had left him at the octopus's cave.

"I feel it is my duty not to put myself at undue risk," Octavius explained gravely. "After all, my great brain is a very valuable asset to the whole community."

Rani was sure that it was, but at the same time she was petrified by the idea of swimming off into the Deep Blue by herself. She had only been in the Deep Blue a few times before with her father who had made her stay very close by his side the whole time. Murdoch made many expeditions into the Deep Blue with the other mermen to collect medicine plants and food and other essential things and he had told them stories about the creatures that lived there. Rani knew that many were friendly like the dolphins and the whales but that others were dangerous, like the sharks and the giant sea-spiders who would catch you and eat you, and the

Yellow-back jellyfish who would kill you with one sting.

"Don't worry," Octavius said. "I've sent a starfish to tell Morva you're coming. She'll be looking out for you. Now, listen carefully. I'm going to tell you how to get to the Secret Cave . . ."

Octavius explained the secret route twice and made her repeat it after him. She was to look out for three landmarks: a craggy rock that was completely covered in limpets; a huge flowering sea-cactus; and a tall bush that pointed upwards in the shape of a needle.

"What if I can't find them?" Rani asked.

"You will," Octavius said. "And when you get there, I want you to give Morva this from me." He handed her a little shell-container. "Hurry now."

Rani looked out anxiously into the dark water of the Deep Blue. Plucking up all her courage, she thrashed her tail and propelled herself over the edge of the reef.

It was much darker in the deep water, and colder too. Rani shivered as she swam down deeper and deeper to reach the seabed. She saw the rock covered in limpets that Octavius had told her to look for and turned left straight after it just like Octavius had said. Then she started to look for a bushy sea-cactus with blue flowers. As she swam past it a shoal of rainbow fish scuttled out from underneath, making her jump.

"There's a shark about," they told her.
"Watch out."

Rani shivered, but it was too late to
turn back. She thanked them for the
warning and continued on her way.

After what seemed like a long time she
saw the needle-shaped bush standing on
its own in a sandy clearing on the seabed.
She had to start swimming upwards now,

Octavius had said. But how could a cave be situated *above* her? It had to be on the seabed or in a rock somewhere.

But since the bush was definitely pointing upwards she decided she had better do what Octavius had said. Then, all of a sudden, the way up was blocked. She stopped dead and looked above her.

In the water above her head was what looked like a huge flat rock stretching out in all directions as far as she could see. She started to swim downwards away from it, thinking that perhaps it wasn't a rock but some huge sea-creature, when she heard a whispery voice calling, "*Look above you, Rani!*"

She looked, and this time she spotted an opening in the rock. And from the opening, a rope of seaweed was dangling down.

Up and up the rope she climbed, through the dark vertical tunnel, until it finally came to an end and all of a sudden she was inside a beautiful underwater cave.

The water inside the cave was crystal clear and beautiful yellow and purple fish swam around playfully. In one corner, two bright orange lobsters were dozing, their large pincers draped lazily round each other. The walls of the cave were decorated with brightly coloured murals of different kinds of sea-creatures, including mermaids, swimming around amongst the pink and purple coral.

Rani turned to look at the wall behind her and gasped.

In the middle of the wall was a picture of a mermaid with red hair and an orange tail, swimming down into the centre of what looked like a burst of golden light!

Rani held in her breath as she swam closer to study the picture. Just as she was almost touching it she heard a noise behind her.

She turned to look. There, blocking the entrance to the cave, was the strangest mermaid she had ever seen.

"Hello, Rani," the mermaid said.

"Are you? Are you *Morva*?" Rani stammered.

The mermaid had dazzling orange

scales and red hair so long that it reached the tip of her tail. Rani saw that her eyes looked old and wise. But how could this be Morva? Old mermaids had white hair and wrinkled faces! And Morva wasn't just old – she was ancient!

"Welcome to my floating cave," Morva said, smiling.

chapter Six

The shell-container Octavius had sent turned out to be a portion of his delicious stew. As Rani watched Morva heating up the stew on top of her hot-rock stove she tried not to think about a story her grandmother used to tell her, about a naughty little mermaid who ran off on her own into the Deep Blue and ended up becoming the tenderest ingredient in a sea-witch's supper.

"I thought you'd look much older," Rani said shyly. "Like my grandmother.

She's got white hair."

"I expect I'm twice as old as your grandmother," Morva said. "But one of the advantages of being able to use magic is that you don't have to *look* older!"

Rani swallowed. "They said— They said you used *bad* magic."

Morva stopped stirring her stew, which seemed to be bubbling up to ten times the quantity as she chanted over it.

"Let me tell you what really happened," she said.

And Morva told her that she came from a different group of mermaids a long way away from here and that, when she was young, she had met a merman from Tingle Reef when she was out

exploring in the Deep Blue. The
merman had swum farther than usual
because he was searching for a rare type
of plant with healing powers. The plant
was needed urgently because the baby of
one of the community leaders was very
sick. Morva had helped him to find the
plant and they had returned to Tingle

Reef together. Morva and the merman, who was called Murdoch, fell in love.

"That's the same name as my father!" Rani interrupted her.

Morva just nodded and carried on.

Morva and Murdoch were very happy apart from one thing. There was another mermaid who was in love with Murdoch and she was very jealous of Morva. When the community leader's baby started to get sick again, Morva offered to make a magic healing potion but the jealous mermaid secretly substituted salt for the potion and the baby died. The jealous mermaid spread the rumour that Morva had used bad magic and Morva was banished. Murdoch tried to go with her but Morva knew he would be unhappy away from Tingle Reef so she wouldn't let him.

But instead of returning home Morva used her magic to create a special floating cave on the edge of the reef. That way she could stay and watch over Murdoch, who eventually did fall in love again with someone else and had a family. Morva made it her business to watch over them, staying in her secret cave for many years, until Murdoch finally died. Then, just as she was thinking about returning to her own people, she heard that a baby mermaid with an orange tail and red hair had arrived in Tingle Reef inside a shell.

"*Me!*" Rani gasped.

"Yes, and the grandson of *my*

Murdoch found you and adopted you." She smiled. "And I decided to stay a while longer until you grew old enough for me to teach you how to use your magic."

"*What* magic?" Rani exclaimed.

"What do you think that tingling feeling is in your body? And how do you think you can hear other creatures' thoughts, if not by magic? It's very weak at the moment, only just beginning to show itself. But in a little while it will be as powerful as mine, so it's very important that you learn how to use it properly."

"But how . . ." Rani trailed off. She had so many questions to ask that she didn't know where to start.

"I don't know how or why you came to Tingle Reef as a baby, Rani," Morva continued. "But what I do know is that you must have come from the same place as me. And we are different from the mermaids of Tingle Reef, not just because of how we look. We're different because we have magic powers that they don't have."

Rani felt dazed. "If this is true," she stammered. "Then . . . then you must know where I come from."

Morva pointed at the picture of the red-haired mermaid swimming through the burst of golden light. "That," she said, proudly, "is where you come from."

Rani stared at the picture. "But where is it? How do we get there?"

"One day, when your magic is strong enough, I will take you there," Morva said. "Until then you must be patient."

Morva started to tuck into her stew. "Now you must go. You mustn't tell *anyone* that you have met me. Or about what I have told you. Do you understand?"

Rani nodded. "But when will I see you again?"

"Soon. And remember . . . Tell *no one*! Not even your family."

Rani took one last look at the picture, and as she left Morva's cave she tried to imagine herself swimming down through the centre of that golden light to reach her true home.

Chapter Seven

By the time Rani got back to Tingle Reef she felt exhausted. All she wanted to do was to go home and tell her parents and Kai all about it, but she knew she couldn't. Rani *really* wanted to tell Kai. Surely it wouldn't matter if she made Kai promise not to tell anyone else?

As the entrance to her cave came into view, Rani saw that there were lots of other mermaids outside.

"What's happened?" she asked anxiously, as the crowd parted to let her through. Everyone was looking really worried.

As she swam inside, her mother looked up. She was hugging Pearl tightly and her turquoise eyes were full of tears. At first Rani thought there was something wrong with her baby sister and then she spotted her father.

Murdoch was lying on a seaweed mat, completely still.

"What's wrong with Father?" she cried.

"He's been stung by a Yellow-back jellyfish," her mother replied, her voice trembling.

Rani looked down at Murdoch. The jellyfish poison was already in his bloodstream and his upper body was red and swollen. His eyes were closed and he was so weak he couldn't move his tail.

"Rani, isn't Kai with you?" her mother asked.

Rani shook her head. "She went somewhere with the twins."

"Where?"

Rani knew that if she told her mother

that Kai had gone off into the Deep Blue then her mother would be even more worried. So she lied. "She's not far away. Shall I go and fetch her?"

"Yes," her mother said hoarsely. She touched Murdoch's forehead. "But hurry!"

Rani swallowed, fighting back the tears. Her mother expected that her father would die. That was why she wanted Kai to come back so quickly.

"Mother—" she began, but Miriam interrupted her.

"There's no cure for this type of poison, Rani. Now go and fetch your sister."

Rani swam out of the cave and found Roscoe.

"Roscoe, will *you* go and find Kai?"
Rani asked. "There's somewhere else
I need to go right now." And she
swam away before he could ask her any
questions.

Rani swam as fast as she could back to
Morva's cave.

When she reached it, she swam
underneath it until she found the hole
with the seaweed rope.

"Morva," she gasped, as soon as she
was inside the cave. "You've got to help
me!"

Morva was sitting on the furthest away
rock, combing her long hair with a
beautiful shell-comb. She stopped as
soon as she saw Rani.

Rani quickly explained what had

happened to her father.

Morva looked distressed. "I'd like to help," she said. "I could collect some special plants and make a magic healing potion to give you. You can come back and collect it tonight."

"There isn't time for that!" Rani cried desperately. "Father's going to die if you don't come and do something now."

"But Rani, I cannot enter Tingle Reef," Morva said. "It is forbidden. They will never permit me to go into the cave to help your father."

"They will if I take you!" Rani said. "Morva, please, you've got to come."

Morva looked solemn. "I can't. They still think I killed that baby."

"Well, this is your chance to show

everybody that they're wrong," Rani said. "If you make Father better then they'll know you couldn't have killed anyone." Rani was near to tears now. "Murdoch would want you to come!" she burst out. "*Your* Murdoch, I mean. Can't you just try?"

When they got back to Rani's cave some of the other mermaids were still outside. They gasped as they saw Morva. Most of them didn't know who she was, but a few of the older mermaids remembered her from when *they* were children.

An urgent whisper went round. "It's Morva! It's the sea-witch!"

The adult mermaids moved closer

together, blocking the entrance to the cave.

"That child looks just like the sea-witch!" one of them said, pointing at Rani's bright red hair.

"Shhh. You'll frighten Rani," another mermaid said protectively.

Morva looked at Rani. "I knew they wouldn't understand," she said. "I'd better leave."

"But you have to save Father!" Rani cried. "You have to come inside and see him." And she burst into tears.

At that moment Octavius pushed his way through the crowd, shoving mermaids out of his way, eight-at-a-time, until he reached Rani.

"Rani has brought Morva here to help

Murdoch!" he shouted, hooking one arm round Rani's waist and pulling her closer to him. "And since we can't help him ourselves, I don't think we've got anything to lose by letting Morva try, do you?"

"But she's dangerous!" someone shouted. "What about what she did to that baby?"

"Nonsense!" Octavius snorted. "You mermaids are *so* silly! I've read all about what happened in my history book of Tingle Reef. No one ever listened to Morva's side of the story. Unfortunately I hadn't been born then or I would have sorted it all out! Now, move aside and let Rani and Morva enter the cave."

But the adult mermaids didn't move. They didn't like being bossed around by Octavius.

Rani was getting scared that they wouldn't reach her father in time. She tugged at Morva's arm. "*Do* something!"

Morva seemed to whirl into action, flicking her tail so that the water swirled around her. "If you don't move out of the way I'm going to turn you all into

70

sea-frogs!" she hissed. And she started to wave her arms in the water in front of her as if she was casting a spell.

The mermaids started pushing and shoving each other as they struggled to move away from her. Quickly, Morva pushed Rani ahead of her into the cave.

"Mother!" Rani called out from the doorway.

Rani's mother turned round. "Rani—" She stopped, gasping out loud and pulling Pearl closer to her, as she saw Morva.

"Morva is my friend," Rani said. "And she's come to make Father better."

Before her mother could say anything Morva swam forward. "I *can* help him," she said. "*If* you trust me."

"I've heard about you," Rani's mother whispered. "But I never guessed that you . . . that Rani . . ." She trailed off, her gaze flitting between Morva's long red hair and the identical red hair of her daughter.

"There isn't much time," Morva said gently.

Rani's mother looked down at her husband. She kissed his forehead and moved back.

"Go on, then," she said.

Morva swam closer and leaned over Murdoch. She placed both hands, fingers outstretched, over his face. Then she closed her eyes and began to chant something under her breath. As Miriam and Rani watched, Morva's upper body

began to sparkle. The golden glow
started to spread down her arms and
into her hands and then it crossed over
into Murdoch's body which started to
sparkle too.

Slowly, the redness left his skin and the
swelling started to go down. The end of
his tail started to twitch. When Morva
removed her hands, the golden light
vanished and Murdoch's eyes flickered
open.

Rani's mother was trembling. "Oh,
thank you!" she cried. "Thank you so
much!" She rushed forward and flung
her arms around her husband, as Pearl
shrieked with excitement.

Rani flung herself at Morva and
gave her an enormous hug. "I knew

you'd save him!"

Suddenly there was a lot of noise at the cave entrance and Kai swam inside with Roscoe, closely followed by Octavius.

"What is it? What's happening?" Kai asked.

"It's all right now," her mother told her, smiling. "Murdoch is all right now. Thanks to Morva."

"Morva?" Kai stared at the beautiful red-haired mermaid who was holding Rani's hand. "*You're* Morva? But . . . but Morva's meant to be *ugly*!"

Morva laughed, sending golden bubbles spiralling above her head.

"*Kai!*" her mother snapped, but she was too happy to be very cross.

One by one the other mermaids started to come inside the cave to see what Morva had done. When they saw Murdoch sitting up on the mat, they all stared at him in awe.

"Maybe Octavius was right," they mumbled. "Maybe she *didn't* kill that baby."

"Of *course* I was right!" Octavius barked at them. "I'm *always* right. When are you mermaids going to realize that?"

"Of *course* Morva didn't kill that baby," Murdoch called out. "My grandfather was always telling you that, but you never listened!"

All the mermaids stared in admiration at Morva.

"You can come back and live in

Tingle Reef now," Rani told her excitedly.

"Yes, Morva!" one or two of the other mermaids called out. "Come and live here with us."

Morva smiled but she shook her head. "Thank you, I'm very happy living in my floating cave. But I'd like to come and visit you. It gets a bit lonely sometimes, with no other mermaids to talk to."

"Come and visit us whenever you want!" everyone said at once.

And Morva promised them that she would.

Chapter Eight

"Do you think Morva will come?" Kai
asked Rani, as they waited for their
father's speech to finish.

It was market day and Murdoch was
giving a talk to the community about the
seaweed nets they were going to use in
future to catch any dangerous jellyfish.
The one that had stung Murdoch had
been sent back into the Deep Blue but
there was always a risk that another
Yellow-back might find its way inside
the reef.

The market had been in full swing all morning with all sorts of different goods being exchanged. There were lots of delicious things to eat as well as practical things for the home like seaweed mats and shell-crockery. Things had quietened down a bit now that a lot of the stall-holders and shoppers had gathered round to hear what Murdoch had to say.

"Are you sure Morva's coming?" Kai asked her sister again.

"Yes, she'll be here. She's just a bit late, that's all," Rani replied.

"She'd *better* come, after all the time we've spent making this." Kai opened the little shell-box she was holding and the girls looked down again at the beautiful pearl necklace inside.

"I can't believe that oyster you and the twins found actually *gave* you his pearl," Rani said.

"He said he was getting bored with it," Kai explained. "He was extremely happy when I gave him my shell-comb and all my jewellery in exchange for it."

"Are you sure you want *me* to make the presentation?" Rani asked. "After all, it's your pearl."

"I think it's best if you do it," Kai said. "Anyway, she'll know it's from all of us."

Just then Octavius appeared, carrying a seaweed shopping bag in each arm. "I've got so much shopping to do that I don't know whether I'm coming or going," he grumbled.

Someone cried, "Morva's here!"

Rani and Kai looked up. Morva was swimming towards them, her long red hair streaming out behind her.

Murdoch beckoned to Rani to come over to the big rock platform in the middle of the marketplace.

"Here," Kai whispered, handing her the little shell-box.

The whole crowd fell silent as they waited for Murdoch to speak.

"We're very pleased to welcome Morva here today," Murdoch announced. "Morva, I want to thank you once again for saving my life, and Rani has something to give you from all of us."

Rani swam over to Morva and presented her with the little shell-box. Morva opened it and gasped with pleasure as she saw the necklace.

"It's beautiful," she said. "Thank you *so* much."

"Welcome back to Tingle Reef!" Rani said, and everyone cheered.

The excitement died down considerably as Octavius climbed up on to the platform. "If *I* could just add a few words . . ." he began.

The mermaids sighed as they prepared themselves for what they knew was bound to be a very long speech indeed.

That's when Rani noticed that little gold sparks were starting to dance around Octavius's mouth. She looked suspiciously at Morva whose fingertips were giving off a faint glow.

"That's all I have to say!" Octavius said grandly. And, much to everyone's amazement, he climbed straight down again from the platform.

All the mermaids started to clap.

"You see, Rani," Morva's whispery words came floating towards her through the water. "Mermaid magic can sometimes come in *very* useful indeed!"

Rani's Sea Spell

Gwyneth Rees

Rani's grandmother has invited Rani and her family to a party at her house in Deep Blue, a very long swim away from Rani's home in Tingle Reef.

When Grandmother gives Rani a beautiful amber necklace, she knows it must be special. She'll need to ask Morva the sea-witch about it when she gets home.

That's if she can make it past hungry sharks and grumpy whales! Perhaps it's time for a little magic...

The Shell Princess

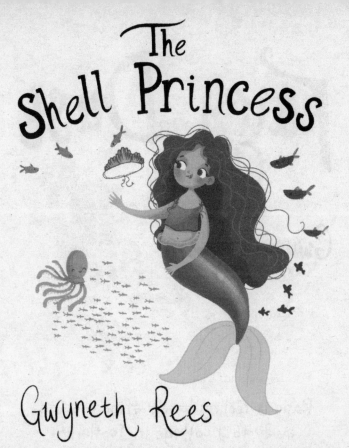

Gwyneth Rees

Rani has a special amber necklace, which hides a message-stone. It shows her long-lost twin brother, who she is desperate to visit, but her family doesn't want her to leave Tingle Reef.

Rani persuades Morva the sea-witch to take her on the long journey through the Deep Blue to the home of the Mer-King and the magic mermaids.

Will she find what she is looking for?

Fairy Dust

Gwyneth Rees

Rosie is feeling lonely after moving
away to a cottage in Scotland.
She misses her dad, and all her mum
seems to do is work. When the lady
next door tells her to watch out for
fairies, Rosie can hardly believe it –
until somebody starts to eat the
chocolates she's been leaving out . . .

Could there really be
fairies out there?

Fairy Treasure

Gwyneth Rees

When Connie is sent to stay with
Aunt Alice in her boring, dusty old
house, she's not very pleased. But
then she meets Ruby – a book fairy!

Ruby is in trouble. She's lost an
important ring and can't get
back to fairyland without it.

Can Connie help Ruby find the
missing ring before the doorway
to fairyland is closed forever?

Fairy Dreams

Gwyneth Rees

Evie and her mum are staying at her
grandma's house – but Grandma is very ill
in hospital. Finding fairies at the bottom
of her bed (fairies who love chocolate),
Evie is whisked away on a magical journey
to fairyland. Her new fairy friends tell her
they cannot make Grandma better, but
they can send Evie and Grandma on
one last magical adventure together.

First, though, the fairies
need Evie's help . . .

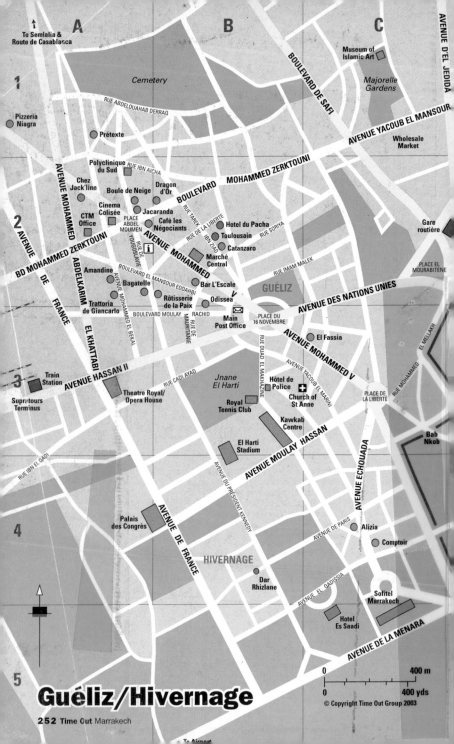

**To Semlalia &
Route de Casablanca**

A   **B**   **C**

AVENUE D'EL JEDIDA

Cemetery

1

Museum of
Islamic Art

*Majorelle
Gardens*

BOULEVARD DE SAFI

RUE ABDELOUAHAB DERRAQ

Pizzeria
Niagra

Prétexte

AVENUE YACOUB EL MANSOUR

Wholesale
Market

Polyclinique
du Sud

RUE IBN AICHA

Chez
Jack'line

Boule de Neige

Dragon
d'Or

BOULEVARD MOHAMMED ZERKTOUNI

Cinema
Colisée

Jacaranda

AVENUE MOHAMMED

CTM
Office

PLACE ABDEL
MOUMEN

Café les
Négociants

Hotel du Pacha

Gare
routière

2

AVENUE MOHAMMED

BD MOHAMMED ZERKTOUNI

RUE DE LA LIBERTE

RUE TAREK

RUE IBN ZIAD

RUE SORIYA

Toulousain

Catanzaro

PLACE EL
MOURABITENE

AVENUE DE ABDELKARIM

Amandine

Bagatelle

RUE DE BOUGUORAVIE

BOULEVARD EL MANSOUR EDDAHBI

Marché
Central

RUE IMAM MALEK

Trattoria
de Giancarlo

AVENUE MOHAMMED EL BEKAL

Bar L'Escale

GUÉLIZ

AVENUE DES NATIONS UNIES

EL KHATTABI

DE FRANCE

Rôtisserie
de la Paix

RUE DE
MAURITANIE

BOULEVARD MOULAY

RACHID

Odissea

Main
Post Office

PLACE DU
16 NOVEMBRE

AVENUE MOHAMMED V

El Fassia

EL MEZIAKH

RUE MOHAMMED

AVENUE HASSAN II

Train
Station

RUE CADI AYAD

*Jnane
El Harti*

RUE OUAD EL MAKHAZINE

Hôtel de
Police

Church of
St Anne

AVENUE YACOUB EL MARINI

PLACE DE
LA LIBERTE

3

Supratours
Terminus

RUE IBN EL QADI

Theatre Royal/
Opera House

Royal
Tennis Club

Kawkab
Centre

Bab
Nkob

El Harti
Stadium

AVENUE MOULAY HASSAN

AVENUE ECHOUADA

4

Palais
des Congrès

AVENUE DE FRANCE

AVENUE DU PRESIDENT KENNEDY

HIVERNAGE

AVENUE DE PARIS

Alizia

Comptoir

Dar
Rhizlane

AVENUE EL QADISSIA

Sofitel
Marrakech

Hotel
Es Saadi

AVENUE DE LA MENARA

5

0   400 m

0   400 yds

© Copyright Time Out Group 2003

Guéliz/Hivernage

To Airport

Edited and designed by
Time Out Guides Limited
Universal House
251 Tottenham Court Road
London W1T 7AB
Tel + 44 (0)20 7813 3000
Fax + 44 (0)20 7813 6001
Email guides@timeout.com
www.timeout.com

Editorial

Editor Andrew Humphreys
Deputy Editor Ismay Atkins
Listings Researcher Younes Cherkaoui
Proofreader Tamsin Shelton
Indexer Jackie Brind

Editorial/Managing Director Peter Fiennes
Series Editor Ruth Jarvis
Deputy Series Editor Lesley McCave
Guides Co-ordinator Anna Norman

Design

Group Art Director John Oakey
Art Director Mandy Martin
Art Editor Scott Moore
Senior Designer Tracey Ridgewell
Designers Astrid Kogler, Sam Lands
Digital Imaging Dan Conway
Ad Make-up Charlotte Blythe
Picture Editor Kerri Littlefield
Acting Picture Editor Kit Burnet
Acting Deputy Picture Editor Martha Houghton
Picture Desk Trainee Bella Wood

Advertising

Group Commercial Director Lesley Gill
Sales Director Mark Phillips
International Sales Manager Ross Canadé
Advertising Sales (Marrakech) Aniko Boehler
Advertising Assistant Sabrina Ancilleri

Administration

Chairman Tony Elliott
Managing Director Mike Hardwick
Group Financial Director Richard Waterlow
Group Marketing Director Christine Cort
Marketing Manager Mandy Martinez
US Publicity & Marketing Associate Rosella Albanese
Group General Manager Nichola Coulthard
Guides Production Director Mark Lamond
Production Controller Samantha Furniss
Accountant Sarah Bostock

Features in this guide were researched and written by Andrew Humphreys, except:
History Hugh Graham. **Marrakech Today** (*The ultimate Marrakech buy* Maggie Perry). **Accommodation** (*Budget beds* Ismay Atkins). **Gardens** Andrew Humphreys, Maggie Perry (*Re-greening the Medina* Maggie Perry). **Restaurants & Cafés** Ismay Atkins, Andrew Humphreys, Cheryl Maiden, Maggie Perry (*Marrakitsch* Ismay Atkins). **Shops & Services** Sheva Fruitman (*By appointment* Sheva Fruitman), Lanie Goodman, Andrew Humphreys, Maggie Perry. **Children** Lynn Perez. **Film** Tom Charity. **Music** Garth Cartwright, Andrew Humphreys (*Maroc 'n' roll* Garth Cartwright). **Nightlife** Andrew Humphreys, Graham Lye (*Gay Marrakech* Graham Lye). **Sport & Fitness** Andrew Humphreys, Matthew Low (*2010: A football odyssey?* Peterjon Cresswell). **High Atlas & the South** Ismay Atkins. **Essaouira** Abby Aron, Jane Loveless, Dave Rimmer. **Getting Started, Casablanca, Fès, Rabat, Tangier** Dave Rimmer. **Directory** Ismay Atkins, Andrew Humphreys, Lynn Perez.

The Editor would like to thank: Mohammed Amine Kabbaj, Herwig Bartels, Abdelatif Ben Abdellah, Fabrizio Bizzarri, Aniko Boehler, Charles Boccara, Younes Cherkaoui, Brahim El Belkani, Anissa El Boukili, Hamid Fardjad, Gadi Farfour, Selwyn Hardy, Richard Horowitz, Chris Lawrence, Richard Lawson, Sam Le Quesne, Alessandra Lippini, Meryanne Loum-Martin, Gaby Noack-Spath, Tourya Othman, Lynn Perez, Clay Perry, Dana Schondelmeyer, Iliass Tafroukht, Florence Taranne, Nicola Thomas and Ahmed Tija.

Maps by JS Graphics (john@jsgraphics.co.uk). The following maps are based on data supplied by New Holland Publishers - Casablanca, Essaouira, Fès, Marrakech, Rabat and Tangier. Maps on pages 65, 67 and 248-51 are based by data supplied by Jean Louis Dorveaux.

Photography by Hadley Kincade except: pages 9 AKG; 141 Sophie Baker; 143 AP/Jalil Bounhar; 14 Cecil Beaton /Sotheby's Picture Library; 181 Corbis; 68 Tony Gibson; 173, 175, 176, 179 Chris Lawrence; 3,11 Topham Picturepoint.

The following photographs were supplied by the featured establishments; 145, 149.

Contents

Introduction

With its deep Islamic faith but parallel belief in everyday magic, a Medina organised around craft guilds and medieval methods, doggedly independent mountain tribesmen and ancient urban cultures, Marrakech is the shortest distance you can travel from Europe and wind up somewhere genuinely different. It's the place where all the clichés come true. It's where the beggars really are blind and snakes are charmed, where mounds of food are delivered on platters as bare-navelled bellydancers shimmy by the table, where herbalists in the souk sell jars of scorpions and exorcists with wildly darting eyes know what to do with them.

There is nowhere so close to London – the flight takes three hours – that gives such a strong sense of foreignness and mystery as Marrakech does, something that neither four-and-a-half decades of French occupation, nor the subsquent influence of tourism, has managed to erode. It's a place where the fantasy of Oriental life can be indulged to the full,

even for just a weekend, and you can still be back in the office by mid-morning Monday.

The current passion for ethnicity and colour has conspired to make Marrakech the destination *du jour*. But that's nothing new. It was abfab in the 1930s when Chaplin and Hayworth dropped in to play, in the '40s when Churchill frequented the Mamounia and in the '60s when it became drop-out central for the boho set. OK, so it went a little quiet for a while but these days such is the parade of A-list names swanning across the concourse of the city's rather modest international airport that one travel agency imposes a ten per cent surcharge on all celebrity bookings.

Marrakech's hip status has been further cemented by a string of stylish accommodations. Tailor-made for days of blissed out indolence, they are completely addictive. Bearing in mind the cheap price of property here, more than a few visitors have returned home to tell friends, 'We liked the hotel so much, we bought one just like it.'

ABOUT THE TIME OUT CITY GUIDES

The *Time Out Guide to Marrakech & the best of Morocco* is one of an expanding series of Time Out City Guides produced by the people behind London and New York's successful listings magazines. Our guides are all written and updated by resident experts who have striven to provide you with all the most up-to-date information you'll need to explore the city, whether you're a local or first-time visitor.

THE LOWDOWN ON THE LISTINGS

Above all, we've tried to make this book as useful as possible. Addresses, telephone numbers, websites, transport information, opening times, admission prices and credit card details are all included in our listings. And, as far as possible, we've given details of facilities, services and events, all checked and correct at the time we went to press. However, in Morocco, opening hours – both of small shops and major tourist attractions – are subject to abrupt changes, the former by personal and the latter by official whim. Before you go out of your way, we would advise you whenever possible to phone and check opening times. While every effort has been made to ensure the accuracy of the information contained here, the publishers cannot accept responsibility for any errors it may contain.

PRICES AND PAYMENT

Prices throughout this guide are given in dirhams (dh). The prices we've supplied should be treated as guidelines, not gospel. If they vary wildly from those we've quoted, please write and let us know. We aim to give the best and most up-to-date advice, so we always want to know if you've been badly treated or overcharged.

We have noted whether venues take credit cards but have only listed the major cards – American Express (**AmEx**), Diners Club (**DC**), MasterCard (**MC**) and Visa (**V**). Some businesses will also accept other cards, including **JCB**. Some shops, restaurants and attractions take travellers' cheques.

THE LIE OF THE LAND

Full-colour maps are located throughout the guide. We have divided the city into areas that correspond to the maps on pages 248 to 252. For a map showing the different city areas and how they relate to each other, *see pp 246-7*. In those chapters where listings are *not* divided by

There is an online version of this guide, as well as weekly events listings for over 35 international cities, at **www.timeout.com**.

area, the area name has been added to the end of the address: note that this is there to help you locate the area on the map more easily; it is *not* necessarily part of the official address. Map references, indicating page and grid reference, are also given for all venues in areas covered by our maps.

TELEPHONE NUMBERS
You must dial area codes with all numbers, even for local calls. Hence all Marrakech land-line numbers begin 044, whether you're calling from inside or outside the city. From abroad, you must dial 212 (the international dialling code for Morocco) followed by the number given, *minus* the zero. Mobile phone numbers begin with 06.

ESSENTIAL INFORMATION
For all the practical information you'll need for visiting the city – including emergency phone numbers, visa and customs information, advice on facilities for the disabled, emergency telephone numbers, a list of useful websites and the full lowdown on the local transport network

in and around Marrakech – turn to the **Directory** chapter. You'll find it at the back of this guide, starting on page 220.

LET US KNOW WHAT YOU THINK
We hope you enjoy the *Time Out Guide to Marrakech & the best of Morocco*, and we'd like to know what you think of it. We welcome tips for places that you consider we should include in future editions and take notice of your criticism of our choices. There's a reader's reply card at the back of this book – or you can email us at guides@timeout.com.

The Time Out City Guides spectrum

Now 43 titles in the series – for more details
go to www.timeout.com

In Context

Koubba El Badiyin.

History

Like the city itself, the story of Marrakech is colourful, turbulent and frequently overheated.

You don't need to read a book to get a feel for the history of Marrakech: its past is laid out bare on the city's streets. There are palm trees that were brought up from the Sahara, Arab mosques adorned with Andalucian trimmings, Jewish ghettoes, imperial palaces, crowded souks, colonial hotels and sprawling shanty towns. The Jemaa el Fnaa, its bustling marketplace, also tells you much about the city's origins. But the real story of Marrakech can be seen in the Medina's imposing walls: for much of the past 1,000 years, this has been a city under siege. Marrakech's backdrop of the Atlas Mountains may be picturesque, but its residents – the warring Berber tribes – have always posed a threat. As Gavin Maxwell wrote in his classic history of the country, *Lords of the Atlas*, 'the whole life in [the Atlas Mountains] was one of warfare and of gloom. Every tribe had its enemies, every family had its blood feuds, and every man his would-be murderer.'

The very fact that the walls still stand over eight centuries since their construction also speaks of resilience: Marrakech has experienced glory, destruction, tyranny and purges, but each time the city has been crushed, it has risen again.

MARRA KOUCH

At the time Marrakech was founded in 1062, what's now Morocco was a former territory of the province of Mauretania. Following more than 1,000 years of rule by the Phoenicians, Romans, Byzantines and Arabs the region had reverted to a chaotic state of warring tribes. These roving peoples were mostly nomadic Arabs who had migrated from the Middle East over the previous few centuries, plus the Berbers (from the Greek for 'barbarian'), a tribe of Caucasian warriors who were direct descendants of the Ibero-Mauretanian Stone Age culture (18,000-8,000 BC). Over the centuries, the Berbers had coalesced into a complex clan system, establishing supremacy in the Atlas Mountains, from where they took delight in launching brutal attacks against whichever imperial forces were trying to impose order down on the plains.

For centuries, imperial rulers had been drawn to Morocco for its control of the caravan routes that ran down through the Sahara to Black Africa, creating a conduit for ivory, rare woods, ostrich feathers, kola nuts, skins, scents and other exotic items, along with slaves, for export to the outside world. By the 11th century the trade routes had become even more

valuable after gold was discovered in Ghana. Competition for control of these routes was fierce, but one loose confederation of Berber tribes, known as the Almoravids, had a natural advantage: these tough herdsmen had lived in the Western Sahara for centuries and had long since learned how to survive, even thrive, in its harsh conditions. They also struck up an alliance with Ghana's gold barons, for whom they became agents.

> **'If trade created Marrakech, then religion – along with a bit of bloodshed – helped it to flourish.'**

To secure their supremacy in the region, the Almoravids established a military outpost in 1062, just north of the most important pass across the High Atlas mountains. The military post quickly became a trading post, the 'gateway to Africa'. It took the name 'Marra Kouch', the meaning of which has baffled historians. It could be tribal dialect for 'Land of the Kouchmen' – a tribe of African warriors from Mauretania. Other tentative decipherings suggest 'cross and hide', a reference to its military origins, or 'do not linger', a warning to travellers to watch out for bandits. Whatever the meaning, the name had great significance – Europeans couldn't pronounce it and the bastardised version eventually became both 'Marrakech' and 'Morocco'.

THE ALMORAVIDS (1062-1147)
If trade created Marrakech, religion – along with a bit of bloodshed – helped it to flourish. The Almoravids were orthodox Muslims; most Berbers had converted to Islam after the Arab conquest of the early eigth century. Their ruler, Youssef Ben Tachfine, was determined to transform an anarchic land into an orderly Islamic state. Rigid self-discipline helped him establish a sizeable empire. From their base in Marrakech, the Almoravids had by the 1080s conquered the whole of Morocco. In 1086 they landed in Spain, defeated the Christians and absorbed much of the Iberian peninsula into an empire that by the early 12th century stretched from Lisbon and the Balearics to West Africa and from the Atlantic to Algeria.

Back in Marrakech, the Almoravids built what was by all accounts a spectacular city. Sadly, no Almoravid architecture survives except for one small but exquisite domed *koubba* (*see p70* **Koubba El Badiyin**). What must the fabled Ali Ben Youssef Mosque have been like if this koubba was just its ablutions fountain?

Despite the lack of buildings, the Almoravid legacy can still be felt in Marrakech, from the palm groves they planted to the city walls they erected. They also used their desert expertise to establish the city's water supply, building long underground pipes that carried water from the High Atlas mountains to the houses and gardens of Marrakech.

THE ALMOHADS (1147-1269)
By the mid 12th century, the Almoravids had overstretched their empire. In Spain, the Christians defeated them in several major battles, and word of their decline reached Marrakech. Scenting blood, a rival confederation of Berber tribes, the Almohads, launched an attack from the Atlas Mountains. Following a bloody seige lasting 11 months, in 1147 the Almohads took Marrakech. Such was their hatred of the Almoravids – the Almohads were even more puritanical than their former rulers – they destroyed the whole city and rebuilt it. To their credit, they did a beautiful job. The monumental architecture of this period still dominates not just Marrakech but the whole of Morocco. Their most stunning achievement was the elaborate Koutoubia Mosque (*see p62*). Built over the ruins of an Almoravid palace by an Andalucian architect, it's considered a masterpiece of Hispano-Moorish architecture. Other significant period pieces include the Kasbah Mosque (*see p76*), the monumental Bab Agnaou (*see p76*) and the glorious Agdal and Menara gardens (*see p84-p87* **Gardens**).

The early puritanism of the Almohad culture was tempered by splashes of Andalucian splendour: Abdel Moumen, the tribe's leader, had reconquered southern Spain, bringing with him Andalucian culture to Morocco. Moumen's army was also victorious in Tunis, Tripoli and southern Algeria. During his reign, Marrakech became something of a bastion of Islamic civilisation and culture, attracting famous scholars and philosophers.

As did their predecessors, the Almoravids, the Almohads eventually began to suffer reverses in Spain at the hands of the resurgent Christians. It was only a matter of time before things went pear-shaped in Morocco too. In 1248 a weakened Almohad army on its way home to Marrakech was ambushed by the Beni-Merens, a nomadic desert tribe. The entire Almohad army was massacred. The Beni-Meren chieftain rode on to capture Fès where he founded a new dynasty, the Merenids. In 1276 the last Almohad sultan was defeated and the Merenids extended their control to Marrakech and the south.

MERENIDS (1276-1554) AND SAADIANS (1549-1668)

After the glory of the Almohad period, Marrakech fell upon hard times, reduced to the status of provincial outpost while all the wealth was lavished on the new imperial cities of Fès, Salé and Meknes. This is the era of the great Muslim historians and explorers such as Ibn Khaldun and Ibn Batuta (the Muslim Marco Polo), but it was a golden age in which Marrakech played little part other than as a bastion against attacks from the south.

Following the pattern established by previous Moroccan dynasties, by the 15th century the Merenids were in decline, largely as a result of state corruption. Morocco suffered repeated attacks by marauding Christians from Portugal and Spain. Not only did these attacks weaken Merenid rule, but they spawned a wave of anti-Christian, Muslim fundamentalism. The Saadians, a southern tribe from the Drâa oasis valley, were quick to exploit the situation gathering an army under the flag of Islam. After a stunning victory against the Portuguese army at Agadir, the Saadian army dethroned the Merenids in Fès (1549).

The Saadian sultans returned the royal court to Marrakech and the city once again had the atmosphere of an imperial capital. The rise in maritime trade renewed the city's strategic importance, and it regained its status as a major trading post.

During the Saadian boom, the ruined city was transformed into the most opulent city in the Arab world. Sultan Moulay Abdellah rebuilt the Almoravids' Ali Ben Youssef Mosque and developed the similarly named *medresa* into the biggest Koranic school in North Africa. He gave the Jews their own quarter (*see p78* **Exodus**), the Christians their own trading centre at the heart of the Medina, roughly where the Club Mediterranean stands today, and sprinkled the city with marble fountains and hammams. To celebrate victory over the Portuguese in 1578 – remembered as the Battle of the Three Kings because three leaders lost their lives during its course, including the Saadian sultan. The succeeding sultan Ahmed El Mansour ('the Victorious'; 1578-1607) oversaw the construction of the most lavish of all royal complexes, the Badii Palace (*see p77*).

Poets of the 16th century compared Marrakech to the semi-mythical Baghdad of *The Thousand and One Nights*, a series of folk stories in Arabic. Some of the wealth and riches of the period can be seen displayed at the Dar Si Said museum (*see p80*), but the clearest impression of this glittering period of Marrakech history can be got from a visit to the mausoleums that the Saadian sultans had built for themselves.

CRUELTY AND NEGLECT

In true Marrakech style, the good times were followed by a period of stagnation. Following the death of Ahmed El Mansour in 1607, the country descended into civil war. Marrakech was repeatedly plundered. Eventually, an Arab prince, Moulay Rachid, seized the throne in 1668 and restored a semblance of order. Although the sultan's reign was uneventful, he left an important legacy: his family still rules Morocco today.

Like any family, there are the members no one likes to talk about – in this case, Rachid's younger brother and successor Moulay Ismail (1672-1727). Ismail hated Marrakech – he considered the city's residents unruly – and accordingly he moved the capital to Meknes. To rub salt into the wound, he stripped the Badii Palace bare (such was the wealth there that the task took a team of labourers 12 years to complete). But the residents of Marrakech were glad to see the back of him. So cruel and depraved was Ismail's rule, the Europeans dubbed him 'the Bloodthirsty'. Reported to have killed 30,000 people with his bare hands, Ismail murdered for entertainment. He organised daily torture shows, routinely disembowelled his staff and decapitated his slaves on a whim. Once, when the idle chatter of some of his concubines began to prove royally irritating, he had all their teeth pulled out. In his most gruesome stunt, he had

LE GÉNÉRAL LYAUTEY S'EST RENDU A MARRAKECH EN AUTO-MITRAILLEUSE

General Lyautey en route to Marrakech, 1912.

Christian labourers embedded into the walls of the imperial palace, where they were left to die slow, agonising deaths.

Ismail also has the dubious distinction of siring the most children in history – 888 according to the *Guinness Book of World Records*. Moroccans may have expelled a collective sigh of relief when his 54-year reign came to its end but not for long because, without his fearsome presence, the country once again descended into anarchy. For the next century, Morocco as a whole remained virtually ungovernable. The authority of the sultan was reduced to the coast and major towns and cities. Under Sidi Mohammed (1757-90) the Atlantic port of Essaouira briefly prospered through trade, until his son and successor decided to sever all contact between Muslim Morocco and Europe, pursuing an almost paranoiac policy of isolationism.

EUROPE COMES KNOCKING

By the early 19th century, Marrakech hadn't progressed much beyond the Middle Ages. Its livelihood was still the same as it had been for almost 1,000 years: olive oil, corn, livestock, tanned leather, slaves and woven goods.

Anxious to modernise, Sultan Abdel Rahman (1822-59) struck up a free trade agreement with Britain in the 1856 Treaty of Tangier. (Britain because Morocco was alarmed by the growing power of France and sought to keep Paris in check by allying with its rival.) As a consequence of the treaty, European influence in Morocco began to grow, particularly in the port cities of Casablanca and Tangier. Marrakech benefited too, and the increased wealth of its rulers and merchants resulted in a building boom that produced the likes of the Bahia and Dar Si Said palaces.

Liberalised trading did little to help ordinary Moroccans: European imports flooded the market, threatening traditional industries, such as metalwork, ceramics and weaving. Not only did Moroccans lose their livelihoods, but their sultans were increasingly rapacious when it came to taxes. When Sultan Abdul Aziz (1894-1908), surrounded by a court of European opportunists and adventurers, started frittering away millions on Western luxuries, his subjects began to get restless.

Meanwhile, oblivious to the sultan's authority, the European powers were cutting deals in a carve-up of North Africa. In exchange for a freehand in Egypt and the Sudan the British backed off the Maghreb; Italy got its paws on Libya and Spain was offered territory in northern and southern Morocco. The French were given wiggle room to proceed as they wished with the rest of Morocco. Their control

was tightened when the greedy Aziz snatched at a loan of 50 million francs dangled by a consortium of French banks. With the sultan heavily in its debt and the French army oozing across the border from Algeria, France needed just one little excuse for direct intervention. Marrakech obliged.

FRENCH RULE

In 1907 a baying mob lynched a French doctor in the Medina. Dr Emile Mauchamp, the first European doctor in the city, made the mistake of attaching an aerial to his roof. Believing it to be an evil charm, a superstitious crowd chased him into an alley and killed him. Lynchings of Europeans also occurred in Casablanca. The French army managed to quell uprisings in both cities, but France needed to consolidate its grip. The sultan of the time, Moulay Hafid (1908-12), was increasingly powerless to keep order. Faced by rebellions in town and country, crippling debts and aggression from the French army, Hafid had little choice but to accept the official imposition of French colonial rule, formalised in the Treaty of Fès in 1912.

> '**Cruelty and corruption were practically job requirements for Moroccan rulers.**'

But the Treaty of Fès was just a piece of paper: it couldn't impose order on anarchy. Two weeks after the treaty was signed, revolution broke out in Fès and 80 Europeans were lynched. In the south, a tribal warlord called El Hiba ('the Blue') raised 12,000 soldiers and captured Marrakech, vowing to drive out all Europeans and restore the country to a pure Islamic state. It took the machine guns and artillery of the French army to dispell the threat.

Keeping control of such an unruly country was going to be a problem. So the first Résident Général of Morocco, Marshal Lyautey, struck a deal with a couple of fearsome warlords from the Atlas Mountains. Thami El Glaoui, a shrewd political operator, was installed as the Bacha (Pasha, or Lord) of Marrakech, where he would rule with an iron fist for 42 years. His brother Madani was appointed Grand Vizier to the Sultan, but he died in 1918.

THE LORD OF MARRAKECH

The French gave El Glaoui cash to build up his army and carte blanche to rule Marrakech and southern Morocco as he saw fit. Ensconced in the lavish palace known as Dar El Bacha ('House of the Lord'), Thami El Glaoui became one of the great despots of Moroccan history, ruling Marrakech as a Mafia boss would. He hung

The last despot

The history of Marrakech is littered with tales of wealth, extravagance and luxury. But of all the rulers, one name stands out: Thami El Glaoui, lord of Marrakech from 1912 to 1955.

When the Europeans discovered him at the turn of the century, he was an uncouth tribal warlord living in the hostile surroundings of the Atlas Mountains. At the time, the Glaoui couldn't speak a word of French, and yet within 20 years, he was one of the most fashionable names in European high society, imbued with all the mystique and grandiosty ofan Indian maharajah. The crème de la crème of the international jet set were entertained at the opulent Dar El Bacha. While his political enemies languished in dungeons below, the Glaoui threw sumptuous banquets and lavished his guests with expensive gifts – from a priceless ring to a girl or boy who took their fancy. While his subjects went hungry, the Glaoui diverted water supplies from farmland to build an 18-hole golf course.

Despite his cruelty, the European elite were thoroughly impressed by his immaculate manners, generosity and bons mots. At one famous dinner party, the Glaoui overheard a young Parisian woman – who thought the Pasha understood no French – call him a pig, but admit to coveting his enormous emerald ring. At the end of the meal, the Glaoui pulled her aside and said, in immaculate French, 'Madame, a stone like this emerald was never made for a pig like me. Permit me to offer it to you'. Another time, when an interloper gatecrashed one of his parties, he forbade his guards from ejecting the man: 'On the contrary, treat him with the greatest consideration, since has taken all the trouble to come without being invited.'

The Glaoui may have gone to extremes to cultivate the image of a European gentleman, but his refined exterior hid a voracious sexual appetite. His harem of African girls was a mere distraction from his real quest: European women. Seduced by his air of omnipotence, European women queued up to be his mistress. But one mistress was never enough: the Glaoui had a comprehensive network of talent scouts scouring the streets of Marrakech for white-skinned conquests. Glaoui would invite the women to dinner and invariably lure them into the bedroom. But as sophisticated as he made himself out to be, he was not always hip to European sexual practices. Once, he threw a European woman out of his bedroom in horror, screaming, 'She tried to eat me!'

The Glaoui (wearing scarf) in London, August 1932.

A lasting affair

Marrakech has attracted many distinguished visitors over the centuries, but there was one famous guest who simply couldn't get enough of the place: Winston Churchill. 'If you have one day to spend in Morocco, spend it in Marrakech,' he famously said. And Churchill, who christened the city 'the Paris of the Sahara', knew what he was talking about. He first visited the city in 1935, and returned almost every winter for the next 20 years.

On his first visit, a working holiday, he wrote newspaper articles and discussed politics with Lloyd George in the winter sun, but soon became distracted by the glorious sunsets and painted seven canvases. On subsequent visits, he mostly stayed at the Mamounia Hotel where he would sit on his balcony with the view of the Atlas Mountains and his box of watercolours.

'I am captivated by Marrakech,' he wrote on one visit. 'Here in these spacious palm groves rising from the desert the traveller can be sure of perennial sunshine, of every comfort and diversion, and can contemplate with ceaseless satisfaction the stately and snow-clad panorama of the Atlas mountains. The sun is brilliant and warm but not scorching; the air crisp, bracing but without being chilly; the days bright, the nights cool and fresh.'

the heads of his enemies from the city gates. He controlled the city's 27,000 prostitutes, collecting a portion of their earnings. His spy network patrolled the city, briefing him each evening on the goings-on in the Medina. His secret agents brought him a never-ending parade of suspects to be tried in his own personal *salon de justice*. As the Glaoui's darkened dungeons filled with prisoners and his coffers with cash, henchmen combed rural villages for girls to stock the harem. The Glaoui's cruelty was matched only by his notoriously extravagant lifestyle (*see p11* **The last despot**), which he funded by establishing local monopolies in hemp, olives, almonds, saffron, dates, mint and oranges. Soon, the Glaoui enjoyed greater power than the sultan himself, and Marrakech rivalled the importance of the capital, Rabat.

The Glaoui's exploits were nothing unusual: cruelty and corruption were practically job requirements for Moroccan rulers. But his tyranny was particularly odious to Moroccans because it was being carried out on behalf of the French. Today, the Glaoui's treachery has even been immortalised in the French language: the word *glaouise* means 'betrayed' in French political jargon.

THE NOUVELLE VILLE

Despite his rapacious rule, the Glaoui enjoyed the wholehearted support of General Lyautey and the French administration. In the paternalistic terms of the time, France could bring enlightenment to Morocco while preserving its indigenous culture. After all, the Glaoui's despotic regime left them free to do what colonial powers did best: exploit the host country's national resources: Morocco was a rich source of phosphates, iron, anthracite, manganese, lead and silver; agriculture also flourished, as French companies turned traditional olive groves and orchards into industrial-style farms.

Beyond question, there was give as well as take. Lyautey had grand schemes ('I have always had two passions – policies regarding the natives and town planning.') involving the entire organisation of the country. He ordered

the Moroccan National Railroad Company which was extending the railway deeper into Morocco and needed a place to accommodate those who were en route to other parts of Africa.

Even to take the charitable view, as noble as Lyautey's intentions may have been, by building Guéliz away from the Medina he maintained a wide gulf between natives and Europeans. Guéliz received an impressive network of roads, railway connections, hospitals and schools, while the Medina remained in squalor.

By the 1930s there were 325,000 Europeans in the country. The staggering inequality between the 'colos', as they were known, and the natives was a major factor in stoking up support for a nationalist movement that found political voice with the formation of the Istiqlal (Independence) Party. World War II provided further momentum. The French army had relied on 300,000 Moroccan soldiers, who had acquitted themselves so capably that Franklin D Roosevelt, who had travelled to Casablanca to meet Churchill for a conference (*see p12* **A lasting affair**), hinted to Sultan Mohammed V that, after the war, the country would become independent.

TOWARDS INDEPENDENCE

Membership of the Istiqlal Party mushroomed, and the French began to get nervous. When the sultan began pushing for independence in 1953, the French sent him into exile – achieved with the coniving help of the Glaoui (who imprisoned his own son for nationalist sympathies). Banning the sultan proved a mistake and Mohammed V became a nationalist figurehead. His expulsion sent the country into a turmoil, triggering riots in Marrakech and Casablanca. Both cities became police states, with curfews, multiple arrests and interrogation under torture. A week after his expulsion, 13,000 Moroccans had been arrested for treason. By the summer of 1955 a campaign for his return had escalated into armed rebellion. In Casablanca, terrorists threw a bomb into a café killing seven Europeans. In Marrakech, a bomb was thrown into the Berima Mosque where Ben Arafa, the puppet sultan of the French, was praying. In the mining town of Oued Zem 49 Europeans were slaughtered in their beds.

The Glaoui's advice to the French was to 'do as the British did with the Mau Mau' – a reference to a particularly brutal suppresion in Kenya, when nationalists were slaughtered in their thousands. Unsurprisingly, this attitude toward his fellow Moroccans meant that when being driven around Marrakech in his Bentley the Glaoui felt safest prone on the floor clutching a submachine gun.

Churchill's most famous visit occurred in 1943, after a wartime conference in Casablanca with Franklin D Roosevelt. After the conference had finished, the US president was all set to return to America. Churchill was horrified. 'You cannot come all this way to North Africa without seeing Marrakech,' he insisted. 'Let us spend two days there. I must be with you when you see the sun set on the Atlas Mountains.' Roosevelt agreed, and before long the two were gazing at the purple hills from the balcony of their villa. As the sun went down, the American president – who was reclining on a divan at the time – was so moved by the scene he said to Churchill, 'I feel like a sultan: you may kiss my hand, my dear.' After their blissful break in Marrakech, the two leaders said their goodbyes and Churchill embarked on a truly punishing work schedule, zigzagging across the globe for war talks. As the year progressed, the exhausting workload took its toll on the statesman's health. Diagnosed with pneumonia, his doctor insisted on a three-week convalescence. When asked where he would like to recuperate, Churchill didn't hesitate: Marrakech. 'It is the most lovely spot in the whole world,' he said.

---

the transfer of the capital from Fès to Rabat and founded a completely new city 45 kilometres (30 miles) to the north (Port Lyautey, now Kenitra). He created a new harbour at Casablanca and in all major urban centres of size he added new European quarters. Thus Marrakech acquired a *nouvelle ville* a short distance north-west of the Medina walls, later to become known as Guéliz. Lyautey was explicit that these new quarters had to be separate from the old medinas in order to 'protect the autonomy of each'. This can be read two ways: a respect for the Moroccans and a commendable desire not to interfere with the traditional organisation of their cities, or enforced segregation.

A town planner named Henri Prost was brought in to lay out a scheme of large *rondponts* connected by wide leafy avenues overlooked by buildings of a Moorish style. A military fort, Camp Guéliz, on a rocky outcrop just north of the new town provided security. Almost as significantly, Prost was one of the architects behind an opulent new hotel called the Mamounia, built in 1922 by

Keith Richards and a shadowy
Cecil Beaton (1967). *See p16.*

Hands already full with a bloody nationalist revolt in Algeria, the French decided to cut their losses in Morocco. In November 1955 Mohammed V was permitted to return. The Glaoui was furious. Nevertheless, he kissed the feet of the sultan and begged for mercy. Punative measures were unnecessary because the Glaoui was already dying of cancer. On 30 January 1956 he died in his palace.

What should have been a joyous occasion for the citizens of Marrakech quickly turned ugly – as if even in death the Glaoui still had the ability to bring terror to the streets of the city. An angry mob took to the streets chanting 'Death to the traitors!'. Old allies of the Glaoui were hunted down, stripped, stoned and dragged outside the city walls where they were doused in petrol and set alight. Children gathered around, laughing and cheering as victim upon victim was thrown onto the bonfires. The new governors of Marrakech did nothing to halt the rioting but placed guards round the smouldering bodies so that women could not take pieces of them for use in black magic.

The corpse of the Glaoui himself was spared any indignities and was interred at the Shrine of Sidi Ben Slimane. People say that each Friday night, a black cobra slithers out of the tomb and remains poised to strike until the sun comes up.

In March 1956, three months after the Glaoui's death, Morocco was granted independence.

THE NEW MOROCCO

Following independence, the first act of the sultan was to restyle himself as King Mohammed V, a modern constitutional monarch. Not too modern, however: the monarchy was still at the centre of political life, and the king kept the military and police on a short leash. He was worried that the jubilation that followed independence would be short-lived, and he was right: the nationalist movement quickly disintegrated into a series of rival factions. The left-wing of the Istaqlal Party broke away to form a socialist party. The Berber-speaking tribes of the mountains formed the conservative Mouvement Populaire.

The king never lived to see the country's first democratic election. Presided over by his son, King Hassan II, the 1963 elections were won by a coalition of royalists and the Mouvement Populaire. The heavily rigged elections were widely considered to be a joke, fuelling the revolutionary zeal of the socialists. Its leader, Ben Barka, denounced the monarchy and was promptly exiled to Paris, where he was assassinated by secret agents. So much for the new Morocco.

Much of the civil unrest of the period was the result of poverty compounded by what can only be described as divine malice: in 1961 an invasion of locusts devastated the crops around Marrakech. A series of droughts added to the country's woes, as did the catastrophic 1961 earthquake in Agadir, which killed 15,000. Hassan II nationalised much of the economy, expropriating land from French companies but most of this land was reserved for export crops, such as citrus fruits, wine and vegetables, and did nothing to feed the domestic population. By the mid 1960s Morocco – once called 'the bread basket of the Roman Empire' – had become a net importer of cereals.

As poverty increased, mass migration to Europe followed: by 1986 there were more than one million Moroccans living abroad. But they didn't all go overseas: many rural Moroccans just emigrated to cities. During the 1960s the population of Moroccan cities doubled. Sprawling, overcrowded shanty towns – known as *bidonvilles* – sprang up on the edge of Marrakech and other major cities. A whole uncontrolled economy developed. Marrakech was soon packed with illegal taxi drivers, street peddlers and unofficial tourist guides. By 1971 some 69 per cent of the urban working population worked in the informal sector. The rise of hashish farming also fuelled the black economy and helped spawn a brand new kind of tourism.

MARRAKECH EXCESS

North Africa had long held a romantic resonance for European intellectuals: a haven for 19th-century bohemians, it had been a source of inspiration for writers and painters from Gustave Flaubert and Eugène Delacroix to André Gide and Henri Matisse.

The bohemian tradition continued into the 20th century when Tangier, designated as an International Zone free from French rule, became a haven for dissolute Americans and Europeans attracting the likes of Paul and Jane Bowles and William Burroughs (*see p212*). When the International Zone was abolished, the expats drifted south to Marrakech, entranced by the balmy climate, colourful exoticism and the quasi-mysticism of the sorcerers and trippy musicians.

In accordance with the prevailing Beat philosophy of the time, the spiritual went hand in hand with the sexual. The Marrakech brothels were infamous, particularly among gay men who found it easy to locate willing partners at a safe enough distance that their activities would go unreported at home (sun and sex in Marrakech remains a favourite with ageing American and European queens to this day). And, of course, there was the *kif*, or cannabis, which was smoked openly.

Brian Jones of the Rolling Stones made his first trip in 1966 with his girlfriend Anita Pallenberg. He brought the rest of the band with him on the next visit; they drove from Tangier to Marrakech and checked into the Hotel Es Saadi, where they tripped on LSD and ran into Cecil Beaton, who photographed Mick and Keith by the pool. At the centre of the scene were the American oil heir John Paul Getty Jr and his wife Talitha. The Gettys owned a place in the Medina, where they were famously photographed in kaftans up on the roof terrace against a backdrop of the Koutoubia Minaret and Atlas Mountains. Here they hosted parties that went on for days at a time. An entry in John Hopkins's *The Tangier Diaries* for 1 January 1968 reads: 'Last night Paul and Talitha Getty threw a New Year's Eve party at their palace in the Medina. Paul McCartney and John Lennon were there, flat on their backs. They couldn't get off the floor let alone talk. I've never seen so many people out of control.'

> **'While the foreigners carried on with their easy drugs and risky sex lifestyle, members of the royal court were plotting how to get rid of their ruler.'**

THE KING OF COOL (I)

While the foreigners carried on with their easy drugs and risky sex lifestyle, members of the royal court were plotting how to get rid of their ruler. In 1971 the king's 42nd birthday party was gatecrashed by 1,400 army cadets who loosed machine-gun fire at the 800 or so diplomatic guests lounging around the pool. The coup leader was accidentally killed in the crossfire and the cadets panicked, at which point the king, who had hidden in a bathroom, emerged and coolly stared down his would-be assassins, who dropped their weapons and rushed forward to kiss his hands and feet. The failed coup had left 98 guests dead.

The following year, the king's Boeing 727 was attacked in the air by six F5 fighters from his own airforce. One of the jet's engines was destroyed but it managed to land at Rabat, where the rebel aircraft continued to strafe it and the groups of officials who had been waiting to greet the flight, until the king grabbed his plane's radio and shouted, 'Stop firing! The tyrant is dead!'. The minister of defence committed suicide, there were summary executions and then the king got back to ruling the country.

In 1975 he seized the Spanish colony of Rio del Oro, in the Western Sahara. He did so by organising the 'Green March', in which 350,000 citizens marched from Marrakech to the Western Sahara. General Franco had just died and Spain relinquished the colony without much fuss. But the colony's residents had other ideas: Polisario, a nationalist group comprised of the indigenous Sahrawi tribe, proclaimed a republic. Backed by the Algerians, they waged a guerrilla war of independence against Morocco until a ceasefire in 1991. To this day, the dispute has yet to be fully resolved.

The same year as the Polisario ceasefire, the king dispatched 1,200 troops to Saudi Arabia as a gesture of support to the US Gulf War operation. It was not a popular move – Arab versus Arab – and resulted in rioting on the Moroccan streets. Although a moderate country, the violence has continued. In 1994 Islamic extremists attacked a hotel in Marrakech, spraying the lobby with machine-gun fire and killing two Spanish tourists. In 2002 a Moroccan El Qaeda cell was arrested for plotting attacks on American and British ships in the Strait of Gibraltar.

Many of the fanatics came from the ranks of unemployed youth – always fertile recruiting ground for the Islamicists. But in fact, social deprivation had long been top of the state agenda. Throughout the 1980s Morocco had been on a privatisation drive aimed at reducing the state sector and bolstering the country's oil, chemical and fishing industries. Today, for example, Morocco yields the world's largest annual catch of sardines (not many people know that). The biggest cash cow, however, remains tourism.

THE KING OF COOL (II)

During the 1990s almost two million visitors a year came to Morocco. Not only were they flocking to newly developed coastal resorts like Agadir, but Marrakech achieved levels of hipness not seen since the '60s. Inspired by what one travel writer called 'ethno-chic tourism', the fashionistas and interior designers rediscovered the pink city, snapping up riads in the Medina or villas in the Palmeraie.

The city's profile was further boosted by the accension to the throne in 1999 of a new young monarch. Dubbed 'the Beatles of the Arab World' by the press, *Time* magazine cover star King Mohammed VI is seen as the country's great modernising force, a bridge between Islam and the West. Although the official royal residence is in the capital, Rabat, the 39-year-old spends as much time as he can

The **'Green March'**, 1975, portrayed at the Café Atlas. *See p16.*

living it up in Marrakech, where he is often seen jogging in the streets in a muscle shirt and Nike trainers, or smoking Marlboros at restaurants in the Medina. The king was instrumental in setting up the Marrakech International Film Festival in 2001, and in his biggest publicity stunt yet, he threw a star-studded birthday bash for the rapper Puff Daddy at the Bahia Palace.

He regularly gives interviews to the press – unheard of for a Moroccan monarch – and, in an unprecedented move, married a 24-year-old computer engineer in 2002, getting rid of his father's harem in the process. Not only was it the first time a Moroccan monarch had married a middle-class, professional woman, but it was the first time a Moroccan royal wedding had been splashed all over the papers.

Despite the *Hello!*-style profile, it seems Mohammed VI is also serious about his politics. Shortly after stepping up to the throne, the new king promised to tackle the problem of rural poverty and illiteracy. He lifted restrictions on the press and released thousands of political prisoners.

The country's most recent elections, in 2002, were the fairest in Morocco's history. The king appointed a socialist, Driss Jettou, as the new prime minister, and for the first time, there are two women in the cabinet. However, he failed to appoint a single representative of the Islamic Justice Party (PJD) to his cabinet, despite its successes in the elections.

Torn between modern, liberal capitalism and the Islamic world, Mohammed VI clearly has his work cut out for him in the coming years. Tellingly, most of the supporters of the PJD are Morocco's working class, the majority of whom are illiterate and live on less than a dollar a day. Marrakech, for instance, might be the chic destination *du jour*, but its newfound glamour is undercut by a worrying divide between the rich and the poor. Unless that gap is somehow reconciled, the history of the city looks set to continue on its restless rollercoaster ride. Still, like the glorious epochs of the Almohads and the Saadians, Marrakech seems to be on a roll again. If the city's tumultuous history is anything to go by, you better enjoy it while you can.

Marrakech Today

Real estate, riad culture and royal patronage are driving the modernisation of Marrakech.

The scene: 1.30am one night in October 2002. A red carpet runs between two kneeling camels, placid creatures that barely bat an eyelid despite the proximity of prancing fire-eaters who belch out plumes of orangey flame. As guests in tuxedos and cocktail dresses tread the red carpet to enter the villa, girls scatter handfuls of pink rose petals from the balcony above. Inside is deep crimson and crowded with chatter. Drinks are delivered by dwarfs, long-haired transvestites consort with regal-looking Africans in white robes, and everyone looks good in the flickering half-light of candles. It could be a scene from something by David Lynch, which is entirely appropriate given that he's expected to drop by tonight. In the event he doesn't, but Francis Ford Coppola looks in as do a handful of French starlets. This is the opening night of the International Film Festival and for sheer drop-dead glamour it out Cannes Cannes. How did a small, provincial, near-dry (in all senses) city in North Africa get to be so damn hip?

Fast rewind to the 1960s. It was back then that the foundations were laid for the Western fantasy of Marrakech, a city where all

eccentricities are permitted, solitude is not considered antisocial, genuinely individual style has room to flourish and lassitude is never out of season. There were Mick and Keith being photographed by the pool while bright young hope of the fashion world Yves Saint Laurent came house-hunting, along with Diana Vreeland of *Vogue*, the Gettys, the odd Rothschild, and sundry rich and famous. It was the alter ego of London and Paris, a place where the fast-living jetset went to shed their social skins and professional identities. As Saint Laurent described it, the city was a 'place out of time' – but that was probably just the *majoun*.

In fact, Marrakech had been fulfilling much the same role since the 1920s, when the same mixture of local colour, Orientalist mystique and a liberating remove from the West captured the imagination of an earlier generation of millionaires and aristos. The social circle then revolved around the Villa Taylor, built in 1923 by the Taylors of Newport, Rhode Island, who came to Morocco on a steam yacht. Its guest rooms played host to Rita Hayworth and Charlie Chaplin, Winston Churchill (see p12

A lasting affair) and Franklin D Roosevelt. The story goes that when Mrs Taylor learned that FDR had spent the night at her house, she refused ever to set foot in it again and the place was sold to the Countess Boul de Breteuil (who, according to John Hopkins' *The Tangier Diaries*, had a seamstress who'd undergone a mastectomy and used her false breast as a pincushion). Anyway, for all those '60s *arrivistes*, a homage-paying stop at the Villa Taylor was an essential part of the Marrakech social itinerary.

When the scene moved on, as scenes do, and everything went a bit *Hideous Kinky* – all tie dyes and cheesecloth – not all of the seasonal migrants departed. Figures such as American interior designer Bill Willis, Spanish-born antique dealer Adolfo de Valesco, the Dutch collector Bert Flint, French designer Jacqueline Fossaic and Yves Saint Laurent stayed on. Having settled on Marrakech, they wanted to make their homes in traditional houses rather than heading for the New City (location of Villa Taylor), so many began restoring and creating homes for themselves in the Medina.

FLIGHT TO THE MEDINA
It seems obvious now that the Medina is where anyone would want to live, but during the French Protectorate, which ended only in 1956, the Old City suffered. In their respect for indigenous life, the French authorities left the Old City well alone and built their new European quarters outside the city walls. What nobody perhaps foresaw was that the Moroccans also preferred to live in the new European neighbourhoods, where houses had modern amenities such as plumbing and the streets were surfaced and wide enough for cars. Money began moving out of the Medina, a trend that continued long after the French had gone. The effects of those decades of neglect continue; barely a week after the 2002 Film Festival party, a bunch of Europeans gathering for dinner at a house near Jemaa El Fna received the fright of their lives when the building next door suddenly collapsed into a great pile of shattered mudbricks. Pure neglect. It's not an uncommon occurrence.

However, that first European and American incursion into the Medina set in motion a sea change from which the city is currently reaping the benefits. Where Willis and Co went others followed. Their numbers were small but the investment was significant, not just in terms of hard cash but also in revitalising traditional skills like tiling, stucco-carving and woodworking. Not since the days of the Glaoui, the early 20th-century warlord of extravagant tastes (*see p11* **The last**

despot), had there been so many moneyed patrons of artisans in Marrakech. The market for high-quality craftsmanship boomed, and soon local Marrakchis began to pick up on what was going on.

In 1990 entrepreneur Abdelatif Ben'Abdellah bought his first riad, renovated it with the help of young Belgian architect Quentin Wilbaux, and sold it on. While searching for other suitable properties, Ben Abdellah and Wilbaux became alarmed by the state of houses they were seeing, so they went to the Ministry of Culture to talk about what could be done to preserve the city's heritage. 'What heritage?' said the Ministry. So the pair set up Marrakech Medina, a company devoted to restoring as much of the Medina as two driven individuals could possibly manage.

To date, the number of old houses worked on by Abdelatif is into double figures but along the way the whole scenario acquired momentum beyond anyone's imaginings. The catalyst can be pinpointed with absolute accuracy: a French TV feature on Morocco screened in the mid 1990s, during which the presenter reported that for the price of a small flat in Paris one could buy a palace in Marrakech. The next day Ben Abdellah's phone went mad with excited calls from France wanting to know if he'd got any palaces he could sell them.

A little over five years on and at last count over 600 houses in the Medina had been bought by foreigners, mainly French, although the Italians and Brits are fast catching up. Prices have skyrocketed and, for a Moroccan, real estate is the business to be in (although they are no longer interested in selling to locals because foreigners pay so much more). Even at the most inflated rates, a pretty little Marrakchi *dar* (house) or *riad* (a house with courtyard garden) still represents an attractive buy. A property with perhaps three bedrooms and a couple of spare salons arranged around a planted inner court open to the sky probably sets you back around £40,000. What's that in London terms, a garden shed in Dagenham? Most of the foreign-bought properties are converted into guest accommodation, either rented out whole or run as maisons d'hôte.

Riad fever has made Marrakech a staple of the glossy travel porn spreads. *Elle Decoration*, *Homes & Gardens* and *Wallpaper** are read more avidly in Guéliz coffeeshops than any daily newspapers. This brings problems, as each new arrival on the Marrakech scene now has to outdo its predecessors to be sure of coverage (proud owners carry the clippings in top pockets). Sleek and stylish is no longer enough. New properties have to razzle and dazzle with stage-set decor: a central water

basin the size of a football pitch; waterways snaking round the property; re-creations of Alhambran courts. They have to up the ante on services offered, adding cigar lounges, 'house' camels or pick-ups from the airport in an air-conditioned London Hackney cab.

All of this comes at a price and room rates of £250 a night are pretty standard for Marrakech. Which is piffling really given that the arrival of the Amanjena in 2000 pushed the upper limits to around £1,400. Rather than acting as a deterrent, the sky-high bracketing only increases the exoticism and allure. Sting was set to hire out the whole Amenjena for his 50th (scuppered by the events of 11 September), while more recently Puff Daddy blew into town for his birthday bash.

With the architecture of many new developments teetering towards parody – 'traditional' Moroccan via the filter of West Coast America – Marrakech has come to resemble a kind of North African Las Vegas.

FOREIGNERS WELCOME

All those Manola Blahniks tottering through the dusty alleys of the Medina – you have to wonder what the locals make of it. More to the point, 600 foreign-owned residences represents about five per cent of Old City occupancy. On some streets there is barely a single Moroccan family remaining. But on the whole locals see this mild foreign infestation as a good thing. There's the odd instance of cultural clash – topless Spaniards on the terraces, boozy English singalongs with the call to prayer – but ask around and most locals will tell you that the majority of foreigners are properly respectful of Moroccan ways and traditions.

Not that any great concessions have to be made. Morocco might be Islamic but in terms of severity it's closer to Bradford than Tehran, while Marrakech is so far removed from the national centres of political power (Rabat) and religion (Fès) that it enjoys an even greater degree of liberalism. For every regular mosque-goer there are ten people who won't see the inside of a prayer hall until their corpse is laid out in one. For every *haj* who's made the pilgrimage to Mecca there are many more who've visited America. For every woman in a *hijab* there's her equivalent in a sleeveless T-shirt and tight Levis. And the fact that non-Muslims can't enter mosques and other religious buildings (as opposed to Egypt, Syria, Turkey and even Iran) is a French rule laid down during the Protectorate in the interests of harmonious relations.

The religious secular split is given physical form in the city's municipal organisation. The Old City and the New are separate entities, each with its own mayor and ruling body, each with its different regulations. Buildings in the

Riad rescuer **Abdelatif Ben Abdellah**. *See p19.*

Dreaming of 10 million tourists: **Mohammed Zkhiri**. *See p22.*

Medina, for example, can't go above three storeys in height; in Guéliz they can climb to five or six. Alcohol is banned in the Medina but there's little problem getting a licence in Guéliz. Marrakchis move easily between the worlds of old and new.

Any gulf between foreign residents and locals is going to focus not on religion but on money. The country as a whole suffers from widespread poverty, illiteracy and more than 20 per cent unemployment. Moroccans are putting their hopes in their new king. Under 40 and dynamic, Mohammed VI (M6 to his young fans) won great initial approval when soon after ascending to the throne in 1999 he sacked scores of government officials to make way for reform. Then, when the story got round that after dining at the Mamounia the king pulled out his wallet to settle the tab, his popularity went through the ceiling.

The new king also happens to like Marrakech and his patronage is the other major factor in the city's current high profile. His intentions were signalled when he built himself a new modestly sized residence just inside the city walls as a more homely alternative to the rambling palace favoured by his predecessors, and by his appointment of the new *wali*. The wali is the governor and the guy who actually runs the city. The person that the king chose for the job is, like his boss, relatively young,

reputedly dynamic and an ex-chairman of Royal Air Maroc – that is, someone who understands tourism. This is important given that the king has stated his wish to see the present figure of 2.5 million visitors to Morocco per year boosted to ten million by 2010.

Together, M6 and the wali are on the right track. One of their first initiatives, for example, was to snip away at the red tape and make it easier for foreigners to acquire property. This was aimed specifically at encouraging the growth of riad-style accommodation. 'It's a formula that is working very, very well,' the king told an interviewer in 2001, noting that riads create jobs while helping to preserve the Medina. After a survey showed that few first-time visitors to Marrakech desired to return, the dynamic duo also cracked down on the legions of aggressive touts who used to make trips into the souk unbearable.

The clean-up campaign, the easing off of bureaucracy and the general buzz around King Mohammed VI are also luring back Morocco's own people. Marrakchis who had emigrated West are now returning to cash in and investment in the city is spiralling. Among many projects on the drawing board in spring 2003 were an ambitious new restaurant and nightclub complex across from the Mamounia, a museum of civilisations combined with concert hall in the southern Medina, a recording studio

and performance space in the northern Medina and a scheme for 40 luxury villas on the edge of the Palmeraie.

Meanwhile, Marrakech is busy creating a framework for this growth. A team of UK consultants has been advising a local steering committee on expansion and development. According to Mohammed Zkhiri, a dapper local businessman, owner of the acclaimed Dar Yacout restaurant and British honorary consul to boot, the main thrust of what they're about is increasing the number of guest beds in Marrakech by 150 per cent. To this end a

100-hectare site on the outskirts of town has been set aside as an 'international hotel and restaurant' zone. Along with it, says Zkhiri, comes new infrastructure, such as roads, and more things for people to do, such as museums and cultural centres.

All of which begs the question, what happens when a city that thrives on exclusivity and vicarious tourism becomes inundated? Can Marrakech sustain its special identity in the face of a possible onslaught of Hiltons, Inter-Continentals and Best Westerns? Our advice: book that flight now.

The ultimate Marrakech buy

A month spent in Marrakech in the 1970s kicked off the affair. I fell in love and my husband sighed and hoped it would pass. It did and for a while I flirted with Crete instead. But then a return visit to Morocco in 1996 on a quest for winter warmth rekindled the 'Marrakech project' took hold. In 1999 we began combing the ancient alleys of the Old City. We were looking for a house we could run as a B&B to cover costs

and then we could always refuse bookings when we felt we needed a North African break from life in London. Aided by two local friends, over the course of three visits we looked at around 100 different properties. Nothing was suitable. We were on the verge of giving up when we walked into the courtyard of one last riad and knew instantly that it was the one.

The house was in a state of total neglect but the structure was sound. We swiftly agreed a price and visited the *notaire* to put down the customary ten per cent deposit. The notaire's job is to establish that deeds are 'clean' – that is, that everybody who owns the house agrees to sell. Because of the laws of inheritance Marrakech houses are typically owned by dozens of family members and every last one of them has to agree to the sale. It can take weeks, months or even years to track them all down. Fortunately, that wasn't the case with our house.

The riad needed complete restoration. We had architect friends in the UK draw up plans and located a local builder in Marrakech. Foolishly, we paid the builder in three tranches according to an agreed contract, and as soon as the third payment was made work fizzled out well short of completion. We turned to another friend, Iliass Tafroukht, who called in builders from his local mosque as well as assorted relatives to make curtains and mattresses. The work was completed on schedule. The riad was kitted out by local craftsmen (five brothers handcrafted the furniture) and from the neighbouring souks.

From start to finish the project took a year. We now have a gorgeous second home, a thriving little business (managed by Iliass) and, best of all, a whole bunch of loyal Marrakech friends.
By Maggie Perry, of Riad Magi (see p51).

Architecture

Arab artisans and Berber mud builders conspire in high art.

When the Arab commander Oqba Ben Nafi spurred his horse into the surf of the Atlantic in AD 682 and swore, 'O God, I take you to witness that there is no ford here. If there was I would cross it', it marked the completion of the Islamic conquest of North Africa, confirmed when Idris II established the wholly Islamic city of Fès. In 818 a failed rebellion in Córdoba sent a flood of Arab refugees to Fès, and a decade later a similar rebellion in Tunisia brought more. In just a few decades Morocco had gained its defining architectural influences and the communities of craftsmen that would give it shape and form.

GAINS FROM SPAIN

Morocco became the inheritor of the architectural and craft traditions of Muslim Spain and the Córdoban empire (whose glory was enshrined in the glorious Mezquita, Córdoba's Great Mosque). The Almoravids (1062-1147), who were the next dynasty to reunite Morocco after the country dissolved into principalities on the death of Idris II, further opened the doors to the influx of Spanish Muslim culture. They founded Marrakech (1062) as their capital and, under the influence of the Spanish, built some monumental structures, importing into Morocco for the first time the horseshoe arch and cusp arch (the one that looks like a broccoli section). Under the Almoravids the fine carving of stucco also first appears. Incredibly, some of those earliest designs (stylised, paisley-like flowers), which

appear in the *mihrab* (prayer niche) of the Karawiyin Mosque in Fès and are reproduced in the erudite *A Practical Guide to Islamic Monuments in Morocco* by Richard Parker, are still being reproduced in Marrakech in 2003 by young craftsmen furiously chiselling swirls and flourishes into bands of damp plaster before it sets.

In terms of surviving monuments, the only complete Almoravid building in the whole of Morocco is Marrakech's **Koubba El Badiyin** (*see p70*), which displayed for the first time many of the elements and motifs that have since come to characterise Moorish building.

During the reign of the successors to the Almoravids, the Almohads (1147-1269), the Spanish-Moorish synthesis reached its peak. Moroccan architectural styles were developed dramatically. Building materials of choice remained mud brick and *pisé* (reinforced mud), but stone was employed for certain structures, notably the splendid Marrakech gate known as the **Bab Agnaou** (*see p76*). Decoration was simplified and made more masculine; according to Parker, whereas the Almoravids went in for flowers, their successors favoured geometric patterns. However, even these austere rulers seemed to have eventually softened to some degree, as can be seen in the lovely trellis-like brickwork and faience tiling lavished on the minarets of the **Koutoubia Mosque** (*see p62*) and the **Kasbah Mosque** (*see p76*) – as well as **La Tour Hassan** (*see p207*) in Rabat and the

sublime Giralda in Sevilla, Andalucia, a territory reconquered by the Almohad Sultan Abdel Moumen.

Under the Merenids (1276-1554), Marrakech may have languished as attention switched to the northern imperial cities of Fès, Meknes and Salé, but artistic interchange continued with Spain. Some of the Merenids' finest monuments – including the **Karaouiyine Mosque** and **Bou Inania Medersa**, both in Fés; *see p198* – share similarities with the other great Moorish architectural achievement of the time, the extraordinary Alhambra palace complex, just across the Strait in Granada.

THE ART OF ZELIJE

It was the Merenids who introduced most of the familiar interior design repertoire into Morocco, including carved stucco (previously largely confined to the outside of buildings) and carved wood, as well as *zelije*, the creation of intricate mosaic design using hand-cut tiles.

> '**The Berbers added pink, purple, orange, red and yellow to the existing blue, green and white palette of Islamic culture.'**

Islamic tradition forbids any representation of living things, a policy defined in the formative years of the religion when the Prophet Mohammed first started preaching

against the idol worshippers of his home town of Mecca. Hence, with very few exceptions, creativity flourished in more abstract forms. The tradition of tiling was carried west by the Arabs, who had been inspired by the bright turquoise domes and mausoleums of ancient Persia and Samarkand. The Central Asians, in their turn, had picked up the idea from Chinese porcelain, hence the devotion to blue. The Moors of Morocco and Andalucia took the art form into a whole new area by widening the colour palette courtesy of the influence of the Berbers. Tribal inhabitants of the Atlas Mountains that separate Morocco from the rest of Mediterranean North Africa, the Berbers added pink, purple, orange, red and yellow to the existing blue, green and white palette of Islamic culture.

Zelije takes the form of complex geometrical patterns executed in small glazed tiles like a massive jigsaw puzzle. The tiles are formed in large, not small, sizes and have to be cut to shape. This remains the case even today. Visit a building under construction and there will be a group of craftsmen employed to do nothing but cut tiles, which are then stockpiled awaiting the attention of the *zelayiya*, the zelije master craftsman, who will assemble them according to designs passed from father to son and retained in memory only.

There are, it is claimed, 360 different shapes of cut-clay pieces, called *fourma*, and the permutations of colour and pattern are endless. The craft has always been a speciality of the artisans of Fès where the best examples of work are to be found, but Marrakech has no shortage of kaleidoscopic tiling either, exhibited in its various palaces and religious monuments.

DOORS AND SCREENS

The other great Merenid addition to the architectural repertoire is woodworking. Morocco is almost unique among the Islamic countries of North Africa and the Middle East in that it has an abundance of trees (concentrated primarily in the Middle Atlas region). Wood has rarely been used as a primary structure (walls, floors and columns are made of mudbrick and stone) but it was frequently employed for ceilings, lintels, column capitals and, of course, doors. Doors are a big thing in Moroccan architecture, frequently massive and imposing pieces of work, and typically decorated with carving, incising and inlays.

The other notable application of woodworking skill is in the wooden screens known as *mashrabiya*. These are formed from a series of lathed bobbins stuck together in geometric patterns. They were made to be

The best Buildings

For formative stylings
Koubba El Badiyin. *See p70.*

For zelije tiling
Saadian Tombs. *See p77.*

For fancy woodworking
Dar Si Said Museum. *See p80.*

For lacy stucco
Ben Youssef Medersa. *See p70.*

For domestic elegance
Dar Cherifa. *See p146.*

For Mauresque
30 rue de la Liberté. *See p82.*

For Marrakech modern
Theatre Royal. *See p82.*

Stucco and zelije at **Dar El Bacha**. *See p75.*

installed in the women's quarter (*harem*) of palaces and grander houses, so that the ladies could push their noses up against the screens and observe what was going on on the other side without being seen themselves. The screens' function has become obsolete in these more progressive times but the skill survives, and mashrabiya is still manufactured in souks throughout the country, purely for its decorative value and saleability to collectors.

Unfortunately, much of the best woodworking has traditionally been reserved for holy institutions such as mosques, shrines and *medersas* (Koranic schools; a building type also introduced by the Merenids), all of which are, with very few exceptions, off-limits to non Muslims. However, some impressive examples of historic craftsmanship can be seen in Marrakech at the engrossing **Dar Si Said Museum** (*see p80*).

PALACES AND HOUSES

Post Merenid, Moroccan architecture went into a period of stagnation. The Moors had retreated from southern Spain in the late 15th century and the Moroccan empire had collapsed inwards. Under the Saadians (1549-1668), Marrakech became the capital again and was embellished with grand new monuments, including the delightful **Ben Youssef Medersa** (*see p70*) and the dazzling **Saadian Tombs** (*see p77*). The former is notable for its acres of carved stucco and wood, the latter for floor-to-ceiling zelije. In the opinion of architectural historians these buildings are of little importance and are dismissed as inferior repetitions of earlier techniques and motifs, created by artisans rather than architects. That may be so, but at least through them the visitor gains an idea of the glories of previous buildings which have since been lost.

What the Saadians excelled at were palaces. Sultan Ahmed El Mansour (1578-1607) took 25 years over the building of the **Badii Palace** (*see p77*). Unfortunately, throughout history Moroccan dynasties have not only had a habit of shifting the centre of power around and constructing new monuments of grandeur, they've also been inclined to destroy whatever had been created by their predecessors. So, right at the start, the Almohads pulled down the original founding fortress of Marrakech to replace it with the Koutoubia Mosque, and, later, Moulay Ismail, who succeeded the Saadians, dismantled the Badii Palace – all that remains are impressive ruins.

Essentially the palaces echoed the design of a traditional house or *dar*. Both followed the principle of an anonymous exterior of blank walls with an entrance leading via a passage – kinked so that anyone at the door or gate couldn't see directly inside – to a central open-air court. The whole palace or house looks inward rather than outward, with windows and terraces addressing the courtyard, which serves to introduce both light and air into the rooms set around it. On the ground floor these are public reception rooms and salons; the private quarters are above.

The central open spaces are also rooms in themselves, used for eating and entertaining. In larger houses the courts often have *bahou*, small recessed seating areas. A *douiriya*, or annex, contains the kitchens and servants' rooms. At roof level, flat terraces provide additional space for storage, drying washing or keeping goats and chickens.

KASBAHS AND KSOUR

All that has been described so far is essentially Arab architecture, imported into Morocco since the arrival of Islam. But Marrakech is notably different from the imperial cities of the north – Fès, Meknes, Rabat and Salé – because of the influence of the indigenous Berbers.

These desert and mountain tribal people were the original inhabitants of Morocco long before the Arabs and their city of Fès, long even before the Romans established their outpost at Volubilis. Their architecture is quite literally of the earth. The typical fortified Berber village, known as a *ksar*, or *ksour* in the plural, has traditionally been built of soil reinforced with lime, straw and gravel, mixed into a thick mud paste and applied by hand to a wooden frame. It dries so hard that it takes a hammer and chisel to mark it. At the same time, it has a beautifully organic quality; if another home or extension is needed it's simply welded on and the village grows like a bees' nest. (Interestingly, the one other place this kind of hive construction appears is at the oasis of Siwa in Egypt, which is a lone desert Berber outpost in another Arab land.)

> **'With French rule came a new style of architecture, a mix of European modernistic and Moorish, dubbed "Mauresque".'**

Similar to the ksour is the *kasbah*, which can be described variously as a castle, a fortress, a palace or a garrison – the key to its definition is that it is the residence of a tribal ruler. These ancient structures predominate in southern Morocco, built as much to protect the Berbers from one another as from outside invaders. They are often sited on a hill or other strategic feature of the landscape, with towers at each corner serving as lookout posts. The interiors are simple, often claustrophobic, with narrow windows, so rely on terraces and courtyards to bring in light – the model for the Arab dar and palace. They might rise to four or five storeys, with the living quarters and grander reception rooms on the upper floors. Decoration is in the form of bold geometric motifs – the Berbers were early converts to Islam so share the Arab aversion to figurative representation. At the same time, they held on to many pre-Islamic superstitions and commonly adorned walls with simple motifs carved into the drying mud that were designed to ward off evil.

Because of the materials used to build these structures, a popular way to break down the defences of a kasbah is to reroute a river and wait for the water to wash away the fortification's foundations.

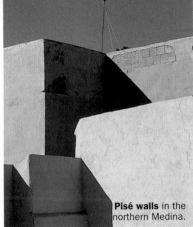

Pisé walls in the northern Medina.

Sadly, many kasbahs and ksour have been abandoned over the decades as tribal power has waned. The south of Morocco, especially the High Atlas region, is studded with decaying hilltop ruins, most spectacularly at **Telouet** (*see p175*), the former stronghold of the Glaoui tribe, whose leader took up residence in Marrakech and gained international infamy as the last great Moroccan despot (*see p11*). There have been several failed attempts to rescue the kasbah – all foiled by complicated inheritance laws, which mean the site is jointly owned by all the descendants of the Glaoui whose myriad permissions would need to be sought before any transfer of ownership could be made. In other cases, rescue attempts have prevailed and impressive partially and wholly restored kasbahs can be visited at **Ait Benhaddou** (*see p176*), **Skoura** (*see p181*), **Taourirt** and **Tiffoultoute** (for both *see p177*).

UNTIL TODAY

Following the Saadian dynasty, Marrakech and Morocco as a whole endured a succession of weak, ineffectual imperial figureheads who were largely unable to halt the country's descent into intermittent civil war. Architecture rarely flourished. Marrakech briefly grew wealthy during the reign of free-trade fan Sultan Abdel Rahman (1822-59), with the wealth accrued resulting in the building of the **Bahia Palace** (*see p78*). Half a century later the Glaoui's rapacious taxes financed the **Dar El Bacha** (*see p75*). However, if the Saadian monuments were just imitations of greater glories past then these later buildings are third-hand pastiche, only sporadically enlightened by the skills of local artisans.

The arrival of the French in 1912 drew a line under all that had gone before. With foreign rule came a new style of architecture, a mix of European modernistic and Moorish, dubbed 'Mauresque'. Marrakech gained a new town but

few buildings of distinction – unlike Casablanca, which is one of the undiscovered gems of 1920s and '30s city planning and the beneficiary of a vast legacy of sleek and elegant art deco design (*see p192* **Deco dreams**). Thankfully, the city is wising up to this cultural lodestone and has embarked on a programme of preservation and restoration.

In Marrakech, the Protectorate was a mixed blessing. The city was introduced to new architectural ideas, but traditional forms and crafts were largely sidelined in the process. It's only recently, almost 50 years after the departure of the French, that architecture in the city has begun to move on. Gratifyingly, the inspiration for much of what is happening is Berber simplicity, with current high-profile architects such as Charles Boccara (*see p31*) and Elie Mouyal (*see p33*) looking to the logic, economy and organic-stylings of mud building.

According to Boccara, when he first began working in Marrakech in the 1980s there was 'no competition'; now he estimates there are maybe more than 50 small architectural practices. He singles out for attention Mohammed Amine Kabbaj, originally from Casablanca, trained in Strasbourg with a diploma from Paris and resident in Marrakech since 1980. Along with two partners, Kabbaj operates out of a hi-tech basement office in the New City, balancing big-bucks projects like a new factory for Coca-Cola with *riad* rebuilds in the Medina and a personal project to revitalise the small Berber town of Tamesloht and conserve its kasbah.

At the same time, thanks to the patronage of a new wave of designers and decorators, the traditional skills of the city's artisans – zelije workers, the wood and stucco carvers – are also back in vogue. After what has been the best part of four centuries of lassitude, a new Marrakech style looks set to shake things up.

The New Marrakech Style

How the marriage of simple forms, indigenous artisanship and vibrant colours took over the style mags.

Every so often some magazine lifestyle pundit says that Moroccan as a style is 'over'. Really? Tell that to Mourad Mazouz, whose Sketch restaurant recently opened in London to the staccato clatter of a collective dropping of jaws, and which makes more than a nod to Moroccan mod. That's not to mention his signature restaurant Momo, still one of the hottest dinner reservations in London and totally Maghrebi. Tell that to leading interiors guru Jonathan Amar, designer of Paris' OTT Moroccan-themed Nirvana Lounge, current haunt of a flashy film and fashion crowd. Tell that to American restaurateur Terry Alexander who hired designer Suhail to create a trippy Moroccan fantasy for his chic Chicago eatery Tizi Melloul. Or, for that matter, to the UK's Building Designers Association, which, when announcing the winners of its annual excellence awards in September 2002, noted that minimalism and Moroccan remain the two biggest influences in the field of design.

Now check out some of the titles down at your local Borders bookstore: *Moroccan Interiors*, a huge doorstopping catalogue of Oriental homes to die for published by Taschen; *Morocco: Decoration, Interiors, Design*, published by Conran Octopus (complete with an appendix of home accessories stockists); and *Morocco Modern*, published way back in 1996 by Thames & Hudson and written by one Herbert Ypma before he moved on to hip hoteldom. Is it too fanciful to suppose that the hotels Herbert saw in Morocco (Villa Maroc in Essaouira; Dar Tamsna, Les Deux Tours and the Tichka Salam in Marrakech) and described in his first book gave him the inspiration for his bestselling series? Could it be that this quartet of southern Moroccan hotels are the prototype of the 'hip'? Quite possibly.

If there's one thing that Marrakech has in abundance it is cool style and design. Fès is too fussy, the walls of its buildings frequently garish with glazed tiles. Tangier is overly Andalucian, overwrought with curling iron and rendered extra chintzy by pastel baby hues. Casablanca suffers a colonial hangover, eager to imitate past masters and prove that it can do everything independently, including erect its own carbuncles in concrete. Only Marrakech seems to have the self-possession to cut its own cloth, and do so in the most elegant of fashions. Why? It's a Berber thing. It's the combination of simplicity of form – itself dictated by the materials (mud, mudbrick, tree trunks and branches) – with the addition of the vibrant

Charles Boccara (*above*), architect of **Le Deux Tours** (*below*). *See p31.*

colours of the Atlas: red earth, fruity orange, rose pink, lemon yellow, cobalt sky blue.

But for Berber traditions to come to the attention of the likes of the mass international DIYing public picking up their earth-glazed dishes at Habitat, terracotta kitchen tiles from Fired Earth and metalwork lanterns from Ikea required some form of intermediary. Step forward Bill Willis.

AN AMERICAN IN MARRAKECH

If anyone can claim credit for reigniting interest in traditional Marrakchi styles it would be Willis. He claims credit for other discoveries too. 'I discovered cocaine in Italy, turned Robert [Fraser] on to that and then he turned the Rolling Stones and the Beatles on to it,' (from *Groovy Bob: The Life and Times of Robert Fraser* by Harriet Vyner). Willis was an interior designer and architect hanging out in '60s London with Jagger and Marianne Faithfull, Groovy Bob and the whole hippy deluxe crowd. He first travelled to Marrakech in 1968, accompanying Paul Getty Jr and his wife, who were looking for a house. He found himself mesmerised by 'a rhythm of life I used to know as a child growing up in Memphis, Tennessee,' he explained in a 1986 magazine interview. 'I was fed up with big cities. Paris, Rome, New York – I'd tried them all. Here it was very slow and easy-going, a sleepy gracious, Southern kind of thing.' Once Getty had found his house, Willis went to work.

Through a string of subsequent clients, including the Rothschilds, Yves Saint Laurent (*see p84* **All about Yves**) and sundry local industrialists, Willis developed a style based on traditional Moroccan references (arches, painted woodwork, geometric patterns in tiling, plaster carving), but imbued with a wry, almost camp sense of humour of his own. Just take a look at his dandy, candy-striped, onion-domed fireplaces at Dar Yacout (*see p102*), the Felliniesque salons at the Trattoria Giancarlo (*see p112*) or the tongue-in-cheek palm tree columns at the Tichka Salam hotel (*see p51*).

> **'The difference is that Marrakech is a city of artisans, and remains largely pre-industrial.'**

While his particular twists are wholly modern, the techniques employed in achieving the finished result are age-old, involving intricate mosaic work, wood carving and stone masonry. Because of the demands placed on local *maalim* (master craftsmen), forcing them to adapt, relearn and stretch themselves,

Willis's interiors are credited with almost single-handedly reviving artisan traditions in Marrakech. This may not be entirely true; according to Herbert Ypma's book, an ambitious programme of palace restoration by Hassan II, the father of the present king, boosted the number of *zelije* (tiling) artisans in Fès from 50 to 700, while the construction of the mammoth mosque in Casablanca, which employed 30,000 artisans, also played a major part in the renaissance of Moroccan craftsmanship. What is amazing, though, is that at the end of the 20th century these essentially medieval crafts were still around to be revived. Can you imagine in Britain trying to put together a bunch of builders to kit out your mansion with sculpted stone spandrels and coffered ceilings in oak?

The difference is that Marrakech is a city of artisans. It remains largely a pre-industrial city that still gets by on trade, commerce and small-scale manufacturing – plus, these days, tourism, which in itself is another perpetuator of handicrafts. The ability of its craftspeople astounds. One local furniture designer tells the story of how he took a prototype lantern in tin to a metalworker to have it refashioned in copper. Less than 48 hours later the model was all over the souk after being copied in a dozen workshops or more. Capitalising on such infinite and ingenious creative skills, an American woman, Dana Schondelmeyer, has set up a company, Made in Marrakech, supplying costumes and props to Hollywood. Here in the Medina her artisans have manufactured Tibetan sandals for Martin Scorsese's *Kundun*, US-style military flak jackets for *Blackhawk Down* and all-leather attire for the Egyptian armies of *The Mummy Returns*.

THE TADELAKT KING

Bill Willis still lives in the holy heart of the northern Medina, between a mosque and a cemetery, in the harem section of an 18th-century palace, but he rarely accepts commissions any more. Charles Boccara, sometime partner of Willis (they worked on the Tichka hotel together), makes up for both with his prolificacy. While Willis is a decorator, Boccara is an architect. Born in Tunisia, educated in Morocco and trained in Paris at the Ecole des Beaux-Arts, he's a force of nature, a big bear of a man, who packs Italian, French and English all into the same sentence. Like Willis, he has seized on traditional elements of local design. He constructs in concrete but plasters in *pisé* (mud). His interiors make stunning use of *tadelakt*, the polished wall finish traditionally employed in *hammams* (bathhouses), where heat and moisture are a problem. It's a technique to create steam-proof

Bill Willis at Dar Yacout.

walls. Surfaces are trowelled in a plaster of powdered limestone with a small amount of coloured dust mixed in to provide the desired colour. After the plaster is set, it's painstakingly polished with flat stones approximately the size of a hand, which makes it as hard as marble. To seal the material further, the surface is painted with a glaze of egg whites. Finally, there's one last polish with a cake of locally made back soap. The finished result looks like soft leather and is as smooth as lather to the touch.

Boccara is the man credited with bringing tadelakt out of the steam room and into style. His buildings make great use of it in almost every room. Since the example set by his signature Les Deux Tours (*see p56*), completed in the early 1990s, Marrakech has gone tadelakt mad. The mantra now seems to be that if an interior surface is flat, it gets tadelakt'd.

But Boccara's architecture goes far beyond surface. He's a man who values surprise and even folly, who believes that getting lost is one of the real pleasures of a house. At Les Deux Tours his bathrooms are astounding, featuring soaring ceilings of mudbrick domes pierced by round holes that emit shafts of light. Ceilings in other rooms are panelled with oleander branches and then brightly painted in vivid geometric patterns like backgammon boards.

With projects like hotels Les Deux Tours, Tichka Salam and Dar Rhizlane (*see p52*), and the as-yet-unfinished Theatre Royal (*see p82*), Boccara has managed to create an architecture that conveys a strong sense of place while striking an unmistakably modern pose. It combines the comforts of modern life – plumbing, bathrooms, fully fitted kitchens – with the mood, texture and ambience of Marrakech's history and culture.

MUD MODERN

Transplanted Parisian Jacqueline Fossaic arrived around the same time as Bill Willis,

although she has far more in common with Charles Boccara. She's mud mad, and over the past three decades has taken the traditional peasant clay or mud house and turned it into something quite sophisticated.

She shares her passion with a protégé of Charles Boccara, native Moroccan Elie Mouyal, and the two have worked together on a number of projects, including several houses for Fossaic in the Palmeraie. The dwellings are constructed entirely of handmade mudbricks echoing the traditional Berber *kasbahs* and *ksours* of southern Morocco. Far from appearing primitive, the buildings are pure rustic chic with high vaulted ceilings, domes and cupolas. They are entirely terracotta in tone, inside and out, enlivened with weavings, painted doors and windows, and white-canvas hangings to provide shade on the terraces.

'Dar Tamsna, the prototype boho-chic villa, introduced Marrakech to the pages of the international life-style press.'

Fossaic now works for clients on restoration projects in the Medina, as well as on more new-build houses in the Palmeraie. Mouyal has moved onwards and upwards and the building he's now most closely associated with is the gleaming white, 30-storey-plus World Trade Centre (not, we should point out, made of mudbrick) at the heart of Casablanca. However, the duo's experiments in raw-earth construction have made a lasting impression and continue to be an inspiration – for instance, in the development of Caravanserai and Tigmi (*see p58* for both): two almost organic Berber-style hotel complexes that blend seamlessly into their local village settings.

Tigmi. See p33.

MOROCCAN MINIMALISM

French-Senegalese Meryanne Loum-Martin first came to Marrakech from Paris in the late 1980s in search of a holiday property that would be accessible to her and her scattered relatives. She found a half-built concrete shell in the Palmeraie and decided to finish the job. Throughout the early '90s she made frequent trips to Morocco and enrolled on a self-taught crash course in the country's traditional crafts and building methods. The result was Dar Tamsna, perhaps the prototype boho-chic villa and the place that introduced Marrakech to the pages of the international lifestyle press – with eight pages in *Condé Nast Traveller*, no less.

An architect by training, a lawyer in practice and a perfectionist by nature, in Dar Tamsna Loum-Martin came as close as any, according to style arbiter Herbert Ypma, to 'providing the essential Moroccan experience'. As Bill Willis before, she adapted local ingredients and reinterpreted them. In the instances where she instructed her craftsmen to use zelije she kept the tiling to a single colour; similarly the tadelakt, which is a deep and lustrous tobacco tone throughout. The Moroccan rugs and carpets are uniformly deep red and the wood work and *mashrabiyas* (fretworked wooden screens) all stained dark. Walking into one of the stately rooms the initial effect is of coolness and restraint, but look closer and the micro detail and intricacy are mesmerising.

In 2002 Loum-Martin completed a new hotel project, Jnane Tamsna (*see p55*), but this time the whole complex was built from scratch. It refines the MLM formula even further with architecture that's grounded in southern Morocco by its absolute simplicity and clarity of form, but with the added zest of some sublimely understated flourishes, such as Moorish keyhole arches and cloister-like arcades. The colours are mango, sand and tan. It's a stage set for *Beau Geste* reworked as a

musical. No surprise that the place is constantly in demand as a location for international fashion shoots.

In the few years between Dar Tamsna and Jnane Tamsna the whole *riad* scene in the Medina exploded (*see p19*). All of a sudden it seemed that behind every door in the Old City artisans were beavering away fashioning ever more neo-Moroccan fantasies. Each took as its starting point the same set of references, but the beauty of the whole modern Marrakech thing is how readily the architecture and traditional crafts lend themselves to experimentation and innovation. Hence hotels Riad Enija (*see p42*), which takes trad Moroccan into the realm of gothic fantasy; Riad Kaiss (*see p47*), which plays heavily on colour and patterning; Riad Malika (*see p47*), fashioned by designer/owner Jean-Luc Lemée as a unique fusion of Moorish and art deco – tadelakt meets bakelite! And there are countless, countless others. No wonder that by the time Jnane Tamsna came along, this time around Loum-Martin's new creation was only able to command a single page of *Condé Nast Traveller*.

Despite the variations on the theme, there is now an established riad design checklist. Tadelakt walls (tick). Carved stucco trim (tick). Beaten copper handbasins (tick). Zelije tiled basin surrounds (tick). Funny-shaped shower cubicles (tick). Kilims and rugs, walls only (tick). Bare terracotta flooring (tick). White canvas sun canopies (tick). Lanterns and tea candles (tick). But when a formula works this beautifully, it would be truly perverse not to pay heed.

Another trend common to *the style* is to utilise older elements, such as aged wooden doors and window frames, marble washbasins, wooden columns or even plumbing fixtures from the 1920s, to create intriguing juxtapositions. Some of the elements become transformed from their original function, such

Alessandra Lippini & **Fabrizzio Bizzarri**. *See p36.*

Ministero del Gusto.

as wooden columns from a baldaquin bed re-employed to hold up a roof terrace pergola. For all would-be designers (and there's something about the air here that effects a transformation; three days in Marrakech and even the most cack-handed and colour-blind suddenly come over all Laurence Llewelyn-Bowen) the local equivalent of Habitat is the Souk El Khemis (*see p132*), an open-air flea market in the northern Medina that is home to a great many architectural salvage merchants.

THE PROFESSIONALS

Not everybody wants to go it alone and there's a decent living to be made in Marrakech as a designer-for-hire. Jennifer Lloyd is an English sculptress who relocated to Marrakech (via Essaouira) after two decades in Norway. Since completing her own house (a colonial bungalow next to the Majorelle Gardens; *see p55* **Having it all**), she's now applying her unique mix of sober Scandinavian and Moroccan style to other design projects. She recently finished an interior makeover for Jasper Conran and film directing partner Trevor Hopkins, and her next big commission is to kit out a Palmeraie villa bought by Katrina Boorman, daughter of John Boorman (Marrakech is beginning to resemble a cross between a North African *Changing Rooms* and *I'm a Celebrity, Get Me Out of Here!*). 'There's enough people doing that thousand and one nights thing', says Lloyd, whose own approach is uncluttered and comes across as Ikea but in mud. In the context of Marrakech it's beautifully refreshing.

Lloyd believes things are moving on in terms of design. Copyism has had its day and she and others of a similar mind are now working closely in conjunction with a new wave of non-traditional creatives. Lloyd now works with the pottery people Akkal (*see p133*) and candlemakers Amira (*see p128*) to create large sculptural pieces to adorn her houses. Other

designers have employed the services of Bridgette Perkins (*see p134* **By appointment**) to supply custom-made fabrics, and even, in one case, called on fashion hotshot Noureddine Amir (*see p127* **Roots couture**) to knock up staff outfits. Lloyd also recently learned of a new artisan in town, Bernard Heriot, whose workshop (trading under the name Peau d'Ane) produces reproduction 1940s furniture in shark skin (shagreen) finish. Expensive, apparently, but already doing well in the local market.

If there's one designer in town who would go for sharkskin it would be Alessandra Lippini. Arguably the most glamorous lady in the Medina, she trips through the souk in kitten heels and a party dress on her way each day to the Ministero del Gusto (*see p132 and p146*), the delirious gallery-cum-workspace she shares with partner Fabrizzio Bizzarri. The pair design trippy interiors for a roster of wealthy clients, mainly from the Italian fashion world. If there's one word that characterises their work together it's 'fun'. Their shared Medina home is a riot of star-studded floorings, spidery chandeliers, Arabic stencils, Fauvist colour schemes and Flintstone furniture – so totally batty and bold that it made the perfect location for Bryan Ferry's video to 'Mamouna'. Their latest work is a riad just off rue Dar Doukkala completely done out in geometric black and white – with a ceiling-high, leopard-skin bed headboard, just for the hell of it. Amazingly, it works.

And that's the thing about Marrakech style. Flexibility. It's not about lanterns or tassles or dressing up in fezzes; it's a style based on indigenous values of simplicity and practicality. At root it's about basic building materials and using them to strike a harmonious balance between outside and in, by use of courtyards, terraces and gardens. Beyond that, architects and designers can be as imaginative and creative as they like. Now how can that ever go out of fashion?

Accommodation

Accommodation   **38**

Features

Accommodation

Less lodgings than lifestyle locations, hotels in Marrakech are hip, happening and desirable destinations in themselves.

It's because of the accommodation that many visitors come to Marrakech. Look at the photos on the following pages: these places are gorgeous, with perfect little courtyards, fountains and orange trees, candles, drapes and scattered rose petals, domed ceilings and softly rounded bathrooms with silky walls. It's all a world away from the standard idea of the hotel with its connotations of corridors, uniforms, franchise boutiques, tacky theme bars and Euro discos. Which, like everywhere else, is what Marrakech had until perhaps a decade ago, with just the Mamounia (*see p41*) upping the ante with a bit of blue-blooded class. But then in the mid 1990s came Les Deux Tours (*see p56*) and La Maison Arabe (*see p41*), two very different new ventures – one a conversion of an old townhouse, the other a new-build gated compound on the outskirts of town – but both employing aeons-old local architectural and craft traditions to glamorous, sophisticated, 21st-century effect. The two provided a blueprint for the explosion in boutique hotels (or *maisons d'hôtes* in local parlance) that has since transformed the city.

Most visitors choose to stay in a cool and stylish *riad* (*see below*) in the teeming alleyways of the Old City, but gaining in favour is the idea of the out-of-town retreat – the Palmeraie or even further afield – somewhere to chill out totally and spend days doing little other than laze beside the pool while being pampered and primped by cooks, masseurs, manicurists, maids and teams of attendant flunkies.

Whichever way you choose to go, the madness of the Medina or hedonistic retreat (and the ideal is probably a combination of the two), we highly recommend pushing the budget. Marrakech is not a place to scrimp on the hotel, not when – muslin-draped four poster! metre-deep baths! moonlight plunges! – it could so easily turn out to be the highlight of the trip.

THE RIAD THING

A lot of the Old City accommodation is riad this and riad that. The definition of a riad is a house with a garden. That's it. But for garden in most cases read courtyard, typically planted with a few citrus trees and often with a small central fountain. The riads are organised around one or more of these courtyards, reflecting the traditions of Moroccan domestic architecture, which are inward looking and intimate, with thick blank walls to protect the inhabitants from heat and cold, and the attentions of the outside world. Some of the grander riads might involve two or more houses knocked together, but most consist of just a half-dozen to a dozen rooms. They're all – so far – small-time, privately operated affairs, which generally means excellent personal service and a great degree of individuality.

In all but the cheapest, rooms have en suite bathrooms, but TVs, air-con, telephones and the like are usually dispensed with in the name of

The best Hotels

For artful posing
Jnane Tamsna (*see p55*) and **Riad Enija** (*see p42*) often double as fashion-shoot sets.

For art lovers
Riad El Cadi (*see p47*) comes with its own carpet and textile museum.

For artists in retreat
Dar Zelije (*see p45*) offers seclusion in the company of like-minded people.

For health and beauty
Kasbah Agafay (*see p58*) and **Riad Mehdi** (*see p48*) come with full spa facilities.

For water babies
The biggest and best pools are at the **Hotel Es Saadi** (*see p52*) and **Tichka Salam** (*see p51*).

For eco friendliness
Ethnobotanist Gary Martin grows his own kitchen produce at 'Moorish hacienda' **Jnane Tamsna** (*see p55*), and the Kasbah **Agafay** (*see p58*) has an organic walled garden.

For good times had by all
Caravanserai (*see p58*) and the **Grand Tazi** (*see p49*) are two of the few non five-stars to have a house bar.

Mamounia: grande dame of Marrakech hotels. *See p41.*

authenticity. Breakfast is nearly always included, commonly taken on a roof terrace shielded from the sun under tent-like white awnings, while lunch and dinner are provided on request from a menu presented in the morning. Several of the riads have truly excellent cooks producing food as good as anything dished up in local restaurants – in some cases (El Cadi, Mabrouka and Noga spring to mind) better. Expect to pay around 150dh for lunch, 200dh-250dh for dinner.

Virtually all riads are tucked away at the end of long, nameless alleys, and signs and nameplates are rare. Guests are met at the airport (for which there may or may not be an additional charge in the region of $10-$15), but after that it's just you and your sense of direction. It's wise to carry your riad's business card to show locals in case you get lost.

RATES AND BOOKING

There are significant seasonal variations in room rates, with prices at some hotels rising by up to 25 per cent at peak periods. What constitutes peak period varies by establishment (where known, we've listed seasonal variations in our reviews), but generally speaking you'll pay considerably more for a room any time over Christmas/New Year and Easter, plus from late September through to October, when the fierceness of the summer heat has abated and the temperatures are near perfect. Despite the price hikes, rooms are still scarce at these times and booking well in advance is a must.

When it comes to making a reservation, even though most hotels boast websites, note that the internet is a relatively new technology for Marrakech and still prone to meltdown. Book by email or through the website by all means but be sure to follow up with a phone call.

We've divided the chapter by area, then price category, according to the average cost of a low-season standard double room: **deluxe** from 3,200dh (currently around £200), **expensive** 1,920dh-3200dh (£120-£200), **moderate** 800dh-1,920dh (£50-£120) and **budget** up to 800dh (£50). Payment is typically cash only and it must be made in local currency. Even those places that purport to take credit cards usually prefer cash in practice – you might too, given that a five per cent surcharge may be added on top to cover the administration costs of the transaction.

Medina

Aka the 'Old City'. A room here puts you right in among the souks and sights, and the nearer to the ground zero of Jemaa El Fna the better. Remember that much of the Medina is inaccessible by car, so accommodation close to a taxi-friendly main street or square is always preferable.

Deluxe

Villa des Orangers

6 rue Sidi Mimoun, place Ben Tachfine (044 38 46 38/fax 044 38 51 23/www.villadesorangers.com/ message@villadesorangers.com). **Rates** (incl breakfast & light lunch) 2,900dh-4,800dh per room. **Credit** MC, V. **Map** p250 B7.

TAMSNA
Since 1989

La Mamounia

Almost since opening in 1923, the Mamounia has been so famous as to be practically synonymous with Marrakech. It was the palace of the crown prince of Morocco when the French administration annexed it for a hotel. During that romantic era of early travel, the Mamounia was not just a hotel, it was a way of life, where a small exclusive community of expats, colonial rulers and adventurers would lazily sip Scotch in the hotel's well-watered gardens, away from the North African heat and dust. In post-war years it was a favourite haunt of Winston Churchill, who declared the views from its roof as 'paintaceous' and executed a number of watercolours to prove his point (there's now a 15,000dh-a-night suite named after him).

The place seems to have had great appeal for rotund and jowly Englishmen, as not long after, Alfred Hitchcock checked in to film *The Man Who Knew Too Much* (in which James Stewart and Doris Day occupy room 414). But in 1986 when a conference centre was added and the hotel was refitted, the cool elegance of the past was sacrificed in a kitsch makeover. This was doubly unfortunate in that it was around this time that the first of Marrakech's famed hip hotels appeared, and the grande old dame began to find herself outclassed.

Its rooms (of which there are now 230) remain spacious, particularly the various suites, but the theming – 19th-century, Orient Express, 1930s, nuptial, Moroccan – is pure Vegas (one suite has a seven-foot harp, another a toy parrot in the bathroom). By contrast, the endless expanses of blank carpeted corridors are corporate characterless. More objectionable are the supercilious staff and their unnecessarily haughty service. The celebs still come, as the hotel's promotion material is at pains to point out, but even there the quality has declined dramatically: Chelsea Clinton, Ted Dawson and Frank Leboeuf anyone?

Do visit for the excellent Italian restaurant (*see p106*), the Churchill Piano Bar (*see p152*) and to peek at the fine marquetry in the lifts. The buffet lunch is also splendid, served beside the pool in the marvellous gardens (*see p84*), but beware the hotel's erratically enforced no-jeans policy.

Mamounia

avenue Bab Jedid, Medina (044 38 86 00/ fax 044 44 44 09/www.mamounia.com/ resa@mamounia.com). **Rates** *24 June-8 Sept* 2,000dh-4,000dh standard rooms; 3,000dh-9,000dh suites. *9 Sept-23 June* 3,000dh-5,000dh standard rooms; 4,000dh-15,000dh suites. **Credit** AmEx, MC, V. **Map** p250 A6. **Hotel services** *Air-conditioning. Art gallery. Bars (4). Beauty centre: hairdresser, massage room, sauna. Business centre. Casino. Conference rooms. Fitness centre. Nightclub. Pool (outdoor). Restaurants (5). Safe. Shops. Tennis.* **Room services** *Air-conditioning. Telephone. TV.*

Built in the 1930s as the residence of a judge, the Villa des Orangers was acquired by a French husband and wife team with a successful hotel business in Paris, and after gaining an additional storey, it opened to paying guests in December 1999. The style is Moorish palatial and it has 16 rooms and suites arranged around two beautiful courtyards – one of them filled with the eponymous orange trees, the other lavishly decorated with lacy carved plasterwork. Six suites have private upstairs sun terraces, although all rooms have access to the roof for the pool along with matchless views of the nearby Koutoubia minaret – doubly enchanting when the storks come wheeling round at dusk. The service here is outstanding and management couldn't be more helpful. It's closed from mid July to mid August.
Hotel services *Babysitting. Cook. Laundry. Newspapers. Pool (outdoor). Safe.* **Room services** *Air-conditioning. Heating. Minibar. Safe. Telephone. TV: satellite.*

Expensive

La Maison Arabe

1 Derb Assehbe, Bab Doukkala (044 38 70 10/ fax 044 38 72 21/www.lamaisonarabe.com/ maisonarabe@iam.net.ma). **Rates** (incl breakfast & afternoon tea) *14 June-12 Sept* 1,500dh-2,000dh double; 1,300dh-4,800dh suite. *13 Sept-13 June* 1,900dh-2,300dh double; 1,700dh-6,000dh suite. **Credit** MC, V. **Map** p248 A4.
Maison Arabe began life in the 1940s as a restaurant run by two raffish French ladies. It rapidly gained fame through popularity with patrons such as Winston Churchill. The last tajines were served in '83 and the place lay dormant for more than a decade before reopening under new ownership (the Italian prince Fabrizio Ruspoli) in January 1998 as the city's first maison d'hôtes. There are 13 rooms and suites set around two flower-filled courts. The style is Moroccan classic with a French colonial feel – lots

Terrace living at beautiful **Villa des Orangers**. *See p39.*

of Orientalist paintings and antiques, high-backed armchairs and a cedarwood library. The rooms are supremely comfortable, most with their own private terraces and a couple with fireplaces. Our favourite is 'Sabah' (the rooms all have names), which is ingeniously fitted around the curve of a dome. The full-size hotel pool may be a 20-minute drive away on the outskirts of town (serviced by hourly shuttles) but it does have a lovely garden setting where lunch is also served. The hotel restaurant (*see p102*) is one of the best in town and guests can also take cookery courses (*see p114*).
Hotel services *Babysitting. Car park. Hammam. Newspapers. Pool (outdoor). Restaurant. Safe.* **Room services** *Air-conditioning. Heating. Minibar. Safe. Telephone. TV: satellite.*

Riad Enija

9 Derb Mesfioui, off rue Rahba Lakdima (044 44 09 26/fax 044 44 27 00/www.riadenija.com/ riadenija@iam.net.ma). **Rates** (incl breakfast) 2,300dh-3,500dh per room. **Credit** MC, V. **Map** p249 D5.
Anyone lacking the pose and hauteur of a Karl Lagerfeld model risks being made to look shabby by comparison with the drop dead gorgeousness of their surrounds at Riad Enija. Its eight rooms and suites (four more due in 2003) boast glorious old wooden ceilings, beds as works of art (wrought iron

gothic in one, a green muslin-wrapped four-poster in another), minimal furnishings of a strikingly modernist nature and bathrooms resembling subterranean throne chambers. Central to the two adjoined houses (which originally belonged to a silk trader from Fès and 64 members of his family) is a Moorish courtyard garden gone wild where red-uniformed staff flicker through the greenery. Distractions like TV and telephones are dispensed with – although there is a 'communication centre' with online laptops – but alternative services include anything from a visiting aromatherapist and masseurs to heli-skiing excursions (in season). Service and food are both excellent and the riad is just a few minutes' walk from Jemaa El Fna.
Hotel services *Beauty treatments. Business centre. Cook. Garden (courtyard). Massage. Plunge pool (outdoor). Safe.*

Moderate

Dar Attajmil

23 rue Laksour, off rue Sidi El Yamami (044 42 69 66/darattajmil@iam.net.ma). **Rates** (incl breakfast) 800dh-1,000dh double. **Credit** MC, V. **Map** p248 B5.
Hidden along a winding alley in the Laksour quarter, Attajmil is only a few minutes' walk from the action on the main square. With just four rooms,

Riad Enija: impeccably stylish. *See p42*.

expect a cosy ambience and highly personalised service from the small body of staff. The reasonably sized, spotlessly clean doubles are decorated to a high standard, with warm rusty tones, plenty of dark wood and mosaic-lined showers. Two small lounges look on to a courtyard with young banana and coconut palms – but the astonishingly peaceful roof terrace is the place to really kick back, with cushions and wicker chairs and sofas. Dinner – trad Moroccan with Italian leanings – is available on request (150dh per person). Note that the hammam and massage carry a supplementary charge.

Hotel services *Cook. Hammam.* **Room services** *Heating. Library. Massage.*

Dar Les Cigognes

108 rue Berima, Berima (044 38 27 40/ fax 044 38 47 67/www.lescigognes.com/ lescigognes@iam.net.ma). **Rates** (incl breakfast & afternoon tea) *Low season* 1,300dh-1,800dh double; 2,200dh suite. *High season* 1,500dh-2,000dh double; 2,500dh suite. **Credit** MC, V. **Map** p251 D7.

Facing the eastern ramparts of the Badii Palace where the storks (in French, 'cigognes') stand sentinel, this was originally a merchant's home and dates in part back to the 17th century. Restoration has been sensitive and walls of white and muted tones serve to highlight fine carved dark wood details around the central court. At present there are

just four rooms and a suite (six more suites will be added when work on a neighbouring house is complete). Decor ranges from the sublimely chic to the wonderfully ridiculous, as in the 'Sahara' room with a painted desert landscape (complete with camels) on a blue *tadelakt* wall, and the 'Silver' room with all-over silvery-grey tadelakt and carved plasterwork glitzed up to look like a wedding cake doily; ideal for honeymooning couples, perhaps. *Directrice* Beatriz Maximo is an absolute sweetie and supremely well informed on all things from Marrakchi haute couture to Berber tribal life (she spent two years south of the Atlas).

Hotel services *Cook. Dry cleaning. Garden. Hammam. Laundry. Library.* **Room services** *Fan. Heating.*

Dar Doukkala

83 Derb Arset Aouzal, off rue Bab Doukkala (044 38 34 44/fax 044 38 34 45/www.dardoukkala.com/ dardoukkala@iam.net.ma). **Rates** (incl breakfast) *6 Jan-19 Dec* 1,600dh-1,800dh double; 2,100dh-2,400dh suite. *20 Dec-5 Jan* 2,400dh-2,700dh double; 3,150dh-3,600dh suite. **Credit** MC, V. **Map** p248 B4.

Opened to paying guests only as recently as January 2003, this is a strange but appealing mix of 1940s English country mansion and Moroccan townhouse, executed by inspired Frenchman Jean-Luc Lemée (who also owns nearby Riad Malika, *see*

Dar Les Cigognes

Guesthouse | Maison d'Hôtes

Luxury, comfort and service

The Silver Room

Refined elegance
in the heart of historic Marrakesh

www.lescigognes.com
Tel. +212 (0) 44 38 27 40

p47). The four bedrooms and two suites are filled with gorgeous period details and furnishings, including in the bathrooms claw-foot bathtubs and chunky pedestal basins (one of the suites has a battleship of a bath). This is what the rooms at the Mamounia should look like. Other wonderfully eccentric touches include Guimard-like glass canopies projecting into the central garden courtyard, and an artful array of lanterns patterning the wall behind the terrace-level swimming pool. For the money, this is one of the most fun and delightful maisons d'hôtes in town – and the location is good too, opposite the wonderful warehouse of Mustapha Blaoui and a few hundred metres from the taxis ranked outside Dar Marjana. Note, staff speak no English.

Hotel services *Cook. Pool (outdoor).* **Room services** *Air-conditioning. CD player. Cook. Hammam. Heating. Laundry. Pool. Safe.*

Dar Zelije

46 Derb Ihihane, Sidi Ben Slimane (044 42 64 63/ fax 044 42 65 11/www.marrakech-riads.net/ dzillije@iam.net.ma). **Rates** (incl breakfast) *7 Jan-31 Mar, 1 June-24 Oct, 4 Nov-19 Dec* 1,000dh per room. *Apr, May, 25 Oct-3 Nov, 20 Dec-6 Jan* 1,200dh per room. **Credit** MC, V. **Map** p248 C2.

Part of the Marrakech Riads group, Zelije is a 17th-century house of impressive proportions and exquisite architectural detailing. Renovation has been sparing: the result, a balance between the majestic and the monastic. Some may find it too spartan, but it operates successfully as an aesthetes' retreat, welcoming contemplatives and creatives, providing peace and seclusion in simple suites with attached small courts and chambers to serve as private work spaces. The ground-floor suite is arguably the most beautiful room in all Marrakech, yet it costs less than 1,000dh a night. There are plans to install a recording studio in the immense salon off the main courtyard, where musos can dabble under a carved wooden ceiling to equal any museum piece. The location, deep in a contorted warren of alleys in the little-visited northern part of the Medina, could be a plus or it could be a minus; either way it's a factor to bear in mind.

Hotel services *Cook.*

Les Jardins de la Medina

21 Derb Chtouka, Kasbah (044 38 18 51/fax 044 38 53 85/www.lesjardinsdelamedina.com/ info@lesjardinsdelamedina.com). **Rates** (incl breakfast) 1,200dh-2,025dh single; 1,600dh-2,700dh double. **Credit** AmEx, MC, V. **Map** p250 C9.

Pitched somewhere between the stylish intimacy of a riad and the modern corporate efficiency of a hotel, Les Jardins is a 36-room complex centred on a large palm-filled garden courtyard with glistening turquoise-blue pool. Rooms range from standard to superior to suites, the latter two categories coming with seating areas and, in some cases, a private walled terrace. Guests in standard also benefit from

Dar Zelije. Monastic yet majestic.

plenty of attractive patios, platforms, pathways and sundry public spaces. This is also one of the very few hotels to offer a room adapted for the handicapped. Its restaurant serves Thai food (in addition to Moroccan and Mediterranean), which could come as a welcome break after several days of tajines. The location, right on the very southern edge of the Medina near the Grand Méchouar, makes Les Jardins de la Medina highly accessible for drivers and taxis, but it's a hell of a trek to get anywhere on foot (20 minutes to Jemaa El Fnaa, for example).

Hotel services *Babysitting. Bar. Car parking. Car rental. Garden. Hammam. Massage. Pool (outdoor). Restaurant. Shop.* **Room services** *Air-conditioning. Heating. Minibar. Safe. Telephone. TV: satellite.*

Maison Mnabha

32-3 Derb Mnabha, off rue de Kasbah (044 38 13 25/fax 044 38 99 93/ www.maisonmnabha.com/kasbah@iam.net.ma). **Rates** (incl breakfast) 730dh-810dh single; 890dh-970dh double. **Credit** MC, V. **Map** p250 C9.

Originally bought as a residence by two English brothers ten years ago, Mnabha has been receiving guests for the last three. The place was part of a bigger house attached to the court (the Royal Palace is a neighbour), hence the opulent first-floor reception room with its fabulous 17th-century-style painted cedarwood ceiling. The rest of the house, however, is far more modest in both decor and scale. Four light and spacious guest rooms are off an upper

Riad Mabrouka: très chic. *See p47.*

patio, each simply decorated and homely; all have direct access to an upper sun terrace. (There's also one cheaper ground-floor room). The location deep in the Kasbah quarter means that it's a trek to get anywhere, but the neighbourhood is quiet, clean and less intimidating than the Jemaa El Fna area. Maison Mnabha is closed throughout August.

Hotel services *CD player (with library). Cook. TV: satellite. Video library.* **Room services** *Air-conditioning. Fridge. Heating.*

Riad El Cadi

87 Derb Moulay Abdelkader, off Derb Debbachi (044 37 86 55/fax 044 37 84 78/www.riyadelcadi.com/ riyadelcadi@iam.net.ma). **Rates** *1,000dh single; 1,200dh-1,500dh double; 2,000dh-2,400dh suite.* **Credit** MC, V. **Map** p249 D5.

Comprising eight (!) interconnected houses, El Cadi is a rambling maze of a residence in which getting lost is a joy. Its 12 (supremely comfortable) suites and bedrooms, as well as the various salons, corridors and landings, also double as gallery spaces for an outstanding collection of art and artefacts gathered by 'genetic collector' and genial host Herwig Bartels, a former German ambassador to Morocco. The reception area alone gathers an ancient Berber textile with a Bauhaus chair and a Rothko-like abstract; 'Great art,' says Bartels, 'has a common language.' Despite the rich details, the overall feel is uncluttered, cool and contemporary. Accomplished cooking (lunch and dinner to order) and extensive roof terraces with tented lounging further add to the appeal of what, for the money, is some of the classiest accommodation in town.

Hotel services *Cook. Hammam. Library. Plunge pool (outdoor). Shop. TV.* **Room services** *Air-conditioning. Heating. Telephone.*

Riad Ifoulki

11 Derb Moqqadem, route Arset Loghzail (tel/fax 044 38 56 56/www.riadifoulki.com/ riadifoulki@riadifoulki.com). **Rates** (incl breakfast) 800dh double; 1,500dh double; 3,000dh suite. **Credit** MC, V. **Map** p251 D6.

This may be the only riad in town at which Latin is spoken; Latin and nine other languages, in fact, including Danish, which is the nationality of owner Peter Berg. It's a former palace (or at least, four-fifths of one) with a total of 14 rooms arranged on several levels around numerous whitewashed courtyards, large and small. Parts of the riad are self-contained with their own door, ideal for families, and with gates at the top of stairs for child safety. Rooms are lovely and cool with big beds swathed in translucent shimmery fabrics. The riad has an excellent small library with volumes on Morocco in various languages, some of which are signed by their authors with gratitude to the erudite Berg. Airport transfers are free.

Hotel services *Babysitting. Cook. Fitness room. Hammam. Library. Massage. Plunge pool (outdoor). TV.* **Room services** *Safe.*

Riad Kaiss

65 Derb Jedid, off Riad Zitoun El Kedim (tel/fax 044 44 01 41/www.riadkaiss.com/ riad@riadkaiss.com). **Rates** (incl breakfast) 1,430dh-2,200dh per room. **Credit** MC, V. **Map** p250 C7.

Renovated, owned and managed by architect Christian Ferré, who lives on the premises, Kaiss is small (eight rooms) but exquisite. Its Rubik's Cube layout has rooms linked by galleries, multi-level terraces and tightly twisting stairs all around a central court filled with orange, lemon and pomegranate trees. Decor is trad Moroccan: earthy ochre walls with chalky Majorelle-blue trim, stencilled paintwork (including some gorgeous ceilings), jade *zelije* tiling and frilly furniture (including four-poster beds). Guests are greeted by red rose petals sprinkled on their white linen pillows. It's the Merchant Ivory of riads. Modern tastes dictate a cool plunge pool on the roof and a well-equipped fitness room – it's worth a workout for the ache-relieving pleasures of the in-house hammam that comes afterwards.

Hotel services *Cook. Fitness room. Hammam. Plunge pool (outdoor).*

Riad Mabrouka

56 Derb El Bahia, off Riad Zitoun El Jedid (tel/fax 044 37 75 79/www.riad-mabrouka.com/ info@riad-mabrouka.com). **Rates** (incl breakfast) 1,400dh double; 1,800dh suite. **Credit** MC, V. **Map** p251 D6.

The Mabrouka is a vision of cool elegance. Architect Christophe Siméon has gone for a Moroccan minimalist look with whitewashed walls, billowing canvas in place of doors and some fab painted ceilings and shutters plus kilims adding selective splashes of colour. The result is stylish, but also very comfortable. Bathrooms are seductively sensuous, all soft corners and rounded edges looking like they've been moulded out of coloured clay – one comes with a deeply sunken bath that you have to climb steps up to. With just two suites and three doubles it's very intimate. There's a pleasant cactus-potted roof terrace, with a canvas-shaded breakfast area, and a good kitchen turning out Moroccan, Mediterranean, French and Italian cuisine.

Hotel services *Beauty treatments. Cook. Fitness room. Hammam. Massage.*

Riad Malika

29 Derb Arset Aouzal, off rue Bab Doukkala (tel/fax 044 38 54 51/www.riadmalika.com/ jean.luc@iam.net.ma). **Rates** (incl breakfast) 800dh double; 1,000dh suite. **Credit** MC, V. **Map** p248 B4.

A hideaway tailor-made for Ladbroke Grove hipsters. Owner Jean-Luc Lemée has a fascination with '20s and '30s design and his riad (which itself dates from the 1920s) is crammed full of a Portobello's worth of chrome, black leather, Bakelite, Day-Glo colours and dramatic deco stylings – all sourced from junk shops and house sales in Morocco. The result is characterful without being overly kitsch. There are two double rooms and five suites, most of

Accommodation

which are spacious, bright and airy thanks to great expanses of windows. We also like the wild courtyard with its unkempt fruit-bearing trees.
Hotel services *Cook.* **Room services** *Air-conditioning. CD player. Heating.*

Riad Mehdi

2 Derb Sedra, Bab Agnaou (044 38 47 13/fax 044 38 47 31/www.riadmehdi.com/contact@ riadmehdi.net). **Rates** 1,000dh double; 2,000dh-2,500dh suite. **Credit** MC, V. **Map** p250 B8.
Mehdi's pitch in the increasingly crowded maison d'hôtes market is an appeal to health and beauty. Its five suites and four double rooms are just one half of the operation: the other is a compact spa complex (*see p166*). The dual functions are housed in one dusky-pink house ranged on two levels around adjoining courtyards. Rooms are pleasant and comfortable, if not quite as stylish as elsewhere, and the suites all come with their own terraces. One unique feature is that Mehdi abuts the city wall, which forms one side of the outer courtyard; guests can float in the open-air pool watching the storks perched up top of the battlements. Few other small hotels can boast a bar either. The location just inside the Bab Agnaou (immediate first right) is a plus: easy to find, plentiful taxis around, and no more than a ten-minute walk to Jemaa El Fna.
Hotel services *Bar. Cook. Hammam. Massage. Pool (outdoor). Spa.* **Room services** *Air-conditioning. Heating. Internet sockets. Telephone.*

Riad Noga

78 Derb Jedid, Douar Graoua (044 37 76 70/fax 044 38 90 46/www.riadnoga.com/riadnoga@iam.net.ma). **Rates** (incl breakfast) 1,390dh-2,020dh per room. **Credit** MC, V. **Map** p251 D5.
One of the most homely of Marrakech riads. Behind salmon-pink walls is a bougainvillaea and orange tree-filled courtyard (complete with chatty grey parrot) serving as an antechamber to an inner, more private court centred on a shimmering green-tiled solar-heated swimming pool. Noga is very spacious (it's three old houses knocked into one) and shared by just seven bed chambers, all bright, bold and cheery, and displaying the hospitable touch (small libraries of holiday-lite lit, for instance) of the garrulous German owner, Madam Gaby Noack-Späth. Expansive roof terraces filled with terracotta pots and lemon trees offer terrific views over the Medina and make for the perfect spot to enjoy aperitifs or fine cooking from the excellent in-house Moroccan chefs. Noga is closed during August.
Hotel services *Cook. Pool (indoor). Safe.* **Room services** *Air-conditioning. CD player. Heating. Internet sockets. Telephone. TV: satellite.*

Riad 72

72 Derb Arset Aouzal, off rue Bab Doukkala (tel/fax 044 38 76 29/www.riad72.com/ riad.72@wanadoo.net.ma). **Rates** (incl breakfast) 1 July-31 Aug 900dh-1,400dh double; 2,000dh suite. 1 Sept-30 June 1,000dh-1,600dh double; 2,500dh suite. **Credit** AmEx, MC, V. **Map** p248 B4.

Italian owned and, boy, doesn't it show. This is one sleek and sexy-looking place – Marrakech has it away with Milan. The resulting union is a trad townhouse given a black and white and lipstick-red makeover. The structure, spatials and detailing are Moroccan, the furniture and fittings imported. There are only four guest bedrooms, including a master suite that's laugh-out-loud large, five meters or more high and crowned by an ornate octagonal fanlight. The roof terrace boasts one of the best views in town with the green-tiled roofs of the Dar El Bacha in the foreground and beyond a cinemascopic jagged mountain horizon. Being that much higher than the neighbours means sunbathing is no problem (many other riads are overlooked so modesty can be an issue).
Hotel services *Cook. Hammam. Plunge pool (outdoor).* **Room services** *Air-conditioning. Heating. Safe.*

Riad Zina

38 Derb Assabane, Riad Larousse (tel/fax 044 38 52 42/www.riadzina.ma/ riadzina@iam.net.ma). **Rates** (incl breakfast) 1,000dh-1,200dh double; 2,000dh suite. **Credit** AmEx, MC, V. **Map** p248 C3.
A large central courtyard belies the modest nature of the Zina, just four rooms small: two upstairs, two down. The first-floor main suite is spectacular with a separate salon, private terrace, crushed velvet amber curtains and a glorious painted ceiling that owner Beate Prinz reckons is 350 years old. The other room on this floor sleeps three, while of the two rooms downstairs only one has an en suite bathroom. These latter rooms open directly on to the cactus-filled courtyard, which has some fantastic furniture, including the widest long leather benchsofa you've ever seen. Additional lounging space is provided by a small, multi-level roof terrace colonised by yet more cactus. Carrot motifs and a passion for copper and orange hint at Ms Prinz's vibrancy, humour and hair colour.
Hotel services *Cook.*

Tchaikana

25 Derb El Ferrane, Kaat Benahid (tel/fax 044 38 51 50/www.tchaikana.com/info@tchaikhana.com). **Rates** (incl breakfast) 6 Jan-15 Mar, 1 July-31 Aug 800dh double; 1,300dh suite. 15 Mar-1 July, 31 Aug-6 Jan 900dh double; 1,500dh suite. **No credit cards. Map** p249 D4.
Run by a young and charmingly idealistic Belgian couple (Jean-François and Delphine), Tchaikana is just four rooms small. However, those four rooms are enormous, particularly the two suites, each of which measures 11m by 5m (36ft by 16ft). The decor is beautiful, with a sort of *Vogue* goes Savannah look, and the central courtyard, laid out for dining, is gorgeously lit at night. Rates are per room, and given that all have banquettes in addition to double beds, each could sleep four or more impecunious souls – Jean-François has no objections (although no more than four breakfasts per room). Soft drinks and

Riad Noga. *See p48.*

orange juice are also free, and there's a great library of kids' books (mainly in French) and a tiny TV room to keep youngsters occupied. In case you're wondering, a 'tchaikana' is a Central Asian teahouse.
Hotel services *Children's library. Cook. TV room (with video library).* **Room services** *Air-conditioning. Central heating.*

Budget

Dar Sara

120 Derb Arset Aouzal, off rue Bab Doukkala, Medina (044 42 64 63/fax 044 42 65 11/ www.marrakech-riads.net/dzillije@iam.net.ma). **Rates** (incl breakfast) *7 Jan-31 Mar, 1 June-24 Oct, 4 Nov-19 Dec* 500dh-600dh per room. *Apr-May, 25 Oct-3 Nov, 20 Dec-6 Jan* 600dh-720dh per room. **Credit** MC, V. **Map** p248 B4.

This is one of six smart guesthouses operated by Marrakech Riads (*see p45* Dar Zelije), a small privately owned outfit captained by Abdelatif Ait Benabdallah, one of the prime movers behind the recent revitalisation of the Medina. It's the most modest (and the cheapest) of the lot, but still quite lovely with a cool blue and white motif throughout. There are just five rooms, only two of which have en suite bathrooms. A first-floor salon acts as a formal dining area but most guests prefer to eat in the cushion-strewn alcove of the courtyard. The location is good, just a few minutes' walk from the Dar Marjana restaurant, which is a busy pick-up and drop-off point for taxis.
Hotel services *CD player. Cook.*

Grand Tazi

Corner of avenue El Mouahidine & rue Bab Agnaou (044 44 27 87/fax 044 44 21 52). **Rates** 246dh single; 293dh double. **Credit** MC, V. **Map** p250 C6.
More accurately, the 'No Longer So Grand Tazi' – although we doubt it was ever that salubrious to start off with. It's a two-storey, two-star establishment that retains its popularity because of its plum location a minute's walk from Jemaa El Fna, combined with cheap room rates. Rooms vary wildly in quality: some have ragged curtains only just hanging from the rails, greying towels that tore when used too vigorously and an unpleasant bathroom, but others are considerably nicer. Up on the first floor, what must be the longest corridor in Marrakech leads to a good-sized swimming pool. In the evening the area beside reception takes on a life of its own as a lounge bar (*see p153*).
Hotel services *Bar. Car hire. Pool (outdoor). Restaurant.* **Room services** *Air-conditioning. Telephone. TV.*

Hotel Gallia

30 rue de la Recette, off rue Bab Agnaou (044 44 59 13/fax 044 44 48 53/www.ilove-marrakesh. com/hotelgallia). **Rates** (incl breakfast) 410dh double; 265dh single occupancy. **Credit** MC, V. **Map** p250 C6.
The warren of narrow roads off rue Bab Agnaou – seconds from the Jemaa El Fna – are thick with budget options (*see below* **Budget beds**), but Gallia comes top of the class. This small, French-owned operation gets ticks in all the right boxes: it's smack-bang central, impeccably clean and aesthetically

---

Budget beds

Let's just reiterate this: Marrakech is not the place to scrimp on accommodation. But for those who just don't have the cash there are enough budget hotels touting for business in the narrow alleys south of the Jemaa El Fna to keep a *Lonely Planet* researcher scribbling notes for months. They're concentrated between rue Bab Agnaou and Riad Zitoun El Kedim. There isn't much to separate one from the next: most of them have basic rooms (usually with a washbasin), communal showers/toilets, a courtyard, a roof terrace and – frankly – not a lot else. The main distinguishing factors are the levels of friendliness and cleanliness, and of course bathroom conditions (watch out for squat toilets and be aware that some hotels charge extra for hot showers). Expect to pay 80dh-120dh (roughly £5-£7.50) for a double, more in high season.

After the **Hotel Gallia** (*see p50*) and **Sherazade** (*see p51*), pick of the bunch is probably **Hotel Central Palace** (59 Derb Sidi Bouloukat, 044 44 02 35, www.marrakechconnect.com/hcp), which has a particularly pleasant central courtyard, friendly staff and almost 360° views from the high terrace. Some of the rooms are a bit poky (there are 'de luxe' options) but the communal lounges are large enough to make up for it.

Nearby **Hotel Afriquia** (45 Derb Sidi Bouloukat, 044 44 24 03) has good, clean rooms and a verdant patio area. The unusual broken-tile motif is a love it or hate it affair. Rooms at the **Hotel Essaouira** (044 44 38 05, 3 Derb Sidi Bouloukat) are on the small side but clean. **Hotel Ali** (rue Moulay Ismail; 044 44 49 79) is a something of a backpacker hang-out, very popular with trekking groups. Go for a dorm bed for rock-bottom prices. Unusually, Ali has internet, currency exchange and bike rental.

pleasing. Nineteen en suite double rooms open on to two picture-pretty, flower-filled courtyards, where an excellent breakfast is served. Bathrooms are big, modern pink affairs with limitless hot water. The well-kept flowery roof terrace is an ideal spot for lounging. Unsurprisingly, Gallia is popular. Bookings should be made by fax and it is advisable to book at least one month in advance.
Room services *Air-conditioning. Heating. Telephone.*

Riad Magi

79 Derb Moulay Abdelkader, off Derb Dabbachi (tel/fax 044 42 66 88). **Rates** (incl breakfast) 560dh single; 800dh double. **No credit cards.** **Map** p249 D5.

Petite, unpretentious and homely, Riad Magi has six carefully colour-coordinated rooms tiered in three levels around its central orange-tree shaded courtyard. The first-floor blue room is particularly lovely with its step-down bathroom. Breakfast is taken in the courtyard (which is now sadly minus its chameleons) or on the roof terrace; other meals are available by arrangement. When in town, English-owner Maggie Perry holds court from her corner table, organising guests' affairs and spinning stories of local absurdity – at such times Riad Magi becomes easily the most fun hangout in Marrakech. The location's good too, just a few minutes' walk away from Jemaa El Fna.
Hotel services *Cook. Massage.*

Sherazade

3 Derb Djama, off Riad Zitoun El Kedim (tel/fax 044 42 93 05/www.hotelsherazade. com/sherazade@iam.net.ma). **Rates** 150dh-250dh single; 200dh-600dh double. **Credit** MC, V. **Map** p250 C6.

The Sherazade is probably the most popular budget accommodation in the Medina. Why so? Well, probably because it's so much better run than most of its competitors. The desk staff speak a variety of languages, English included, rooms come with meal menus, services and trips out of town, the place is cleaned regularly, and there's a general air of competency, which isn't always a given down at this end of the market. Some rooms are better than others; those on the roof share toilets and get overly hot in summer, while the 'suites' – which come with a kitchen – are an expensive waste of time. There's an attractive roof terrace, good for getting to know one's fellow boarders, with an excellent tented chill-out area, all crimsony and strewn with cushions. Rooms are subject to a 50dh 'high season' supplement during April, August, October and over the Christmas and New Year period; reservations are a must year-round.
Hotel services *Cook. Laundry.* **Room services** *Fan.*

Villa El Arsa

18 Derb El Arsa, off Riad Zitoun El Jedid (044 42 63 26/). **Rates** (incl breakfast) 640dh-960dh. **No credit cards.** **Map** p251 D6.

Owned by a British couple, David and Susie Scott, this is a modest little house, but utterly charming with it. There's a rustic, vaguely Spanish air about the place, conveyed by whitewashed walls, potted plants, and bare, weathered wooden doors and furniture. There are two attractive cushion-filled lounging salons off the central courtyard and a tub-sized plunge pool; the four bedrooms are ranged off the irregularly shaped upper gallery. Two of the rooms are a bit on the small side, but the other pair are generous; all are rendered in calm neutral tones with splendid en suite bathrooms. Plus, there's the ubiquitous roof terrace, in this case with an open fireplace for chill winter evenings.
Hotel services *Cook.*

Guéliz

Aka the 'New City'. Less intense than the Medina, Guéliz offers a continental-style café scene, boutique shopping, good eating and what passes locally for nightlife. It's a good antidote to the foreignness of the Old City, which is still only five minutes away by taxi.

Moderate

Tichka Salam

Route de Casablanca, Semlalia (044 44 87 10/ fax 044 44 86 91/www.groupesalam.com/ tichkasalam@iam.net.ma). **Rates** *6-31 Jan, 1 June-31 Aug, 1 Nov-21 Dec* 950dh single; 1,200dh double; 1,700dh-2,700dh suite. *1 Feb-15 Mar, 1 Apr-31 May, 1 Sept-31 Oct* 1,000dh single; 1,300dh double; 1,800dh-3,000dh suite. *16 Mar-30 Apr, 22 Dec-5 Jan* 1,100dh single; 1,300dh double; 2,000dh-3,300dh suite. **Credit** AmEx, MC, V. **Map** p246 B1.

Jaws dropped when the Tichka first opened in the '70s. It's said that Jagger checked out of the Mamounia and executed a snake-hipped shimmy straight over here. The society-page people followed. The big wow was the design, courtesy of louche Texan Bill Willis. Since then, Marrakech has been hip-hoteled to excess and much of the sheen has come off the Tichka, but the public spaces are nevertheless still huge fun, particularly the bar and restaurants, which are a riot of rich colouring and tongue-in-cheek detail – check out the palm-leaf column capitals. Plus the back garden pool, complete with giant birdcage on stilts, remains arguably the best in town. However, rooms (130, plus eight suites), though blessed with Willis furniture, are badly in need of a little TLC, especially the drab bathrooms. Another drawback could be the out-of-town location: close to nowhere and a ten-minute taxi ride to the Medina.
Hotel services *Bar. Conference rooms. Garden. Hammam. Laundry. Massage. Pool (outdoor). Restaurants (2). Safe. Shops.* **Room services** *Air-conditioning. Hairdryer. Heating. Minibar. Room service (24hrs). Safe. Telephone. TV: satellite.*

Budget

Hotel du Pacha

33 rue de la Liberté, Guéliz (044 43 13 27/fax 044 43 13 26). Rates 250dh single; 360dh double. No credit cards. Map p252 B2.

A standard two-star joint, nondescript and of a kind common to cities the world over. The only indication that this is Morocco is a handful of aged tourist office posters. The better rooms have small balconies overlooking a central courtyard. All are in need of a little spending, with guest-worn furniture and broken fittings, but the beds are comfortable and the en suite bathrooms are kept clean. For the price it's a reasonable deal and one that has considerable appeal with independent tour groups, judging by the logo stickers on the door. The hotel business card announces that it has a 'restaurant gastronomique' but it's not – hardly a problem, though, as there are plenty of good dining options in the neighbourhood.

Hotel services *Bar. Laundry. Restaurant. Safe. TV lounge.* **Room services** *Air-conditioning. Telephone. TV.*

Hivernage

Aka the 'international enclave'. Between the airport and the Old City walls (five minutes from each), so the location is good, but the architectural neighbours are puffed-up villas and civic buildings and it's a taxi journey to get anywhere of interest.

Expensive

Dar Rhizlane

avenue Jnane El Harti (044 42 13 03/fax 044 44 79 00/www.dar-rhizlane.com/ rhizlane@iam.net.ma). Rates (incl breakfast) July, Aug, Nov, Dec 2,300dh double; 3,630dh suite. Jan-June, Sept, Oct 2,540dh double; 4,235dh suite. Credit MC, V. Map p252 B4.

Among the international chain hotel enclave that is Hivernage, Dar Rhizlane sets out to offer five-star accommodation with personality. Purpose-built and opened only in 2001, it's styled as a country villa, set in its own extensive grounds just a few minutes by taxi from the walls of the Medina. The architecture (by Charles Boccara) is imposing, even severe, but the 19 rooms and suites are all very comfortable, if a little staid. Other than the pool area and garden (with open-air bar and a separate restaurant building), common areas are few and we imagine staying here might be like temporarily inhabiting an exclusive apartment block. Several rooms offer a further level of privacy in the form of their own small, high-walled gardens.

Hotel services *Babysitting. Bar. Garden. Massage. Pool (outdoor). Restaurant. Safe.* **Room services** *Air-conditioning. Central heating. Minibar. Telephone. TV: satellite.*

Sofitel Marrakech

rue Harroun Errachid (044 42 56 00/fax 044 42 56 50/www.sofitel.com/H3569@accor-hotels.com). Rates (incl breakfast) 1,600dh-2,950dh per room. Credit AmEx, MC, V. Map p252 C5.

Hivernage is home to several big international five-stars (*see p56* **The chain gang**), but this is the pick of the bunch. None of them is particularly characterful, but at least the Sofitel boasts a lovely garden area with a great big pool beside which breakfast is taken. It's also the closest to the Medina walls and within walking distance (roughly a mile) of Jemaa El Fna. There are 260 rooms and suites, each with private balcony or terrace (ask for one south-facing overlooking the garden with the mountains in the distance), as well as all the usual facilities. The house restaurants are no great shakes but there are plenty of alternatives a short taxi ride away. The Sofitel has been open only since June 2002: in the early months of operation its staff weren't yet quite up to speed and service wasn't what it should be, but that should change – and the rates represent good value.

Hotel services *Bars (3). Business centre. Conference rooms. Disabled rooms (2). Garden. Health & fitness centre. Parking. Pool (outdoor). Restaurants (3). Safe.* **Room services** *Air-conditioning. Central heating. Hairdryer. Internet sockets. Minibar. Radio. Telephone. TV: satellite.*

Moderate

Hotel Es Saadi

avenue El Qadissia (044 44 88 11/fax 044 44 76 44/ www.essaadi.com). Rates 4-31 Jan, 7 June-20 Dec 1,500dh-1,800dh double; 2,800dh-3,600dh suite. 1 Feb-6 June, 21 Dec-3 Jan 1,800dh-2,100dh double; 3,100dh-3,900dh suite. Credit AmEx, MC, V. Map p252 C5.

The Saadi has been around forever. Cecil Beaton snapped the Rolling Stones beside its pool back in the late '60s. Undoubtedly, then it looked like the chicest thing on the planet; now it looks more like a municipal hospital. Guests tend to be of the same era as the hotel, that is a good few decades past their prime, but a lot of them are repeat customers, so folk are obviously well looked after here. Rooms (150 of them) are dated but comfortable, but get one south-facing, overlooking the gardens. We like how the glass rear wall of the lobby slides up during the day so that the hotel blends seamlessly with the poolside terrace – and the irregular-shaped pool remains one of the biggest and best in town. Even if you aren't staying here, the terrace is a great place to come for lunch (sandwiches, brochettes, burgers, salads and so on are priced at 50dh-120dh, and the bar does cocktails). Equally unmissable is the three times weekly dinner show staged at the Casino (*see p111*).

Hotel services *Bar. Casino. Conference rooms. Golf practice. Hairdressing salon. Hammam. Massage. Pool (outdoor). Restaurants (2). Sauna. Tennis courts.* **Room services** *Air-conditioning. Minibar. Radio. Telephone. TV: satellite.*

The simple charms of **Riad Magi**. *See p51.*

Jnane Tamsna: calm among the palms. *See p55*.

Palmeraie

Location of choice for the moneyed and famous, accommodation in the palms is strictly select and top end. Personally, we find the 15-minute drive into town a drag (not to mention expensive; 50dh by taxi) but if luxury isolation's your thing, look no further.

Deluxe

Dar Ayniwen

Tafrata (044 32 96 84/fax 044 32 96 86/www.darayniwen.com/ayniwen@iam.net.ma). **Rates** (incl breakfast) *7 Jan-14 Mar, 20 May-19 Dec* 3,300dh-4,500dh per room. *20 Dec-6 Jan, 15 Mar-19 May* 3,960dh-5,400dh per room. **Credit** AmEx, MC, V.

This place began life as a luxurious family residence until the kids grew up and moved out and Dar Ayniwen started accepting paying guests to fill the vacant rooms. There are seven of those (six are suites with associated lounges, salons, terraces and patios), all huge and lavishly furnished, mixing mod cons with home-style comforts (lots of deep sofas and open fires) and an eclectic assortment of antiques amassed over the years by household head Jacques Abtan. Son Stephane (a former Parisian hotelier with an MBA from Miami) now manages the residence, its large team of liveried staff and its magnificent walled gardens complete with citrus groves. If money's no object, go for the Galaxie suite with a private terrace overlooking the sparkling turquoise pool and a backdrop (heat haze permitting) of the Atlas Mountains.

Hotel services *Babysitting. Business centre. Cook. Garden. Hammam. Massage. Pool (outdoor). Room service (24hrs). Sauna.* **Room services** *Air-conditioning. CD player. Heating. Minibar. Safe. TV: cable.*

Jnane Tamsna

Douar Abiad (044 32 94 23/fax 044 32 98 84/ www.tamsna.com/info@tamsna.com). **Rates** (incl breakfast & 1st night dinner) 2,800dh-4,500dh per room. **Credit** MC, V.

Having it all

Riads lend themselves to being rented out in their entirety – for get-togethers, weddings, special anniversaries, bar mitzvahs... They offer the freedom of a rented villa with the service of a hotel. Most of the riads listed in this chapter will quote *pour le riad complet*, although typically the price is simply the non-discounted standard room rate times the number of rooms. Haggling is recommended, particularly in low season.

For real exclusivity, nothing beats a villa. The most select are located out in the Palmeraie, with the nearest neighbours several copses distant and protective, bougainvillea-swathed walls ensuring complete privacy – very necessary for the kind of A-list figures some of these places attract. Brad & Jennifer, David & Iman and the one-time Tom & Nicole all grace the leather-bound guest book at **Jnane Tamsna** (044 32 94 23/fax 044 32 98 84/ www.tamsna.com/info@tamsna.com; *see also p55*), twin villas where the outsider's fantasy of Moroccan life can be indulged to the fullest. Both come complete with gracious staff including driver (and, naturally, a car). Full board costs 25,000dh per week based on eight people sharing.

Nearby, the **Orchard of the Shooting Star** (Verger de L'Etoile Filante, 044 32 94 56) is owned by former US ambassador Frederick Vreeland (son of Diana Vreeland).

It comprises two residences with a total of eight bedrooms accommodating up to 15 people. There are multi-level salons, Balinese doors, Indian chests, Tibetan wall hangings, a swimming pool, tennis court, staff of five, chauffeur-driven car and 'Jamil' the house camel. The minimum stay is one week and that should set you back approximately 35,000dh per house.

In the Medina, **Medani** is where – so we were told – Jeffrey Archer bolted to when things got a bit hot in Britain. It's so secret we don't even have an address, but we do know that it's owned by a Brazilian-born Parisian and has 13 rooms, including 'La Charlotte', after former guest Ms Rampling. It costs from 2,672dh per night; call Stephen Collins (068 94 68 20).

Altogether more modest is the **Garden Room** (tel/fax 044 33 16 10/ lloyd_project@hotmail.com), a tiny lodge in the garden of a small colonial house just behind the Majorelle Gardens. It belongs to artist Jennifer Lloyd, who provides breakfast on the lawn, or in her gorgeous library if the weather's dreary; the cost is 640dh per night.

For details of other riads for rent contact UK-based specialist Best of Morocco (www.morocco-travel.com), or visit Marrakech Riads (www.marrakech-riads.net) or www.riad-2000.com; to check out more villas visit www.villa-rentals.com.

The chain gang

A growing number of global chains have branches in Marrakech (including **Sofitel**, see p52), with many more on the way. Don't, as a rule, expect a great deal of individual character, but do rest assured that you'll get the same standard of service and level of comfort you last found at the same chain's outlets in Dallas, Kuala Lumpa, Zurich… wherever, really.

● **Sheraton Marrakech** (avenue de la Menara, Hivernage, 044 44 89 98, www.starwood.com/sheraton) has 219 rooms, ten suites, a royal villa and a club floor for SPG members, plus five restaurants, a bar, a pool, a putting green and tennis courts.

● **Le Meridien N'Fis** (avenue de France, Hivernage, 044 44 87 72, www.lemeridien.com) offers 278 rooms including 12 suites, two restaurants, a bar, Avenue nightclub (see p158), a tearoom, a pool and all other usual amenities.

●The **Kempinski Mansour Eddahbi** (avenue de France, Hivernage, 044 33 91 00, www.kempinski-marrakech.ma) is just about the biggest joint in town with 403 rooms and 38 suites, plus five restaurants, a bar, Paradise nightclub (see p158), three swimming pools, a hammam, gym etc, plus a state-of-the-art conference/convention centre.

A creation of designer Meryanne Loum-Martin and her ethnobotanist husband Dr Gary Martin, Jnane Tamsna is a 'Moorish hacienda' with ten opulent rooms set around two central courtyard gardens. The architecture is vernacular chic, coloured in the palest tones of primrose, peppermint and clay and enhanced by Loum-Martin's own inspired furniture. Surrounding fruit orchards, herb and vegetable gardens provide fragrance and organic produce for the kitchen. A second kitchen is used for 'culinary adventure' programmes (see p114). Overflow from the main building is taken up at an adjacent smaller villa of six double rooms, the decor of each inspired by a different Islamic culture. The combination of rural tranquillity, Zen-like aesthetics and ecological initiative makes for an almost utopian (no locks on the doors!) scenario. Special packages can be arranged that combine time at Jnane Tamsna with several nights in a Medina riad lowering the overall cost of a week's stay.

Hotel services *Cook. Garden. Laundry. Massage. Pool (outdoor). Safe. Tennis courts. TV: satellite. Video library.* **Room services** *Air-conditioning. Central heating.*

Ksar Char-Bagh

Palmeraie (044 32 92 44/fax 044 32 92 14/ www.ksarcharbagh.com/info@ksarcharbagh.com). **Rates** 5,500dh-8,500dh per suite. **Credit** MC, V.

As we go to press this is *the* villa of the moment. It takes the whole Moroccan fantasy trip to its absolute extremes. A charming French couple (she in advertising, he publishing) have recreated an Alhambran palace court that defies belief. It's been built from scratch on a kasbah-sized scale. A massive moated gatehouse with six metre-high beaten metal doors fronts an arcaded central court with a fountain pool fit for gondolas. Extensive grounds contain separate English, herb and flower gardens, a fruit orchard, an open-air spa and the deepest of pools. OTT indoor amenities include a cigar salon (!) and wine cellar selected by the house sommelier (!!). All this is shared by just a handful of suites, each with its own private garden or terrace, one with its own exclusive swimming pool. Look out for it soon in a Condé Nast magazine spread near you.

Hotel services *Billiard room. Cook. Garden. Gym. Hammam. Laundry. Library (books, CDs, DVDs). Massage. Pool (outdoor). Safe. Tennis courts. Wine cellar.* **Room services** *Air-conditioning. CD player. Heating. Minibar. TV: DVD, satellite.*

Expensive

Les Deux Tours

Douar Abiad (044 32 95 27/fax 044 32 95 23/ www.deux-tours.com/deuxtour@iam.net.ma). **Rates** 6-31 Jan, 16 June-30 Sept, 1-19 Dec 1,750dh double; 2,500dh deluxe; 3,750dh suite. *1 Feb-15 June, Oct, Nov, 20 Dec-5 Jan* 2,000dh double; 3,000dh deluxe; 3,750dh suite. **Credit** MC, V.

One of the longer established guesthouses in the Palmeraie, Les Deux Tours (named for its distinctive twin-towered gateway) is the sublime work of premier Marrakchi architect Charles Boccara. Approached via a cactus-lined driveway, it's a walled enclave of clustered villas that together offer 24 rooms and suites (with more on the way) in a lush blossom and palm garden setting. No two rooms are the same but all feature glowing tadelakt walls and zelije tiling with the most stunning of sculpturally soft bathrooms, several seductively lit via glassy punch-holes in pink mud-brick domes. Guests share the most attractive of outdoor pools, keyhole shaped and fringed by grassy lawns, as well as a stunning subterranean hammam.

Hotel services *Cook. Hammam. Massage room. Pool (outdoor).* **Room services** *Air-conditioning. Telephone.*

Moderate

Topkapi

rue El Atlas, route de Fès, km4 (tel/fax 044 32 98 89/topkapi_marrakech@hotmail.com). **Rates** (incl breakfast) 1,500dh single; 1,700dh double. **Credit** MC, V.

Topkapi offers an affordable alternative to the more expensive Marrakech retreats; it's out of town, on the edge of the Palmeraie. It's tranquil and self contained, but it's also a hotel rather than a private villa, so room rates are less prohibitive. Opened in March 2002, it's custom-built, low rise and *Elle Decoration*-chic with a central pink-brick pavilion housing reception, a lounge and bar, then out back an expansive garden with a great pool. A second building, octagonal in shape with a central area open to the sky, accommodates ten rooms arranged on two levels. All are spacious and each has its own colour scheme with fabrics to match by Bridgette Perkins. Ground-floor rooms have small garden patios; upper-floor rooms have balconies. Plus there's a lovely roof terrace. The place is run by a young French couple who are eager to please.

Hotel services Bar. Cook. Hammam. Massage. Pool (outdoor). **Room services** Air-conditioning. Heating. Telephone.

Further afield

All of the places below are a 15- to 30-minute drive from the Medina – far enough away to be rural, close enough to pop to Jemaa El Fna for dinner.

Deluxe

Amanjena

Route de Ouarzazate, km12 (044 40 33 53/ fax 044 40 34 77/www.amanresorts.com/ amanjenares@amanresorts.com). **Rates** 8,000dh pavilion; 9,000dh pavilion bassin; 17,000dh maison; 22,000dh maison jardin. **Credit** AmEx, MC, V.

You did convert those prices right: rooms from $800 to $2,200. That's not to mention the 10% service charge and 10% government tax that gets slapped on top. The Amanjena is part of the Amanresorts group, the world's most luxurious international hotel chain. It caters to a very specific and highly pampered clientele: Aman-junkies are not the kind to worry about a couple of hundred dollars here and there. What they get for their money is an exclusive gated complex some five miles south of town, well away from the masses (and secure from paparazzi). The architecture is low-rise palatial, rose pink and frilly, trimmed with green tiled roofs. At the heart of the resort is the *bassin*, a massive fish-filled reservoir of water that feeds two shallow canals running between the 34 'pavilions' and six *maisons*. These are vast and lavish private residences, some of them with their own walled gardens, all of them filled with every conceivable luxury. Services range from spas and facials to hot-air ballooning and the loan of clubs for use on the 18-hole Amelkis golf course next door. Yes, that might be Sting by the pool, but if you can afford to stay here you're probably every bit as rich and famous as he is.

Hotel services Bar. Beauty centre. Bicycle rental. Car rental. Gym. Hammam. Library (books, CDs, DVDs). Massage. Pool (outdoor). Restaurants. Shops. Tennis courts. **Room services** Air-conditioning. CD player. Heating. Minibar. Room service (24hrs). Safe. Telephone. TV: cable, DVD, video.

Tigmi: a roof with a view. *See p58.*

Expensive

Kasbah Agafay

*Route de Guemassa (044 36 86 00/fax 044 42 09 70/
www.kasbahagafay.com/info@kasbahagafay.com).*
Rates (incl breakfast) 4,000dh kasbah rooms;
5,000dh tents. **Credit** MC, V.

A 150-year-old hilltop fort formerly owned by a local
holy man, the Kasbah Agafay has been rescued from
dereliction and transformed into a striking piece of
fantasy accommodation. It appears as some sort of
monastic retreat or convent, solitary on a hillock
among sun-browned fields and olive groves. Inside,
18 minimally furnished (but highly stylish) rooms
are grouped around small private courts, most with
direct access to one of the kasbah's varied and gorgeous gardens. There are also four air-con Caidal
tents the size of pavilions, each with two double beds
and grand bath and shower facilities. A new addition is the spa, offering, among other treatments,
open-air massage and mud and algae baths after
which guests take herbal tea on the lawn overlooking the walled garden where vegetables, herbs and
aromatic plants are grown for the kitchens and the
cookery courses (*see p114*). Lunch (a buffet for
around 300dh per person) and dinner (à la carte) are
ideally taken among the olive trees beside the generously sized garden pool. At 20 miles south-west of
Marrakech, distance could be an issue; then again,
you could look at Agafay as a destination in itself
with the bonus of a rather nice city close by.
Hotel services *Cook. Cookery lessons. Gardens.
Hammam. Pool (outdoor). Spa. Tennis courts.*

Tigmi

*Douar Tagadert El Cadi, km24 route d'Amizmiz
(www.tigmi.com/tigmi@morocco-travel.com).*
Rates (incl breakfast & lunch or dinner) *1 June-31
Aug* 1536dh suite; *1 Jan-10 Apr, 21 Apr-31 May, 1
Sept-20 Dec* 1,760dh suite. *10-20 Apr, 21-31 Dec*
2,560dh suite. **Credit** MC, V.

The ultimate rural retreat, Tigmi is a mud-walled
eight-suite haven of solitude lying in the middle of
nowhere, halfway to the foothills of the Atlas, some
15 miles or so south of Marrakech. The architecture
and interiors are rustically simple but fashion-shoot
stylish – lots of whitewashed arches, arcades and
alcoves, covered walkways and terraces with beguil-
ing views over raw, dusty pinkish landscapes (think
Sergio Leone with citrus fruits). Most suites have
courtyards (one has its own pool), terraced chill-out
areas and simple, cosy bedrooms with fireplaces (lit
in winter). There's a TV room, a pool, food (and
wine) when you want it and a small Berber village
for company, but no phones and otherwise little to
do but kick back and relax. A rental car would
extend your options but, then again, as David Byrne
once sang, 'Heaven is a place where nothing ever
happens'. Reservations must be made through Best
of Morocco (*see p55* **Having it all**).
Hotel services *Car rental. CD player. Cook.
Garden. Hammam. Pool (outdoor). TV: cable, DVD.*

Villa Dar Zina

*4 Jnane Brika, Targa (044 34 66 45/fax 044 49 56
55/www.villadarzina.com/info@villadarzina.com).*
Rates (incl breakfast) *July, Aug* 1,980dh double;
2,780dh suite. *Sept-June* 2,480dh double; 3,480dh
suite. **Credit** MC, V.

Not so much a hotel as an exclusive retreat, Dar
Zina is a luxurious terracotta-toned villa 3.5km (two
miles) north-west of the Medina in a bucolic, semi-
rural neighbourhood. It boasts four double rooms
and four suites, all exquisitely decorated and furnished in modern, elegantly restrained Moroccan
style, each slightly different in character. All
address the lush palm-fringed garden and its azure-
blue pool – illuminated by candlelight throughout
the night to maximise the enchanting effect. The
intention, according to Parisian owner Pierre
Guillermo (a former journalist: first assignment,
1971, three days in the company of John Lennon), is
that guests should feel as though they are kipping
over at a (very rich) friend's house. To this end service is ultra-discreet. There's no restaurant but an
on-site and highly accomplished chef takes orders
for lunch and dinner to be eaten wherever you
fancy. The distance from town could be an issue
except that once installed at the villa it's easy to forget the rest of the world exists.
Hotel services *Car park. Car rental. Cook.
Garden. Fitness room. Laundry. Massage room. Pool
(outdoor). Safe. Sauna. TV: satellite.* **Room services**
Air-conditioning. CD player. Safe. Telephone.

Moderate

Caravanserai

*264 Ouled Ben Rahmoun (044 30 03 02/
fax 044 30 02 62/www.caravanserai.com/
info@caravanserai.com).* **Rates** (incl breakfast)
700dh-1,250dh single; 1,250dh-2,500dh double;
1,750dh-3,250dh suite; 3,250dh-3,500dh Majorelle
suite; 3,750dh-4,000dh pool suite. **Credit** MC, V.

Outwardly indistinguishable among the collection
of compressed mudbrick walls that make up the
small sun-baked hamlet of Ouled Ben Rahmoun, but
behind its wooden door Caravanserai offers a super-
sophisticated take on rural life – right down to a
water-mist cooling system. It's a seductive ensemble of pale pink walls, rough-hewn eucalyptus
ceilings, earthenware fittings and plenty of white
canvas-draped banquettes for indolent hours spent
lounging. Best of all is the magnificent central
swimming pool, framed by a massive gate-like structure escaped from *Waterworld*. There are 17 rooms
and suites, including a couple that feature their own
courtyards and pools. For guests who can tear themselves away, a minibus shuttles into central
Marrakech three times a day (15 mins) and there's a
24-hour taxi service. Reservations recommended.
Hotel services *Bar. Beauty treatments. Car park.
Cook. Garden. Hammam. Massage. Pool (outdoor).
Shop.* **Room services** *Air-conditioning. Fridge.
Heating. Telephone.*

Sightseeing

Introduction

Before you begin, get your bearings here.

Marrakech is not a city of great monuments. In total there are hardly more than a half-dozen mosques, palaces or museums to detain the tour bus crowds. Visitors bound by tight itineraries can be round the highlights in a few hours with still time enough to be fleeced in the souk before dinner. Poor them. This city doesn't work like that. Much of what's best is hidden and it takes time, luck or fortuitous acquaintance to winkle it out. The more hours spent idly wandering, pausing and observing, the greater the chance of having one of those experiences (the opening of a closed door; a supper shared with locals; an evening astray in bad company) that'll later become the stuff of dinner table anecdote.

The area in which to idle is the **Medina**, Arabic for the 'city', by which is meant the old walled historic heart of Marrakech. As a visitor this is where you are going to be spending the greater part of your walking hours. What monuments the city possesses are here, typically well hidden deep among labyrinthine alleys and dead-end backstreets, most of which don't bear names. There's little logic in the layout but navigation is at least aided by two major landmarks: the vertical signpost of the Koutoubia Minaret, which helpfully flags the location of the adjacent big central square, the **Jemaa El Fna**, aka 'la place'. This is the sink hole around which Marrakech swirls. Seemingly whichever way you walk, you always end up here. Its vast open space also neatly divides the Medina into two zones for exploration: north of the square is commercial (the vast souks), south is imperial (the palaces).

North-west of the old walls is the 'New City', a French colonial creation of the 1930s, which goes by the name **Guéliz**. Old City and New are connected by the broad, tree-lined avenue Mohammed V (pronounced 'M'hammed Sanc'), the Champs Elysées – and we write that tongue firmly in cheek – of Marrakech. It's the main street of Guéliz. Few short-term visitors bother with this part of town but middle-class Marrakchis and serious expats favour it for car-friendly streets, modern apartment blocks and a semblance of 21st-century living. It's also home to a lot of the city's better restaurants and choice shopping, as well as what passes for the local nightlife. A short distance further north again is **Semlalia**, a rapidly expanding, edge-of-town, highway strip of motel-hotels, petrol stations, supermarkets, the city's first McDonald's and other similarly dubious aspects of modern urban life. Beyond that lies 250 kilometres (155 miles) of next to nothing until Casablanca.

South of Guéliz, and immediately west of the city walls, is **Hivernage** (drop the aitch), a small, low-density neighbourhood of villas and international five-star hotels. Also out this way are some of the trappings of civic society:

The best Sightseeing

For the total tourist trip
Climb into a horse-drawn **calèche** for a circuit of the city walls. *See p62.*

For imperial excess
Check out the apartments of the concubines at the **Bahia Palace**. *See p78.*

For spiritual serenity
Cool white marble and a beautiful ablutions pool induce calm at the **Medersa Ben Youssef**. *See p70.*

For oriental intensity
Main square **Jemaa El Fna** is chaotic and enthralling at any time, but doubly so by night. *See p65.*

For haunting ruins
Muse on how the mighty fall at the denuded and stork-festooned **Badii Palace**. *See p77.*

For time stood still
Trade and manufacturing remain pre-industrial in the Medina's many old **fundouks**. *See p70.*

For greenery (and blue)
Planted by a painter, nurtured by a couturier, the **Majorelle Gardens** mix horticulture with art. *See p84.*

For time out
Gorgeous exhibition space **Dar Cherifa** serves mint tea to weary explorers. *See p72.*

the railway station, new Opera House, Palais des Congrès and airport, all quite grand, all sorely underused.

On the opposite (north-east) side of the Medina is a vast bare-earth oasis of well-spaced palm trees, known, prosaically enough, as the **Palmeraie**. While not particularly pretty, its distance from the hoi polloi, ultra-low population density (there are more trees than people) and unbounded opportunities for lavish construction have made it a favourite locale for the homes of the rich and wealthy – both Moroccans and foreigners.

GETTING AROUND

The only real option for getting to grips with the Medina is to go at it by foot. It looks daunting on the map but the area within the walls isn't really that large – although with all the wrong turns and backtracking you're bound to make, the miles do add up. Besides which, a lot of the streets are too narrow to accommodate cars, hence the swarms of motorcycles, scooters and pushbikes that make negotiating the city so bloody lethal to pedestrians. Just occasionally, a taxi might be necessary, but more for navigation purposes than for anything else – some restaurants and hotels are so well hidden that the only way to find them is to be chauffeured by a native, who at least has the language skills to ask the way when he too invariably gets lost.

Taxis are necessary for shuttling between the Medina and Guéliz (and any other New City destinations), only a five-minute ride (10dh) but the best part of a half-hour walk. The green-painted horse-drawn carriages (known as *calèches*) are pretty impractical as a form of transport, but they are a pleasant way to go about sightseeing and aren't prohibitively expensive. Rental of a two-wheeler is also a fun option, especially for exploring around the New City and the Palmeraie.

For more information on getting around the city, *see p220-p224*.

GUIDES

Hotels all but push them on clients and guidebooks collude, warning of the dangers of unaccompanied exploration, but do you really need a guide? The answer is an unequivocal no. Yes, you'll probably get lost a few times but never for long. There are no no-go areas. And if you do really get stumped, then stop any local and they'll graciously set you back on track. In any case, in a city of so many hidden surprises, there's no such thing as a wrong turn, only alternative routes.

However, if you do have special interests or wish to hire someone whose knowledge goes

(That means 'Stop!', by the way.)

beyond the extents of this book, then we can recommend **Ahmed Tija**, who's been guiding visitors around for the best part of 50 years, and was a friend to author Gavin Maxwell, whose *Lords of the Atlas* is the definitive local history book. We've also heard good things about **Moulay Youssef**, **Mustapha Chouquir** and **Mustapha Karroum**, all of whom speak English and ply their trade with some of the better hotels. Alternatively, ask at your hotel reception or at the tourist office. Beware picking up unofficial guides in the Medina (official guides carry accreditation) as they usually turn out to be an expensive waste of time.

Ahmed Tija

044 30 03 37/mobile 061 08 45 57. **Rates** 300dh per half-day.

Moulay Youssef

Moible 061 16 35 64. **Rates** 200dh per half-day.

Mustapha Chouquir

Mobile 062 10 40 99. **Rates** 200dh per half-day.

Mustapha Karroum

Mobile 061 34 07 78. **Rates** 200dh per half-day.

The Medina

Short on monuments but big on sights, sounds and smells, Marrakech Medina is an intoxicating realm of the senses.

The numerous gates that puncture the ribbon of pink wall binding the Medina act like time travel portals. On the outside is a familiar world of blue skies above roads and pavements and orderly arrangements of glass and concrete blocks. But step through certain of the gates and suddenly the sky all but disappears as blank-faced buildings crowd in on alleys soaked deeply in shadow, while sight-lines shrink to just a few metres and the next twisting corner. Madcap cyclists and moped riders keep pedestrians on their toes. It's very disorienting, possibly even slightly daunting.

WHERE TO START

Ease your way in by starting with an exploration of the main square Jemaa El Fna (*see p65*) and the area around the adjacent Koutoubia Mosque (*see below*). A ride around the ramparts in a horse-drawn carriage also helps with orientation (*see below* **Walls & gates**).

The fibrous network of souks lies to the north of Jemaa El Fna, as do three of the city's major must-see monuments – the Musée de Marrakech, Koubba El Badiyin and Ben Youssef Medersa. South of Jemaa El Fna are the Bahia and Badii Places along with the melancholic Saadian Tombs.

Away from well-trodden tourist paths, alleys rapidly become more shambolic. Stray into neighbourhoods like Aylen and El Moukef in the eastern Medina to experience a little-seen, backstage world of Marrakech *au naturel*.

Although not always apparent, there is some kind of street etiquette: pedestrians stick to the right leaving the centre free for two-wheeled and four-legged traffic.

Walls & gates

The Medina began life as a garrison camp in 1060, under the leadership of the Almoravid leader, Youssef Ben Tachfine. As the nomadic tent dwellers converted to a settled lifestyle, the city grew. Around 1126, in the face of threat from the Almohads to the south, Sultan Ali Ben Youssef decided to encircle the new city with walls. Within a year a circuit of ten kilometres (six miles) of ten-metre (30-foot) high wall defended by 200 towers and punctuated by 20 gates had been completed.

There have been constant repairs and some expansion, but the original walls probably followed roughly the same lines as the reddish *pisé* (dried mud mixed with lime) walls of today.

Although strikingly beautiful at times – especially when glowing under a setting sun – the walls are fairly featureless. There are no ramparts to ascend, and a walk around the whole circuit is a bit of a slog. It makes for a great whirl in a **horse-drawn calèche**, though. Drivers and their carriages wait in line on the north side of place de Foucault (just follow your nose). A complete circuit, heading north up avenue Mohammed V and right out of the Bab Nkob, will take the best part of an hour and costs around 60dh; state-fixed prices are posted on the carriages.

Koutoubia Mosque

Maps p65 & p250

Paris has its Eiffel, 21st-century London its Eye; Marrakech has the Koutoubia. Its square-towered minaret is the modern city's pre-eminent landmark. At 77 metres (252 feet) it's not actually that high (the Eiffel Tower is over four times taller at 321 metres), but thanks to Marrakech's flat topography and a local planning ordinance that forbids any other building in the Medina to rise above the height of a palm tree, it towers majestically over its surroundings. As such, the minaret is the first thing that any visitor sees when approaching the city from afar. Unfortunately, up close the view remains largely restricted to the tower because the precincts of the mosque (including the interior of the minaret) are off-limits to non-Muslims.

The Koutoubia gets its name (Mosque of the Booksellers) from the cluster of Koran merchants, parchment dealers, binders, copyists and scribes that at one time filled the surrounding streets. They're all long gone and instead the shadow of the minaret falls across a small modern plaza where the tour groups congregate, mingling with the faithful on their way to pray. Small, fenced, sunken areas on the plaza are the remains of reservoirs that belonged to the **Dar El Hajar** (House of Stone), a fortress built by city-founder Youssef Ben Tachfine towards the end of the 11th

The **Medina walls**.

Koutoubia Mosque. *See p62.*

century, and the first permanent structure
in the encampment that became Marrakech.
The fortress was short-lived, destroyed by
the conquering Almohads who replaced it
with a mosque in 1147.

The extensive ruins of that first mosque,
in the form of the foundations of columns
that supported the roof, cover a large area due
west of the plaza. The Koutoubia Mosque was
built in 1158 adjoining the Almohad mosque,
presumably because the earlier structure was
no longer big enough to accommodate the city's
expanding population. The two would have
functioned as one mosque through connecting

doors until the Almohad mosque fell into
disrepair and eventually collapsed following
an earthquake in 1775.

The Koutoubia's celebrated minaret
was added by Yacoub El Mansour, an
architectural patron of vertical delights;
El Mansour was also responsible for La
Tour Hassan in Rabat and the Giralda in
Seville. Like the Giralda, the Koutoubia
Minaret has an ascending ramp inside,
which is broad and tall enough for the
muezzin (whose job it is to call the faithful
to prayer five times a day) to ride his horse up
to the top. The pale brick façade was originally

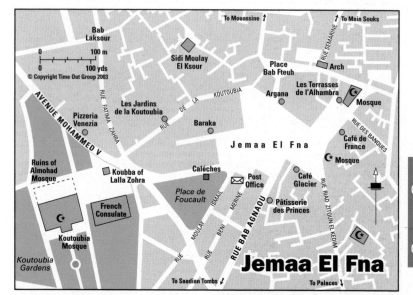

See map above and p250

completely encased in ceramics and stucco but all that remains is a single narrow blue-tiled frieze beneath the saw-tooth crenellations.

Legend has it that the four brass balls that top the domed lantern were originally made of solid gold, cast from the melted-down jewellery of the sultan's wife as her penance for having eaten four grapes during the Ramadan fast. Hardly more credible is the claim that in times past only blind muezzins were employed because from the summit a sighted individual would have been able to gaze into the royal harem. The gibbet beside the balls is used to hoist a white flag that indicates prayer time for the deaf.

The small white domed structure on the plaza is the **Koubba of Lalla Zohra**, a shrine that used to be open to the public until the inebriated son of a former city mayor ploughed his car into the structure and, as part of the repairs, the door was sealed up.

It's possible to walk around the Koutoubia, clockwise following the wall that encloses the grounds of the French Consulate, or anti-clockwise along the top of the Almohad ruins. South and west of the mosque are the rose-filled Koutoubia Gardens. Across avenue Houman El Fetouaki a high wall cuts off from sight a modest crenellated building; this is the humble **Tomb of Youssef Ben Tachfine**, founder of Marrakech. A padlocked gate ensures that the great desert warrior rests in peace, his tomb off limits to the public.

Jemaa El Fna

See map above and p250

It's the main open space in Marrakech but to call Jemaa El Fna a public square is misleading. Uncontained, disorderly, untainted by grandeur or pomp, untamable by council or committee, Jemaa El Fna is nothing less than bedlam. It's an urban clearing, irregular in shape as an accident of nature, and thronged day and night with a carnival of local life – totally at odds with its name, which roughly translates as 'Assembly of the Dead'.

The square is as old as Marrakech itself. It was laid out as a parade ground by the Almoravids in front of their royal fortress (the Dar El Hajar, *see p62*). When the succeeding Almohads built a new palace complex a little way to the south the open ground passed to the public and became – as it remains now – a place for gathering, for trading, for entertainment and even the occasional riot. The name (which is pronounced with its consonants tumbling into each other to come out something like 'jemaf'na') references its past role as a venue for executions, with the decapitated heads then put up for public display on spikes. The French put a stop to that.

In more recent times, during the 1970s the municipality attempted to impose order with a scheme to tarmac the square and turn it into a car park. It was opposed and defeated. Since

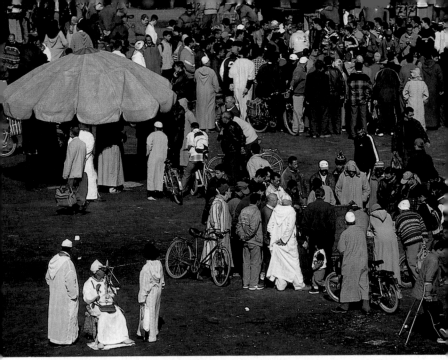

Life as a spectator sport: **Jemaa El Fna** by day. *See p65.*

then, thanks in part to the lobbying efforts of Spanish writer Juan Goytisolo (who has lived just off the square since the late 1970s), Jemaa El Fna has been recognised by UNESCO as part of the 'oral patrimony of mankind' and its preservation is secured.

A DAY IN THE LIFE

During the early part of the day the square is relatively quiet. The orange-laden carts of the fruit-juice sellers line the perimeter, wagon-train fashion, but otherwise there's only a scattering of figures, seated on boxes or rugs, shaded under large shabby umbrellas. The snake-charmers are early starters with their black, rubbery reptiles laid out in front or sheltered under large tambourine-like drums (be careful what you kick). For a few dirhams visitors can have a photograph taken with a large snake draped over their shoulders; for a few more dirhams they can have it removed. Other hunched figures may be dentists (teeth pulled on the spot), scribes (letters written to order), herbalists (good for whatever ails you) or beggars (to whom Moroccans give generously). Overlooking all, the prime morning spot for unhurried businessmen and traders is the patio of the landmark **Café de France** (*see p115*), which has been resident on the square for at least the last 50 years.

The action tends to wilt beneath the merciless heat of the afternoon sun, when snake-charmers, dancers and acrobats can barely manage to stir themselves at the approach of camera-carrying tourists. It's not until dusk that things really kick off.

As the light and heat fade, ranks of makeshift kitchens set up with tables, benches and hissing flames, constituting one great open-air restaurant where adventurous eaters can masticate on anything from snails to sheep's head (*see p98* **Street eats**).

Beside the avenues of food stalls, the rest of the square takes on the air of a circus. Shoals of visiting Berber farmers from the surrounding plains and villages join Medina locals in crowding around the assorted performers. These typically include troupes of cartoon-costumed acrobats, musicians and their prowling transvestite dancers, storytelling magicians and boxing bouts held between underage boys who can hardly lift their hands in the heavy leather gloves. The tourists and visitors who provided the *raison d'être* for the afternoon entertainers are now negligible in this far more surreal evening scene.

Approaching midnight the food stalls begin to pack up, the performers wind down, sending the contributions cap on one last round, and the

crowds thin. Only the musicians remain, purveyors of seedy mysticisms, attended by small knots of wild-eyed devotees giddy on repetitive rhythms, helped along by hash. At the same time, the place becomes one great gay cruising ground, busy with tight-shirted, tight-trousered teens, sharp and savvy beyond their years, well-practised peddlers of ass for cash.

THE OVERVIEW

The best place to be at any time of the day is in among it all (watch your wallet and bags), but several of the peripheral cafés and restaurants have upper terraces with fine ringside seating, among them the **Argana** (*see p101*), **Les Terrasses de l'Alhambra** (*see p109*) and – with the best view of the lot – the **Café Glacier**, which is above the Hotel CTM, where the compulsory purchase of one soft drink (9dh) gives access to the rooftop terrace with its 270° sweeping panorama.

Day or night, whether you choose stealthy observation from the terraces or a headlong plunge into the mêlée, Jemaa El Fna always remains somewhat elusive. 'All the guidebooks lie,' writes Juan Goytisolo, 'there's no way of getting a firm grasp on it'.

North of Jemaa El Fna

Map p248-249

Stretching north of Jemaa El Fna are the *souks* (markets), with alleyway upon alleyway of tiny closet-sized emporia – a hundred of them in a hundred metres. In the most densely touristed areas, the overwhelming number of shops is offset by the fact that most seem compelled to offer exactly the same non-essential goods; in particular, canary-yellow slippers, embroidered robes and etched brass platters the size of manhole covers. Slip away down the side alleys and you'll find that things improve; our **Shops & Services** chapter (*p117-p136*) picks out some of the highlights.

The two main routes into the souks are rue Semarine and rue Mouassine; the former offers the more full-on blast of bazaar, the latter is a more sedate path leading to choice boutiques.

THE MAIN SOUKS

Entrance to the **rue Semarine** (aka Souk Semarine) is via an elaborate arch one block north of Jemaa El Fna – reached via either the spice market or the egg market, both pungent experiences, one pleasant, the other not. It's a relatively orderly street, broad and straight with overhead trellising dappling the paving with patterns of light and shadow. Every section of the souk has its own speciality and here it has traditionally been textiles, although

these days the cloth merchants have been largely supplanted by souvenir shops.

About 150 metres along, the first alley off to the east leads to a wedge-shaped open area known as **Rahba Kedima**, or the 'old place'. (The way between Semarine and the Rahba Kedima is a perpetual crush because it also leads to a small court, the **Souk Laghzel**, formerly the wool market but now a car-boot-sale of a souk where women– and only women – come to sell meagre possessions like a single knitted shawl or a bag of vegetables.) The Rahba Kedima used to be the city's corn market but it's now given over to spices and 'magic' stalls – *see p68* **Jinn and tonics**.

The upper storeys of the shops on the northern side are usually hung with carpets and textiles, an invitation to search for the partially obscured passageway that leads through to the **Criée Berbère** (Berber Auction). These days this partially roofed, slightly gloomy section of the souk is the lair of the rug merchants, but until well into the 20th century it was used for the sale of slaves, auctioned here three times weekly. According to North African historian Barnaby Rogerson, the going rate was two slaves for a camel, 10 for a horse and 40 for a civet cat.

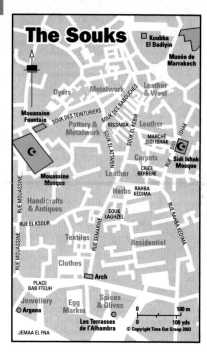

Jinn and tonics

Abdelhamid Oulhiad wears a grey wool rollneck, khaki canvas pants and a black donkey jacket. He looks every inch the young (late thirtyish), stylish modern Moroccan. It's only when he removes his shades to display red-rimmed, nervously darting eyes that a note of the other-worldly creeps in.

Abdelhamid battles *jinn*. Created from fire, the jinn are souls without bodies and a tendency towards malice. Belief in these troublesome spirits is widespread throughout Morocco, even in the most urbane of social circles. On the occasion of a death in the house, a run of bad luck, uncharacteristically antisocial behaviour or inexplicable illness in a loved one, worried parties seek out Abdelhamid. Practitioners like him can often succeed where more conventional methods fail. He tells of a case where a woman was inexplicably paralysed following the death of her husband. The doctors couldn't understand it until an exorcist discovered she was being held captive for sex by the spirit of her recently deceased partner. A cure was effected. Honest.

The worst of the jinn is one-eyed Aicha Kandicha, a female spirit with a donkey's tail who plagues men. But the types and varieties are legion, with one set that operates exclusively by day and a whole other army that appears only by night.

To do battle, Abdelhamid relies on the Koran and a complex hand-drawn reference chart that takes into account numerology and astrology to indicate which are the best days to fight and when it's expedient to lay low. There are also myriad incenses and compounds required in different measures for each and every situation.

Herbalist Abdeljabbar Ait Chaib on the Rahba Kedima at the heart of the Medina stocks most ingredients, from jars of leeches to dried chameleons, good for warding off the evil eye: toss it into a small wood-fired oven and walk around it three times. If the chameleon explodes, it's bye-bye evil eye. But if the chameleon melts, you're still in the shit.

And the little black scorpions? Nothing to do with black magic – they're good against haemorrhoids, apparently. 'What do you do?', we asked. 'You kill them first,' replied Abdeljabber dryly. Black magic with humour.

Back on rue Semarine, just north of the turning for the Rahba Kedima, the street forks: branching to the left is the Souk El Attarin (*see below*), straight on is the **Souk El Kebir** ('Great Souk'). Between the two is a ladder of narrow, arrow-straight passages, little more than shoulder-width across and collectively known as the **Kissaria**. This is the heart of the souk. Stallholders here specialise in cotton, clothing, kaftans and blankets.

Further along the Souk El Kebir are the courtyards of carpenters and wood turners, before a T-junction forces a choice: left or right. Either way, the alleys disgorge into a hub of streets that are once again wide enough for the passage of cars. Just north of here is a cluster of noteworthy sights, including the Musée de Marrakech: *see p69* **A Museum and Two Monuments**.

THE DYERS' QUARTER

Contrary to the name, **Souk El Attarin** ('Spice Souk') no longer deals in the hot and flavoursome stuff. Instead its traders largely traffic in tourist tat, from painted wooden thingamies to leather whatjamacallits. Almost opposite the subdued entrance to a workaday mosque is the **Souk des Babouches**, a whole alley devoted to soft-leather slippers (and their almost identical synthetic counterparts). Pick a colour, any colour, so long as it's garish – though personally we prefer the models fashioned from snakeskin.

Further along Attarin, ringing blows announce the **Souk Haddadin**, the quarter of the ironworkers. One of the most medieval parts of the souk, it's full of dark, cavern-like workshops in which firework bursts of orange sparks briefly illuminate tableaux of grime-streaked craftsmen like some scene by Doré.

The **Dyers' souk.** *See p68.*

West of Attarin three alleys run downhill into the **Souk des Teinturiers**, the dyers' quarter. Labourers with arms coloured to their elbows rub dyes into cured hides (to be cut and fashioned into babouches) and dunk wool into vats of dark-hued liquids. The resulting brightly coloured sheafs of wool are then hung over the alleyways in a manner irresistible to passing photographers.

The three alleys converge into one, which then doglegs between a squeeze of assorted artisans' salesrooms (lanterns, pottery, brass- and copperware) before exiting under an arch beside the Mouassine fountain and mosque; *see p72* **Mouassine**.

A MUSEUM AND TWO MONUMENTS

Inaugurated in 1997, the **Musée de Marrakech** is a conversion of an opulent early 20th-century house formerly belonging

to a Marrakchi grandee. Entering the outer courtyard, there's a pleasant café off to one side and a bookshop opposite. Within the museum exhibits rotate. On our last visit we found two rooms devoted to 20th-century Moroccan art and the rest filled with fine examples of old ceramics from Fès. But the star attraction is the building itself, particularly the tartishly tiled great central court, roofed over and hung with a chandelier like the mothership from *Close Encounters*. The former hammam is lovely and makes a fine exhibition space for the prints and photos on show. If nothing else, the museum is a cool refuge from the blazing heat outside. And as Joulia from Greece writes in the guest book, it has 'amazing toilets'.

Departing the museum, directly in front is the dusty open plaza of the place Ben Youssef, dominated by the **Ben Youssef Mosque**. The

original mosque went up in the 12th century and was the grandest of the age, but what stands now is a third and lesser incarnation, dating from the early 19th century. Non-Muslims may not enter.

Across from the mosque, set in its own fenced enclosure and sunk several metres below the current street level, is the **Koubba El Badiyin**. It looks unprepossessing but its unearthing in 1948 prompted one French art historian to exclaim that 'the art of Islam has never exceeded the splendour of this extraordinary dome'. It's the only surviving structure from the era of the Almoravids, the founders of Marrakech, and as such it represents a wormhole back to the origins of Moorish building history, presenting for the first time many of the shapes and forms that remain the basis of the architectural vocabulary throughout North Africa today.

It dates to the reign of Ali Ben Youssef (1107-1143) and was probably part of the ablutions complex of the original Ben Youssef Mosque. It's worth paying the slight admission fee to descend the brickwork steps and view the underside of the dome, which is a kaleidoscopic arrangement of a floral motif within an octagon within an eight-pointed star.

Backtracking slightly, immediately north of the museum is the **Ben Youssef Medersa**, a monument of less import than the Koubba but with greater impact, courtesy of its size and pristine presentation. A *medersa* is a Koranic school, dedicated to the teaching of Islamic scripture and law. This one was founded in the 14th century, then restored and enlarged to its current dimensions in 1564-5 by the Saadian sultan Abdellah El Ghalib. It was given a further polishing up in the late 1990s courtesy of the Ministry of Culture.

Entrance is via a long, cool passageway leading through to the great courtyard, a place of great serenity centred on a water-filled basin with surrounding façades decorated with tiling, stucco and carved cedar, all executed with restraint. At the far side is the domed prayer hall. Arranged around the courtyard on two levels are more than 100 tiny windowless students' chambers clustered in sixes and sevens about central lightwells. Medieval as it all seems, the medersa was still in use until as recently as 1962. The building stood in for an Algerian Sufic retreat in Gillie Mackinnon's 1998 film *Hideous Kinky*.

North of the medersa, through an arched passageway, there's a large wooden door in the crook of the alley emblazoned with a bird's head: this is **Dar Bellarj**, the 'Stork's House'. It's so called because it was formerly a hospital for the big leggy white birds. Restored in the

1990s, the building now serves as a local cultural centre hosting exhibitions, workshops and performances. Unless you're lucky enough to drop in on a happening there's little to see; the courtyard is attractive with seating and caged songbirds and sweet tea is offered to visitors, but you may still find yourself wondering exactly what it was you paid the 15dh admission for.

Ben Youssef Medersa

Place Ben Youssef (044 39 09 11/2). **Open** 9am-6pm daily. **Admission** 20dh. **Map** p249 D4.

Dar Bellarj

9 Toulat Zaouiat Lahdar (044 44 45 55). **Open** 9am-6pm daily. **Admission** 15dh. **Map** p249 D4.

Koubba El Badiyin

Place Ben Youssef (044 39 09 11/2). **Open** 9am-1pm, 2.30-6pm daily. **Admission** 10dh. **Map** p248 C4.

Musée de Marrakech

Place Ben Youssef (044 39 09 11/2). **Open** 9.30am-6pm daily. **Admission** 30dh. **Map** p249 D4.

THE TANNERIES

Jogging right and left but maintaining a generally eastward course from Dar Bellarj is **rue du Souk des Fassi**. Most of the open doorways off this rutted trench of an alley admit to large open courtyards enclosed by two storeys of galleries typically busy with half-naked male youths sitting listlessly banging bits of metal, leather or wood. These are old *fundouk*s, the distant forerunners of the modern hotel. Known elsewhere in the Middle East as a khan or caravanserai, the fundouk was a merchant hostel, built to provide accommodation and warehousing for the caravan traders who had crossed the desert and mountains to the south to bring their wares into the marketplaces of Marrakech. A fundouk offered stabling and storage rooms on the ground floor, bedrooms off the upper galleries, and a single gated entrance to the street that was locked at night for security. Most of the city's remaining fundouks now operate as artisans' workshops; one has been converted into a fashionable bar-restaurant: *see p106* **Foundouk**.

Continuing due east and encountering rue Essebtiyin (where the alley opens out into a small plaza filled with tradesmen for hire), Souk des Fassi becomes rue de Bab Debbagh and makes a beeline for the gate ('bab') of the same name. This is the **tannery district** – something that's quickly apparent to anybody in possession of a nose.

The tanners have been here since the city was founded, and the treatment of the skins

Roll 'em up, roll 'em up at the **Criée Berbère**. *See p67.*

remains a pre-industrial process. It begins with a softening soak, then the hair is scraped off by hand. This is followed by more soakings in a variety of solutions to make the skins thinner, smoother and more supple, before they're scraped again in preparation for receiving the dyes. The animal hides are mostly sheep, goat and less often camel. At one time antelope hide was tanned to order, but no more, and the trade in lion skins has dwindled too since the last Atlas lion was shot dead in 1912.

The tanneries are hidden from view but a loitering youth will always approach unaccompanied foreigners and offer his services as a guide. The tanneries fill large yards and, with rows of lozenge-shaped pools of various hues, look like giant paintboxes. However, closer up the bubbling pits are more like cess pools with surfaces of floating bubbling crud; the hides piled up beside look like rancid tripe. Pity the poor labourers who wade in the noxious fluids up to mid-thigh ladling the skins from one pit to another (now here's suitable prison-release work for Jeffrey Archer). Guides sometimes hand out sprigs of mint to hold under your nose to block out the abattoir air and reek of pigeon shit (which is used to soften the hides) but it's ineffective. Sensitive stomachs may rebel.

The results of the process can be seen and purchased at the leather shops near the gate, but you may prefer just to get the hell out of the quarter and go purge yourself in the nearest hammam or sauna. Taxis can be caught outside the **Bab Debbagh** (where a stair inside gives access to the roof of the gatehouse) on the route des Ramparts ringroad.

MOUASSINE

Although far from immediately apparent, **Mouassine** is rapidly becoming the most chic of Medina quarters. Spreading west of the main souk area and north of Jemaa El Fna, it's home to a growing number of smart boutiques, cutting-edge galleries and hip *maison d'hôtes*.

Immediately on entering rue Mouassine from place Bab Fteuh is Beldi (*see p120*), must-stop shop for the likes of Jean Paul Gaultier and sundry international fashion moppets. Ahead, where the way crosses with rue Ksour, is the atelier belonging to local fashion designer Kenza Melehi (*see p127* **Roots couture**) and at 1 rue Ksour is **Kulchi**, the newly opened boutique from Florence Taranne of Comptoir (*see p123*).

At the point where the street widens to embrace the walls of the **Mouassine Mosque** (which lends its name to the quarter and was erected in the 1560s by Saadian sultan Abdellah El Ghalib) a sidestreet off to the west bends

around to reach a large wooden doorway with a signplate reading **Dar Cherifa**. Inside is a stunning late 15th-century riad with filigree stucco and beautiful carved cedar detailing. It operates as a gallery and performance space (*see chapter* **Galleries**), doubling as a mint tea café during the day.

Where rue Mouassine hits rue Sidi El Yamami, a dim little archway under a sign reading 'A la Fibule' jogs left and right to the fantastical façade of the **Ministero del Gusto** (*see p131*), an extraordinary gallery-cum-sales space executed in an architectural style that co-creator Alessandro Lippini describes as 'delirium'.

Following Sidi El Yamami west leads past a clutch of high-end restaurants to the city gate **Bab Laksour**; in the opposite direction, a few paces east, is the **Mouassine fountain** with triple drinking bays, two for animals and one – the most ornate – for people. It's here that the character Louis Bernard is fatally stabbed in Hitchcock's 1955 *The Man Who Knew Too Much* – although not so fatally that he can't first stagger half a mile to Jemaa El Fna to expire in the arms of Jimmy Stewart.

Beyond the fountain is an arch through to the Souk des Teinturiers (*see p69*), while continuing north, at 192 rue Mouassine is a large fundouk that featured extensively in the film *Hideous Kinky*; it served as the hotel in which Kate Winslet and daughters lodged. Up on the first floor, the 'room' numbers painted by the film production crew remain – Winslet's room was No.38, the only one with a bright new door. Another grand fundouk across the street is thought to be the oldest surviving example of its type in the Medina.

CITY SAINTS AND SHRINES

A few steps north of the fundouks is a cross-roads: go left for the Dar El Bacha (*see p73*) or right to the Souk des Teinturiers, but only adherents of Islam should proceed straight ahead, according to a sign that reads 'Non Moslem interdit'. Up this particular alley is the **Shrine of Sidi Abdel Aziz**, resting place of one of the seven saints of Marrakech. Collectively known as 'El Sebti', this group of holy men have been venerated for centuries as guardians of the city. Each has a nice new shrine erected by Sultan Moulay Ismail in the 18th century. All the shrines are within, or just outside, the walls of the Medina and once a year they are the focus of an official seven-day *moussem* (pilgrimage).

Sidi Abdel Aziz's shrine can be skirted, zigging east then north, then east and north again on to rue Bab Taghzout, which runs north to the most renowned of the saintly

Cures effected (possibly) at the **Shrine of Sidi Bel Abbas**.

resting places, the **Shrine of Sidi Bel Abbas**. (En route is a beautiful Marrakech cameo that brings together the stately **Chrob ou Chouf** – 'Drink and Look' – a monumental 18th-century fountain, and, directly opposite, a chickenshit amusement arcade where kids batter the hell out of pixilated Ninja warriors on gaming machines scarcely less ancient than the neighbouring water trough.)

Soon after widening to accommodate a local bus halt and scrubby park, the rue narrows again to squeeze through an ornate gateway with six-inch thick wooden doors (**Bab Taghzout**); this was one of the original Medina gates until the walls were extended in the 18th century to bring the shrine within the city. Through and a few steps to the right is an even more elaborate arched gateway, executed in carved alabaster, and beyond an arcade that would formerly have been lined with herbalists, faith healers and quack doctors here to minister to/prey on the sick and the ailing drawn to the tomb to bask in its saintly *baraka* (blessings). Such beliefs remain strong and the courtyard of the shrine – adorned with Marrakech's only

sundial – is always filled with the crippled and infirm. If things don't work out, a shaded arcade on the south side harbours a decrepit gathering of largely blind characters all of whom belong to a special sect of priesthood specialising in the ministering of last rites. The sanctuary itself is off limits; instead depart the courtyard on the western side where a large open plaza affords a photogenic view of the shrine's pyramidal green roofs.

Returning back through Bab Taghzout, a right turn leads down to the **Shrine of Sidi Ben Slimane El Jazuli**, another of the patron saints of Marrakech. Active in the 15th century, he was an important Sufi mystic and his *Manifest Proofs of Piety* remains a seminal mystical text.

DAR EL BACHA

Just a few minutes' walk south and west of the city's holy shrines is the high-walled former residence of the most unsaintly Thami El Glaoui, 'Lord of the Atlas' and ruler of Marrakech and southern Morocco throughout much of the first half of the 20th century (*see p11* **The last despot**). Known

So long as it's pink

The old Henry Ford maxim ('Any colour – so long as it's black') acquires a wry twist in Marrakech. An ordinance set in writing during the time of French rule specifies that all buildings in Marrakech must be painted pink. In fact, it's not exactly pink, the colour is ochre, which is the natural hue of the rich earth on which the city's planted. Throughout its history earth has been the prime building material, mixed with crushed limestone and straw (a mix known as pisé): no painting required. You'll note that all the local pottery neatly matches the architecture too. It's only when the French began building the New City

in the early 20th century and introduced new building materials such as concrete that colour became an issue.

There's no prescribed paint number or swatches to match, and as a result the tones vary from pale flesh to fiery vermilion. It's all highly practical, as the colour takes much of the glare out of the often harsh sunlight (by contrast Casablanca, which frequently labours under overcast skies, is, as the name suggests, uniformly white). And just think of all the time saved at the local equivalent of Homebase when it comes to sprucing up the walls.

locally as **Dar El Bacha** ('House of the Lord'), it's here that the Glaoui entertained luminaries such as Churchill and Roosevelt until his death in 1956 unleashed widespread rioting and looting (*see pp13-14*).

The complex dates from the early 20th century and turns out to be a dull setting considering all the spicy stories originating from the place. Visitors pass through several mundane administrative chambers (the complex now belongs to the Ministry of Culture) into a large courtyard, overwrought with carved plaster and woodwork, and excessive tiling. A passage snakes through to a second courtyard, which served as the harem. Once again the decoration is laid on thick, but some of the work is impressive, particularly the column capitals.

Facing the side wall of the Dar El Bacha is another property with pedigree – owned previously by the chamberlain of the Glaoui, later by French *haute couturier* Pierre Balmain ('Dressmaking is the architecture of movement') and now, as a large sign announces, the premises of **Dar Moha** (*see p102*), arguably the finest restaurant in Marrakech.

The stretch of rue de Bab Doukkala just west of Dar El Bacha was the location for a car chase in Stephen Sommers' 1999 remake of *The Mummy*. Further west at Nos.142-4 is **Blaoui** (*see p130*), venue for some of the best shopping in the Medina. The major monument round here is the **Bab Doukkala Mosque**, built in 1558 by the mother of the Saadian sultans Abdel Malek and Ahmed El Mansour. It's fronted by the **Sidi El Hassan fountain**, now dry, fenced around and used as an occasional exhibition space. Across from the fountain, a small whitewashed building houses a 400-year-old hammam (men only) with a fantastic cedarwood ceiling in the reception area. Behind the fountain a faint hand-painted 'WC' signposts the city's oldest toilets, built at the same time as the Doukkala Mosque opposite. They're still in use.

The westernmost stretch of rue de Bab Doukkala is the domain of the butchers and it verges on the macabre with prominent displays of decapitated heads and mounds of glistening offal. Note that all the hanging bits of carcass display testicles: Moroccans don't eat female meat so butchers are mindful to prove the masculine provenance of their meat.

The massive Almoravid gate of **Bab Doukkala** is now bypassed by a modern road that breaches the city walls. There's a petit taxi rank at the foot of the gatehouse.

Dar El Bacha (Dar El Glaoui)
Rue Dar El Bacha (no telephone). **Open** 9am-2pm Mon-Fri. **Admission** 10dh. **Map** p248 B4.

Bab Agnaou. *See p76.*

South of Jemaa El Fna

Map p250-251

Although little different in feel to the northern part of the Medina, almost since the founding of Marrakech the southern area has been the domain of the sultans. The present Royal Palace is built on the site of the earliest Almohad palaces and covers an absolutely vast area, equivalent to a whole residential quarter. Youthful King Mohammed VI, however, is a little more modest in his requirements and has had a new bijou residence built nearby. Neither of these two royal precincts is open to the public but visitors are permitted to explore two 19th-century viziers' palaces, the Bahia and the Dar Si Said, as well as the impressive ruins of the grand Saadian-era Badii Palace.

THE KASBAH AND TOMBS

Running south-west off Jemaa El Fna, pedestrianised rue de Bab Agnaou is budget-tourist central, lined with banks, ATMs, moneychangers, téléboutiques, internet centres and too many dodgy eateries. At the far end is the famed roost for decades of impecunious

Polychromic spree at the **Saadian Tombs**. *See p77.*

travellers, the Grand Tazi – and one of the few places in the Medina where it's possible to get a beer (*see p50*). Past the Tazi the street runs in the shadow of high walls: not the city walls, but a wall that formerly sectioned off the royal *kasbah* (palace) from the rest of the Medina.

The traditional entrance to the kasbah is via the gorgeous **Bab Agnaou** (Gate of the Gnawa, named after the black slaves brought from Africa to the south of the city), built on the orders of the Almohad sultan Yacoub El Mansour in 1185. It's one of the very few stone structures in this otherwise mudbrick city, and has weathered in such a way that the aged limestone now resembles heavily grained wood.

Across the street is the original southern gate to the Medina, the **Bab Er Rob**, which is now filled by a pottery shop and bypassed by the traffic, which exits through a breach in the wall.

A short distance inside the Agnaou gate is the **Kasbah Mosque**, constructed in 1190, again during the reign of Sultan Yacoub El Mansour (hence its alternative name of El Mansour Mosque). It has been renovated on numerous occasions since (most recently during the reign of Hassan II, father of the current king) but the cut-brick-and-green-tile decoration on the minaret is original. The plaza in front is usually busy with guide-led tourist groups. They're not here for the mosque, which, of course, they're

forbidden to enter, but for what lies hidden in the lee of its southern wall: the **Saadian Tombs**.

In the early 1920s the French authorities noticed two green-tiled roofs rising above the shanty quarters. Inquiries made of the locals were met with evasive answers. The persistence of one curious official was eventually rewarded when he discovered a narrow, dark lane, wide enough for a single person, that ended in a tiny arched door. He pushed through to enter a courtyard garden and see what apparently no 'infidel' had ever seen before – the holy tombs of the Saadian sultans. According to the account in a 1928 travelogue *The Magic of Morocco*, the Frenchman was then accosted by a wizened guardian who said, 'You have discovered our secret, but beware what you do with the knowledge. You cannot make it a mere show for your people to come and gaze at'. Well, tough luck, pal, because that's exactly what has happened: the tombs are possibly the most visited site in Marrakech.

Entrance is via that same constricted passage and it gives access to an ancient walled garden, the use of which far pre-dates the time of the Saadians. There are a great many early mosaic graves dotted around the shrubbery of which the identity of the interred is long lost. Attention instead focuses on the three pavilions constructed during the reign of Saadian sultan Ahmed El Mansour. Despite the numbers of visitors drawn to the tombs, it's a far from spectacular ensemble, and the setting is so modest that it's reminiscent of an English parish churchyard.

First on the left is the Prayer Hall, which was not intended as a mausoleum but nevertheless holds numerous graves mainly of Alaouite princes from the 18th century. Their resting places are marked by what looks like offcuts from a marble mason's yard. Next to it is the Hall of 12 Columns, a far more ornate affair with three central tombs surrounded by a dozen ornate marble pillars. The tomb in the middle is that of Ahmed El Mansour, flanked by those of his son and grandson. The third, stand-alone pavilion has fine Andalucian-style ornate entrance portals.

Following rue de Kasbah south leads to the **Grand Méchouar**, or parade grounds of the Royal Palace, but the way is closed whenever the king is in town. It's more interesting to duck into the warren of alleys behind the tombs, where a small square at the conjunction of four alleys hosts a morning market of fruit, vegetable, meat and fish vendors.

Saadian Tombs

rue de Kasbah, Bab Agnaou (no phone). **Open** 8.30-11.45am, 2.30-5.45pm daily. **Admission** 10dh. **Map** p250 C8.

THE BADII PALACE

Barely 400 metres east of the Saadian Tombs is the city's other great monument of that era, the Badii Palace. However, while secrecy ensured the intact survival of the sultans' mausoleums, the scale and ostentation of their triumphal residence marked it out for special attention and it survives only as a denuded ruin.

The palace was constructed during the reign of Sultan Ahmed El Mansour (1578-1607), funded by the wealth accrued through victories over the Portuguese. Walls and ceilings were encrusted with gold from Timbuktu (captured by El Mansour in 1598), while the inner court had a massive central pool with an island, flanked by four sunken gardens filled with richly scented flowers and trees. At the centre of each of the four massive walls were four pavilions, also flanked by arrangements of pools and fountains. It took some 25 years for the labourers and craftsmen to complete the palace. Surveying the achievement, the sultan invited opinion from his fool and received the prophetic response that the palace 'would make a fine ruin'. And it does. El Mansour was spared that vision because barely were the inaugural celebrations over before the ageing sultan passed away. His palace remained intact for less than a century before the Merenid sultan Moulay Ismail had it stripped bare and the riches carted north for his new capital at Meknes.

The palace is approached via the open plaza of place des Ferblantiers and a canyon-like space constricted between two precipitous walls, the outer wall meant to keep the Medina at a respectful distance from the royal domains. The former main gate is collapsed and gone, and entrance is through a gaping hole in the fortifications directly into the great court. It's a vast empty space the size of a couple of football pitches ringed around by pockmarked mudbrick battlements that act as apartment blocks for pigeons and have their tops adorned with the wiry afros of stork nests. The sunken areas that were once gardens still exist, as does the great dry basin that was the ornate central pool. On the west side (right of the entrance) are the skeletal ruins of the Pavilion of 50 Columns; a small area of mosaic remains on the floor, but the colours are badly dulled by exposure to the elements. In the south-eastern corner of the court a gate leads through to a walled yard with the excavated remains of troglodytic chambers and passages.

The palace comes back to life once a year when a giant screen is set up on the central island for the International Film Festival (*see p143*).

Badii Palace

Place des Ferblantiers, Mellah (no phone). **Open** 8.30-11.45am, 2.30-5.45pm daily. **Admission** 10dh. **Map** p250 C7.

Exodus

Talk about population shifts: in the early years of the 20th century there were some 36,000 Jews living in Marrakech; the current best guess total is 260, according to the keeper of one of the three surviving synagogues.

Jews have been present in Morocco since Phoenician times. Later, protected by the walls and gates of their own quarter, and by the express patronage of the sultans (who valued their abilities in trade, linguistics and crafts), the Jews flourished as middlemen between local Muslims and visiting Christian merchants. They were inevitably viewed with mistrust, especially in times of strife, but that didn't prevent the community from growing. However, from the end of the 19th century the pull of Zionism and the struggle for a homeland in Palestine (culminating in the creation of Israel in 1948) triggered mass emigration. King Mohammed V (who during World War II had refused to comply with any of the Vichy regime's anti-Semitic decrees) passed laws to prevent a mass exodus – fearing adverse effects on the economy – but Mossad, the Israeli secret service, smuggled out 18,000 Jews between 1958 and 1961. Arab-Israeli conflicts in 1956, '67 and '73 engendered such bad blood that even non-Zionists felt it expedient to relocate. Jews with money went to Canada, France and Israel; those less well off sought refuge in the more international climes of Casablanca. The only Jews to stay were those who absolutely couldn't afford to go anywhere, hence the decrepit state of the Mellah today.

THE MELLAH

Hugging the eastern walls of the Badii Palace are the narrow gridded alleys of the Mellah, the old Jewish quarter. The name translates roughly as 'Place of Salt', a reference to the Jews' historic monopoly on the trade in mineral salts from the Atlas Mountains, which was traditionally used as a preservative. Although the number of Jews in Marrakech is now negligable (see p78 **Exodus**), evidence of Jewish heritage is still abundant to anyone who knows where to look. In the nearby Marché Couvert (also known to locals as the Jewish Market), some of the signboards still bear Hebrew lettering. Some of the houses in the neighbourhood have external balconies,

which in Marrakech is peculiar to the Jews; some have Hebrew letters on the metal grills above the doors. There's even an occasional Star of David.

Across the road from a newly laid-out Rose Garden, a green-painted arch leads through into a street market. Following this south and east, past stalls of gaudy beaded necklaces (made in Hong Kong) and bright pyramids of spices, and windows of the lurid sweets known as Pâte Levy, leads deep into the Mellah. The streets here are some of the narrowest, not to mention poorest, in the Medina and in places crude scaffolding is required to stop the houses collapsing.

At the heart of the quarter is a small square, **place Souweka**, now disfigured by a badly sited concrete building. Along the street that runs north just beyond the square, at No.36 is one of the three last working synagogues in the Medina (from a one-time total of 29). It occupies a large hall off the open courtyard of a well-maintained community centre. Judging by the plentiful supply of new prayer books and other contemporary trappings, the synagogue is kept alive by remittances from Marrakchi Jews abroad, but the advanced age of the congregation suggests that more than just money is required to keep the community alive.

On the very eastern edge of the Mellah is an extensive Jewish cemetery; the sheer numbers of modestly marked graves (tens of thousands) are probably the best remaining testament to the one-time significance of the Jews in the history of Marrakech.

THE OLIVE GARDEN ROADS

On the northern edge of the Mellah is the **Bahia Palace**, built principally by Ba Ahmed Ben Moussa, a vizier to the royal court in the 1890s and a man of 'no particular intelligence, but of indomitable will, and cruel' (*Morocco That Was*, Walter Harris; 1921). Entered via a long garden corridor, it's a collection of paved courtyards, arcades, pavilions and reception halls constructed in a modern style but smothered in traditional Moroccan decoration (lots of unnecessary *zelije* tiling, sculpted stucco and carved cedarwood embellishments). It includes extensive quarters for Ba Ahmed's four wives and 24 concubines.

On Ba Ahmed's death (exhaustion maybe?), the palace was completely looted by the sultan Abdel Aziz. Caravans of donkeys staggering under the weight of furniture, carpets and crates made their way the short distance from the Bahia to the Royal Palace. Between then and now it served as the living quarters of the French resident-généraux (Edith Wharton guested here at this time, described in her *In Morocco*; 1927) and it's still occasionally used by the current royal family – King Mohammed VI threw a party here for Puff Daddy in 2002.

Denuded and stork haunted: the **Badii Palace**. *See p77.*

Stork city

It's one of the most magical sights: as the sun dips and the sky turns brilliant shades of orange, to a soundtrack of the muezzins' calls to evening prayer the sky fills with great wheeling birds. The stork is holy to Marrakech. There are countless tales to explain its exalted status, and the impression it gives of prayer-like prostration when at rest. The most commonly repeated is of a local *imam* (the Islamic priest), dressed in traditional Moroccan garb of white jellaba and black robe, drunk on wine, who then compounds the sin by climbing to the top of the minaret and blaspheming. Shazam! Man suffers the wrath of god and is transformed into a stork. Even before the arrival of Islam, an old Berber belief also had it that storks are actually transformed humans.

Until qiute recently a hospital existed in Marrakech to care for the injured birds, where they could recover or die peacefully (*see p70* Dar Bellarj), and to this day the offence of disturbing a stork carries a three-month prison sentence. Just in case you were tempted.

Outside the main palace gate, **rue Riad Zitoun El Jedid** runs narrow but straight. The name means the 'new olive garden road' but the only olive trees in the area these days are newly planted in the modern Rose Garden and they've failed to take root and have died. (Rue Riad Zitoun El Kedim, or the 'old olive garden road', runs parallel and is full of budget accommodation.)

Just east off Zitoun El Jedid, beside the Préfecture de la Medina is **Maison Tiskiwin**, a private house belonging to Dutch anthropologist Bert Flint but open to the public for viewing of his rich collection of trad Moroccan decorative art (carpets and clothing).

A couple of twists of sidestreet to the north is the **Dar Si Said Museum**, the former home of the brother of Ba Ahmed, builder of the Bahia. It's less grand in scale but more impressive in detail. It's home to an absorbing collection of Moroccan arts and crafts. Displays change but the core exhibits include beautiful examples of carved cedar rescued from the city's various lost dwellings – polychromic painted doors, window shutters, fragments of ceilings and the like. There's also one room devoted to 'rural' woodwork that includes some primitively worked and painted Berber doors. Such items are very much in vogue with collectors these days and exchange hands for vast amounts of cash.

Although you'd never guess it from the low-key presentation (stuck in a tiny room, no access, visible only through apertures, no explanatory text), the museum's prize item is what's known as the Koutoubia minbar, a transportable stepped pulpit formerly used in the city's great mosque. It was fashioned in the early 12th century by Cordoban craftsmen and the 1,000 decorative panels that adorn the sides supposedly took eight years to complete.

Also in the neighbourhood is **Riad Tamsna**, restaurant, gallery, boutique and bookshop (for directions *see p106*), and a beautiful building in its own right with a gorgeous central courtyard overlooked by high galleries.

Bahia Palace
Riad Zitoun El Jedid (044 38 92 21). **Open** 8.30-11.45am, 2.30-5.45pm Mon-Thur, Sat, Sun; 8.30-11.30am, 3-5.45pm Fri. **Admission** 10dh. **Map** p251 D7.

Dar Si Said Museum
Riad Zitoun El Jedid (044 38 95 64). **Open** 9am-noon, 3-6pm Wed-Mon. **Admission** 20dh. **Map** p251 D6.

Maison Tiskiwin
8 Derb El Bahia, off Riad Zitoun El Jedid (044 38 91 92). **Open** 9.30am-12.30pm, 3-6.30pm daily. **Admission** 15dh. **Map** p251 D6.

Guéliz

The New City features rarely on visitors' itineraries – and understandably so. But it does have its moments.

Breakfast is a good time to be around Guéliz (pronounced 'gileez', rhymes with 'please'). As a change from the standard hotel morning fare of boiled eggs, bread and apricot jam, there's coffee and croissants at Café Les Négociants served by grouchy uniformed waiters who generate a great air of efficiency while being brusquely indifferent to the customers. It's pleasing to find that almost 100 years on the ground rules laid by the French are still so lovingly adhered to.

Marrakech's New City came into being shortly after December 1913, which is the date of the arrival of Henri Prost, the young city planner imported into Morocco to assist in the town planning schemes of French résident général Marshal Lyautey (*see p12*). One of his early sketches survives and it illustrates how he took the minaret of the Koutoubia as his focal point and from it extended two lines: one north-west to Jebel Guéliz, a rocky outcrop north-west of the Medina, the other south-west to the pavilion of the Menara Gardens. In the pie slice between these lines (which have since become avenue Mohammed V and avenue de la Menara) is the original nucleus of the new European city.

HOLY BEGINNINGS

One of the first and most important buildings was the church, or *église* – a word that was corrupted into the name Guéliz. This wasn't the first church in Marrakech; in 1908 a French priest consecrated a house in the Medina in the neighbourhood of what is now the Dar Si Said

Museum. A Christian cross fashioned into the wrought iron grill over one of the windows survives as evidence; the priest lasted nowhere near as long, murdered within two years of setting up shop.

The Guéliz église is now the Catholic **Church of St Anne** and it stands barely a communion queue from the northern walls of the Medina. It's a modest affair with a bell tower very deliberately overshadowed by the taller minaret of a mosque built adjacent following Moroccan independence. The congregation notes are printed in six languages but Protestants are relegated to using the library for their services.

PARKS AND AVENUES

One block over from the church is the **Jnane El Harti** park, which was originally laid out as a French formal garden with 'hedges' higher than head height, and a zoo. In a 1939 essay entitled 'Marrakech', George Orwell writes of feeding gazelles here and of not being able to look at the animals' hindquarters without thinking of mint sauce. The park is in a bad way at present, displaying the signs of years of neglect but there's an ambitious scheme well under way to re-landscape with fountains, ponds and play areas.

The north-east corner of the park connects with **place du 16 Novembre**, the hole in the middle of Guéliz's spider's web street pattern. Sadly, instead of developing as the grand *rondpont* of Prost's vision, it has been

Bloomin' lovely: the **Marché Central**. See p82.

disfigured by some grotesque intrusions, including the Soviet-stylings of the central post office, two mammoth concrete frameworks frozen in a skeletal state for some ten years as a result of land disputes, and a roadside McDonald's. Rumour has it that the reason McDoh! was able to wangle such a prime site is because a member of the royal family is the franchisee.

Until the 1970s there were two lines of parking down the centre of the avenue, but the increase in the volume of traffic has done away with them. Shame, because standing in the middle of Mohammed V presents one of the city's best views; in one direction the Koutoubia Minaret, in the other a high rocky outcrop topped by a pink wall of a former French Foreign Legion fortress.

CENTRAL GUELIZ

At the junction of avenue Mohammed V and rue de la Liberté is an elaborate piece of colonial building with pavement arcades, art deco lines and Moorish flourishes – a style termed 'arabiasance'. It dates to 1918 and is just about the oldest surviving bit of architecture in the New Town. This was also the address (30 rue de la Liberté) of the city's first tourist office and a gallery of faded decades-old hand-painted scenes of Morocco line the hallway.

The eastern stretch of rue de la Liberté is the local maid market. Every morning the pavements are busy with knots of poorly dressed women hanging around on the chance of some cleaning work or similar. Behind them is the **Marché Central**, focal point of Guéliz life. It's where locals (middle-class Marrakchis and tons of expats) come for groceries, of course, but also for booze, flowers, plates and dishes, last-minute gifts, and where they post flyers for lost Scottie dogs and ads for second-hand Renaults, best offer accepted.

At the western end of rue de la Liberté, where it meets rue de Yougoslavie, is a throwback to a forgotten bit of Marrakech history: a narrow alley planted with mulberry trees and crammed with terraces of single-storey dwellings daubed in a multitude of colours (it may be the only non-pink street in Marrakech). This is the old **Spanish quarter**, a reminder of the city's once significant Hispanic population.

BRIGHT LIGHTS, LITTLE CITY

Towards the northern end of Mohammed V is **place Abdel Moumen**, which is about as close as it gets in Marrakech to a Piccadilly Circus. It's the hub of an area of cafés, bars, restaurants and nightclubs; it's even got neon. If Les Négociants is the café of choice in the morning, the **Café Atlas**, which it faces, has it

White elephant? No, **Theatre Royal.**

in the evening, especially if you like your beer with added entertainments (see p155). Sadly, everybody's favourite, the Renaissance, which boasted fantastic views from its seventh-floor terrace, was boarded up at the time of writing.

From place Abdel Moumen, it's an easy 20-minute walk to the Majorelle Gardens (see p84), while to the west, Guéliz more or less peters out at the expanse of the avenue de France. There's an attractive little colonial-era **railway station**, which rises from its drowsy torpor a couple of times a day for the train to Casablanca. The junction with avenue Hassan II is lorded over by the impressive new **Theatre Royal/Opera House**, designed by local star architect Charles Boccara. It's a monumental piece of work, planned to seat 1,200 people. But more than ten years after it was begun the interiors have yet to be completed due to the spiralling costs.

Two blocks south is a similarly over-ambitious complex in the form of the **Palais des Congrès**. Constructed in 1989, it's a mammoth five-storey edifice, which was used for the signing of GATT trade agreements in 1994. It's never been busy since. Still, if you should find yourself in need of a couple of halls the size of a modest Baltic state, you know where to look.

Sightseeing

Gardens

Ingenious irrigation makes Marrakech the pink city with green fingers.

Desert dwellers have always known how to manage water. So despite the arid climate and parched plains all around, ever since the Almoravids moved out of the Western Sahara to found Marrakech back in the 11th century, it has always been a garden city. They brought in water from the Ourika Valley by means of *khettara*, long irrigation pipes made of baked mud, the remains of which can still be found in the Palmeraie on the outskirts of the city. They used the water to nurture *jnane* (market gardens) and *agdal* (walled private gardens), as well as public gardens, which the city has always possessed in abundance.

The **Menara Gardens** (*see p87*), for instance, go right back to the 12th century and the era of the Almohads, as do the royal **Agdal Gardens** (*see below*). When the Saadian Sultan Ahmed El Mansour built the show-stopping Badii Palace in the late 16th century, visitors marvelled at its architecture and gilded, bejewelled embellishments, but more than anything they were also awestruck by its multi-level gardens, orchards and 700 fountains.

Neither were gardens the preserve of royals. Wealthy merchants, judges, master craftsmen and petty officials dwelt in riads, townhouses built around courtyard gardens, usually designed symmetrically with four beds planted with trees, underplanted with perfumed flowers and the all important central fountain. The microclimate created provided shade, cooled the air, gave off sweet smells and encouraged songbirds.

All credit to the French who continued the horticultural tradition under the Protectorate. In the Nouvelle Ville of Guéliz (*see pp81-2*) many of the boulevards are lined with jacaranda trees that bloom in electric blue each spring. Bougainvillaea and vines clothe the boundary walls of the villas, cactus abound, jasmine perfumes the evening air and hibiscus flowers add spots of vibrant colour. Then there are the orange trees. The streets of Guéliz are lined with them. The combination of blue sky, pink walls, green leaves and orange fruit is a knockout; it's like walking in a Matisse landscape painting. All this and free fruit too? But that would be just too perfect and the oranges are in fact way too sour to eat or juice. Instead, the prize is the orange blossom, which is highly valued for its scent. Every year the rights to a city-wide harvest are bought up by a major international perfume company and armies of local women are sent out on to the streets to lay sheets under the trees and start banging the hell out of the branches.

PUBLIC GARDENS

Besides the gardens described in this chapter, there are several other public gardens within the ramparts of the Medina. Most notable is the massed greenery of the **place de Foucault**, between Jemaa El Fna and the Koutoubia Mosque. It's a tight triangle of great palms soaring above the surrounding buildings, with benches down at their bases. In spring these gardens are full of Candidum lilies.

Over the far side of the mosque are the **Koutoubia Gardens**, planted heavily with roses that are seemingly permanently in flower. Roses flourish in this climate and seem impervious to the heat of summer. Carefully shaped topiary hedges fringe the pathways. To the north, flanking main avenue Mohammed V, is the **Arset Abdelsalam**, an extensive area of scrubby lawns, palms and pathways that are a favourite with promenading couples and civil servants from the grand Hôtel de Ville opposite enjoying an open-air afternoon siesta. All snoozing is shortly to be disturbed as plans are in the offing to propel the park into the 21st century with shopping kiosks and public internet booths courtesy of Maroc Télécom, which is sponsoring the scheme.

Agdal Gardens

Laid out in 1156-7 by the Almohads, the royal Agdal are several hundred years older than those most celebrated of Islamic gardens at the Alhambra. They cover a vast 16 hectares (40 acres) stretching south for a couple of kilometres from the back door of the Royal Palace. At the centre of the Agdal is a massive pool, the Sahraj El Hana, so large that the sultan's soldiers used it for swimming practice. In 1873 Sultan Mohammed IV drowned in it while boating with his son; the servant who managed to swim to safety was executed on the spot for failing to save his lord. The rest of the area is divided into a variety of different kinds of orchards and gardens, including an orange grove, vineyards, areas of pomegranates and figs, masses of walnut trees and palm groves. There are several ornamental pavilions, and it's possible to climb on to the roof of one of them, the Dar

El Hana, beside the pool, for an impressive view of the gardens and the High Atlas beyond.

To get to the Agdal take the path off the south-western corner of the Méchouar Intérieur (*see* map p251 D9).

Agdal Gardens

Open irregularly but usually weekends; closed if the king is in residence at the Royal Palace. **Admission** free. **Map** p247 E5.

Majorelle Gardens

Now privately owned by Yves Saint Laurent (*see below* **All about Yves**) – but open to the public – the gardens were created by two generations of French artists, Jacques and Louis Majorelle, in the 1930s. Although small in scale and located out on the edge of the New City, the glamour of the YSL connection ensures that the gardens are usually packed well beyond comfort by coachloads

of visitors. The juxtaposition of colours is striking, plants sing against a backdrop of the famous Majorelle blue (*see p144*), offset with soft ochres and terracottas. Bamboo groves rustle in the soft breeze, great palms tower over all, sheltering huge ancient cacti. Rills lead into pools floating with water lilies and flashing with golden carp, terrapins paddle languidly and frogs croak. Great pots overflow with succulents and birds sing. For the botanically curious, everything is clearly labelled.

Jacques Majorelle's former studio has been turned into a fine little **Museum of Islamic Art**, recently renovated and reorganised to display a collection of traditional jewellery, fine embroidery, illuminated manuscripts, carved wooden doors and Majorelle lithographs of the High Atlas. Air-conditioned and dimly lit, the museum makes for a welcome refuge from the intensity of light and colour outside. Labelling of the exhibits is also in English.

All about Yves

If Churchill was the totemic Marrakech visitor of the 1930s and '40s (*see p12* **A lasting affair**), then Yves Saint Laurent has been the name attached to the city from the 1970s until today. He and partner Pierre Bergé first visited in 1962, escaping the mixed reviews that followed the debut of the first YSL couture collection in Paris. The couple spent their days lounging on the terraces of the Mamounia, Saint Laurent, who had been brought up in Oran, Algeria, revelling in the remembered sun and colour of Africa.

By 1967 YSL was established as the fashion figurehead for the Pop age and could contemplate buying a house in Marrakech. He and Bergé found a place in the Medina known as Dar El Hanch ('House of the Serpent'). Unsurprisingly, the city made its influence felt in the next YSL collection, which featured transparent silk blouses and safari jackets. A floating garland of flowers wrought into the initials 'YSL' was photographed floating in the basin of the Menara Gardens as part of an advertising campaign for a perfume launch.

Greater success equalled bigger Marrakech houses with a step up to a new villa, the Dar Es Saada ('House of Happiness'), a 1930s colonial building in the grounds of the family home of Jacques Majorelle. When rumours began to fly that the adjacent gardens laid out by Majorelle were being sold to make way for urban apartment complexes, YSL and Bergé arranged to purchase them, reportedly

through sources close to the royal family. The couture twosome then groomed the gardens to a state of Rousseau-like feral picturesqueness and opened them to the public. Along with the gardens came a new house, the Villa Oasis. With the assistance of American decorator Bill Willis (*see* chapter **The New Marrakech Style**) the house was done over in an Orientalist style and filled with items from Paris auction houses; according to YSL biographer Alice Rawsthorn, he shipped over 200 cases of furniture, paintings, sculpture and books, the latter all re-covered in Morocco leather or snakeskin. The work took four years to complete, with one room alone, the 'red study', taking nine months to complete.

Marrakech became Saint Laurent's escape, so much so that by around 1990 he was holed up in the Villa Oasis on two bottles of whiskey a day stumbling round the Medina and screaming hysterically if anyone broached the subject of going back to Paris. When his presence was absolutely required the fashion house had to fly someone down to Marrakech to escort him back.

'I love the feeling here of mystery on every side,' said Saint Laurent. 'For me, Marrakech is the Venice of Morocco.'

Saint Laurent still has the villa (it's the one bhind the petrol station) and continues to spend a part of the year in Morocco, but is rarely ever seen in public these days.

Majorelle Gardens with that powder blue hue.

Menara Gardens, a place for quiet reflection.

Re-greening Marrakech

As if Marrakech wasn't already absurdly pretty enough, several schemes are under way to further beautify the place. One that has shown immediate results in a short space of time has been the planting of trees and flowers along the airport and Medina ring roads. The city ramparts are now surrounded by beds of roses, hibiscus and jasmine. A part of the money for the planting has been donated by the king.

While the perimeter of the city is being transformed into one great loop of a garden, the area within the walls is also undergoing change. Worried by the gradual disappearance of nature within the Medina, a charitable foundation, ARCH, in conjunction with the Global Diversity Foundation (GDF), is working to initiate the restoration of traditional vegetation. Individual strands of the project involve inventorying the Medina's remaining cultivated plants, surveying key places that once contained important gardens and restoring existing agdal, arsat, jnane and riads.

In a similar spirit the municipality has recently completed a new rose garden in the Mellah, opposite the place des Ferblantiers. The planting also includes mature olive trees, and a pergola shelters benches.

There's plenty of grass roots (ha ha) enthusiasm for such schemes and locals have been spontaneously contributing with green-painted oil drums full of vines, runner beans and brightly coloured flowers. In Derb Moulay Abdel Kader, off Derb Dabbachi, attendees of the alley mosque have filled the area with plants and strung trellises of vines overhead.

'One hundred years ago,' says Dr Gary Martin, director of GDF, 'this was one of the greenest cities in North Africa, and we hope it will be so again.'

To get to the garden walk from central Guéliz (it's about two kilometres, or just over a mile, east along boulevard Mansour Eddahabi) or take a petit taxi, which should cost 5dh-6dh from Guéliz or about 10dh from the Medina. Note that picnics, children and dogs are not allowed; it's a shame the prohibitions don't extend to coach parties.

Majorelle Gardens
avenue Yacoub El Mansour, Guéliz (no phone). **Open** *Summer* 8am-noon, 3-7pm daily. *Winter* 8am-noon, 2-5pm daily. **Admission** 20dh; Museum of Islamic Art 15dh. **Map** p252 C1.

Mamounia Gardens

The world-famous Mamounia (*see p41* **La Mamounia**) takes its name from its gardens, the Arset El Mamoun, which predate the hotel by more than a century. They were established in the 18th century by Crown Prince Moulay Mamoun on land gifted to him by his father the sultan on the occasion of his wedding. A central pavilion served as a princely residence, occasionally lent out to visiting diplomats, until the onset of French rule when it was transformed into a hotel. The gardens remain. They're designed in a traditional style, on an axis, with walkways, flowerbeds, orange groves and olive trees and attended by 40 gardeners who, twice a year, plant 60,000 new annuals. Non-guests can visit but it's preferred that they do so in the context of a buffet lunch or afternoon tea at one of the terrace cafés. Dress smartly (no jeans or shorts) or you risk being sent packing.

Mamounia Gardens
Mamounia Hotel, avenue Bab Jedid, Medina (044 38 86 00/www.mamounia.com). **Open** no set hours. **Admission** see text. **Map** p250 A6.

Menara Gardens

Coming in to land at Aéroport Marrakech Menara, alert passengers snatch a glimpse of a large rectangular body of water to the left. It's the basin of the gardens from which the airport takes its name. They've been there since around 750 years before man took to the air, which is to say that, like the Agdal, the Menara Gardens were laid out by the Almohads during the 12th century. They fell into disrepair and their present form is a result of restoration carried out under the Alouites in the 19th century. Sultan Mohammed V added the impressive and highly photogenic green tile-roofed picnic pavilion that overlooks the basin in 1869. Climb to the first-floor balcony for a wonderful view over the water or, better still, stroll around to the opposite side for the celebrated view of the pavilion against a backdrop of the High Atlas. Great ancient carp live in the basin; buy some bread, toss it in and watch the water churn as the fish go into a feeding frenzy.

The Palmeraie: humping ground for the rich and famous.

To get to the Menara Gardens take a petit taxi, which should cost about 15dh from just about anywhere in the Medina.

Menara Gardens

avenue de la Menara, Hivernage (no phone).
Open 5am-6.30pm daily. **Admission** free; picnic pavilion 15dh. **Map** p246 A5.

The Palmeraie

Legend has it that the Palmeraie was born of the seeds cast away by date-chomping Arab warriors centuries ago. A nice story but it fails to accord due credit to the clever minds that designed an underground irrigation system that carried the meltwater from the foothills of the High Atlas all this way north to create a massive oasis of several hundred thousand palm trees north-west of the Medina. The ancient khettra system now has only historical curiosity value because the water supply is guaranteed by several reservoirs along with a substantial network of artesian wells.

It's not what anybody would call a pretty oasis: many of the palms are the worse for wear and the ground from which they sprout is dry, dusty and lunar-like. Even so, this is probably the most prime real estate in all North Africa. Ever since the 1960s when King Hassan II granted the first permission for the sale of what is still fiercely protected by zoning regulations Palmeraie land has been the plot of choice for the rich and even richer. This has become the Beverly Hills of Morocco. Land is only available in parcels of more than one hectare and any building that takes place is not allowed to interfere with, damage or destroy any palms. Huge fines are levied for any tree disturbed. Narrow lanes that carry so little traffic that they're almost private drives, slalom between copses, occasionally squeezing by high walls surrounding the typically massive grounds of highly discreet residences. It's just possible to make out the turrets, spires and domes of the upper storeys poking over the top.

Other than pricey accommodation, there isn't much to see in the Palmeraie (ramshackle villages, grazing camels, lots of building sites) but it does make for a good place to cycle around. The ideal half-day ride is to east along the main route de Fès taking a left on to the route de Palmeraie (look for signs for the Tikida Gardens hotel), which winds through the oasis to exit north of the city on the Casablanca road. For details of bike hire *see chapter* **Directory**.

Around Marrakech

Verdant valleys, snow-capped mountains, buzzing markets: all are within a day's reach of the city.

It can take just a matter of minutes to get out of Marrakech. While modern, low-cost, mid-rise apartment blocks roll out along the road west to Essaouira and highway debris blights the route north to Casablanca, to the south and east the city barely extends beyond its ancient walls. These latter two directions lead to the foothills of the High Atlas Mountains, a pretty region of undulating green terrain, gradually rising to the rugged peaks beyond (for more information, *see p173-181*).

WHERE TO GO
No fewer than four roads radiate south from the city, plus there's the Tizi n Tichka road, which branches off the eastward-heading route de Fès. The routes and highlights are:

The route de Fès
The P24 is for walks around the **Lac des Ait Aadel** and the most impressive waterfall in Morocco, the **Cascades d'Ouzoud**.

The Tizi n Tichka road
The P31 is the road for the weekly market of **Ait Ourir**, high mountain pass antics and the imposing ruined fortress of **Kasbah Telouet**.

The Ourika Valley road
The S513 is for fine scenery, garden lovers (**Aghmat** and **Ourika**) and **Setti Fatma** with its waterfall walk – plus in winter, the ski resort of **Oukaimeden**.

The Taroudant road
The S501 is the route for weekly markets at **Tahanaoute** and **Asni**, and onwards and upwards either to the **Tin Mal Mosque** or to the village of **Imlil** and the **Kasbah du Toubkal**.

The route d'Amizmiz
This goes via the village of **Tamesloht** with its ruined kasbah up to the **Barrage Lalla Takerkost** for lakeside dining, finishing up at **Amizmiz** for trekking.

Each of the above routes constitutes a half-day to a full-day excursion. All the roads run along valley floors or via mountain passes and are separated from one other by high terrain with no connecting roads. What this means is that you can't get from the Ourika Valley to Asni, for example, without backtracking all the way to Marrakech.

Go shopping for sheep at **Ait Ourir**'s weekly market. *See p91.*

GETTING AROUND

Almost all the places described in this chapter are accessible by public transport in one form or another; we give the relevant details in the 'Getting there' sections. However, taking public transport can be time-consuming – waiting for buses to arrive and grand taxis to fill – and limiting. We recommend hiring a taxi or car, especially if you intend visiting more than one place at a go. A taxi can be arranged through your hotel and, depending on how far you are travelling, should cost around 400dh a day. This is about the same as a hiring a car (*see p221*). If you are looking to hire a taxi yourself then note that petit taxis cannot go outside the city limits, only grand taxis (the big Mercedes).

If you fancy total delegation of planning responsibilities, then many Marrakech hotels and riads organise their own excursions. You don't always have to be a guest to sign up. As an example, budget hotel Sherazade (*see p51*) charges 650dh per person to Telouet, 550dh to the Tin Mal Mosque, 450dh to the Ourika Valley and 400dh to the Barrage Lalla Takerkost. At the other end of the scale (practically off the scale, in fact), the Amanjena (*see p57*) asks its guest for 1,200dh per person to visit Asni, Ouirgane and Tin Mal. Expect to pay somewhere in between these two extremes.

Weekly markets

Almost every town in the Atlas region has a weekly 'country' market. Villagers from the locale ride in on their bikes and donkeys (the 'Berber Mercedes'), as much for the buzz as the trade. The typical market spreads over several roadside fields (one of which will be for donkey parking). At its heart are the stalls and groundsheet pitches of agricultural produce – although forget all that stuff about 'country fresh', because all the best fruit and veg goes straight to the cities and what you're left with at the market is bargain-basement fodder.

There will also be sellers of groceries and cigarettes, cheap clothing, cassettes (music and Islamic sermons), farming equipment and implements, and lots of and lots of bric-a-brac. Sheep and cattle are auctioned off to one side. This is also the place to come to for a haircut – there's a typically a row of busy barbers each in their own little makeshift, roofless cubicle – or to get a tooth pulled.

Fascinating though these markets are, the people attending are dirt poor, and if you visit we recommend leaving the flash camera gear and expensive shades back at the hotel. Not that they're liable to get stolen, but you might feel a little self-conscious about any such ostentatious displays of wealth.

Markets are held on the following days:
● Monday: **Dar Caid Ourika** (*see p91*).
● Tuesday: **Amizmiz** (*see p94*) and **Tahanaoute** (*see p93*).
● Thursday: **Azilal** (*see below*); **Ouirgane** (*see p93*); **Setti Fatma** (*see p91*) and **Touama** (32 kilometres/20 miles east on the Tizi n Tichka road).
● Friday: **Aghmat** (*see p91*); **Ait Ourir** (*see p91*) and **Tamesloht** (*see p94*).
● Saturday: **Asni** (*see p93*)
● Sunday: **Chichaoua** (52 kilometres/32 miles east of Marrakech on the Essaouira road).

The route de Fès

The route de Fès runs east out of Marrakech. After ten kilometres (six miles) there's a right-hand turn for road 6112, which runs to the towns of Demnate and Azilal. Beyond is what's known as the High Atlas of Azilal, a verdant region of high mountains and deep valleys well worth exploration but not feasible as a day trip. Instead, after 40 kilometres (24 miles) look for a right turn down to the village of Timinoutine, which is on the edge of the **Lac des Ait Aadel**. Also known as the Barrage Moulay Youssef, it's a large reservoir with the High Atlas mountains as backdrop. The gorgeous scenery is great for tramping and it's a popular weekend picnic spot for fresh-air fancying Marrakchis.

Continuing eastward, road 6707 loops through **Demnate**, where a side road runs down to **Imi n Ifri**, which has a natural rock bridge, a slippery grotto and fossilised dinosaur footprints.

From Demnate return to the S508, which runs east to the signposted turn-off for the **Cascades d'Ouzoud**. This is the site of the highest waterfall in Morocco, with a picturesque plunge pool at the bottom over-looked by several waterside cafés. By car it should take about two to two-and-a-half hours from Marrakech. For anyone who doesn't fancy returning on the same day, there are several small hotels in the village by the Cascades, including a recently-opened riad.

Getting there

To get out this way by public transport, take a bus to **Azilal** (of which there are two a day) and either ask to be let off at the Cascades turning (and then hitch the last ten kilometres/ six miles) or stay on until the end, then hire a grand taxi for the 20-minute ride back to the falls. Make the trip on a Thursday to coincide with Azilal's weekly market.

The Tizi n Tichka road

This is the road that leads over the mountains to Ouarzazte. Leave Marrakech on the route de Fès (P24) and eight kilometres (five miles) out branch off on to the P31 for **Ait Ourir**, a small village 36 kilometres (22 miles) from the city, worth visiting only for its weekly market (held on Friday and visible from the highway). Beyond Ait Ourir the road winds between the two parts of the village of **Taddert** before snaking through the stunning **Tizi n Tichka** pass. Beyond the crest, as the road begins to dip, is the signposted dirt road up to the fortress eyrie of **Kasbah Telouet**. Most people visit en route to Ouarzazte (the pass and kasbah are described more fully on *p174*), but, given that the kasbah is only a shade over 100 kilometres (62 miles) from Marrakech, it is quite possible to make it there and back in a day.

High Atlas valley.

Getting there

Telouet is a fantastic trip, but you need your own transport; a grand taxi hired in Marrakech should do it for around 400dh-500dh.

The Ourika Valley road

The Ourika Valley road (S513) goes nowhere, but you'll have a beautiful time getting there. It passes through green terraced fields for 34 kilometres (21 miles) before a small road off to the left signposted **Aghmat** (or maybe Rhmate – various spellings are used). This was the first Almoravid capital of the region and boasts a shrine to El Moutamid, the poet king of Andalucía. Aghmat is also where most of the plants for the city's gardens are grown. A quiet young man named Abdulhak manages the **Pépinière Agricole**, a nursery and garden that plant lovers might enjoy. Visit on Friday for the weekly souk.

A short distance further south along the valley from Aghmat, another left turn leads to **Dar Caid Ourika**, the main market town for the region; here the traders gather on Mondays. Horticulturalists, herbalists and assorted therapists might also be interested in the garden of Dr Jaleel Bekamel, an eminent botanist who's created an aromatic garden. He grows herbs and aromatic plants that he distills to produce essential oils. Some of these are beautifully packaged and sold commercially (the Amanjena puts them in all its rooms).

Back on the main road, ten kilometres (six miles) further, a turn-off to the right leads to the 'ski' resort of **Oukaimeden** (*see p162*).

The valley road ends at **Setti Fatma**, a small village spoiled by some unfortunate breeze-block housing, but with opportunities for pleasant riverside walking; it takes about 30 minutes to reach a series of seven cascades.

Getting there

Buses and grand taxis head out along the Ourika Valley from the Bab Er Rob gate in the southern part of Marrakech Medina (map p250 B8). They go all the way up to Setti Fatma (one hour, 20dh) but will drop off anywhere en route. To get to Aghmat, expect to have to hitch the last couple of kilometres from the main highway to the village. There are also daily buses direct to Oukaimeden, also from Bab Er Rob, but these run only in the winter.

The Taroudant road

The S501, which heads directly south out of Marrakech, runs over the Tizi n Test pass and

Sightseeing

all the way down to the Atlas city of Taroudant, 223 kilometres (138 miles) away. The first stop south of Marrakech is **Tahanaoute**, a regional administrative centre that contains nothing to look at – unless you're passing through on a Tuesday, which is the local market day.

Soon after Tahanaoute the road chicanes through several gorges before dropping and passing a right-hand turning for **Moulay Ibrahim**; this is a small village a few kilometres off the highway reached by a narrow curving road. It's a popular weekend destination for Marrakchis, who come to visit the green-roofed shrine of the saint after whom the place is named.

The Moulay Ibrahim turn-off is on the outskirts of **Asni**, an extensive little town, but with nothing to see other than the weekly souk (held on Saturday). The road splits here, the right-hand fork continuing on to the Tizi n Test and the Tin Mal Mosque, the left-hand one heading for Imlil.

TIN MAL MOSQUE

The former holy city of the Almohad dynasty (1147-1269), Tin Mal offers the opportunity to visit one of the country's earliest mosques (and one of only two mosques in all Morocco that non-Muslims are allowed to enter). It lies around 100 kilometres (62 miles) south of Marrakech on the Taroudant road (S501), which represents about a two-hour drive. The scenery en route is stunning. The road also passes by **Ouirgane** (pronounced 'Weer-gan'), a beautiful little village best known for the **Résidence La Roserie** (044 43 20 94), a peaceful hotel set in well-planted gardens of succulents and roses. It's a good place for lunch. The **Tin Mal Mosque** was completed in 1154 and heavily restored in the 1990s. It remains roofless but has beautiful arcaded columns and pleasingly restrained decoration.

IMLIL AND KASBAH DU TOUBKAL

Heading due south from Asni leads to Imlil. The road hugs the side of a broad valley, its bottom a wide bed of shale. Not far out of Asni, surrounded by high walls and cypresses, is the restored **Kasbah Tamandout**, owned until recently by Richard Branson; the road passes right by its lion-guarded gates. Further up the valley, across on the far side and perched above green pastoral enclosures and walnut groves, is the hilltop hamlet of **Aksar Soual**, also known locally as 'Clintonville'. In 1999 the place was descended on by a fleet of big black SUVs with

accompanying helicopter support. It was Hillary, visiting her niece who lives up here and is married to a local Berber guide.

At the head of the valley the road comes to a halt at **Imlil**, a small village that serves as the centre for trekking in the region. The place is big with both walkers and climbers, lying, as it does, at the foot of **Jebel Toubkal**, which at 4,167 metres (13,667 feet) is North Africa's highest peak. By the time you've got here from Marrakech (the drive takes about one hour 45 minutes), it doesn't leave time to do anything too ambitious, but you can carry on walking up the dirt track that extends east of the village in the direction of Sidi Chamharouchouch and Jebel Toubkal. Guides can be hired at the Bureau des Guides in the centre of the village. There are also several small café/restaurants and basic budget accommodation. However, for anyone interested in staying overnight, we recommend **Kasbah du Toubkal**.

Kasbah du Toubkal

Kasbah Toubkal, BP31, Imlil, Asni (044 48 56 11/ fax 044 48 56 36/www.kasbahdutoubkal.com/ kasbah@discover.ltd.uk). **Rates** dorm 300dh; double 1,200dh-1,700dh; suite 2,500dh-4,000dh. **Credit** MC, V.

A stunning restoration of an abandoned kasbah by two English brothers and their local Moroccan part-ner, Toubkal is one of the most atmospheric places to stay in southern Morocco. Guests are transport-ed up from Imlil by mule (an adventure in itself) and enter the compound beside a tower constructed for the filming of Scorsese's *Kundun*. Key scenes were shot here and some of the abandoned props remain, notably a Tibetan prayer wheel. Rooms range from 'mountain hut' dorms to a split-level, glass-walled suite that's like a Bond villain's shag pad. The views from the various terraces are breathtaking, with Jebel Toubkal rising up sheer behind. The people at Toubkal can arrange transfers from Marrakech. They also offer day trips (850dh per person): at 9am a car picks you up in the city, ferries you to the kas-bah for a Berber lunch and a spot of walking, then delivers you back again by 6pm . One other big plus: the kasbah is also a flagship for sustainable tourism and works closely with the local community.

Hotel services *Bicycles. Car hire (4X4). Conference facilities. Cook. Garden. Hammam. Library. Mountain guides. Mules. Trekking.*

Getting there

There are regular buses and grand taxis for Asni from Marrakech's Bab Er Rob gate. Hop off en route for Tahanaoute or Moulay Ibrahim. In Asni it's possible to pick up another grand taxi onwards to Imlil. For Ouirgane and Tin Mal, catch a Taroudant bus or grand taxi direct from Marrakech, but check that it is going via the Tiz n Test road.

Lunch terrace at the **Kasbah du Toubkal**.

The route d'Amizmiz

Take the main S501 road out of Marrakech then fork right soon after the Royal Club Equestre – where the looping racetrack is not for horses but for camels (there's no regular programme, unfortunately). After a further 15 minutes' driving, fields of terracotta pottery announce the turning for **Tamesloht**, home of a potters' co-operative. The village also boasts ancient olive oil presses with gigantic grind stones driven by mules – only recently decommissioned when the villagers were given modern machinery. They are located 'derrière la commune'. There's also a rambling kasbah, looking like something out of *Gormenghast*, and still partially occupied by descendants of the village founders. Beside the kasbah is the Shrine of Moulay Abdellah, with a minaret that appears to be toppling under the influence of the enormous storks' nest it carries. The village is well worth investigation and visitors can drop by the offices of the Association Tamesloht (place Sour Souika) for additional information and directions.

South of Tamesloht, the fertile landscape becomes a brilliant patchwork of greenery. Visible off to the left is **Kasbah Oumnast**, location for Scorsese's *The Last Temptation of Christ* and Gillies MacKinnon's *Hideous Kinky*. French- or Arabic-speakers could probably persuade the guardian to show them around for a little baksheesh. A kilometre or so south of the

kasbah in the village of Tagadert is the chic rural retreat of **Tigmi** (*see p58*).

A further eight kilometres (five miles) south and the road swings on to a perilously narrow-looking bridge over the Oued N'fis river before looping around to hug the shore of the **Barrage Lalla Takerkost**. This is a sizeable reservoir, which although a little dry in recent years appears almost Alpine when viewed with the snowy Atlas peaks as a backdrop. There are several restaurants and campsites in the area, the best of which is the **Relais du Lac** (061 24 24 54/061 18 74 72), which has a grassy garden beside the water's edge where daily specials (usually tajine and couscous) are served al fresco for about 80dh per head.

The road ends at **Amizmiz** (pronounced 'Amsmiz'), 55 kilometres (34 miles) south-west of Marrakech. The town has a semi-ruined kasbah and a former mellah, as well as a weekly market (held on Tuesday) that's one of the biggest in the region. Amizmiz is also a popular base from which to set out trekking into the mountains to the south and west; respected climbing and adventure activity outfit, High Country (*see p160*), has its main office here.

Getting there

There are regular bus and grand taxi links between Marrakech (Bab Er Rob) and Amizmiz. The journey takes just over an hour.

Aksar Soual: as visited by Hillary Clinton. *See p93.*

Eat, Drink, Shop

Restaurants & Cafés

Restaurants may be limited in number but food is never in short supply.

Eat, Drink, Shop

Moroccans are not a nation of people who eat out. A person who dines out is to be pitied because everyone knows that the best food is served in the home. So tough luck on you the visitor, eh? Well, not really. As an established modern consumer pit stop for well-heeled international weekenders, Marrakech has become a dab hand at finely packaging the Moroccan cuisine experience and feeding it to tables of wide-eyed, open-mouthed diners. Meanwhile, the ongoing love affair European travellers have with the place is resulting in an ever-increasing demand for, and growth of, good-quality food venues.

Good food's only part of the story, though. Dining in Marrakech is typically a full-blown multi-sensual experience. It starts with anticipation and intrigue – some of the restaurants are embedded so deep in the twists of the Medina that uniformed boys wait on the main street to lead in guests. Interiors offer sumptuous visual feasts of tiling and stucco, courtyards open to starry skies, with everything seductively textured and coloured with soft lighting and rich fabrics. Rose petals, jasmine and citrus blossom add scent, splashing fountains and lightly strummed *ouds* provide the soundtrack.

When you've had your fill of Moroccan – which can happen quite quickly given the limited choice on most local menus – variety is offered by a clutch of top-class international (for which read French and Italian) options.

THE MARRAKECH (NON) MENU

Moroccan cuisine is practical and unfussy. Dishes have evolved from Persia via the Arabs, from Andalucía with the returning Moors and from the colonial French – but the overriding principle seems to be throw all the ingredients in a dish and then leave to cook slowly.

Prime exhibit is the national dish of *tajine*. It's essentially a stew of meat (usually lamb or chicken) and vegetables, frequently cooked with olives, tangy preserved lemon, almonds or prunes, typically slow-cooked over a charcoal fire. The name describes both the food and the pot it's cooked in – a shallow earthenware dish with a conical lid that traps the rising steam and stops the stew from drying out.

The other defining local staple is *couscous*, which is again the name of the basic ingredient (coarse-ground semolina flour) and of the dish,

which is the slow-cooked grains topped with a rich meat or vegetable stew, not unlike that of a tajine. It's a full meal not a side dish.

Don't expect a menu in most traditional restaurants – customers are seated and the food simply arrives, course after course after course. First to be delivered to the table will be a selection of hot and cold small dishes, called salads, but, which actually are spiced purées of carrots, peppers, aubergine, tomatoes and the

The best Restaurants

For going native
Chez Chegrouni (*see p101*).

For light lunching
Bar L'Escale (*see p109*). Les Jardins de la Koutoubia (*see p106*). Les Terrasses de l'Alhambra (*see p109*).

For haute Moroccan
Dar Marjana (*see p102*). Dar Yacout (*see p102*). El Fassia (*see p109*). Ksar Es Saoussan (*see p102*). La Maison Arabe (*see p102*). Marrakchi (*see p102*). Tobsil (*see p105*).

For haute Française
Jardin des Arts (*see p112*). Pavillion (*see p106*). Prétexte (*see p112*).

For culinary innovation
Dar Moha (*see p102*). Riad Tamsna (*see p106*).

For outdoor dining
Alizia (*see p113*). Bagatelle (*see p109*). Dar Moha (*see p102*). El Fassia (*see p109*). Pizzeria Venezia (*see p106*). Rôtisserie de la Paix (*see p112*). Trattoria de Giancarlo (*see p112*).

For seeing and being seen
Comptoir (*see p113*). Foundouk (*see p106*). The Thai Restaurant (*see p114*).

For anything but tajine
Catanzaro (*see p109*). Dragon d'Or (*see p111*). KM9 (*see p114*). Pizzeria Niagra (*see p112*).

Dar Moha (celebrity chef not pictured).
See p102.

Street eats

As the sun sets on central Jemaa El Fna, the stew of musicians, snake charmers, dancers, dentists and herbalists shift their pitches to accommodate the early evening arrival of massed butane gas canisters, trestle tables and tilly lamps. With well-practised efficiency, within a matter of an hour around 100 food stalls are set up in tightly drawn rows, benches for the diners, strings of lights overhead and masses of food banked up in the middle. Stallholders fire up the griddles and the smoke drifts and curls to create a hazy pall over what must be one of the world's biggest open-air eateries.

Most stalls specialise in one particular dish, and between them they offer a great survey of Moroccan soul food. Several places do good business in ladled bowls of *harira* (a thick soup of lamb, lentils and chickpeas flavoured with herbs and vegetables). Similarly popular are standbys of grilled *brochettes* (kebab), *kefta* (minced, spiced lamb) and *merguez* (spicy sausage; stall No.31 apparently sells the best in all Morocco). Families perch on benches around stalls selling boiled sheep heads, scooping out the jellyish gloop inside with small plastic forks. Elsewhere are deep-fried fish and eels, bowls of chickpeas drizzled with oil, and mashed potato sandwiches, while a line-up of stalls along the south side has boys presiding over great mounds of snails, cooked in a broth flavoured with thyme, chilli, pepper and lemon, served in a bowl. Humblest of the lot is the stallholder selling nothing more than simple hard-boiled eggs.

Menus and prices hang above some of the stalls, but not everywhere. It's easy enough to just point, and prices are so low that they're hardly worth a thought anyway. Etiquette is basic: walk around, see something you like, squeeze in between fellow diners. Discs of bread serve instead of cutlery. For the thirsty, orange juice is fetched from one of the many juice stalls that ring the perimeter of the square.

The food is fresh and prepared in front of the waiting diners, so you can actually see the cooking process. Few germs will survive the charcoal grilling or boiling oil; plates and dishes are a different matter. The single same bucket of water is used to wash up all night, so play safe with your stomach and ask for the food to be served up on paper.

OFF THE SQUARE

There's further atmospheric eating in the covered market on the eastern edge of the Jemaa El Fna; narrow **rue Bani Marine** is lined with small restaurants specialising in charcoal-grilled meats, including merguez, lamb brochettes and cutlets, kefte and liver, all displayed under glass, and covered with parsley to repel the flies. Similarly, **Souk El Bhaja** (daytime only) is a wonderful street of great bubbling pans of stews, frying fish and vast bowls of piled couscous.

For food on the hoof, or something to take back to the riad, buy some fresh bread from a street vendor and follow your nose to the corner of rue Kassabine; there **El Haje** (28 Souk Abou El Kassabine) does the most succulent *mechoui*, lamb slow roasted here in a wood oven until it falls off the bone. Buy it by the weight – insisting on some crispy skin – and make your own sandwiches. Nearby, **Chez Sbai** (91 Kassabine) does the best grilled chicken in town – marinated and cooked over charcoal. Easy to find, it's in the far south-east corner of the Jemaa El Fna, at the start of Derb Debbachi. Perfect for takeaway picnics.

like, as well as diced sheep brains and chopped liver. Next, *briouettes* – little envelopes of paper-thin *ouarka* (filo) pastry wrapped around ground meat, rice or cheese and deep fried. Next, *pastilla*, ouarka pastry filled with a mixture of shredded pigeon, almonds and spices, baked then dusted with cinnamon and powdered sugar. Next, a tajine. Next, a couscous. Next, dessert of flaky pastry drizzled with honey and piled with fruit. Next, indigestion and the beginnings of a long-term aversion to all foodstuffs delivered in pottery dishes with lids.

All the above is delivered with Moroccan wine (very drinkable, especially the *vin gris*, a type of dry rosé produced in the region around Meknes), and finished off with mint tea and, gawd help us, more pastries.

A la carte Moroccan menus are available in only a few blessed places.

PRACTICALITIES

Ring ahead if you don't eat meat, although chances are the only alternative will be a vegetarian tajine/couscous. Be aware that the better the restaurant, the worse it is for

The world's biggest open-air restaurant?
Jemaa El Fna by night.

**BAR
RESTAURANT**

37 Rue Berger
75001 Paris
Tél.: 01 40 26 26 66
Fax: 01 42 21 44 24
Email: comptoir.paris@wanadoo.fr

PARIS - MARRAKECH

www.ilove-marrakesh.com/lecomptoir.html

**RESTAURA
BOUTIQ**

Avenue Echouhada, Hivern
Marrakech, M
Tél.:(212) 44 43 77 0
Fax:(212) 44 43
(212) 44 44
Email: comptoirdarna@iam.ne

Hep cat hangout **Chez Chegrouni**.

vegetarians, as meat is synonymous with wealth. Strict veggies may want to inquire about the cooking process because in a dish like vegetable couscous the odd mutton bone may have been used for flavour. Our top vegetarian-friendly venues would include Catanzaro (*see p109*), KM9 (*see p114*), Pizzeria Niagra (*see p112*), Pizzeria Venezia (*see p106*) and Les Terrasses de l'Alhambra (*see p109*) – but this is very much the pick of a poor bunch.

Reservations do need to be made for more popular places (noted in our reviews), especially during peak season (Christmas/New Year, Easter, September and October), when tables at some of the more high-profile restaurants are booked out weeks in advance.

PRICES AND PAYMENT

Prices fluctuate between the unbelievably cheap (a handful of dirhams for a full meal at Chez Chegrouni, *see below*) to the unpalatably expensive (around 50 quid per head). On average, expect to shell out around 200dh (roughly £12) for dinner. The 'average' prices we give in the text are based on a two-course meal per person without drinks.

The more upmarket the restaurant, the more likely that service will be included. You will, nonetheless, see the look of anticipation.

While many places display the symbols of major credit cards, it's common for management to claim that the machine is broken. If you insist and are willing to endure a 20-minute standoff, the machine may miraculously start working again but it's a lot easier to anticipate having to pay cash.

Restaurants

Medina

Moroccan

Argana

Jemaa El Fna (044 44 53 50). **Open** 5am-11pm daily. **Average** 80dh-120dh. **No credit cards.** **Map** p248 C5.
A no-frills (plastic tablecloths, garden furniture) eaterie on the edge of Marrakech's mayhemic main square, Argana's formula of pack-'em-in seating, canteen catering and ringside views makes it a big hit with tour groups. A stair at the back of the ground-floor café (good ice-cream, pastries, tea and coffee) leads up to two floors of restaurant terrace. Choose from a trio of three-course set menus (90dh, 100dh or 120dh), or order à la carte from a basic menu (in English) of not very good salads, ten kinds of tajine, or meat from the grill. The quality is so-so, but portions are large. It makes for a good lunch spot, but the views are best at dusk.

Baraka

Jemaa El Fna (044 44 23 41). **Open** noon-2.30pm, 7.30pm-midnight daily. **Average** *Prix fixe* 300dh-400dh. **Credit** DC, MC, V. **Map** p248 B5.
Tucked away in a westerly corner of the Jemaa El Fna, near the police station, Baraka ('Blessing') is nothing if not convenient. Shame that so many tour operators think the same – the place is often swarming. This isn't a reason not to go, however, since Baraka serves up well-executed traditional Moroccan cuisine in the sumptuous setting of an old Medina mansion. Expect all the usual suspects on the four set menus: excellent pigeon pastilla, high quality tajines – lemon chicken recommended – and local speciality tangia Marrakchia, a slow-cooked meat dish. Several large salons decorated in trad fashion – surround an elegant courtyard big enough to seat some 50 diners. Come nightfall, musicians and a belly dancer add further spice.

Chez Chegrouni

Jemaa El Fna (065 47 46 15). **Open** 6am-11pm daily. **Average** 30dh-50dh. **No credit cards.** **Map** p248 C5.
Everybody's favourite cheap restaurant in the Medina, Chez Chegrouni is as humble as they come. It looks like a garage space with a small terrace out front, but it's clean, well run and hugely popular

with both locals and tourists. All the usual dishes (salads 6dh-8dh, grills 20dh-30dh, couscous and tajines 40dh) are served briskly, accompanied by big baskets of fresh bread. Note to vegetarians: there is no meat stock in the vegetable couscous and the vegetable soup is also excellent. Menus are in English and the glasses on the tables contain paper napkins on which you scribble your order and then hand it to a waiter; it comes back as your bill at the end.

Dar Marjana

15 Derb Sidi Ali Tair, Bab Doukkala (044 38 51 10/ fax 044 42 91 52/www.dar-marjana.com). **Open** 8pm-midnight Mon, Wed-Sun. **Rates** *Prix fixe* 650dh (incl drinks). **Credit** AmEx, MC, V. **Map** p248 B4.
Alongside fine traditional Moroccan cuisine, Dar Marjana serves up the kind of effortlessly upbeat, warm atmosphere that other restaurants only dream of. Of course, this may not be entirely unconnected to its alcohol-inclusive prices, but we like to think it has more to do with the genuinely friendly staff. Set in a luxurious riad (still a family home), guests are led down a candlelit passageway and invited for aperitifs in the courtyard, before being escorted to their rose petal-strewn tables. Come expecting a veritable onslaught of food, starting with ten different cold dishes (including sheep brain), followed by the likes of *trid*, pigeon wrapped in a crêpe, and lamb with sweet tomatoes. The hard spirit digestifs come – appropriately – moments before the music and dancing starts. Book in advance, tables are limited.

Dar Moha

81 rue Dar El Bacha (044 38 64 00/ www.darmoha.ma). **Open** noon-3pm, 7.30pm-late Tue-Sun. **Average** *Prix fixe* 220dh lunch; 420dh dinner. **Credit** AmEx, MC, V. **Map** p248 B4.
And the award for the best Marrakech restaurant goes to... Dar Moha! Cue applause. Owner Moha Fedal is the closest Marrakech comes to a celebrity chef. He learnt his trade over 14 years in Switzerland and the result is a kind of Moroccan fusion cuisine – traditional dishes with a twist. We recommend sampling a standard tajine or couscous elsewhere first, then come here and delight in the difference. Both lunch and dinner are set-course affairs but there is some choice of dishes. Prime seating is outside around the pool, serenaded by musicians, with the overspill accommodated inside in premises that were once home to designer Pierre Balmain. Service is exemplary and the gregarious Moha usually flits from table to table. Reservations are recommended.

Dar Yacout

79 rue Ahmed Soussi, Arset Ihiri (044 38 29 29/ www.yacout-marrakech.com). **Open** 7pm-1am Tue-Sun. **Average** *Prix fixe* 700dh dinner. **Credit** AmEx, DC, MC, V. **Map** p248 B3.
Yacout's fame – and 20 years on from opening, it's still the destination restaurant in town – rests as much on its art of performance as it does on cooking. The building itself is all show, a madcap mansion designed by Bill Willis complete with flowering

columns, candy striping, fireplaces in the bathrooms and a yellow crenellated rooftop terrace. Guests are led up to the latter on arriving or invited to take a drink (included in the price, so feel free) in the first-floor lounge, before being taken down, past the pool and across the courtyard, to be seated for dinner at great round tables inset with mother-of-pearl. On comes the food, delivered with pomp to the accompaniment of musicians, course after course, quickly passing the point where you'd wish it would stop. It's a feast fit to bursting for both eyes and belly, but one thing's for sure, your wallet will leave considerably slimmer. Reservations are essential.

Ksar Es Saoussan

3 Derb El Messaoudyenne, off rue des Ksour (044 44 06 32). **Open** 8pm-1am Mon-Sat. **Average** *Prix fixe* 350dh/450dh/550dh. **Credit** V. **Map** p248 B4.
Yet another historic-house/fixed-menu combination, but one possessed of a uniquely peculiar old world charm. The tone's set by the shuffling elderly French gent who greets guests with an invitation to ascend to the roof for the splendid view of an illuminated Koutoubia. Then back down to be seated in silk-cushioned corners with gentle piano concertos filling the space where other diners' conversation would be (the number of covers barely reaches double figures). Stiffly formal African giants in uniform take the orders from a choice of four set dinners; all but the most ravenous should be satisfied by the three-course 'petit' option (350dh), which comes with aperitif, a half-bottle of wine and bottled water.

La Maison Arabe

1 Derb Assehbe, Bab Doukkala (044 38 70 10). **Open** 7-11pm daily. **Average** 200dh-300dh. **Credit** MC, V. **Map** p248 A4.
Other than the address, the house restaurant of the hotel of the same name (*see p41*) has no connection to the original and legendary La Maison Arabe. But the food's commendable and the surroundings are beautiful – a grand dining room under a brilliant blue-hued Persian-style ceiling with heavily draped tables generously spaced and discreetly attended by liveried staff. It feels more like an exclusive private club than a restaurant. Order à la carte from a choice of around a dozen tajines (including the excellent lamb and pear; all 150dh) and four kinds of couscous (120dh-200dh). Be warned, however: portions are meagre, so starters (soup, briouettes, pastilla) are a good idea. Afterwards, take tea or coffee out in the charming little candlelit courtyard with trompe l'oeil façade. Reservations are recommended.

Marrakchi

52 rue des Banques, Jemaa El Fna (044 44 33 77/ www.lemarrakchi.com). **Open** 11.30am-11pm daily. **Average** 160dh-250dh. **Credit** MC, V. **Map** p248 C5.
There are two huge factors in favour of this place: one's the location, on the edge of Jemaa El Fna, the second is that it serves Moroccan food à la carte – although you can go down the set-menu route if you

Never mind the food – just check out the decor at **Dar Yacout**. *See p102.*

timeout.com

The online guide to the world's greatest cities

Foundouk – design showroom with food. *See p106.*

wish (choose from 220dh or 310dh meals). It's found up a steep staircase two floors above Chez Chegrouni (*see p101*). Crude modern repro tiling and stuck-on wooden ceilings don't quite disguise the concrete and aluminium nature of the host building, but dim lighting helps, as does the diverting performance of resident *gnawa* musicians. The menu holds no surprises (tajines at just over the 100dh mark, couscous at 120dh-160dh) but the food is good, and there's an accompanying short list of local wines.

L'Mimouna

47 place des Ferblantiers, Mellah (044 38 68 68/ www.restaurant-lmimouna.com). **Open** 7-11pm Mon, Wed-Sun. **Average** 240dh-300dh. **Credit** MC, V. **Map** p251 D7.

Tucked hard against the wall that separates the public quarters from the royal precincts of the Badii Palace, L'Mimouna fills a wonderfully restored and imaginatively embellished old Jewish house. A ground floor of khaki *tadelakt* walls and beautifully dressed tables, candlelit and strewn with red petals,

is overlooked by a heavy wooden first-floor gallery (there's also seating on the roof terrace, weather permitting). The detailing is fantastic, like the house logo discreetly sewn in white on white tablecloths and fireplaces in the washrooms. We found the food less impressive – a limited menu of Moroccan standards – however, the place had only been open a matter of weeks, and changes were already planned, including the introduction of Italian dishes. The wine list runs from 120dh to 2,200dh a bottle, and the eucalyptus outside the front door is supposedly the oldest in Marrakech, at 400 years old.

Tobsil

22 Derb Abdellah Ben Hessaien, Bab Ksour (044 44 40 52). **Open** 7.30-11pm Mon, Wed-Sun. **Average** *Prix fixe* 550dh dinner. **Credit** MC, V. **Map** p248 B5.

Considered by some to be Marrakech's premier Moroccan restaurant, Tobsil offers a lesson in local gastronomy. There is no menu. On being led by a uniformed flunkey to the door (the place is otherwise impossible to find), diners are greeted by owner

Christine Rio then seated either downstairs in the courtyard or upstairs in the galleries. And so the endurance test begins. Aperitifs (included in the price of the meal, as is the wine) are rapidly followed by a swarm of small vegetarian meze dishes. Then comes a pigeon pastilla, followed by a tajine, then a couscous dish, and finally fruit and tea or coffee accompanied by cakes or pastries. It's all delicious but by about the pastilla stage you begin to feel like an overstuffed boa constrictor. Reservations (and a doggy bag) are recommended.

International

Foundouk

55 rue du Souk des Fassi, Kat Bennahïd (044 37 81 90). **Open** 7.30pm-late Tue-Sun. **Average** 160dh-200dh. **Credit** MC, V. **Map** p249 D4.

You need faith to find Foundouk. Why? Because the rutted trench of a street that leads to this restaurant appears so unpromising that many probably turn back. Those who locate the two lanterns marking the door enter to a huge round table to seat a dozen, at its centre a flower-filled sunken water tray, above, a massive spindly chandelier from the skewed fantasies of Tim Burton. Softly glowing side rooms are filled with plush sofas and armchairs: one holds a shimmering bar, one with a cascading water feature turns out to be the toilets. Diners are led upstairs to candlelit tables ranged around an upper gallery open to the sky. Unfortunately, it's downhill from here. The food (French-Moroccan) is no better than average, the service amateurish. Thankfully, prices are reasonable and worth paying for the decor alone. Reservations are recommended.

L'Italien

Mamounia Hotel, avenue Bab Jedid (044 38 86 00/ www.mamounia.com). **Open** 6pm-midnight daily. **Average** 300dh-460dh. **Credit** AmEx, MC, V. **Map** p250 A6.

There are five restaurants at the Mamounia but this is the one that draws the raves. Most of the plaudits are lavished on the gorgeous deco surrounds of a dining room that resembles the lounge bar of a classic Cunard liner with rosewood-panelled walls, cloudy trompe l'oeil ceiling and sleek and angular fittings. A ship's-bridge arrangement of windows overlooks a nightclub below. Cutlery is monogrammed and wine glasses are exquisitely engraved with the Mamounia imprint. And the food? It's good. In fact, very, very good – but that's to be expected at these prices (minestrone soup 140dh?). Jackets are supposedly required of gents; we turned up without and were served, albeit with pointed sniffiness.

Les Jardins de la Koutoubia

26 rue de la Koutoubia (044 38 88 00). **Open** 12.30-4pm, 7.30-10.30pm daily. **Average** 40dh-70dh. **Credit** MC, V. **Map** p248 B5.

Les Jardins de la Koutoubia is a recently built five-star hotel a few minutes' walk from central Jemaa

El Fna. It's derided for its gauche architecture and the sterility of its public spaces. However, its Piano Bar (*see p153*) is a fine spot for an early evening cocktail, while the poolside terrace is an equally pleasant place to take lunch. The setting is a spacious central court with grassy, shrubby verges flanking the large rectangle of invitingly blue water. Choose from a menu of salads, hugely substantial sandwiches (served with pommes frites), omelettes and a few pasta dishes. Prices are reasonable.

Pavillion

Derb Zaouia, Bab Doukkala (044 38 70 40). **Open** 7.30pm-midnight Mon, Wed-Sun. **Average** 200dh-300dh. **Credit** AmEx, MC, V. **Map** p248 A4.

The French cuisine served at Pavillion is as good as any we've tasted. The setting is equally superlative: the courtyard of a splendid old house where tables are squeezed under the spreading boughs of a massive tree. Several small salons provide for more intimate dining. In typical French fashion, the day's menu is scrawled out on a white board presented by the waiter. Offerings change regularly but expect the likes of *agneau*, *canard* and *lapin*, all exquisitely presented accompanied by seasonal veg and rich wine sauces. The staff can be supercilious, but otherwise this is a classy affair through and through. The place is a little difficult to find, but if you can locate the alley with La Maison Arabe (which is signposted), then Pavillion is 100 metres north, hidden down the next alley but one. Reservations are recommended.

Pizzeria Venezia

279 avenue Mohammed V (044 44 00 81). **Open** noon-3pm, 6pm-midnight daily. **Average** 50dh-100dh. **Credit** MC, V. **Map** p248 B5.

It's worth eating at the Venezia at least once, if only for the view: it occupies a rooftop terrace opposite the Koutoubia minaret and overlooking Mohammed V with its shoals of darting mopeds. Although it's only a pizzeria, general manager Ahmed Bennani is fussy about the quality and freshness of ingredients, so the wood-oven cooked pizzas (45dh-60dh) are as good as it gets this side of the Med. The menu also stretches to salads (30dh-45dh) and meat dishes, including a good fillet steak in a green peppercorn sauce (70dh). On Friday and Saturday there's a self-service buffet (120dh) with an enormous choice including vegetable dishes and puddings. Given the terrace, on hot summer nights dinner often comes with complimentary cooling breezes.

Riad Tamsna

23 Derb Zanka Daika, off Riad Zitoun El Jedid (044 38 52 72/fax 044 38 52 71/www.tamsna.com). **Open** 10am-midnight daily. **Average** 250dh. **Credit** MC, V. **Map** p250 C6.

Owned by Meryanne Loum-Martin, the talent behind Jnane Tamsna (*see p56*), this is a sublime courtyard restaurant (with boutique and gallery attached, *see p130*) in cool white Moorish surrounds. Ecclesiastically styled chairs and tables sit under

Moreish Moorish
at **Riad Tamsna**.
See p106.

What
Londoners
take when
they
go out.

angular white sunshades, and every detail is just-so, right down to the pebble-like salt and pepper shakers. There's a set menu with a choice from two starters, two mains, two desserts, plus juice and tea or coffee. It makes for a pricey lunch but a reasonable value dinner. The food (a Moroccan-Mediterranean fusion) is first rate, wine is served, the service immaculate and the cool jazz soundtrack is a refreshing change from the ubiquitous gnawa. If you were lunching with Anna Wintour, this is where you'd bring her. And afterwards, go upstairs and purchase the dinner service. To find Riad Tamsna, coming along Riad Zeitoun El Jedid look for a small, shabby pâtisserie next to an arched entrance (it's on the right approached from Jemaa El Fna); go down the arched passage, bear right and look for the black door with a No.23.

Les Terrasses de l'Alhambra

Jemaa El Fna (no phone). **Open** 8am-11pm daily. **Average** 50dh-100dh. **No credit cards.** **Map** p248 C5.

Opened in the summer of 2002, Les Terrasses is a hugely welcome addition to the dearth of lunchtime dining options around the central Medina. It's a clean, smart, French-run operation on the east side of the main square (across from the landmark Café de France, *see p115*). The ground floor and patio is a café for drinks and ice-cream; the first floor with terrace is for diners; the top-floor terrace is for drinks (non-alcoholic). The menu is brief – salads, pizzas and pasta (all around the 50dh mark, plus a few desserts, ice cream and milkshakes – but the food is very good. If you're new to Marrakech, it's somewhere you can eat and feel confident that your stomach will hold up. Settle in air-con comfort indoors or slow roast out in the open air overlooking the madness of Jemaa El Fna below.

Guéliz

Moroccan

El Fassia

232 avenue Mohammed V (044 43 40 60). **Open** noon-2.30pm, 7.30-11pm daily. **Average** 120dh-180dh. **Credit** AmEx, MC, V. **Map** p252 C3.

One of the scarce few posh Moroccan restaurants in town that allow diners to order à la carte, El Fassia is also unique in being run by a women's co-operative – the chefs, waiting staff and management are all female. We'd recommend skipping starters (which are mainly pastillas), not because they're not good (they are), but because the mains alone are so huge. Choose from ten tajines or three types of couscous (all approximately 100dh) – mostly meaty (chicken, lamb or rabbit), although there are a couple of vegetarian options. The decor's a bit drab, service can be grumpy and there's no alcohol, but who cares when the food's this good? El Fassia is located on the main avenue halfway between the Medina and Guéliz proper.

International

Bagatelle

101 rue Yougoslavie (044 43 02 74). **Open** noon-2pm, 7-11pm Mon, Tue, Thur-Sun. **Average** 120dh-150dh. **Credit** MC, V. **Map** p252 A2.

With its modest open-air patio overhung by vine-trailed trellising that bows under the weight of clustered grapes, and with tables divided by ferns and bushy plants, lunch at Bagatelle's can resemble dining in a greenhouse. The menu is substantially bistro French: salads and standard entrecôtes, escallopes and fillets. They are supplemented by a few Moroccan dishes and a typed page of daily specials (from which we enjoyed *tajine de lapin aux prunes*; 70dh). Beer and wine are served. Bagatelle is particularly popular with lunching mademoiselles on time out from raiding the nearby boutiques.

Bar L'Escale

rue de la Mauritania (044 43 34 47). **Open** 11am-11pm daily. **Average** 50dh-70dh. **No credit cards.** **Map** p252 B2.

It's primarily a bar (*see p154*), but L'Escale's also a good place for a quick cheap lunch – although not if you're a vegetarian. The humble house special is marinated grilled chicken, leg (*la cuisse*) or breast (*le blanc*), which comes with an excellent tomato and onion salsa and a basket of bread for mop-up. The spicy merguez sausages are pretty good too. There's a back-room specifically for dining beyond the front bar but prime seating is at one of the half-dozen sun-shaded tables out on the pavement. It's across from the Marché Central.

Catanzaro

42 rue Tarek Ibn Ziad (044 43 37 31). **Open** noon-2.30pm, 7.30-11pm Mon-Sat. **Average** 80dh-120dh. **Credit** MC, V. **Map** p252 B2.

It's just a rustic-styled neighbourhood Italian (red-checked tablecloths, faux-woodbeam ceiling) with a homely air and reliable cooking, but Catanzaro is probably the most popular eaterie in town. White-hatted chefs work an open kitchen with a big wood-fired oven turning out excellent thin-crust pizzas (average 45dh). Alternatives include various grills and steaks (70dh-80dh), with a good selection of salads to accompany and plenty of choice of wine by the bottle or half-bottle. The dessert list includes a tiptop crème brûlée. Customers all seem to be regulars – most are greeted by name as they arrive – and, although the place seats 60 or more, reservations are recommended in the evenings. It's very easy to find: one street back from avenue Mohammed V, behind the Marché Central.

Chez Jack'line

63 avenue Mohammed V (044 44 75 47). **Open** noon-2.30pm, 7-11pm daily. **Average** 80dh-120dh. **No credit cards.** **Map** p252 A2.

Resolutely old school, Jack'line's is a sepia-toned French bistro complete with Parisian mementoes (posters, street signs), a shuffling aged waiter given

Eat, Drink, Shop

Les Terrasses de L'Alhambra. *See p109.*

to reminiscing and, overseeing all, the elderly madame with a little white yappy pooch. She still greets every diner with a description of the day's special: the fact that the special has remained the same for what seems like years – a small pigeon pastilla – is neither here nor there. Although the menu lists frogs' legs and eggs in aspic many of these dishes are echoes of better days and are no longer available. Instead, play safe with meat in sauces. Prices are cheap and there's an excellent value 80dh set menu of three courses. Most patrons forsake the chintzy but charming interior (complete with squawking parrot) for the wrought iron enclosed area of pavement seating.

Dragon d'Or

10 boulevard Mohammed Zerktouni (044 43 06 17). **Open** noon-2pm, 7-11pm daily. **Average** 120dh-220dh. **Credit** MC, V. **Map** p252 B2.

This is about as far removed from Marrakech as it gets without crossing international borders. Pass under the gilt-and-red dragon gate into a gilt and red interior, complete with fully-ticked checklist of restaurant Asiatique fittings and accessories: black lacquered surfaces, lanterns, tassels and la-la sing music. The menu is surprisingly extensive with a major in Vietnamese specialities (the spring rolls on a bed of coriander are great). The overall quality of the dishes is high with a greater authenticity than might be expected in near-Saharan North Africa. Beer and wine are served and they do take outs too..

Jacaranda

32 boulevard Mohammed Zerktouni (044 44 72 15/ www.lejacaranda.ma). **Open** noon-3pm, 6.30-11pm daily. **Average** 200dh-300dh. **Credit** MC, V. **Map** p252 A2.

With large picture windows looking on the traffic tango of place Abdel Moumen, Jacaranda's the place for an urban dining experience. Inside it's hardly less busy: a crush of furniture, chintzy table settings and assorted paintings spill down from the mezzanine gallery cluttering all available wall space. But it's friendly and comfortable. The kitchen specialises in *cuisine française* with plenty of *viande* and *poisson*, but it's hardly haute cuisine and as such a bit overpriced with entrées at 70dh-95dh and mains at 110dh-150dh. However, decent value is offered by a lunchtime two-course *menu rapide* at 85dh or the *menu tourisme*, three

Marrakitsch

As all wised-up travellers know, one fail-safe way of sabotaging any culture is to put it into a touristic dinner-show formula and slap on a high price tag (with discounts for tour groups, of course). But those from the 'so bad it's good' school who actively seek out exotic kitsch will find plenty to delight at Marrakech's 'folkloric' dinner shows.

Now in its 25th year, **Chez Ali** tops the bill of Moroccan extravaganzas. It occupies a mammoth 27-acre site outside the city on the Casablanca road. With a capacity of 2,000 and its own hotel, it's pitched as something of a folkloric wondervillage. For full effect, come for an early dinner before the show. Guests are ushered, via various strategically placed all-singing, all-dancing groups in traditional dress, to tables in one of several grand carpet-lined tents arrayed around a central arena, all filled by innumerable tour buses' worth of blinking, elderly and slightly bewildered fellow seekers of the exotic.

As diners negotiate the largest portion of lamb in culinary history, on comes an army of costumed drummers, the warm up to a spectacle that includes herds of horsemen dashing around the arena displaying acrobatic feats and swordplay, and firing off rifles. There's even a flying carpet finale to boot.

Hivernage hotel **Es Saadi** (*see p52*) puts on a floor show in its 'casino': in reality a dimly lit dining hall with a few slot machines and aesthetic crimes aplenty – think gold nylon tablecloths, silver bowed chairs and liberal pink-red clashes. Just as you're tucking into your pigeon pastilla and suffocating on the wafts of aftershave from neighbouring middle-aged businessmen, distraction arrives in the form of music, dancing, acrobats and snake charmers.

For a subtler – not to say classier – folkloric dining experience, try **Dar Marjana** (*see p102*), while the supremely hip **Comptoir** (*see p113*) also entertains with a troupe of fleshy belly dancers, complete with candelabras balanced on head – it's all done tongue-in-cheek, or at least we hope it is, otherwise that's its credibility blown.

Chez Ali

Route de Safi, km12 (044 30 77 30/ www.ilove-marrakech.com/chezali.html). **Open** 8.30-11pm daily. **Price** *Prix fixe* 400dh. **Credit** AmEx, MC, V.

Es Saadi

avenue El Qadissia (044 44 88 11/ www.essaadi.com). **Price** *Prix fixe* 280dh. **Open** 12.30-2.30pm, 7.30-11pm daily. **Credit** AmEx, DC, V. **Map** p252 C5.

courses for 105dh. In the evenings there's a *menu du marché* for 180dh. In addition to beer and wine, the tiny bar counter stretches to apertifs and a small selection of cocktails. Chin chin.

Jardin des Arts

6-7 rue Sakia El Hamra, Semlalia (044 44 66 34). **Open** 7-11pm Mon, Tue, Thur-Sun. **Average** 180dh-250dh. **Credit** MC, V. **Map** p246 A1.

Way off the radar as far as most visitors are concerned, Jardin des Arts is beyond Guéliz, a five-minute taxi ride up the Casablanca road; it's next to the cluster of big hotels of which the Tichka Salam (*see p51*) is part. But boy, is it worth the (brief) ride. The place is a modern villa, elegantly done out in mustard and dusky pink tones with nice touches like spidery starburst wall lights and shawl-draped seating – or you can dine in the garden, overlooked by the main salon through arched French windows. The menu's also French and includes dishes not seen elsewhere, such as loin of pork (this is an Islamic country, remember), plus it's also strong on seafood (110dh-145dh). The cooking is highly accomplished (although the chef has just changed as we go to press) and the service refreshingly discreet. Alcohol is served. We like.

Odissea

83 boulevard El Mansour Eddahbi (044 43 15 45). **Open** noon-2.30pm, 7-11pm Mon, Tue, Thur-Sun. **Average** 150dh-200dh. **Credit** MC, V. **Map** p252 B2.

There's a kind of an excesses of the Roman Empire thing going on here: heavy stucco detailing, plaster busts, big cat artwork, leopard print chairs, golden tablecloths and pretty-boy waiters in floridly patterned silk shirts. Very droll, very Versace. We expected to be offered nightingale tongues or roast heart of kitten, but no, just pizzas, pastas and an array of meat and fish standards. Nothing terribly exciting, but all competently done and reasonably priced. The wine list is wholly local but extensive. Upstairs is a wonderful rubeous private dining area and bar with a supremely decadent air, just the place for your next Marrakech orgy.

Pizzeria Niagra

31-2 Centre Commercial El Nakhil, route de Targa (044 44 97 75). **Open** 12.15-2.15pm, 7.15-11pm Tue-Sun. **Average** 60dh-130dh. **Credit** MC, V (over 150dh only). **Map** p252 A1.

One of three adjacent pizza joints five minutes' walk north of central Guéliz on the road out to the French Lycée, and easily the best (although neighbouring Pizzeria Exocet shades it in the name stakes). An excellent menu of far more than just pizza (pasta, escalopes, steaks, fillets, plus 14 salads) at cheap prices ensures that the place is packed most every lunch and dinner – the latter often quite boozy given that beer and wine are sold at almost supermarket prices. With pink and chintzy decor, it's far from being an event restaurant, but if you lived here it'd certainly become a much loved local.

Prétexte

9 rue Ibn Zaidoun (044 43 94 26). **Open** noon-2pm, 8-11.30pm Tue-Sun. **Average** 250dh-350dh. **Credit** MC, V. **Map** p252 A1.

Prior to 2003 this was Les Cépages, one of the city's best respected – and ponciest – restaurants. Other than ownership and the name, little appears to have changed. It's a highly formal and traditional French affair occupying the ground floor of a fine villa on a leafy arcing sidestreet a few minutes' walk from central Guéliz. The interior's a bit starchy but pretty – though the jury's out on the homoerotic Orientalist canvases. The menu is limited and contains little to set pulses racing, but an entrecôte with roquefort sauce and veal à la crème (both around the 180dh mark) are very good, and the silver salver service is fun as the assembled waiters carefully synchronise the lifting of the covers. The core clientele appears to be diplomatic folk, and anyone turning up in jeans and a T-shirt can expect a significant reduction in the quality of service.

Rôtisserie de la Paix

68 rue Yougoslavie (044 43 31 18). **Open** noon-3pm, 6.30-11pm daily. **Average** 100dh-150dh. **Credit** AmEx, MC, V. **Map** p252 B2.

Flaming since 1949, the 'peaceful rôtisserie' is a large garden restaurant with seating among palms and bushy vegetation. Simple and unpretentious, it's utterly lovely, whether lunching under blue skies (shaded under red umbrellas), or dining after sundown when the trees twinkle with fairy lights. (In winter dining is inside by a crackling log fire.) Most of the menu comes from the charcoal grill (kebabs, lamb chops, chicken and own-made merguez sausage; average prices 55dh-85dh), but there are also delicacies such as quail, and a selection of seafood. We recommend the warm chicken liver salad, listed on the menu as a starter but easily a meal in itself and a bargain at 65dh. If you have an afternoon flight, farewell lunch here is the ideal way to bid Marrakech goodbye.

Trattoria de Giancarlo

179 rue Mohammed El Bekal (044 43 26 41/ www.latrattoriamarrakech.com). **Open** 7.30-11.30pm daily. **Average** 200dh-300dh. **Credit** AmEx, MC, V. **Map** p252 A2.

La Trattoria is possibly Marrakech's finest Italian restaurant, serving superb food in the most enchanting of surroundings. The Felliniesque interiors (lush, occasionally lurid and more than a little louche) are by local legend Bill Willis and are a delight, but the best tables are those overhung by oversized greenery out on the tiled garden terrace beside the large luminous pool. In the evening the place is lit by lanterns and candles to ridiculously romantic effect. While the menu is hardly extensive, it holds plenty of appeal (salads, vegetarian pastas, meat and seafood dishes). Service is excellent going on obsequious: 'Would sir like his beer with a head or without?'. Reservations are recommended.

The Gypsy Rose Lee boudoir awaits at the **Trattoria de Giancarlo**. *See p112.*

Hivernage

International

Alizia

Angle rue Ahmed Chouhada Chawki (044 43 83 60).
Open noon-2.30pm, 7-11pm daily. **Average** 120dh-180dh. **Credit** MC, V. **Map** p252 C4.

Presided over by Madame Rachida (who studied English in Bayswater, London), this is an intimate Italian that in addition to the expected pizzas (30dh-50dh), pastas (60dh-80dh), meaty fillets and steaks (around the 100dh mark) also serves some wonderful fish dishes. How about a starter salad of small red mullet fillets flamed in balsamic vinegar, followed by fillet of John Dory in a prawn bisque sauce, with exotic fruit salad, seasoned with cinnamon and served with cream to finish? There's a very decent wine list too (local and imported). Although the pitch is upscale (with overly fussy waiters), the atmosphere is very relaxed, especially if you're seated in the bougainvillea-draped garden.

Comptoir

avenue Echouada (044 43 77 02). **Open** 5.30pm-2am daily. **Average** 180dh-300dh. **Credit** MC, V. **Map** p252 C4.

Its sultry exotic-East-meets-moneyed-West style is an absolute winner, and until the next big thing comes along, Comptoir remains *the* nightspot in town (*see p154*). The food is a little more hit and miss. The menu's divided into *saveurs d'ici* (tajines and couscous) and *saveurs d'allieurs* (Frenchified meat in sauces), a smart move that satisfies both the visitor fresh off the plane and eager for a taste of Morocco, as well as the more jaded palate that blanchs at the whiff of yet another pastilla – in other words, the visitor who's been in town for two days or more. The quality of the dishes varies wildly, influenced perhaps by cloud formations, coffee grinds, the Nikkei index, or maybe just by whichever chef's working the kitchen. What is a constant is the fantastic party atmosphere, brought to a raucous climax around 11pm each weekend evening with the arrival of a troupe of belly dancers. Audience participation is encouraged.

Eat, Drink, Shop

International

KM9

Route de l'Ourika, km9 (044 37 63 73). **Open** noon-2.30pm, 8-11pm daily. **Average** *Prix fixe* 170dh/190dh/210dh/280dh. **Credit** MC, V.

Without your own car it's a nuisance to get to KM9 (expect to pay around 100dh each way in a taxi), but the good news is, it really is worth it. From the outside it's a kind of roadhouse in the middle of nowhere but the interior is supremely seductive with a bar-lounge area up front and dining areas at the back. Choose from four good-value set menus, each of which kicks off with a superb antipasto buffet. One menu choice follows up with six small, delicate pasta dishes (judged by one expat to be the best pasta in town – and this from a woman so particular she trucks in her food from Bologna). Other menu options are more meaty. Staff are charming, and if you drop in on a summer weekend there's likely to be a party in full swing (*see p156*).

The Thai Restaurant

Amanjena, route de Ouarzazate, km12 (044 40 33 53). **Open** 11.30am-3.30pm, 8-10.30pm daily. **Average** 300dh-400dh. **Credit** AmEx, MC, V.

The ultra-exclusive Amanjena resort (*see p57*) has two formal dining options: the sublime onyx-columned 'Moroccan', which is beautiful but serves nothing that can't be had at plenty other restaurants, and this prosaically named place, a venue for which wealthy Marrakchis climb into their 4x4s and drive for top-rank Thai food. The chef is formerly of the highly regarded Celadon restaurant in Bangkok and

under his direction the kitchen turns out raved-over flavours featuring the likes of fried fish salad or green duck curry. Dishes are 200dh-300dh – pricey, but you're paying for the regal 'Aman experience'. Although the restaurant's open for lunch, the complex is at its best by night illuminated by flickering torchlight. Reservations are recommended.

Tivoli

Route de Casablanca (044 31 35 28). **Open** 11am-2.30pm, 7-11.30pm Mon-Sat. **Average** 150dh-250dh. **Credit** MC, V.

It's approached via a mini-Japanese garden, but that's the only flair about the Tivoli, which otherwise is a sober affair resembling a prefabricated pavilion (or is that pagoda?). Instead, the art is reserved for the cooking, which is a highly accomplished (if slightly over-salted) rendering of northern Italian cuisine (predominantly meat and fish options, plus pastas). The regular menu is supplemented by a half-dozen regularly changing daily specials. Staff are smart and efficient with a sassy line in table talk. It's out on the Casa road, on the left just before the Marjane hypermarket; a petit taxi should cost 15dh, but you'll also need picking up.

Cafés

Traditional Moroccan cafés are thin on the ground. Instead, thanks to the French, Marrakech has a legacy of continental-style places where you are likely to find croissants and pastries, as well as the ubiquitous oversweetened green mint tea and thick gritty coffee. They open early for breakfast and tend to close early too.

Kitchen breaks

Just can't get enough of those tajines? Then sign up for lessons in how to make your own. La Maison Arabe (*see p41*) offers cooking workshops held in a purpose-built teaching kitchen in a small villa in verdant surrounds on the edge of town. Each session is preceded by a brief introduction to Moroccan cuisine and a gathering of herbs and spices from the garden. Participants lunch beneath olive trees on the meal they've prepared. Jnane Tamsna (*see p55*) and Kasbah Agafay (*see p58*) also offer similar; call for details.

UK-based Rhode School of Cuisine constructs whole holidays around the kitchen. Its courses, held at a luxury Palmeraie villa called Dar Liqama ('House of Green Mint'), run for a whole week, although daily lessons last only about two hours – the rest of the

time is spent making forays into the souk for ingredients, or snoozing off the food with poolside lounging.

La Maison Arabe

1 Derb Assehbe, Bab Doukkala (044 38 70 10/www.lamaisonarabe.com). Workshops are held on demand for a minimum of two people (charged at 1,600dh per person), a maximum of eight (500dh per person).

Rhode School of Cuisine

Hambledon House, Vann Lane, Hambledon, Surrey GU8 4HW (01428 685140/ www.rhodeschoolofcuisine.com). Courses are held January to April, October and November. Prices per person per week – including accommodation, food, tours and classes, but not flights – start at £1,395.

Lots to see at the **Café de France**.

Medina

Café de France

Jemaa El Fna (no phone). **Open** 6am-11pm daily.
No credit cards. **Map** p248 C5.
The most famous of Marrakech cafés is distinctly
grotty but it boasts a prime location right on the
main square. No one seems to know exactly how old
the place is but it crops up as a landmark in Peter
Mayne's *A Year in Marrakech*, written in the early
1950s. It remains a prime meeting place for both
travellers and for locals with business in the Medina:
assorted Morocco guidebooks and copies of the
day's Arabic-language press are present in about
equal numbers. Neither category is favoured and
prices are posted ensuring fair trade for all.

Pâtisserie des Princes

32 rue Bab Agnaou (044 44 30 33). **Open** 5am-
11.30pm daily. **No credit cards**. **Map** p250 C6.
A weak-kneed wobble (the heat! the heat!) from
Jemaa El Fna, des Princes offers gloriously icy air-
conditioning in a dim coldstore of a back room.
Sounds gloomy, but we guarantee, the hotel swimming pool aside, there's no better retreat on a sun-
hammered afternoon. Front of house is taken up by
glass display cabinets filled by frilly, puffy, creamy
cakes and pastries to be accommpanied by cappuc-
cino (10dh), English tea (10dh), *jus d'orange* (8dh) or
shakes (18dh). There's another large salon upstairs.

Guéliz

Amandine

177 rue Mohammed El Bekal (044 44 96 12). **Open**
6am-11pm daily. **No credit cards**. **Map** p252 A2.
Amandine comes in two parts: there's the smart
pâtisserie with a long glass display cabinet layered
with continental-style cakes and pastries and a few
chairs and tables in front, or next door is a proper
café space with high bar counter, fewer cakes but
far more atmosphere. Both spaces are air-conditioned but we prefer the café, where efficient table
service provides the usual coffees and (mint) teas,
plus hot savouries and things like croissants and
French toast. It's bright and cheerful and very
female-friendly – and highly popular with young
Marrakchi dating couples too.

Boule de Neige

*Angle rue Yougoslavie, off place Abdel Moumen,
(044 44 60 44)*. **Open** 5am-11pm daily.
No credit cards. **Map** p252 A2.
Don't come particularly for the coffee or food, but do
come for a look. The setting's a large room coloured
a fetching mint green and pink, with tables laid out
canteen style. There's a food counter at one end with
things shiny, gelatinous and best left well alone.
There's also an extensive breakfast menu but it only
baffles the staff if you attempt to order from it.
Instead, just nip next door to the Pâtisserie Hilton

Bitter black coffee, flaky croissants and perhaps a shoe shine at **Café Les Négociants**.

and bring something back – it's permitted, even encouraged. Then settle in and watch the almost sitcom-like spectacle of staff chasing cats chasing other cats dodging men eyeing single girls looking bored exchanging knowing smiles with the staff, who are chasing cats… Huge fun.

Café Les Négociants

place Abdel Moumen, avenue Mohammed V (044 43 57 82). **Open** 6am-11pm daily. **No credit cards**. **Map** p252 A2.

Far classier than the endearingly sleazy Café Atlas (*see p155*), which it faces across the *place*, Les Négociants is a Parisian boulevard-style café with acres of rattan seating and round glass-topped tables crowded under a green-and-white striped pavement awning. We like it for breakfast: café au lait, orange juice and croissants, plus the papers from the international newsagent across the road. It's somewhere that women obviously feel comfortable judging by how many family groups and girls frequent the place.

Shops & Services

Hey lady! Wanna buy a carpet? Glasses for tea? How about a Jean Paul Gaultier knock-off? Welcome to souk couture.

Prices may have soared in recent years, but Marrakech remains a superb place to shop. The souks represent head-spinning, circus-crazy commerce at its most intoxicating – a riot of dazzling primary colours, seductive shapes and exoticism with a price ticket. The snap impulse is to go for a Moroccan makeover on the pad back home and embark on a mass shop for all the requisite props. Fine, but just be aware that once back in drizzly, grey northern Europe those bright oranges and reds can just look garish, the brass lanterns are the height of tackiness and the curly yellow slippers, well, best just hide them at the back of the wardrobe, eh?

Some of the best shopping is well beyond the walls of the Medina, up in the *nouvelle ville* of Guéliz. On and off avenue Mohammed V are plenty of smart and sophisticated little boutiques stocking exclusive designer items and one-offs superior in style and quality to anything found in the souks – and without the hassle of hard sell, haggling and interminable mint teas.

Committed shoppers might want to take a ride out to the Quartier Industriel at Sidi Ghanem (taxi up the Casablanca road, left just before the McDonald's on to the route de Safi, left again opposite the mosque); it's about eight kilometres (five miles) north of town and, as the name suggests, not somewhere you head for the views. This is the warehousing belt and it's home to several fine factory showrooms including notably those of **Akkal** (pottery, *see p133*), **Amira** (candles; *see p128*), **La Medina** (home accessories and furniture, *see p130*) and **Mia Zia** (fashion, *see p123*).

Recommended good buys include Moro couture clothing, brightly coloured fabrics, spices, natural oils and pottery, but there's even more fun to be had with the odd, impractical and function-free purchase – a pair of shoulder-high brass candlesticks? Mother-of-pearl inlaid dowry chests? Spangly belly-dancing outfit? Mummified baby alligator? Above all else, shopping in Marrakech is a hoot.

I SPIT ON YOUR OFFER

It's a drag, but when shopping in the souk haggling is expected, even demanded. There are no hard and fast rules as to how to do it,

but when you've spotted something you want it's smart to do a little scouting around and get a few quotes on the same or similar item at other stores before making your play. Don't feel you need to go through the whole silly charade of offer and counter-offer like in some B-movie dialogue; simply expressing interest then walking away on being told the price is usually enough to bring about radical discounting. Otherwise, try shopping at either the **Centre** or **Ensemble Artisanal** (for both, *see p120*), both of which display fixed prices, or at the boutiques in Guéliz – where you might still be paying over the top but at least the onus isn't on you to do anything about it.

OPENING HOURS

Just as prices are highly elastic, so are hours of business. We've done our best to extract from recalcitrant shop owners the times they're likely to be open and trading, but it's all a bit *inshaallah* (God willing). A chance meeting with a colleague in the street and the *fermé* sign can stay in place all morning. As a rule of thumb, the working day stretches from around 9am to 7pm with a break of a couple of hours for lunch and a snooze. Shops in the souk will often close on the Muslim holy day of Friday, at least for the morning; shops in Guéliz take Sunday off. Some places take both. During Ramadan it's even more unpredictable, but there's a general shift for businesses to open and close later.

PAYMENT

Generally speaking, it's dirhams only. Some shops are authorised to take euros, pounds sterling or US dollars, particularly the more heavily touristed emporia. However, this won't be self-evident and the only way to find out is by asking. Many shops purport to take credit cards, but in practice they'd much rather not and will press for cash. Payment by plastic also often incurs a five per cent surcharge (to cover processing costs). If you find yourself short of the cash, shops are often prepared to deliver to your hotel and accept payment on receipt.

Note that there are no added taxes on purchases, and hence nothing to be claimed back.

Beldi's slinky, silky stuff.
See p120.

BRINGING IT ON HOME

Lots of shops offer a shipping service for foreign visitors. Beware. Tales of goods last seen somewhere in Marrakech are legion. Unless we're talking about a container load, the best advice is to take care of transporting purchases home yourself. The most straightforward option is to bite the bullet and pay the excess baggage fee. On British Airways this is about 100dh per kilogram (32 ounces). Alternatively, you can use an international courier service; DHL and FedEx both offer what they call an 'artisanal rate'. This is specifically geared to the shipping of handicrafts and souvenir buys, which is around 150dh per kilogram. For couriers, *see* chapter **Directory**.

There is a levy of between five and 15 per cent payable on anything above the 2,300dh duty-free customs allowance.

One-stop shopping

Aswak Assalaam

avenue du 11 Janvier, Bab Doukkala (044 43 10 04). **Open** 8am-10pm daily. **Credit** MC, V. **Map** p248 A2.

Across the main road from the *gare routière* at Bab Doukkala, this is a decent-sized supermarché, and the closest good grocery shopping to the Medina. No booze though (the owner's a religious man). It has less choice than Marjane (*see below*) and it's pricier, but it's also a whole lot more convenient for anyone without a car.

Marjane

route de Casablanca, Semlalia (044 31 37 24). **Open** 9am-10pm daily. **Credit** MC, V.

How did Marrakech manage before Marjane? This massive hypermarché is the utimate shopping destination for the city's middle and upper classes. It combines a supermarket (food and plentiful booze, clothes, household items, electronics, white goods, CDs, computers) with a Kodak Express Lab, McDonald's, Lacoste, Yves Rocher and Caterpillar franchises, plus banks, Méditel and Maroc Télécom, and a pharmacy. It's about 8km (five miles) north of town and a petit taxi will get you out there for around 30dh each way.

Antiques

Antique is a manufactured style here, and few things in Marrakech are as old as they would first appear. Added to which, fraud is

widespread. Buy it because you like it, and if it turns out to be worth what you paid, well, that's an added bonus.

Amazonite
94 boulevard Mansour Eddahbi, Guéliz
(044 44 99 26). **Open** 9.30am-1pm, 3.30-7.30pm Mon-Sat. **Credit** AmEx, MC, V. **Map** p252 B2.
Probably the only shop in town where you have to ring a doorbell to enter. It's a cramped three-storey repository of all manner of objets d'art, top quality Berber jewellery, early 20th-century oil paintings (displayed in the basement), a stunning collection of ancient silk carpets (stored in fine armoires), plus miscellaneous ethnic trappings, including old marriage belts. It's a place for serious buyers in search of rare finds.

El Badii
54 boulevard Moulay Rachid, Guéliz (044 43 16 93). **Open** 9am-7pm daily. **Credit** AmEx, MC, V. **Map** p252 A3.
Two floors of museum-quality antiques, hand-picked by owners Najat Aboufikr and his wife, featuring a dazzling array of gold and silver jewellery, unusual lamps, carved Berber doors, ornate mirrors, and a huge choice of carpets downstairs. Pride of house are the ancient ceramics from Fès in traditional yellow and cobalt blue. This is where the likes of Brad Pitt, Tom Cruise and Hillary Clinton come to browse (the photos are on the wall to prove it), but the fixed prices and warm welcome are for everyone.

Bazaar Ikhouan
15 Marché Sidi Ishak, off rue Sidi Ishak, Medina (044 44 36 16). **Open** 9am-8pm daily. **Credit** AmEx, MC, V. **Map** p248 C4.
Just how antique most of these pieces are and how much of it is just junk is open to debate – antiquity is in the eye of the beholder. Anyway, curious excavators can sift through piles of tarnished jewellery, dull-bladed curved daggers, trays and teapots, greening brass lanterns, fancy-headed walking sticks, silver Koranic carry-cases, gunpowder flasks and ivory handled muskets. Owner Khalid is a real charmer and speaks fluent English.

Moha
73 Laksour Sabet Graoua, Mouassine, Medina (044 44 37 81). **Open** 9am-8pm daily. **No credit cards**. **Map** p248 C5.
One of several objets d'art shops around Mouassine, this place offers a good selection of choice, if not always particularly old, doors, large vases, armoires and chests. The owner – Moha – speaks English and will happily hold court in his modestly sized showroom over mint tea while discussing purchases. He also has a second shop nearby for genuine buyers.

L'Orientaliste
11 & 15 rue de la Liberté, Guéliz (044 43 40 74). **Open** 9am-12.30pm, 3-7.30pm Mon-Sat; 10am-12.30pm Sun. **Credit** MC, V. **Map** p252 B2.

Comptoir Boutique. *See p123.*

L'Orientaliste comprises a small street-front boutique and a huge basement space hidden round the corner, both crammed with fine enticements to purchase. The former is stuffed with a piled selection of inexpensive items – vintage soda siphons, modern Fès ceramics, filigree metal containers, scented candles and perfume bottles, some filled with essences – the latter with pricey antique furniture, watches, turn-of-the-century Moroccan paintings and engravings, and leatherbound notebooks with original watercolours. We defy anyone not to buy.

La Porte d'Orient
6 boulevard El Mansour Eddahbi, Guéliz (044 43 89 67). **Open** 9am-7.30pm Mon-Sat. **Credit** AmEx, MC, V. **Map** p252 A2.
The most mind-blowing of shopping experiences occurs when a door at the back of this cosy shop is opened to a back room, which then gives on to a warehouse-sized space of enormous proportions. The huge space is loaded with an impressive panoply of Berber jewellery, ancient carved doors of fantastic size and patterning, irridescent lanterns, beautiful glass cases of illuminated manuscripts, gilded lion thrones… and the list goes on. What you won't find, however, are too many bargains.

Tinmel

38 rue Ibn Aicha, Guéliz (044 43 22 71).
Open 9am-7.30pm Mon-Sat. **Credit** AmEx, MC, V.
Map p252 B2.
A highly browseable mini-museum of Islamic art with a staggering variety of antiques: aged silver swords, Touareg earrings and pendants, 18-carat-gold jewellery from the early 20th century, colossal bronze lanterns that once adorned palaces, decorative oil jars, mirrors with cedar and camel bone inlays, silk-embroidered camel skin bags, and marble fountains. Phew. And don't miss the exquisitely crafted backgammon tables displayed upstairs.

Arts & handicrafts

Almost every store in the souk is a handicrafts store of some description, but the three places below offer a greater range than most. For anyone pushed for time, the two artisanals are good one-stop options. For other stores selling similar, *see p128* **Home accessories**.

Centre Artisanal

7 Derb Baissi Kasbah, off rue de Kasbah, Medina (044 38 18 53). **Open** 8.30am-8pm daily. **Credit** AmEx, MC, V. **Map** p250 B8.
Don't let the humble entrance fool you – this is the closest thing to a department store Marrakech has seen, albeit a department store selling nothing but Moroccan handicrafts. It's the ultimate souvenir store, with everything from trad clothing (babouches, jellabas, kaftans) to jewellery to home furnishings and carpets stacked high to the ceiling. Prices are fixed and are generally about what you'd expect to pay in the souk, but without the tiresome charade of haggling. The stalker-like behaviour of the sales assistants can irritate.

Darkoum

5 rue de la Liberté, Guéliz (044 44 67 39). **Open** 9.30am-12.30pm, 3-7.30pm Mon-Sat. **Credit** MC, V. **Map** p252 B2.
Ethnic design aficionados are likely to swoon at Darkoum, a sprawling multi-levelled shop that looks more like an art gallery. Beyond a great selection of shiny woven fabrics from Senegal and Morocco (including custom-made curtains), you can pick up inexpensive mosaic tiles or splurge on mother-of-pearl-inlaid stools and chests originating from Syria, or ceremonial African masks, or dazzling silks from India.

Ensemble Artisanal

avenue Mohammed V, Medina (044 38 67 58).
Open 8.30am-7.30pm daily. **Credit** AmEx, MC, V. **Map** 248 A5.
Second major tourist stop after photo ops at the Koutoubia, the EA is another state-sponsored crafts mini-mall like the Centre Artisanal described above – but far more popular because of its highly central location. All the artisans selling within are purportedly here by royal appointment, selected as the best

in their field (a licence therefore to charge higher prices, which are completely non-negotiable). Expect everything from fine embroidered table linen (first floor at the back) to jewellery, clothing, lamps and even knock-off European handbags.

Bookbinding

Abderrhamane El Kadaoui

212 Souk Chkairia, Medina (063 62 64 97). **Open** 9am-8pm daily. **No credit cards. Map** p248 C4.
The leather souk is chocka with stalls selling every kind of bag and belt, both trad Moroccan and in current European street styles, but there are only a few bookbinders left. Mr El Kadaoui can re-cover a book or make an album to order in two to three days for a very reasonable price. He also has small leather desk items and picture frames in fun colours.

Fashion

A word of warning: what wears well in Marrakech will not necessarily have the same glamour in inner-city London or Washington. Kaftans suit souks not subways and suburban streets. Accessories are another matter, and there's some really fun stuff to be found.

Adolfo de Velasco

Mamounia Hotel, avenue Bab Jedid, Medina (044 44 59 00). **Open** call for details. **Credit** AmEx, MC, V. **Map** p250 A6.
De Velasco's what you call 'local colour', a flamboyant raconteur known for his over-the-top parties and friendships with the famous, rich and royal. He also designs fabulous one-of-a-kind women's kaftans (championed in days of old by *Vogue* mistress Diana Vreeland, no less), which he stashes in giant armoires in his Mamounia (where else?) boutique. There's also a hand-picked selection of antiques and objets d'art. Hope that the man himself is present when you call, for entertaining tales to accompany all purchases.

L'Art de la Couture

42-4 rue Rahba El Biadyne (044 44 04 87/mobile 061 34 40 26). **Open** 9am-1pm, 3.30-7.30pm daily. **Credit** AmEx, MC, V. **Map** p248 C5.
It looks nothing from the outside, nor within for that matter, but this tiny shop sells wonderful classic coats and jackets for men and women, and has made to order for the queen. Cuts are simple with embroidered details in subtle colours. The best garments are made from B'zou wools, a fabric speciality of a small mountain town. Prices start at 1,000dh and custom orders take two weeks (shipping available). Coming from Derb Dabbachi, look for a modest light-pine frontage on the right with an AmEx sticker on the glass.

Beldi

9-11 Soukiat Laksour, Bab Fteuh, Medina (044 44 10 76). **Open** 9.30am-1pm, 3.30-8pm daily. **Credit** MC, V. **Map** p248 C5.

Riad Tamsna. *See p130.*

ALCS
association
de lutte
contre
le sida

"AIDS exists in Morocco too... so protect yourself as well as others"

Since its creation in 1988, the Moroccan Association in the Fight Against AIDS (ALCS), the first of its kind in the Arab world, has focused on two objectives: the prevention of HIV infection and the support of those whose lives are affected by HIV.

The very presence of those living with HIV at the ALCS has enabled us to become a focal point for helping all concerned with this virus, by providing access to all information, access to treatment, defending their right to work, their right to live.

In the domain of prevention, we have chosen to get much closer to the public, especially those groups most vulnerable to infection, by putting ourselves in a position to listen to their reality, to their differences, and to their needs.

Our volunteers constantly lead the fight, both day and night, against ignorance, prejudice and denial. Present in schools, cafés, factories, parks, nightclubs, and on the streets, they listen, explain and inform.

If you would like to support the work of the ALCS, then please email us at:
alcsmarrakech@menara.ma

Toufik studied fashion in Germany and, now back in Marrakech, he and brother Abdelhafid have transformed the family tailoring business into maybe the most talked-about bijou boutique in town. They do both men's and women's ranges in the most beautiful colours and fabrics, fashioned with flair and an eye to Western tastes (this is Moroccan chic that you could actually wear in Barbes, Brixton or Brooklyn). Beautiful handmade velvet coats lined with silk start at around 1,600dh; men's shirts in fine linen at about 400dh. Collections change seasonally.

Eva/Adam

144 Souk El Hanna, Medina (044 44 39 69). **Open** 10am-12.30pm, 3.30-6.30pm Mon-Thur, Sat, Sun. **Credit** AmEx, MC, V. **Map** p248 C4.

No high fashion or class cuts, just practical and genuinely comfortable warm weather clothes in neutral colours. Lots of cottons and lightweight wools. Everything is very loose fitting yet elegant. It's the kind of stuff you might actually wear on a day-to-day basis, and prices are reasonable enough. To find it, walk north up Souk El Attarin just past the entrance to the mosque (to your left), look to the right for the word 'Lacoste' painted on a whitewashed arch: Eva/Adam is the first on the right with barely more than a door as shop frontage.

Au Fil D'Or

10 Souk Semmarine, Medina (044 44 59 19). **Open** 9am-1pm, 2.30-7.30pm Mon-Thur, Sat, Sun; 9am-1pm Fri. **Credit** AmEx, MC, V. **Map** p248 C5.

It's near indistinguishable from the multitude of small stores around, but Au Fil D'Or is worth honing in on for the finest quality babouches and wool jellabas, plus fantastic own-label hand-stitched shirts (400dh) in gorgeous deep hues, and finely braided silk-lined jackets (2,200dh) – just the thing should one be invited to the palace. Note that the bulk of the stock is kept in the cellar-like space downstairs, accessed via a trapdoor behind the counter. Watch your head (and your spending).

Intensite Nomade

139 avenue Mohammed V, Guéliz (044 43 13 33). **Open** 9am-12.30pm, 3-7.30pm Mon-Sat. **Credit** AmEx, MC, V. **Map** p252 B2.

IN features owner-designer Frédérique Birkemeyer's own chic 'nomad' line of colourful kaftans, suede skirts, comfy rafia slippers, men's cotton shirts, leather jackets and inexpensive accessories, as well as providing a rare outlet for pieces by celeb couturier Noureddine Amir (*see p127* **Roots couture**). Pickings are mixed but the place draws a glitzy local clientele, poking around the racks for casual prêt à porter.

La Maison du Kaftan Marocain

65 rue Sidi El Yamami, Medina (044 44 10 51). **Open** 9am-7.30pm daily. **Credit** AmEx, MC, V. **Map** p248 C4.

Ever wondered where Samuel Jackson gets the sharp threads? Yep, check out the photo on the back wall. La Maison may have the unloved, run-down look of a charity store, but it also has the widest selection of Moroccan clothing for men, women and children in the souk, housed in what sustained exploration reveals to be a deceptively vast mausoleum of place. Stock ranges from *pantalon turq* (trad men's trousers) to beautiful velvet jackets and vintage kaftans that go for 20,000dh. Scouts for international fashion houses often drop by placing orders and looking for inspiration.

Marion Theard

Dar Cannaria, 54 rue des Banques, Medina (044 42 66 09). **Open** call for details. **No credit cards.** **Map** p248 C5.

Marion Theard was the Marrakech connection for Parisian shoe guru Christian Louboutin, but after a few years of working with him she split off to do her own line of women's accessories. You can see her fabulous embroidered sacks and slippers, plus bath, table and home accessories all in natural fabrics, in a tiny shop she has opened in her own riad just behind Café de France.

Mia Zia

Quartier Industriel Sidi Ghanem No.322, route de Safi (044 33 59 38/www.miazia.com). **Open** 8am-6pm Mon-Fri; 8am-5pm Sat. **Credit** MC, V.

Fashion designer Valerie Barkowski has ultra-chic shops in Paris, Marseille, Geneva and Saint-Barth, but in Marrakech you can visit her factory showroom – full of stripy socks, babouches and jumpers, crisp white cotton bed linen with embroidered borders and plush fringed towels – and pay half what you would in Europe. New designs come and go with the seasons, but stripes are a staple. She shares a showroom with Akkal (*see p133*) – a short taxi ride north of town in the Quartier Industriel; *see p117* for directions.

Tazidriss

13 rue de la Mauritanie, Guéliz (044 44 34 04). **Open** 9am-8.30pm Mon-Sat. **Credit** MC, V. **Map** p252 B2.

Owner Rachid – who speaks good English – stocks traditional Moroccan wear (from simple cotton shirts to elaborate kaftans) at fair fixed prices. Ideal if you can't be hassled with the bustle of the souk. Rachid's happy for customers to try things on and take their time. He also does a large choice of fabrics.

Fashion accessories

Comptoir Boutique

avenue Echouada, Hivernage (044 43 77 02). **Open** 5.30-11pm Mon-Sat. **Credit** MC, V. **Map** p252 C4.

Tucked out back of the fashionable restaurant-club (*see p113/154*), Florence Taranne's small and very pink boutique stocks a quirky hand-picked collection of boho Moro chic, including rafia shoes from Essaouira, leather shopping bags with khamsa ('hand') motif, lamps fashioned from gaudy tin-plate packaging, '70s-patterned babouches, Hassan

Eat, Drink, Shop

Shopping the souk

The souk is, above all else, the scene of an invisible tug of war. Most tourists enter prepared to admire its historical and architectural details, but disinclined to peruse the thousands of shops that are the real reason for its existence. Shopkeepers, for their part, cajole and entreat in a dozen languages and are determined not to permit visitors to indulge in such a non-commercial activity as sightseeing.

The only way to shop the souk successfully is to ignore unwanted overtures. Saunter purposefully avoiding eye contact. Indecision, hesitancy and fatigue will be punished by inveigling offers of tea and assistance. If you have a particular item in mind, head for the section that specialises in it. General handicrafts and great bric-a-brac emporia are scattered everywhere (though particularly concentrated on the two main souk streets of rue Mouassine and rue Semarine), but other trades tend to huddle together, as indicated on the map on page 67.

Debate rages on the issue of guides. Yes, they can zero in quickly on the shops selling the item or items that you're looking for, and yes, they can haggle on your behalf, but wherever they lead it always ends in a commission and that goes on your bill. The size of that commission also determines where you shop, overshadowing any issues of quality and worth that you might have. If you've even a gnat's pimple of independence, forget the guide and go it alone.

Hajjaj T-shirts and Taranne's own-designed summer-of-love clothing (including glamorous see-through jellabas). Look out for her new boutique, Kulchi, which is due to open at 1 rue Ksour in the Medina any day now.

Jewellery

Most of the jewellery for sale in Marrakech is ethnic in either inspiration or origin. Favoured materials are silver, amber and beads, and pieces tend toward heavy and chunky. Nice but monotonous. For something fresher check out the work of Amina Agueznay (see p127 **Roots Couture**), available at the **Amanjena** (see p128) and **Riad Tamsna** (see p130).

Bazaar Atlas
129 boulevard Mohammed V, Guéliz (044 43 27 16).
Open 9.30am-1pm, 3.30-7.30pm Mon-Sat; 9.30am-1pm Sun. **Credit** MC, V. **Map** p252 B2.
A small but eye-catching boutique in central Guéliz (opposite the Marché Central) of one room lined with floor-to-ceiling cabinets filled with jewellery: antique, antique-styled, ethnic (Berber and Touareg) and modern. In among it all is also a smattering of odd gift items including ceramics and everything from tiny silver pill boxes to sculpted gazelle horn and camel bone ink wells and letter openers. The owner speaks fluent English.

Bellawi
Kessariat Lossta No.56, off Souk El Attarin, Medina (044 44 01 07). **Open** 9am-7pm Mon-Thur, Sat, Sun. **No credit cards. Map** p248 C4.
Different spelling but same family: Abdelatif, whose closet-like jewellery store this is, is brother to the famed Mustapha of 'Blaoui' emporium fame (see p130). Here, there's just about room for Abdelatif, his workbench and one customer. The walls are hung with beads clustered like bunches of berry fruits, along with a fine selection of traditional Moroccan-style silver bangles and necklaces, and rings set with semi-precious stones. The shop is along the same narrow passage as Eva/Adam (see p123); no sign in English but just ask for Abdelatif – eveyone knows him, he's been here 39 years.

Boutique Bel Hadj
22-3 Fundouk Ourzazi, place Bab Fteuh, Medina (044 44 12 58). **Open** 9am-8pm daily.
Credit AmEx, MC, V. **Map** p248 C5.
The landmark Café Argana on Jemaa El Fna occupies the south-west corner of an old *fundouk* (merchants' inn); walk right round the corner and into place Bab Ftouh to enter and you'll find Mohammed Bari's shop, which is piled high with a mad assortment of bits and pieces of jewellery, old and new. The range and quality are impressive, the prices are fair and Mohammed will never try and foist off the newly made as antique (not knowingly, anyway).

Micheline Perrin
Mamounia Hotel, avenue Bab Jedid, Medina (044 38 86 00/mobile 061 618 215).
Open 10am-1pm, 4-8pm daily. **Credit** AmEx, MC, V. **Map** p250 A6.
Perrin is one of the old guard who blew into Marrakech during its glamorous '70s heydays. Her jewellery shop is in the little forecourt kiosk around which the Mamounia driveway arcs. She sells self-designed enamelled pieces that are a fusion of Moroccan and Indian stylings, as well as lots of one-of-a-kind necklaces strung from old and new stones. There's usually a display of her creations in the vitrines in the lobby of the hotel.

El Yed Gallery

66 Fhal Chidmi, rue Mouassine, Medina (044 44 29 95). **Open** 9.30am-12.30pm, 1.30-6.30pm Mon-Sat. **Credit** AmEx, MC, V. **Map** p248 C4.

Opposite the side of the Mouassine Mosque, El Yed is a real collectors' haunt, specialising solely in beautiful antique Moroccan jewellery and pottery. Much of it comes from the deep south and it's not for the delicate of frame – bracelets look like great silver sprockets and the favoured stone is amber by the hunk. The owner speaks English and is highly knowledgeable about his stock, and happy to discuss details and provenance, but probably less willing to talk prices, which are fixed and expensive.

Lighten up at **Amira**. *See p128.*

Leather

Galerie Birkemeyer

169 rue Mohammed El Bekal, Guéliz (044 44 69 63). **Open** 8.30am-12.30pm, 3-7.30pm Mon-Sat; 9am-12.30pm Sun. **Credit** AmEx, MC, V. **Map** p252 A2.

A long-established haunt for leather goods from handbags and luggage, to shoes, jackets, coats and skirts, with a sportswear section of international designer labels. The sales assistants aren't particularly helpful and founder Ms Birkemeyer no longer has anything to do with the place (she now owns Intensite Nomade, *see p123*), but you still might stumble across a bargain, such as a beautifully crafted purse for 600dh.

Place Vendome

141 avenue Mohammed V, Guéliz (044 43 52 63). **Open** 9am-12.30pm, 3.30-7.30pm Mon-Sat. **Credit** AmEx, MC, V. **Map** p252 B2.

Owner Claude Amzallag is known for his custom-designed buttery leather and suede jackets, and sleek line of handbags and wallets, which come in every colour from forest green to hot pink. The suede shirts for men and stylish luggage are also big hits with the fortysomething crowd.

Shoes

Atika

35 rue de la Liberté, Guéliz (044 43 64 09). **Open** 8.30am-12.30pm, 3-7.30pm Mon-Sat. **Credit** MC, V. **Map** p252 B2.

This small shop is where well-heeled residents and enlightened tourists flock for stylish and affordable men's and women's ranges – everything from classic loafers and spiky black pumps to natural leather sandals and stylish beige canvas mules. Prices start at 300dh and rarely go beyond 750dh. It also carries a small selection of handbags. There's a second branch a few hundred metres south at 212 avenue Mohammed V.

Cordonnerie Errafia

Riad Zeitoun El Jedid, Medina (mobile 062 77 83 47). **Open** 9am-1pm, 3-9pm daily. **No credit cards**. **Map** p251 D7.

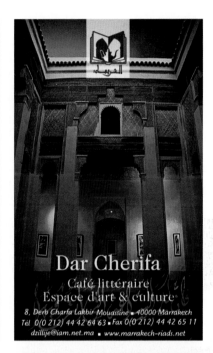

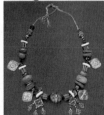

Roots couture

Fashion and Marrakech go way back. Yves Saint Laurent and partner Pierre Bergé moved in on the Medina way back in the 1970s. They picked up on the soft and spicy colours and waft of voluminous fabric, and took the kaftan from hippie to hip. And it's never looked back. Gucci's Tom Ford updated the souk look in 1996 with urban jellabas in figured velvet, black lace and patterned chiffon; Oscar de la Renta used the kaftan as evening wear, adorned with gold lace; Dolce & Gabbana kept the traditional hood but sliced the sleeves off; Jean Paul Gaultier topped his lime-green robe-thing with a fez.

But while Marrakech has long thrilled as a source, it's rarely been a supplier. For Moroccan fashion, read copy-cat dressmaking and tailoring; a craft rather than an art. That is changing. A new wave of young Moroccan designers are rediscovering the traditional shapes and materials of their parents' wardrobes and going at the contents with scissors, pins and thread.

Bright talent of the moment is **Noureddine Amir**, born in Rabat in 1967 but resident since 2001 in Marrakech. He employs natural linens and wools, combining with hand-painting, trad stitching and embroidery to ultra-chic, sophisticated effect. His designs have featured in the work of feted film-maker Shirin Neshat, and in 2003 will be paraded in Antwerp and London. Some of his designs are on sale at Intensite Nomade (see p123) or phone to visit the showroom.

Kenza Melehi also draws her inspiration from traditional Moorish culture – specifically from the Jewish Sephardic community and the styles of Arab-Andalucía. Originally from Assilah near Tangier, she moved south to Marrakech in 1996 in search of 'authenticity'. Her designs incorporate calligraphic, kufic and architectural motifs applied to Indian silks and local wools. The results are very feminine and very sexy. Call to visit her atelier in the Medina.

Trained as an architect, Casablanca-born **Amina Agueznay** traded draughting board for jewellers' loup. She takes antique silver, pearls, ribbon, coral, shells and even buttons and combines with semi-precious stones to create the most flamboyant and strikingly modern jewellery. Some of her work can be bought at Riad Tamsna (see p130) and the Amanjena boutiques (see p128), and shortly at an as yet undecided studio location in Marrakech, following a move to the pink city in early 2003. 'Casablanca,' she explains, 'is the centre of the fashion industry, but Marrakech is its soul'.

Amina Agueznay
Mobile 063 61 88 10. **Open** by appointment.

Kenza Designs
Mobile 061 16 07 09. **Open** by appointment.

Noureddine Amir
Mobile 044 43 12 84. **Open** by appointment.

In a little workshop opposite the Préfecture de la Medina, artisan Ahmed cobbles together classic loafers out of rafia for gents, with more extravagantly coloured and cut stylings for women. Given three or four days, he can also make to order.

Florists

There's a corner given over to florists at the **Marché Central** (see p132 **Markets**) in Guéliz, and an excellent flowerseller at the **Mamounia** (see p41).

Vita
58 boulevard Mansour Eddahbi, Guéliz (044 43 04 90). **Open** 8.30am-12.30pm, 3-7.30pm Mon-Sat; 9am-1pm Sun. **No credit cards**. **Map** p252 B2.
A Western-style florist-garden centre with a decent stock of cut flowers and ready-made bouquets. It also does delivery (local and Interflora), and sells potted plants, seeds and compost.

Food & drink

The greatest range of food and drink is found at **Awsak Assalaam** and **Marjane** (for both, see p118). For fresh fruit and veg there's the Marché Couvert and Mellah market in the Medina, and the Marché Central in Guéliz: see p132 **Markets**.

Entrepôt Alimentaire
117 avenue Mohammed V, Guéliz (044 43 00 67). **Open** 8am-noon, 3-10pm Mon-Sat; 8am-noon Sun. **No credit cards**. **Map** p252 B2.
A dusty little place that appears disorganised, but it does have one of the best selections of wine (Moroccan and French) in town. If you can't see it, ask.

Hassan Oumlile
Marché Central No.19, avenue Mohammed V, Guéliz (044 43 33 86). **Open** 8am-8pm Mon-Thur, Sat; 8am-12.30pm Fri, Sun. **Credit** MC, V. **Map** p252 B2.

Mr Oumlile's small shop in the Guéliz central market is well stocked with a decent selection of local wines and beers, some very good cheeses and imported butter, plus basic groceries. He speaks excellent English.

Jeff de Bruges
17 rue de la Liberté, Guéliz (044 43 02 49).
Open 9am-1pm, 3.30-8pm Mon-Sat. **Credit** MC, V.
Map p252 B2.
The best chocolates in Marrakech bar none. They make a great gift if you're invited to dinner at a local home (Moroccans are notoriously sweet-toothed), but don't expect a share because they'll be hoarded away for later. There's also a branch at Marjane (*see p118*).

Yacout Services
2 rue Yakoub El Marini, Guéliz (044 43 19 41).
Open 8am-9pm daily. **No credit cards**.
Map p252 C3.
Just south of place du 16 Novembre and not far from the church, Yacout is a fantastically well-stocked minimarket with a basement store devoted to booze – local and imported wines, beer and spirits. Plus, next door is a shop that does own-made pasta.

Health food

Marrakech Bio Diététique
91 avenue Houman El Fetouaki, Arset El Maach, Medina (044 42 75 67). **Open** 9am-1pm, 3-7pm daily. **No credit cards**. **Map** p250 C7.
The city's first organic shop is still in its initial stages and supply can be patchy, but on a good day expect the likes of organic aubergines, tomatoes and squash, plus walnuts from the mountains, cold-pressed olive oil, whole grains, wheatgerm and beautifully packaged organic herbal teas (including mint and verveine). More interesting are the various oils and essences, including argan and amlou (a mix of argan, almonds and honey). Marrakech Bio Diététique is opposite the northern end of the Marché Couvert, down a short passageway where crafts are sold.

Home accessories

By which we mean crystal, china and pottery, furnishings and drapes, lanterns and candles, gee-gaws and assorted knick-knacks…
In this city of a 1,001 interior designers, 'home accessories' is just about the biggest business in town.

Amanjena
Route de Ouarzazate, km12 (044 40 33 53).
Open 10am-7pm daily. **Credit** AmEx, MC, V.
In addition to the household range of Aman lifestyle accessories, the three boutiques at this most exclusive of resorts (*see p57*) also specialise in the most desirable of local products. At the time of writing, it's the only place in Marrakech to find the designs

of Valerie Barkowski (*see p123* Mia Zia) and woven fabrics by Bridgette Perkins (*see below*) By appointment), as well as candles by Amira (*see below*) and jewellery by Amina Agueznay (*see p127* **Roots couture**). It's a long way to go just to shop (so phone first to double-check opening times) but tie it in with a fine Thai lunch (*see p114*) beside the pool and it might be worthwhile.

Amira
Lot El Massar No.522, route de Safi (044 33 62 47/ amirabougies@hotmail.com). **Open** 9am-1pm, 2-6pm Mon-Sat. **No credit cards**.
Candles are a core element of magical Moroccan nights, and the best are made by Amira, run by Rodolphe and Geraldine from Brittany. They come in all kinds of unexpected shapes and colours: giant orange or purple cubes, candles that can also be used as vases, knee-high stripy cylinders and candles within candles. Amira also has simple contemporary bases to complement the wax. Selected pieces can be bought at the Amanjena boutiques, but for the full range you need to head out to the factory showroom on the outskirts of town close by the Sidi Ghanem industrial zone; it'll cost about 30dh each way by taxi. The place is near impossible to find so call for directions.

Best Ameublement
rue de la Liberté, Guéliz (no phone). **Open** 8.30am-1pm, 3-8pm Mon-Thur, Sat, Sun. **No credit cards**.
Map p252 B2.
The Barrada brothers have six shops in Marrakech, all selling traditional cushions and banquettes (the long mattresses that line the sitting rooms of most riads) to posh homes, riads and hotels. Theirs is a high quality product, sales service is efficient and prices are reasonable.

Casa Mangani
26 rue Tarek Ibn Ziad, Guéliz (044 43 56 34).
Open 3-7.30pm Mon; 9am-1pm, 3-7.30pm Tue-Sat. **Credit** AmEx, MC, V. **Map** p252 B2.
An upmarket shop specialising in rococo and otherwise florid designs in silver, crystal and fancy china (the latter from Florence), plus tableware, chandeliers, lamps and a sumptuous choice of Moroccan fabrics and cushions fit to grace a photo spread in *World of Interiors* (copies of which are liberally scattered around the shop). Look out for owner Fouzia Bennis's cold-pressed organic olive oil in leather-sleeved bottles from her farm just outside town.

Cherkaoui
120-22 rue Mouassine, Medina (044 42 68 17/ m.cherkaoui@wanadoo.net.ma). **Open** 8.30am-7.30pm daily. **Credit** AmEx, MC, V. **Map** p248 C4.
Opposite the Mouassine fountain, this is one of those glittering Aladdin's cave places full of everything imaginable for home decoration Moroccan style (except carpets). The proprietors, one local (Jaoud) and one German (Matthias), use their own local artisans, working in various media, including wood,

Mustapha Blaoui (the shop not the cat).
See p130.

leather, metal and clay, to supply the store. Customers include the famed restaurant Dar Yacout (*see p102*) and the ritzy Hotel les Jardins de la Koutoubia. Any piece can be made up in eight to ten weeks and overseas shipping can be arranged.

Founoun Marrakech
28 Souk des Teinturiers, Medina (044 42 62 03).
Open 10am-7pm daily. **No credit cards.**
Map p248 C4.
This is the place if you want a lantern (*founoun*) of quality. At first glance it's tiny, but walk through to the glittering back room where there's an impressive choice of truly beautiful things. Rachid El Himel, the owner, is both helpful and charming; ask nicely and he'll take you through to the workshop in which a team of men and young boys hammer and cut at sheets of copper fashioning the goods to fill the shop. To find it, walk east past the Mouassine fountain, then through the arch, and it's the first lantern shop on the left.

Lun'art Gallery
24 rue Moulay Ali, Guéliz (044 44 72 66).
Open 9am-12.30pm, 3.30-8pm Mon-Sat.
Credit AmEx, MC, V. **Map** p252 A2.
Eclecticism reigns supreme at this rather odd gallery-cum-Moro curio shop. It has a garden space showcasing wrought iron garden furniture and heavy mosaic tables, while indoors is a grab bag of modern paintings by Moroccan artists, traditional pottery, tadelakt lamps, bric-a-brac and the odd curveball such as cinema costume accessories (for example, neckties left over from the filming of Scorcese's *Kundun*). Prices at Lun'art Gallery are very reasonable.

La Medina
Quartier Industriel Sidi Ghanem No.24, route de Safi (044 33 61 32/www.la-medina.fr). **Open** 8.30am-12.30pm, 2.30-6.30pm Mon-Sat. **No credit cards.**
Everything designed by Thierry Isnardon for his super-stylish restaurant Foundouk (see p106), from the salt and pepper sets to the tables and chairs, is available to purchase at this warehouse-showroom space. In addition, there's a wide selection of non-Foundouk ceramics and artisana that Isnardon has designed for wholesale distribution to shops and boutiques throughout Europe. For information on how to get to the Quartier Industriel, see the introduction to this chapter on *p117*.

Mustapha Blaoui
142-4 Bab Doukkala, Medina (044 38 52 40).
Open 9am-8pm daily. **Credit** AmEx, MC, V.
Map p248 B4.
This is the classiest, most beloved 'best of Morocco' depot in town. It's a warehouse of a place crammed, racked and piled with floor-to-ceiling irresistibles – lanterns, dishes, pots, bowls, candlesticks, chandeliers, chests, tables and chairs… If Mustapha doesn't have it, then you don't need it. He supplied almost all the furnishings for the sublime Villa des Orangers (*see p39*). Even people who

don't own a hotel will find it almost impossible to visit here and not fill a container lorry. Added to which, Mustapha's a real sweetheart, his staff are ultra-helpful and shipping is a cinch.

Mustapha Latrach
7 Souk Labbadine, Medina (044 44 42 13).
Open 9am-7pm daily. **Credit** MC, V. **Map** p248 C4.
Monsieur Latrach has a gem of a shop not far from the dyers' souk filled with authentic antique mint teapots, including quite a few bearing old English hallmarks – highly collectible and becoming ever harder to find. Prices start at around 1,000dh. You'll also find here all the other accoutrements necessary for the correct setting of a table.

Riad Tamsna
23 Derb Zanka Daika, off Riad Zitoun El Jedid (044 38 52 72/www.tamsna.com). **Open** 10am-midnight daily. **Credit** MC, V. **Map** p250 C6.
Tamsna is a 400-year-old riad owned and restored by Meryanne Loum-Martin, housing a restaurant (*see p109*), gallery, bookshop and small first-floor boutique. All items have been carefully chosen by Loum-Martin and lean toward the exquisite and exclusive: Limoges china à la Maroc designed by Arielle de Brichambaut; hand-woven fabrics from Senegal made up into ethno-chic purses, shawls and slippers; plus limited edition jewellery by local artists. Loum-Martin's own striking furniture and accessories are also available for sale (displayed throughout the riad, as well as at the Dar and Jnane Tamsna houses, *see p65*).

Scènes du Lin
70 rue de la Liberté, Guéliz (044 43 61 08).
Open 9.30am-12.30pm, 3.30-7.30pm Mon-Sat.
Credit MC, V. **Map** p252 B2.

Owned by Anne-Marie Chaoui, this is an ultra-chic fabric store that specialises in linens, and also offers a huge range of brilliant hues in striped woven cloth or delicate pastel organdie. Any combo can be ordered for custom-made curtains, tablecloths or place settings. There's plenty of other top quality stuff besides, including luxurious fringed hammam towels, cushions with Fès embroidery, natural essential oils and unusual contemporary lamps.

Carpets

The greatest concentration of carpet sellers is in and around the Souk des Tapis, which lies immediately north of the Rahba Kedima (map p248 C5), lapping up against the Sidi Ishak Mosque. **El Badii** (*see p119*) in Guéliz also carries an extensive stock in the basement showroom. Prices are wholly dependent on age, quality and type, but for a good-quality piece of carpet of about three by two metres (nine by six feet) expect to pay around 8,000dh and have to drink significant amounts of mint tea.

L'Art de Goulimine
25 Souk des Tapis, Medina (044 44 02 22).
Open 9am-6.30pm daily. **Credit** AmEx, MC, V.
Map p248 C5.
For something a little different, Rabia and Ahmed are two young dealers specialising in Rhamana carpets, which originate in the villages on the plains north of Marrakech. They have a small showroom displaying choice pieces downstairs from the main sales space, where you'll find plenty of all the more usual carpet types at competitive prices.

Bazaar du Sud
117 Souk des Tapis, Medina (044 44 30 04).
Open 9am-6.30pm daily. **Credit** AmEx, MC, V.
Map p248 C5.
This place has possibly the largest selection of carpets in the souk, covering all regions and styles, new and old. The owners tell us that they have 17 buyers out at any one time scouring the country for the finest examples. Although considerable effort goes into supplying collectors and dealers worldwide, sales staff are just as happy to entertain and advise the novice. Prices range from 2,000dh to 350,000dh. Ask for Mustapha, who speaks perfect English.

Bazaar les Palmiers
145 Souk Dakkakine, Medina (044 44 46 29).
Open 9am-7pm Mon-Thur, Sat, Sun. **Credit** AmEx, MC, V. **Map** p248 C5.
Hamid is a fourth-generation carpet dealer. His passion is carpets from the High Atlas, characterised by their beautiful colouring. His pieces take in the old and not-so-old, with prices starting at an affordable 100dh (although all that gets you is a cushion). He speaks English and is happy to expound on his favourite subject over a glass of mint tea.

Furniture

In addition to the places listed below, for something in a traditional vein pay a visit to **Mustapha Blaoui** (*see p130*); for something a little more unique look at the work of Thierry Isnardon at **La Medina** (*see p130*), Meryanne Loum-Martin at **Riad Tamsna** (*see p130*) and that of **Fréderic Butz** and the **Noula** people: *see p134* **By appointment**.

Scenes of **Scènes de Lin.**

Eat, Drink, Shop

Markets

The greater part of the Marrakech Medina is one vast market, but away from the main lanes of the souk are several other areas of concentrated open-air commerce.

Down in the old Jewish quarter of the Mellah there's a daily **street market** (*map p251 D7*) one block east of the place des Ferblantiers. It's very much a local affair with traders selling predominantly fruit and vegetables, herbs and spices. Few tourists venture around here.

Nearby, on the south side of avenue Houman El Fetouaki is the **Marché Couvert** (*map p250 C7*), again a working market supplying fresh produce, meat and fish to the kitchens of the homes of the southern Medina.

At the opposite extreme, in all senses, is the **Souk El Khemis** (*map p249 D2*). At the northern end of the Old City, just inside the Bab El Khemis gate, it's as much rubbish dump as market. A last chance saloon for manufactured goods, stalls here can be no more than a blanket spread with a pitiful heap of cast-offs – single shoes, a box of rusted bicycle gears, a bag of unravelled audio cassettes. But it's also a legendary treasure trove of architectural salvage. Palmeraie villas have been kitted out at the Souk El Khemis, and when the Mamounia underwent its last refit, the discarded sinks, fittings and even carpets all turned up here.

Away from the Medina, the **Marché Central** (*map p252 B2*) on Guéliz's main avenue Mohammed V is a low-slung terracotta building sheltering no more than a couple of dozen stalls. It's where the city's expats come to buy fruit and veg, meat and fish, cheese and wine, Cheerios and Frosties. There are also a number of craft stalls where

quality is high and prices beat those in the souk. The dry central fountain is beloved of neighbourhood cats.

A kilometre east, just off avenue Yacoub El Mansour and in the neighbourhood of the Majorelle Gardens, is the city's **Wholesale Market** (*map p252 C1*). Operating from seven to ten each morning, it's where farmers from outlying villages bring crates of oranges and tomatoes, baskets of dates and grapes. There's little for casual buyers but some great photo opportunities.

Ministero del Gusto

22 Derb Azouz El Mouassine, off rue Sidi El Yamami, Medina (044 42 64 55). **Open** 9.30am-noon Mon-Fri. **Credit** MC, V. **Map** p248 C4.

The Ministero is HQ to ex-*Vogue Italia* fashion editor Alessandra Lippini and her business partner Fabrizio Bizzarri. It's a surreal space – a sort of Gaudi goes Mali with a side trip to Mexico. As well as filling the role of informal social centre for friends and assorted fashionistas and creatives blowing through town, the two floors of Del Gusto also act as a sometime gallery (*see p146*) and showcase for funky 'found' objects (sourced from house clearances) such as African-inspired furniture, chairs by

Eames, plus on our visit a famed *Dr No* Jo Colombo chair, Bernini glassware and also a fun vintage clothing corner.

Glassware

Myriam Roland-Gosselin

6 route de l'aeroport (044 36 19 88). **Open** by appointment only. **No credit cards**.

Roland-Gosselin has a studio in a tranquil garden just off the airport road where she makes delicate hand-blown glass objects for the home. Her collection, exhibited in an adjacent showroom, consists of

vases, tumblers, bowls, wine glasses, candle holders and small lamps. Her colour schemes range from neutral to warm ambers and oranges that bring to mind fiery Moroccan sunsets. Purchases are packaged in her lovely signature boxes.

Metalwork

Artisant Berbere

33 Souk El Attarin, Medina (044 44 38 78). **Open** 9am-8pm daily. **Credit** MC, V. **Map** p248 C4.

A charming dusty old emporium of bric-a-brac, filled with heaps of largely useless items fashioned from brass, copper, pewter and other pliable metals. Lots of trays, pots and lamps, plus ancient flat irons and giant sculpted animals. And you've got to love a place that promises on its business card 'small margin profit'.

Dinanderie

6-46 Fundouk My Mamoun, Mellah, Medina (044 38 49 09). **Open** 8am-8pm Mon-Sat. **Credit** MC, V. **Map** p250 C7.

Moulay Yousef is one of the country's handful of elite artisans. If you need something extravagant wrought from metal – and if you have the money – then Moulay is your man. The bulk of his work is made to order (when we visited his team was putting the finishing touches to a pair of splendid doors to grace the gatehouse of a Palmeraie villa), but adjacent to his workspace is also a crowded gallery of smaller pieces. A little difficult to find, the Dinanderie atelier fills an alley immediately west of the small rose garden across from the place des Ferblantiers.

Mohammed Ouledlhachmi

34 Souk El Hararin Kedima, Medina (066 64 41 05). **Open** 9am-6pm Mon-Thur, Sat, Sun. **No credit cards**. **Map** p248 C4.

Mohammed does copper. Copper trays, copper pots, copper kettles, copper you-name-it. Some of the pieces are new, but the bulk of the stock is aged. Mohammed sometimes has pieces by well-known metalsmiths whose work is highly prized by collectors. To find him, head north up Souk El Attarin and take the second right after passing the entrance to the mosque (which is on the left).

Pottery

In addition to the shops and outlets below, there's a dedicated **pottery market** (map p247 F4) just outside the southern Medina walls, a couple of hundred metres east of the Bab Ghemat. Styles are traditional, but include brightly coloured pieces from Safi, patterned vessels from Fès and plain terracotta from Marrakech.

Akkal

Quartier Industriel Sidi Ghanem No.322, route de Safi (044 33 59 38). **Open** 8am-6pm Mon-Fri; 8am-5pm Sat. **Credit** MC, V.

The Akkal pottery factory does Conran-worthy modern takes on classic Moroccan shapes (tajines to tea glasses) and pick 'n' mix dinnerware, all of which come in the most fantastically rich colours. It's stronger than average Moroccan pottery but not quite as dishwasher-proof as it claims. It still needs handling with care – looks great on the shelves, though. Akkal also offers overseas shipping.

Caverne d'Ali Baba

17A Fhal Chidmi, Mouassine, Medina (044 44 21 48). **Open** 9am-8pm daily. **Credit** MC, V. **Map** p248 C5.

Ali Baba's an Akkal imitator, but a good one. This huge shop is stocked with an incredible array of everything from egg cups to lamp bases in all imaginable colours. In fact, just about any pottery trend that has hit the Medina will very quickly be copied and put on sale here. Especially attractive are the tadelakt-finish items, which have an almost soft leather-like appearance. But beware water leakage from the vases.

Création Chez Abdel

17 Souk des Teinturiers, Medina (044 42 75 17). **Open** 9am-9pm daily. **No credit cards**. **Map** p248 C4.

Another good outlet for tadelakt pottery. This is a small shop packed from floor to ceiling with simple shapes in rich, luminous colours. There are great bowls and lamps, but also more portable items such as candlesticks, ashtrays and bowls for the light traveller. Prices are reasonable. There's no name on the shop so it can be difficult to spot – walk east past the Mouassine fountain and there's a sharp right, then a left, then Abdel's is the pine-framed door on the right.

Textiles

Art Ouarzarzate

15 rue Rahba Kedima, Medina (067 35 21 24). **Open** 10am-6.30pm daily. **Credit** MC, V. **Map** p248 C5.

A small sparsely stocked shop, but with an interesting stock, including beautiful throws handwoven from agave fibres. Colours are jewel-like and prices pretty reasonable. There are also old kaftans and jellabas, and babouches made of silk (about 200dh a pair). Mohammed speaks English and you can accept his offer of tea, without feeling cornered into buying.

Chez Brahim

101 Rahba Lakdima, Medina (044 44 01 10). **Open** 9.30am-6.30pm daily. **Credit** AmEx, MC, V. **Map** p248 C5.

Brahim offers an overwhelming selection of fabulous Moroccan textiles. His collection covers all regions and styles. Many of his textiles are old and it is hard to find things like his elsewhere. Chez Brahim is like going to a museum where everything is for sale. Prices are steep, but these are collectors' pieces.

Riad El Cadi

87 Derb Moulay Abdelkader, off Derb Debbachi, Medina (044 37 86 55. **Open** 10am-noon, 2-6pm Mon-Sat. **Credit** MC, V. **Map** p249 D5.

One of the city's best riads (*see p47*) also contains a small boutique (and you don't have to be a house guest to visit). Proprietor and collector Herwig Bartels sells on some of the pieces that he's acquired but chosen not to keep, including the best of traditional Moroccan designs in textiles, wood and metal. Visit here and you'll get the benefit of an expert eye.

Leisure

Bookshops

This is not a literary city and reading matter in any language is scarce, though particularly so in English. Beyond the places listed below, **Riad Tamsna** (*see p130*) and the **Musée de Marrakech** (*see p66*) both have bookshops, as does the **Mamounia** (*see p41*), but nowhere will you find anything much beyond coffee-table volumes and guides.

ACR Libraire d'Art

Immobelier Tayeb, 55 boulevard Mohammed Zerktouni, Guéliz (044 44 67 92). **Open** 8am-7.30pm Mon-Fri. **Credit** MC, V. **Map** p252 B2.

ACR is a French publishing house notable for its lavish art books. It's also seemingly dedicated to photographing every last mudbrick and orange blosom in Marrakech and publishing the results in a series of coffee-table volumes. Get them all here, along with other (non-ACR) titles on the art and architecture of Morocco and the Islamic world, guides, cookery books and art cards. Mostly in French but some material in English.

Librairie Chatr

23 avenue Mohammed V, Guéliz (044 44 79 97). **Open** 8am-1pm, 3-8pm Mon-Sat. **Credit** MC, V. **Map** p252 A2.

These days it's mainly a stationers, the long bar counter perpetually swamped by short-trousered fiends in search of marker pens and notebooks, but there is a large back room where a heavy patina of dust fogs the titles of what's mainly Arabic and French stock. A single shelf represents the English-language world and most of what it contains is heavier on pictures than words.

By appointment

What started with the likes of American architect-decorator Bill Willis and the French designer Jacqueline Foissac back in the late '60s and '70s – foreign designer settles in town, absorbs ethnic influences – continues today with a new wave of expat designers fusing the skills and talents of local artisans with 21st-century styling. Their work adorns and enhances many of the new wave of *maison d'hôtes*, as well as providing more fab things to shop for.

French designer **Bridgette Perkins**'s passion for textile weaving has resurrected and redefined the craft in Marrakech. Her influence can be seen in all the *sabara* (synthetic silk) striped fabrics hanging in the souk. She uses natural yarns imported from France and Italy and her colour and design sense is excellent. Her latest work is made more extraordinary by the addition of fine embroidery. Some of her textiles are available at the Amanjena boutiques (*see p128*), but for the greatest selection you need to make an appointment to visit her studio.

Fréderic Butz had a blossoming career in Paris but fell in love with Marrakech so settled and set up **FB Design**. He works in stainless steel, creating silvery-grey sculpted

forms that are softened by curves and rounded edges. His range includes cabinets, cupboards, coffee-tables, desks, chairs and beds – the latter adorned by sharply coloured local fabrics. Pieces are made to order but some of the smaller accessories are available to casual callers.

Bernard Schmidt (five years in Marrakech designing in metal) and Alexandrine Soudry (a fabrics specialist) work together under the name **Nouala**, producing furniture and textiles. Oversized metal mirrors, grand candelabras, beds, lamps, chairs and tables, all with hand-hammered textures and sculptural finishing combine with glamorous fabrics shot through with gold and velvet. Accessories include graphically embroidered giant cushions, pillows, curtains, bedspreads and even tent linings. Items are made to order, although certain pieces are available ready-to-go at their showroom.

Bridgette Perkins

044 37 74 16. **Open** by appointment only.

FB Design

044 37 80 78. **Open** by appointment only.

Nouala

044 38 54 15. **Open** by appointment only.

Animal rights activists just love **Ministero del Gusto**. *See p132.*

Maktabet El Chab

rue Mouassine, Medina (044 44 34 17).
Open 8.30am-8.30pm daily. **No credit cards.**
Map p248 C5.
Aka the FNAC Berber bookshop, this corner kiosk claims to be 'La première librairie à Marrakech', founded in 1941. Stock is pitifully limited – a handful of tourist guides, coffee-table volumes and postcards. Still, full marks for perseverance.

Newsagents

The two best newstands are either side of avenue Mohammed V in Guéliz: one outside the Marché Central, the other beside the tourist office, just off place Abdel Moumen. There's also a reasonably good stand outside the Hotel CTM on Jemaa El Fna.

Services

Beauty & hair salons

Suntan lotion is available at pharmacies (*see below*), but the choice is better at **Marjane** (*see p118*).

Salon Jacques Dessange

Sofitel Marrakech, rue Harroun Errachid, Hivernage (044 43 34 95). **Open** 10am-8pm daily. **Credit** call for details. **Map** p252 C5.
A French hairdresser, formerly at the Meridien, with a growing reputation among the moneyed set.

L'Univers de la Femme

22 rue Bab Agnaou, Medina (044 44 12 96).
Open 9am-1pm, 3-8pm Tue-Sun. **Credit** MC, V. **Map** p250 C6.
All beauty treatments are available here, and the well-trained assistants know how to look after you. The pleasant surroundings are perfect for pampering (at affordable prices).

Yves Rocher

13 rue de la Liberté, Guéliz (044 44 82 62).
Open 9am-1pm, 3-7pm Mon-Sat. **No credit cards.**
Map p252 B2.
The French beauty chain has several sites, but the rue de la Liberté branch is the easiest to find. All offer moderately priced beauty products as well as manicures, pedicures, facials and epilation.

Dry-cleaning

Superpressing

12 avenue Oued El Makhazine, Guéliz (044 43 67 62).
Open 8.30am-12.30pm, 2-8pm Mon-Sat. **No credit cards.** **Map** p252 B3.
A professionally run outfit and one of the few to offer a one-hour service (which actually means same-day), but it's still a big improvement on the competition). It's next to the central police station – which must be handy for them.

Electrics

Possibly the best place for everything electric is hypermarché **Marjane** (*see p118*).

Sailane

11-12 avenue Palestine, Daoudiate (044 30 15 15).
Open 9am-1.30pm, 3.30-8.30pm daily **No credit cards.**
A chain store with a reasonably wide choice of items plus, unusually, a good warranty service.

Herbalists

For an explanation of what a dried lizard can do for you, *see p68* **Jinn and tonics**.

Rahal Herbes

43-7 Rahba Kedima, Medina (044 44 00 60). **Open** 9am-8pm daily. **No credit cards. Map** p248 C5.
The west side of Rahba Kedima is lined with herbalists and 'black magic' stores; we recommend Rahal for owner Abdeljabbar's fluency in English and his wickedly dry sense of humour.

Pharmacies

Pharmacie Centrale

166 avenue Mohammed V, corner of rue de la Liberté, Guéliz (044 43 01 58). **Open** 8.30am-12.30pm, 3-7pm Mon-Thur; 8.30am-noon, 3-7pm Fri; 8.30am-1pm, 3-7pm Sat. **Credit** MC, V. **Map** p252 B2.
The most conveniently central pharmacy in the New City. On the door is a list of other city pharmacies which are on 24-hour duty that particular week.

Pharmacie du Progrès

Jemaa El Fna, Medina (044 44 25 63). **Open** 8.15am-12.30pm, 2.15-6.30pm daily. **No credit cards. Map** p250 C5.
An excellent pharmacy with knowledgeable, qualified staff, who will advise you on minor ailments and suggest medication. English is spoken.

Photography

There's also a Kodak Express lab at hypermarché **Marjane** (*see p118*).

Ikram Photo Lab

Centre Kawkab, 3 rue Imam Chafii, Guéliz (044 44 74 94). **Open** 9am-noon, 3-9pm Mon-Sat. **Credit** MC, V. **Map** p252 B3.
A smart and modern Fuji lab near the Jnane El Harti for 24-hour print processing, plus slide and video.

Wrédé

142 avenue Mohammed V, Guéliz (044 43 57 39).
Open 8.30am-12.30pm, 2.45-7.30pm Mon-Sat.
Credit MC, V. **Map** p252 B2.
Staff are friendly and the quality of processing is fine. Slide film is sent to Casablanca and takes three days. Photocopying is available. Some English spoken.

Arts & Entertainment

Children

Marrakchis go ga-ga over kids but do little to keep them entertained.

Children are universally adored in Marrakech. It's not unusual for a group of teenagers or a businessman talking on a mobile phone to stop to smile at a cute kid. There may even be overzealous kissing and hugging of your baby.

Families are very close and it's natural that children should accompany their parents everywhere: shopping, to restaurants, even to work. People generally tend to be very tolerant of other people's kids and unruly behaviour that in other countries would inspire stern looks is here more likely to inspire indulgent cooing.

Despite all that, there isn't much geared to children's needs. Families tend to be large and entertainment comes in the form of brothers, sisters, myriad cousins and neighbours' children. They're allowed the freedom to play in the street. The risks of scrapes and bumps aside, Marrakech is extremely safe, particularly the Medina, which is largely traffic-free. There are few crimes against kids and no parent has any cause to fear when their children are out of sight. It's all reminiscent of the childhoods remembered by your gran and grandad – 'We just had a stick and a tin can in our day and it would keep us happy for hours.' And in Marrakech it does.

Given the scenario above, entertainment aimed specifically at children is scarce. For many families the hottest outing is to Marjane, the hypermarket, where kids can gaze wide-eyed at the shelves of shiny consumer goods, including a toy section. Likewise, petrol stations are a popular place to take boys (really), and anything with a playground such as the McDonald's (see p140) is swamped when school's out.

For the average Moroccan child, school is out for good a lot earlier than for his or her European counterpart. Although Mohammed VI encourages his population to send their children to school through to the age of 16, in many cases economics dictate against. As you wander through the souks the sight of young children in tiny workshops is a common one. This isn't as shocking as it might seem. Apprenticeship in a trade is still very much part of the local working tradition, and the sooner the apprentice begins, the more skilled they become. And the bottom line is that for many families when faced with a choice of sending a child to school (which will cost money) or putting them to work and bringing home an income, there really isn't any choice to be made.

SIGHTSEEING

Sightseeing with very young children is difficult, particularly in the Medina. The heat can be hard on kids who are used to more temperate climates, especially in summer months when temperatures can reach over 40°C (104°F). Avoid sightseeing around midday when the sun is at its strongest. Be sure to take the usual precautions: light, loose cotton clothes, sun hats, high-factor sun cream and plenty of fluids.

Apart from cafés (of which there aren't many), there are few parks or other places to take a break from walking and amenities such as toilets and washrooms are scarce. It's worth making use of toilets in hotels and restaurants wherever possible. And carry toilet roll just in case.

Avoid unpurified water (bottled mineral water is widely available), stay away from uncooked food, such as salads, and be sure to peel or wash fruit and veg. Diarrhoea and stomach complaints are common in Morocco and children are even more susceptible than adults. Pack some rehydration sachets just in case.

Busy Medina streets can be difficult for pedestrians, with bikes and cars coming from all directions, so keep a strong hold of children.

ACCOMMODATION

If you decide to come to Marrakech with your children, the first thing you need to decide is where you want to stay. Although riads are the height of fashion, they are not well suited to children. They tend to be quiet intimate spaces, very peaceful, with all rooms arranged off a central courtyard with no activities or places to play – fine if you have a quiet, well-behaved child, but a potential nightmare otherwise. One riad worth knowing about is the **Tchaikhane** (see p48), which has a library of kids' books and a TV room. **Riad Ifoulki** (see p47) is arranged in such a way that certain parts of the riad can be separated off by doors behind which families can have their own courtyard and rooms.

The alternative is to go for one of the larger five-star-style hotels such as the **Sofitel Marrakech** (see p52) or one of its neighbouring international counterparts (see p56 **The chain gang**) in the Hivernage district. Particularly recommended for kids is the **Coralia Club Palmariva**, one of the few hotels in the city that claims specifically to cater for children. The hotel complex is huge, so much so that Rollerblades are handed out to help get around. Facilities

include the Baboo Kids Village, a playgroup and activity centre for four to 12-year-olds that is open seven days a week. Most of the activities of the hotel are included in the price and include golf, archery and canoeing. There's also the nearby **Palmeraie Golf Palace**, another large resort complex with heaps of activities, including a kiddies' adventure playground, horse and pony stables and camel rides. Both the Palmariva and Golf Palace are out in the Palmeraie some distance north of the Medina, involving lots of taxiing around, which may or may not be an issue. *See also p55.*

The majority of hotels will not charge for children under the age of two. Between two and 12 years, so long as the room is being shared with parents, children are commonly charged around 50 per cent of adult rates.

Note that budget hotels are unlikely to have adequate bathroom facilities for small children – they are often communal.

Coralia Club Palmariva
route de Fès, km6 (044 32 90 36). **Rates** 500dh per person per day (full board); 50% discount under-12s. **Credit** AmEx, MC, V.

Palmeraie Golf Palace
Palmeraie Golf Palace Hotel & Resort, Palmeraie (044 30 10 10/fax 044 30 63 66/www.pgp.co.ma/ golfpalace@pgp.ma). **Rates** 2,200dh double; free under-12s. **Credit** AmEx, MC, V.

TRANSPORT
If you decide to rent a car for a day trip or even plan to do some exploring by taxi, do not expect child seats (or even seat belts in some taxis). Even if you have requested them, child seats aren't guaranteed, and smaller local car hire agencies are unlikely to have them at all. You could bring your own; there is a type that is attachable to the seat belts. The spectacular panoramas out of the car window – especially in the south – should be enough to keep the little ones interested, but it's worth bringing something to keep them entertained on long journeys. Make sure you have enough water and food as shops may be few and far between on the open road.

BABYSITTING
Most riads and hotels can provide babysitters upon request. Most won't speak English but that shouldn't be a problem – the language of play is universal.

Activities

There's not a great deal specifically for children to do in Marrakech. Attempts have been made at creating kids' attractions but they haven't worked. In 2002 a children's activity park opened just across from the airport with mini golf, a pool

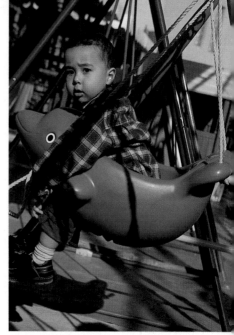

Having a whale of a time.

with slides, various rides, a climbing wall and restaurants. Entry was free and you paid for each activity. It received a huge amount of press and free introductory trips were offered to local schools. It closed in under eight months and has since lain abandoned. Meanwhile, a much vaunted safari park (*see p140* **Bab Africa**) has so far failed to open and a rumoured waterslide park remains just that – a rumour. It appears that there just aren't enough rich kids to make these projects viable and most locals can't afford this kind of luxury entertainment.

Never mind, most kids will be just as taken by the unfamiliar sights, sounds and smells as their parents are. It's not as if Marrakech has any shortage of visual stimulation. For a wonderful take on Marrakech from a child's view read Esther Freud's *Hideous Kinky*.

Carriage rides
place de Foucault, Medina. **Map** p65.
A ride in a brightly painted horse-drawN carriage (*calèche*) is great fun. They seat around four and can be hired for a circuit of the walls, which is a pretty ride, or taken even further afield up and through the Palmeraie. The wall circuit will probably take an hour or more; the Palmeraie run two or three hours. The rate is officially 80dh an hour but be prepared to negotiate down from 100dh or so. Note that the rate is per carriage not per person. Pick them up on the north side of place de Foucault, midway between the Koutoubia Mosque and Jemaa El Fna.

Jemaa El Fna

Map p65.

Children love the Jemaa El Fna. During the day there are dancing monkeys and snake charmers, while the water carriers with their bright red outfits can easily be mistaken for clowns. At night food stalls are set up, displaying of all kinds of strange things to eat and there are acrobats, fire-eaters and magicians.

Kawkab Jeu

1 rue Imam Chafii, Kawkab Centre, Hivernage (044 43 89 29). **Open** 8.30am-10pm daily. **Map** p252 B3.

Next door to the Royal Tennis Club, Kawkab Jeu is a coffeeshop (big on crêpes and fancy ice-creams) with both an indoor play area for the really little 'uns, plus an outdoor playground with swings, slides, climbing frames and so on. For young teens there's also table football, table tennis and video games.

Tansift Garden

Circuit de la Palmeraie (044 30 87 86). **Open** 10am-3pm, 5.30-10pm daily.

Just off the main road that winds through the Palmerie, the Tansift Garden is a combination of playground and coffeeshop. Plastic tables are set up among the palm trees where children can run and play and scream their lungs out bothering no one. There are also slides, swings, monkey bars and camel rides in the parking lot.

Parks & outdoor spaces

There are several parks and gardens around town (*see pp83-7*) but they're going to be of limited interest to most children. The exception is possibly the **Menara Gardens**, which has a big water-filled basin at its centre, home to huge and greedy fish. Children can buy bags of bread from a kiosk and feed them. It's also worth checking on the progress of the **Jnane El Harti** (*see p81*), a landscaped park in Guéliz; as we went to press it was in the process of being redeveloped and when completed it should include several children's play areas.

Also under development in spring 2003 was a new project, the **Bab Africa**, which is supposed to be a safari park with roaming and paddocked wild animals aimed specifically at youngsters. Reportedly, there's big money behind it but on our most recent visit all we were able to see were a signboard and some towering enclosure walls. Call to find out whether or not it's open yet.

Bab Africa

route de Fès (044 30 97 12/fax 044 30 97 90/ecncept@iam.net.ma).

Menara Gardens

avenue de la Menara, Hivernage (no phone). **Open** 5am-6.30pm daily. **Admission** free; picnic pavilion 15dh. **Map** p246 A5.

Sports & leisure

The range of distractions increases with the age of your children. If they're able to swing a club or stay astride, then the **Royal Golf Club** has a kids' club every Wednesday and Saturday and the **Palmeraie Golf Palace** a weekly pony club. The Golf Palace also has a **bowling alley**, open 4pm-midnight daily (also to non-residents).

For a day rate of 190dh per person, including lunch, **Club Med** will bus you to its site in the Palmeraie for pool access and a full range of sporting activities. **Le Relais du Lac**, which is based a half-hour south of the city, offers something similar; a driver will pick you up in Marrakech and drive you down there for a day of darts, canoeing, pedal boats, donkey rides, biking, volleyball and badminton with lunch included. Little children might enjoy it too, as it's a lakeside site with mountain views, and ducks and geese wandering freely. The price is 450dh per person (under-12s half-price).

Club Med

place de Foucault, Medina (044 44 40 16). **Credit** AmEx, MC, V. **Map** p250 B6.

Palmeraie Golf Palace

Palmeraie Golf Palace Hotel & Resort, Palmeraie (044 30 10 10/fax 044 30 63 66/www.pgp.co.ma/golfpalace@pgp.ma). **Credit** AmEx, MC, V.

Le Relais de Lac

barrage de Lalla Takerkoust (mobile 061 24 24 54/061 18 74 72). **No credit cards**.

Royal Golf Club

Ancienne route de Ouarzazate, km2 (044 40 98 28). **Open** *Summer* sunrise-sunset daily. *Winter* 9am-2.30pm daily. **Credit** MC, V.

Restaurants

Shame on us for promoting it, but the kids do love **McDonald's**. Marrakech has two: one up by the Marjane hypermarket, a few minutes' drive north of town on the Casablanca road, the other in central Guéliz on place 16 du Novembre. **Catanzaro** (*see p109*) has a children's menu.

Shopping

For nappies and baby food you'll have to make the trek to **Marjane** (*see p118*), as most small grocery stores don't stock them. UHT and powdered milk, however, are easily available. For clothing try **Jacadi** on avenue Mohammed V in Guéliz. For toyshops, again, hit Marjane or there's **La Drogerie** (163 avenue Mohammed V, 044 43 07 27) in Guéliz, and, just round the corner, **Articles pour le Bébé** (68 rue de la Liberté, 044 43 12 00) specialises in baby needs.

Arts & Entertainment

Film

Hollywood cashes in while the home-grown scene struggles.

Kate Winslet in 1999's **Hideous Kinky**.

'With the end of the second world war, a tortuous roundabout refuge trail sprang up: Paris to Marseilles, across the Mediterranean to Oran, then by train, or auto, or foot, across the rim of Africa to Casablanca in French Morocco. Here, the fortunate ones, through money or influence or luck, might obtain exit visas and scurry to Lisbon, and through Lisbon to the New World. But the others wait in Casablanca. And wait, and wait, and wait.'

You must remember this: the indelible image of Morocco in the movies is always going to be conjured by the name 'Casablanca', no matter that Rick's Café Americain never existed, and Bogart, Bergman et al never left the Warner Bros backlot in Hollywood.

If you're looking for traces of the real Morocco on screen, it comes in many guises – in recent years it's become the exotic backdrop of choice for foreign film-makers, standing in for Tibet in Martin Scorsese's *Kundun*, Somalia in Ridley Scott's *Black Hawk Down* and Egypt in the French hit *Astérix, Obelix and Cleopatra*. It was a generic North Africa for Michael Douglas and Kathleen Turner in *The Jewel of the Nile* and for Timothy Dalton's James Bond in *The Living Daylights*. Even Chilean surrealist Raoul Ruiz shot his typically idiosyncratic *Treasure Island* here.

The country's tradition of religious tolerance has made it a popular substitute for the Holy Land: Ben Kingsley was a cable TV Moses, and

Willem Dafoe was Jesus in Scorsese's *The Last Temptation of Christ*. (And in 2002-3 Paul Schrader went to Morocco for *The Exorcist III*.) Closer to geographical authenticity – and probably the most evocative representation of the landscape's mysterious charms – Bernardo Bertolucci adapted Paul Bowles's *The Sheltering Sky*, filming in the author's old stomping ground Tangier as well as south in the Sahara – and Gillies Mackinnon brought Esther Freud's *Hideous Kinky* to the screen, easily the sparkiest western take on Marrakech and the Moroccans. Then, of course, Ridley Scott shot the North African scenes of *Gladiator* in the Atlas Studios at Ouarzazate, the south of the mountains, desert's edge town that's home to Morocco's biggest film facilities.

SMART ALEX

The $457-million, multiple-Oscar-winning success of *Gladiator* has transformed the prospects for the local industry, inspiring the biggest new wave of 'sword and sandal' epics since the 1960s. Among the projects announced for 2003-4 are Baz Luhrmann's Alexander the Great biopic, starring Leonardo DiCaprio – however, Wolfgang Petersen's Trojan War epic Troy, with Brad Pitt as Achilles, has been removed to Mexico after jitters set in following the US invasion of Iraq.

According to Souheil Ben Barka, film-maker and director-general of the Centre Cinématographique Marocain (CCM), his first inkling that the Hollywood zeitgeist was turning toward Morocco came in 2000, when he received three phone calls in the course of one remarkable day: 'The first was from the producer Dino de Laurentiis, and he said he was making an Alexander film. He was going to send me the script, and please could I give it to Ridley Scott, who was filming here. In the afternoon I received a call from HBO, who said they had an Alexander project, and they wanted to send me a script. I said, "I know, I spoke to Dino this morning" – I thought it was the same one. They said, "Dino? No, this is a different project." After, I received a call from one of Martin Scorsese's assistants, and it was another Alexander film. That was a very strange day. A couple of weeks later Oliver Stone came here researching his Alexander script. So there were four completely different Alexander the Great projects.'

At press time, De Laurentiis is producing Luhrmann's film along with Scorsese, and a new two-square-kilometre studio facility is being built to accommodate it in Ouarzazate.

Why is Morocco such a popular location? 'Because we have 300 clear sunny days a year, and because if they shot Alexander in the US it would cost $300 million; here it will cost $70 million,' Barka explains. 'In America, an extra earns $100 a day. Here, it's $15. A stunt horse in the US is $200 a day. Here, $20.' Nevertheless, he insists, what is good for Hollywood is also good for Morocco: 'They will invest $60 million below-the-line in our country. Maybe 10,000 people will work on this one film as extras and crew, drivers and technicians… the hotels will be full… this is serious business for us.'

Happily, government policies seek to boost the indigenous film sector. To receive a production licence, at least one producer must be Morocco-based and ten per cent of your cinema ticket helps to fund Moroccan movies, of which there are usually between ten and 12 a year. Nevertheless, the industry faces grave problems. In a country of about 150 cinemas, Moroccan films can never hope to be self-supporting, but the local Arabic dialect is not widely understood beyond Morocco and Algeria. In fact, many Moroccan feature films are French co-productions and are often in French. Not surprisingly, emigration to Europe is a common theme (see 2001's *Au-delà de Gibraltar*, for example), though raucous comedies and historical romances are also popular. Few of these films have excited international attention, although the engaging neo-realist fable *Ali Zaoua: Prince de la Rue* (directed by Nabil Ayouch, 2000) was distributed across Europe. The sad truth is, though, you're more likely to find a Hollywood blockbuster, an Egyptian musical or an Asian action movie playing than a home-grown Moroccan movie.

Cinemas

Marrakech has no more than a half-a-dozen or so city centre cinemas, with just a handful more dotted around the outskirts. This is a francophone country with Arabic subtitling, so unless you speak French you're fuqued. Screenings are typically three times daily at 3pm, 7pm and 9pm.

In addition to the cinemas listed below (the pick of a poor crop), films are also shown roughly twice a week at the **Institut Francais** (Route de Targa, Jebel Guéliz, 044 44 69 30, 20dh), an adequate venue with a more eclectic, culturally inclined programming remit, and – during the Film Festival (*see p143*) – in the grand ruins of the Badii Palace.

Cinéma La Colisée

boulevard Mohammed Zerktouni, Guéliz (044 44 88 93). **Tickets** 15dh, 25dh Mon; 25dh, 35dh Tue-Sun. **No credit cards. Map** p252 A2.
The self-proclaimed 'best cinema in Morocco' – and certainly the best in Marrakech. It's a comfortable,

Francis Ford Coppola's back at the Marrakech International Film Festival.

modern, good-size venue with a good rack, excellent sightlines, a balcony and a relatively plush red and black design.

Cinéma Rif

Daouidiat (044 30 31 46). **Tickets** 15dh. **No credit cards**. **Map** p247 D1.
A real Moorish movie palace, a big barn-like building, again with a balcony, red carpets on the steps and (sometimes) tea in the forecourt.

Saada

Quartier Hay Hassani, Douar Laasker (044 34 70 28). **Tickets** 15dh. **No credit cards**.
1950s-style auditorium, again with carpets and tea, in a dusty neighbourhood square off the Essaouira road past the railway station.

International Film Festival

The first Marrakech International Film Festival had the misfortune to kick off in September 2001 – within days of 11 September. Nevertheless, in its second year, the fallout from that day lent focus and definition to an ambitious, multifaceted festival ideally placed between East and West. Sponsored by His Majesty King Mohammed VI – a film buff, apparently – and presided over by the powerful UniFrance chief Daniel Toscan du Plantier (and paid for entirely by commercial interests in France and Morocco), the festival was able to attract a good deal of star-power and (consequently) media attention: Francis Coppola, David Lynch and Matt Dillon all made the trip, Jeanne Moreau was head of the jury, and Catherine Deneuve, Emmanuelle Béart, Anne Parillaud, Johnny Halliday and Charles Aznavour weighed in for the former colonial power. This French-bias didn't seem well suited to position the festival as the foremost in North Africa (local films tended to be shunted into the little-attended French Institute), but at least the foundations are there, and so too is the will to make it happen.

The festival currently takes place in mid September, but plans are afoot for a new November date when Ramadan allows in 2004.

Galleries

Not so very state of the art.

Fine art's had a bit of a slow start in Marrakech. Painting has never really been a Moroccan thing. It wasn't until the first European artists came to North Africa on the back of 19th-century colonial conquest that the country was first captured on canvas. The adventuring artists were captivated by the clear light and richness of colour. It also helped that pictures of fearsome desert warriors and dusky harem girls sold well at home. The painterly products of a visit to Morocco and Algeria by **Eugène Delacroix** in 1823 diverted subsequent generations of French painters from the traditional pilgrimage to Italy and had them swarming all over North Africa instead. 'I am like a man dreaming', wrote Delacroix, 'and who sees things he is afraid will escape him.' Not much did, and he went on to complete 80 canvases with North African themes before he died, defining the style that became known as 'Orientaliste' (Orientalism).

It's an artistic movement widely derided these days for the treatment of its subjects as colourful curiosities (See the mighty negro with his beheaded victim! See the dancing Arab girl with one nipple casually exposed!), but its influence was such that it motivated **Henri Matisse** to explore Morocco in 1912. He settled in Tangier for a highly productive stint, now regarded as the culmination of his Fauve period.

Matisse protégé **Raoul Dufy** followed in the footsteps of the master, travelling to Marrakech and painting the typically cartoony canvas *Couscous Served at the Residence of the Pasha*, among other works, but few other painters made it this far south. The notable exception is **Jacques Majorelle**, a tuberculosis sufferer who came on the advice of his doctor. He settled here in 1923, building a villa at the gates of the city, later adding the gardens that perpetuate his name. Majorelle's work still falls under the heading Orientalist but it's more than redeemed by the artist's apparent sense of empathy with his subjects; that and a superbly graphic sense of draughtsmanship and pattern (some of his most enduring works are a series of striking travel posters promoting Maroc to the French). He's also remembered for his attachment to a particularly virulent shade of powder blue that now goes by the moniker 'Majorelle blue'.

Arts & Entertainment

Elder statesman of the Marrakech art scene **Hans Werner Geerdts**. *See p145.*

Tourya Othman adding the finishing touches at Dar Cherifa.

THE SCENE TODAY

The first impression of visiting art buffs will be that the mainstream Marrakech art scene hasn't moved on since Matisse. The few galleries dotted around town are stuffed full of impressionistic daubings of camels, scurrying veiled women, carpet sellers and sunsets over the city walls. It's faux Orientalism and it's a product of the Marrakchi artisan mentality that whatever sells – be it filigree lanterns, curly slippers, embroidered bedsteads or ethnic bridalwear – should be knocked out in whatever style is required. 'Just picture making', explains **Tourya Othman**, 'and not to be confused with art'.

So where *is* the art? The answer is, it's coming. Othman is one of a number of young Moroccan artists who emigrated years ago but has now been attracted to return by recent political and social changes. She's exhibited internationally and now flits between homes in Bangkok and Marrakech. Similarly **Hassan Hajjaj**, whose family left Morocco when he was 14 to settle in England. He recently came back and now shuttles between London (where he has a café/gallery), Paris (where he's just designed a new restaurant for Mourad Mazouz of Momo fame) and Marrakech, which he considers to be the most exciting of the three.

Othman does video art and bedsheet-sized oils of hyper-magnified bits of microbiology, Hajjaj is pure Pop. They are just two of a floating circle of well-travelled artists and conceptualists, some who have been around a while (like elder artistic statesman **Hans Werner Geerdts**, whose forte is ink-blot people and Pollock-like abstracts), others who have just arrived. They have yet to coalesce into any sort of scene, but give it time.

Already **Dar Cherifa** (*see p146*) has established itself as the focal point of the city's artistic scene and there are several other promising projects in the pipeline, including an ambitious arts performance centre being created in a 17th century riad in the Kasbah quarter by Othman. In the words of Hajjaj, 'It's all just kicking off'.

Galleries

With a just a few of notable exceptions, the city's galleries are fairly uninspiring. The work is astonishingly unvaried and unchallenging – mostly Moroccan variations on an Orientalist theme. They'd make a nice gift for your mum.

In addition to the places listed below the **Musée de Marrakech** (*see p69*) and the restaurant **Jacaranda** (*see p111*) also exhibit art, as does Frédérique Birkemeyer's boutique **Intensite Nomade** (*see p123*), and there's a permanent display of the work of Jacques Majorelle at the **Museum of Islamic Art** (*see p84*) in the Majorelle Gardens.

Also look out for a couple of pocket-sized glossy freebie mags, *Fen'art* and *Scopus*, both devoted to the local art scene (such as it is), carrying listings of current exhibitions; they are distributed free at galleries and boutiques.

Dar Cherifa

8 Derb Charfa Lakbir Mouassine, off rue Mouassine, Medina (044 42 64 63/www.marrakech-riads.net). **Open** hours vary; call for details. **Map** p248 C4.

The most exciting art space in town, Dar Cherifa is also the most gorgeous of Medina townhouses. It dates back to the 16th century in parts and has been lovingly restored by Abdelatif Ben Abdellah (*see p19*), who's taken great pains to expose the carved beams and stucco work while leaving walls and floors bare and free of distraction. Regular exhibitions lean towards resident foreign artists and openings often feature performances from gnawa and Sufi musicians. The space also incorporates a small library and tea and coffee are served.

Darkoum

5 rue de la Liberté, Guéliz (044 44 67 39). **Open** 9.30am-12.30pm, 3-7.30pm Mon-Sat. **Map** p252 B2.

Upstairs from the ethnic knick-knacks and assorted *objets d'art* is a modest but attractive little space. Pieces are big and bold and sold as glamorous home decor accessories but we've seen some striking and interesting work here, mainly from foreign artists living in or inspired by Morocco.

Galerie Bleu

119 Mohammed V, Guéliz (044 42 00 80). **Open** 10am-1pm, 4-8pm Tue-Sun. **Map** p252 B2.

A smart new exhibition space just across from the Marché Central, Galerie Bleu had been open just a few of weeks when we visited. We're told it will specialise in solo shows of cutting-edge contemporary Moroccan artists. The exhibition we saw had large canvases boldly coloured with red earth pigments. The work is displayed to advantage in two cool, bright spaces plus a mezzanine. Very promising, and the kind of gallery Marrakech needs more of.

Marrakech Arts Gallery

60 boulevard Mansour Eddahbi, Guéliz (044 43 93 41/www.art-gallery-marrakech.com). **Open** 9am-1pm, 3-8pm daily. **Map** p252 B2.

More shop than gallery, MAG is a tiny sales space in central Guéliz where the paintings aren't exactly flattered by being displayed en masse, crammed on to the wall like so many posters on a teenage bedroom wall. We didn't see anything to excite but then the gallery had only been open a matter of weeks and might need more time to find its feet.

Matisse Gallerie

61 rue Yougoslavie, No.43 passage Ghandouri, Guéliz (044 44 83 26/matisse_art_gall@hotmail.com). **Open** 9.30am-1pm, 4-8pm daily. **Map** p252 A2.

Enterprising gallery owners Youssef Falaki and Youssef Nabil Moroccan have created an innovative space to showcase contemporary Moroccan artists – albeit contemporary artists working in an historical pastiche fashion. Every now and again there's the odd interesting solo show. Upstairs is a showroom of classic landscape oils and watercolours, plus some repros by masters like Jacques Majorelle.

Ministero del Gusto

22 Derb Azouz El Mouassine, off rue Sidi El Yamami, Medina (044 42 64 55). **Open** 9.30am-noon Mon-Fri. **Credit** MC, V. **Map** p248 C4.

Showroom for the design talents and eclectic tastes of owners Alessandra Lippini and Fabrizio Bizzarri, the Ministero also hosts exhibitions. These change every three months and in recent years have included B&Ws by American photographer Martin HM Schreiber (famous for his Madonna nudes), screen prints by Hassan Hajja and installations by Italian multimediaist Maurizio Vetrugno.

La Qoubba Galerie d'Art

91 Souk Talaa, off place Ben Youssef, Medina (044 38 05 15/www.art-gallery-marrakech.com). **Open** hours vary; call for details. **Map** p249 D4.

Around the corner from the Koubba Badiyin and almost opposite the Musée de Marrakech, La Quobba has regularly changing exhibitions of mainly local Marrakchi artists, both solo and in groups. It's all fairly predictable stuff; you can grab a preview courtesy of the gallery's surprisingly good website which has plenty of links to painters and their work.

Riad Tamsna

23 Derb Zanka Daika, off Riad Zitoun El Jedid (044 38 52 72/www.tamsna.com). **Open** 10am-midnight daily. **Credit** MC, V. **Map** p250 C6.

Tamsna is primarily a restaurant (*see p106*) with a first-floor boutique (*see p130*) attached, but one of the ground-floor salons off the main courtyard also serves as a small but lofty exhibition space. Shows tend to be on a Moroccan theme, curated according to owner Meryanne Loum-Martin's impeccable taste. Works from past shows, as well as antique photos, are available for sale upstairs.

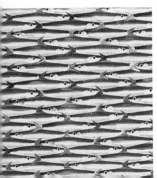 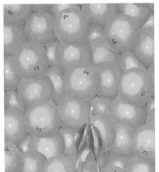 

Music

There's no shortage of Moroccan sounds, just nowhere to hear them.

Gnawa guys. *See p148.*

Arts & Entertainment

Long before the words 'world' and 'music' were first indelibly linked, Moroccan was one of the rare ethnic musics attracting any sort of Western audience. Proximity had a lot to do with it – cultural exchange across the Strait of Gibraltar has been going on for centuries. And when in the late 1960s hippies returned with tales of wild, kif-smoking musicians, Morocco was the place for mind-altered jamming. 'Whoopa, hey mesa, hooba huffa, hey mesha goosh goosh', as Crosby, Stills & Nash so precisely summed it all up in their 'Marrakesh Express' (1969).

But to paint Moroccan music as the exotic soundtrack to a thousand hippie trips is to seriously undersell a rich and varied music-making tradition. Its roots lie in the classical arrangements of Arab Andalucía, in the Jewish folksongs nurtured among the communities of Essaouira, Fès and Marrakech, in the culture of the indigenous Berber people and even in the age-old practice of slave trading.

BERBER BEATS

With its own instruments, tunings, rhythms and sounds, Berber music (called *grika* – 'improvisation') is something entirely different from Arabic music. It's rural music traditionally performed at community celebrations, especially harvest and religious festivals. It's heavily percussive with harsh – to some ears, ugly – shrieks from the *ghaita* (an instrument related to the oboe). The music is composed of several fairly simple parts, which are intricately woven together and extended into performances that can last for days at a time, with some musicians taking breaks and others stepping in to replace them. It's a ritualised formula that's changed little over the last 2,000 years.

Prime exponents of grika – and one of Morocco's best-known exports – are the **Master Musicians of Jajouka**, tagged by William Burroughs as 'the world's oldest rock 'n' roll band'. According to their website (!), the musicians, who are all inhabitants of the small village of Jajouka in the foothills of the Rif Mountains, have been passing their musical traditions from father to son for 4,000 years. Prior to the days of French colonial rule, they were court musicians to seven kings of Morocco and, not unsurprisingly, they're accredited with all kinds of mystical powers – one of which is the ability to captivate foreign rock stars (*see p149* **Maroc 'n' roll**).

MOROCCAN BLUES

If Berber music comes across as elemental, bordering on mystical, it's got nothing on *gnawa* (also spelled gnaoua).

The name refers both to the music and its practitioners. Performances frequently inspire trance-like states in both musicians and listeners, swayed by the rhythm of iron castanets, shaken by the sub-bass thrumming of the *guimbri*. Its intense and looping hypnotic washes commonly induce shuddering, audible moaning and even total collapse. From the outside it appears something like an exorcism, and the gnawa are renowned for their ability to 'cast out evil spirits' and soothe the mentally ill. They're also called upon to purify houses after death. At a time when the concept of 'trance' is endlessly and glibly applied to Western dance tracks, gnawa music is the real deal.

The gnawa trace their ancestry back to sub-Saharan Africa – particularly Ghana, from which the term 'gnawa' supposedly derives – from where they were transported north by Moorish slave traders (Marrakech had a slave market until 1912). Less credibly, the gnawa claim spiritual descent from Sidi Bilal, an Ethiopian slave who was the Prophet Mohammed's first *muezzin* (the gent who calls the faithful to prayer).

The descendants of these early enslaved groups are the present-day 'gnawa brotherhood', concentrated mainly in the southern, more African, less European part of the country – notably Marrakech and Essaouira. A strong oral tradition has kept alive the customs, rituals and beliefs of their ancestors, and gnawa music is the best-preserved manifestation of the black African aesthetic within Morocco. Some of the ancient songs are still sung in Bambara (a Malian dialect), even if the meaning of the language is now lost. The *gimbri*, a long-necked lute almost identical to a West African instrument, is the most popular gnawa instrument and combines a fat acoustic bass sound with a metallic rattle to distinctive effect.

Gnawa lyrics are riddled with references to the pain of slavery and exile, and the turmoil of dislocation. If that sounds familiar, the raw delivery, bluesy riffs and spiritual overtones also reinforce the impression that if Blind Lemon Jefferson were to walk in on a *leila* (an all-night gnawa session), he'd be able to pick up and play without a break.

GNAWA FUSION

Although always on the very periphery of Moroccan society (local cassette buyers favour the latest J-Lo and Limp Bizkit, Egyptian pop and Algerian rai), gnawa has made an impact on both the local and global music scenes. Like reggae, its sound is easily appropriated. A music of gaps, spaces and extended durations, it lends itself easily to fusion experiments, collaborations and remixes. The process has been going on since the 1970s when the torch was lit by one Casablancan group in particular, **Nass El Ghiwane**. They were a long-haired five-piece that came on like a more rootsy version of Hendrix's Band of Gypsies. They played traditional instruments and fused gnawa with elements of popular Egyptian and Lebanese song and a barely concealed political edge. It was a heady brew that resulted in Bob Marley-like status across North Africa. The band leader died in a plane crash in the '80s, but two of the group play on under the original name. The old revolutionary songs are a staple of the jobbing musicians on Jemaa El Fna.

Gnawan fusionist **Hassan Hakmoun** cut his teeth playing ceremonies around Jemaa El Fna before moving to New York in the mid '80s, where he made the impressive *Gift of the Gnawa* (1991), featuring legendary trumpeter Don Cherry and Richard Horowitz, an avant-garde musician and composer (contributor to the soundtrack for Bertolucci's *The Sheltering Sky*), and some-time resident of Marrakech.

Gnawa fusion also made radical moves forward with **Aisha Kandisha's Jarring Effects** who pioneered Arabic techno across several albums – although their momentum has slowed since founding member Habib El Malak left the band to become a politician in Marrakech; Paris-based **Gnawa Diffusion** blend gnawa with strong helpings of ragga and reggae to euphorically funky effect.

In the UK, three-piece **Momo** peddle their version of gnawan 'dar' (house) to a clubbing crowd, while DJ **U-Cef** promiscuously mixes in samples of Moroccan music with just about everything ('You can put Moroccan rhythms with anything – drum 'n' bass, speed garage, house – and it works').

New York, Paris, London: if this gives the impression that Europe and America are the places for cutting-edge gnawa collaborations, then that's a fairly accurate reflection of the truth. There's little market in Marrakech and Morocco for anything too edgy. Instead, home-grown developments have been more along social lines. Recent years have seen the emergence of a women's gnawa scene, with the most high-profile exponents being **B'net Marrakech** (Women of Marrakech). They're a feisty group of five taboo-breaking ladies (gnawa has always been a male preserve) who do weddings, births – and international world music festivals. Their debut CD *Chamaa* includes songs about love and demonic

Maroc 'n' roll

Morocco's musical links with Mediterranean Europe stretch across millennia. Yet the West's greater interest in Moroccan music largely began with recordings author-composer Paul Bowles made in Morocco in the 1950s for the Library of Congress. His recordings appealed to the Beats, many of whom passed through Tangier, and one of whom, Byron Gysin, would turn doomed Rolling Stone Brian Jones on to the Master Musicians of Jajouka (*see p147*). Jones recorded with the Master Musicians in 1968 and an album was issued posthumously on Rolling Stone Records in '71.

In the wake of the Stones other musicians followed: the Beatles holidayed in Marrakech, inspiring Lennon to write a song 'The Road to Marrakech:

On the road to Marrakech
I was dreaming more or less
And the dream I had was true
Yes the dream I had was true

It never made a Beatles' album so he changed the words and it became 'Jealous Guy'. Jimi Hendrix hung out in Essaouira (and supposedly, inspired by local ruins, wrote the track 'Castles Made of Sand') and Cat Stevens came and discovered Islam. Led Zeppelin were enthralled enough by their 1970 visit that when Robert Plant and Jimmy Page reunited in 1994 they made Morocco their base, recording the No Quarter album with local musicians, and filming a video on Jemaa El Fna.

Robert Plant has never lost his passion for Moroccan music. 'I have a great lust for Berber music from Morocco and Algeria,' he says. 'It seems to be the most wailing, plaintive, untouched music I've ever heard. I don't know what the fuck it's all about. But it's stirring, primal stuff. It's not affected by any outside trend. And the songs haven't changed for hundreds of years. All I can tell you is it hits my musical G-spot.'

At the same time many jazz musicians were looking to North Africa for inspiration. African-American pianist Randy Weston settled in Tangier in 1968 and has since recorded many albums with Moroccan musicians. Saxophonist Pharoah Sanders collaborated with Essaouiran Mahmoud Ghania on an album called *The Trance of the Seven Colours*.

If the 1980s were a quiet time for Moroccan music, the '90s found Morocco hip once again with the likes of über-producer Bill Laswell in-country to record several albums – including a powerful new session with the Master Musicians of Jajouka. Less successfully, Talvin Singh attempted to fuse Berber rhythms and dance beats when he produced an album with the Jajoukans in 2000.

Most recently, Blur (pictured) spent a month recording 2003's *Think Tank* in Marrakech. While Damon Albarn stressed that the group was not trying to make 'a world music album', he added, 'Marrakech and its music definitely have an effect on you.' Few would disagree.

Master musician **Brahim El Belkani**.

possession, and an ode to the Moroccan national football team. *Ez zaman yata ghayer*, as it were (the times, they are a changin').

WHERE TO SEE MUSIC

Where to see music in Marrakech? The short answer is 'nowhere'. Or almost nowhere. Music-making remains largely tied to ritual, and performances for performances' sake are rare. Hence an absence of concert halls and live music clubs. The **Musica Bar** (*see p156*) and **Stars House** (*see p158*) both feature live bands but they perform the Arab world equivalent of cheesy cabaret. Jemaa El Fna is filled with musicians, solo and in groups, but these are the equivalent of street buskers. Likewise, the costumed gnawa seen and heard in restaurants.

According to **Brahim El Belkani**, respectable gnawa musicians just don't do that sort of stuff. El Belkani is a *maalim*, or master, one of only eight such gnawa dignitaries in Marrakech (with about the same number in Essaouira, Fès, Meknés and Taroudant). He's scornful of the idea of playing for 'tips' and works professionally as a butcher. Gnawa music exists on a plane beyond that controlled by Mammon. He plays infrequently and then mostly at international festivals – although from the photos that adorn his music room wall, he's not averse to turning out for visiting

musical stars: there's Brahim and Dizzy Gillespie/Santana/Page and Plant.

Chances to witness genuine Berber and gnawa masters like El Belkani occur only on occasions such as major cultural jamborees or exhibition openings (check what's happening at **Dar Cherifa** (*see p145*). Important religious festivals including Aid El Fitr and Milud (for dates *see chapter* **Directory**) also guarantee great music: ask around to find out where, or just follow your ear.

FESTIVALS

There are no festivals in Marrakech, but there is an annual **Essaouira Festival of Gnawa and World Music**. Initiated in 1998 by a Frenchman, a gnawa master musician and an English woman, it's a free and freewheeling four-day event staged each June on the streets and plazas around the coastal town. In 2002 it was attended by more than 200,000 spectators and attracted musicians from all over the world. Past players have included Ali Farka Touré, Archie Shepp, Oumou Sangaré and Orchestre des Barbes jamming with gnawa groups from around Morocco. Paul Simon was spotted in the audience in 2000, Damon Albarn in 2001. For details visit the festival website (www.festival-gnaoua.co.ma).

Also in June is the **Festival of the World's Sacred Music** held in Fès, which is a celebration of international Islamic music.

Nightlife

For a city where supposedly no one drinks, Marrakech nights can be an awful lot of fun.

Being a city in an Islamic country doesn't have to mean an absence of nightlife: Casablanca can be trippy, Cairo goes all night and Istanbul is regularly touted as the next Ayia Napa. The problem with Marrakech is that it's both Islamic *and* parochial.

The Koran cautions against substances that cloud the mind, a much debated injunction that has traditionally been interpreted to mean 'lay off the booze'. But the reality is that attitudes towards drink remain much more ambiguous, if not outright hypocritical – see right **Alco-hypocrisy**.

Generally speaking, Moroccans aren't fussed about alcohol; they're not censorious of foreigners who drink and many aren't averse to the occasional hit of booze themselves, although economics dictate that wine and beer consumption is very much a privilege of the moneyed – and more liberal – middle and upper classes. However, being a small town with a corresponding lack of sexy professional career opportunities, the Westernised rich kids who might support any kind of flourishing bar and club culture are largely absent, removed to the commercial and media capital of Casablanca, or even further afield.

Instead, it's down to foreign support to float Marrakech nightlife: all the clubs except one are attached to large international hotels, and similarly a high proportion of the bars. The current hippest venue in town **Comptoir** (*see p154*) is French-owned, as is the most recent opening, **Bodega** (*see p154*).

DIVE, DIVE, DIVE

The truly local locals' booze scene is far grittier, devoid of sheen and chic, and all the more interesting for it (unless you happen to be a woman, in which case it's just outright alarming). At base level, the business of beer drinking is the province of defiant reprobates of all ages who, encountered in the act, almost seem to revel in their rebel status. They gather principally in a ragtag of bars around the upper reaches of Guéliz (notably rue Mohammed El Bekal), which are filled to bursting each night with suitably raucous behaviour. Mixing it with the men are the local 'ladies' (note those inverted commas), feisty characters of full figure and a way with a six-inch brush and

blusher. Such a display of flesh for cash is in fantastic contrast to the demure modesty exhibited by the majority of Moroccan women, but look at it from the state's point of view: vice happens, so why not at least corral into the one place where it can easily be kept an eye on?

Alco-hypocrisy

How's this for a get-out clause? Morocco has a prohibition against alcohol use but not against its production or sale. Handy when it's the authorities who produce over half of the country's booze.

National production is supposedly earmarked for consumption by non-Muslims and visitors – all 1,200,000 hectolitres (310,000 of wine, 900,000 of beer) annually of it. To ward off errant Muslims, shops that are authorised to sell alcohol also have to display the text of a royal decree of 14 November 1967 forbidding public drunkenness, which is punishable by three months in prison and a 700dh fine. But, of course, Muslims do drink, thereby creating several millions of dirhams in profit for the (largely state-owned) alcohol industry (not to mention all the taxes raked in). According to a report in Moroccan men's mag *Version Homme*, some other state employees also have a nice little side-line in alcohol-related income: the article quotes a shopkeeper in Casablanca who pays a bribe to police every month to preserve his alcohol licence (this after bribing civil servants to get the necessary documentation in the first place). It also reports on the instance of police loitering outside booze shops so as to apprehend customers leaving to confiscate their bottles and extract a fine.

Other curious by-products of the proliferation of alcohol in a country where nobody drinks is that there's no legal drinking age (how could there be when all drinking is illegal?) and no such thing as drunk driving.

THE BOOZE

Beer comes in both local form (Flag Spéciale brewed in Tangier, Stork brewed in Fès and Casablanca, 'the legendary beer from the legendary city') and imported (bottled Heineken and other lowest common denominator international brands). The perfectly adequate local stuff (it's cold and it's wet) sells by the bottle for anything from 13dh to 50dh. In spring look out for the superior Bière de Mars, made only in March with Fès spring water.

Local wines aren't bad, especially the rosés, although you generally won't find them offered outside of restaurants and hotel bars. Spirits are downright expensive; cocktails have scarcely been heard of.

Beware the holy month of Ramadan when all bars other than those in hotels close for the duration: for dates *see chapter* **Directory**.

Bars

Medina

The sale of alcohol in the Medina with its myriad holy sites is strictly regulated. It's practically impossible to get a licence. A few restaurants have persevered and are able to offer beer and wine to diners, but bars are an absolute no no, except in the 'international zones' that are hotels.

Alanbar

47 rue Jebel Lakhdar, Bab Laksour (044 38 07 63). **Open** 8pm-2am daily. **Credit** DC, MC, V. **Map** p248 B4.
Inspired by waning Parisian fashion haunt the Buddha Bar and any number of Bondian film sets, Alanbar tops a grand flight of stairs with a glowing HR Geiger goddess. It also features a baronial fireplace, a grand piano in the corner and a basement palm-court dining area, all of which are rendered completely insignificant by the sheer scale of a place that has the ungainly size, atrium-style layout and acoustics of a shopping mall. You could march the entire population of Liechtenstein inside here and still feel agoraphobic. But it does boast maybe the best-stocked bar in town, and if you tire of Shakira on the banked video screens, move closer to the DJ booth for an earful of the 'Ketchup Song' or similar, or hang over the balcony to catch the cabaret singer below. Who says size isn't everything?

Churchill Piano Bar

Mamounia Hotel, avenue Bab Jedid (044 38 86 00/ www.mamounia.com). **Open** 7pm-1am daily. **Credit** AmEx, MC, V. **Map** p250 A6.
So it's not original and much of the current decor dates from the 1986 refit, but for fans of bar culture – deco bar culture, no less – this one's a beaut.

...under dressed at **Comptoir**. *See p154.*

It's intimate and dark (leather padded walls!) and full of gleaming surfaces, not least the polished pride-of-place grand (hence the name) in its own semi-sunken pit. A backlit painted-glass montage of jazz greats fills up the wall behind like an altarpiece. Leather seats are in British racing green with brass go-faster stripes and there's a proper high bar counter complete with brass foot rail. It's a venue made for dry Martinis, but you could settle for a local beer at 50dh a pop. If you time it right (about 9.30ish most nights) you'll catch a guy at the ivories. Requests to 'Play it again, Sam,' will probably be treated with the disdain they deserve.

Grand Tazi

Corner of avenue El Mouahidine & rue Bab Agnaou (044 44 27 87). **Open** 7-11pm daily. **No credit cards.** **Map** p250 C6.

The Tazi's a godsend – the only place in the central Medina where the weary and footsore can kick back with a cheap beer. There's no real bar as such, just a sofa space off to one side of the lobby (and a large empty room beyond that) where accommodating waiters will fetch a cold one for anybody who succeeds in snaring their attention. You don't have to be a resident, just not too fussy about the company you keep or addicted to quality furnishings. Fellow drinkers tend to be budget travellers annotating their copies of the *Rough Guide* and swapping stories of loose bowels amid the dunes

of Merzouga. For anybody around at the time, the New Year's Eve parties thrown by the Tazi each year are near legendary.

Piano Bar

Hotel les Jardins de la Koutoubia, 26 rue de la Koutoubia (044 38 88 00). **Open** 7pm-midnight daily. **Credit** AmEx, DC, MC, V. **Map** p250 B5.

The Jardins de la Koutoubia is a new-build hotel one block north of central Jemaa El Fna that draws divided opinions on its faux-traditional architecture ('shopping mall Moroccan', in the words of one local critic). We like it, though, for the bar, which is just off the central courtyard, on the far side of the swimming pool from the entrance. A small space in Gucci red and gold, the bar comes complete with piano player who, wreathed in swirls of Gitanes smoke, schmoozes through a repertoire of French *chansons*. Drinks aren't cheap (50dh-70dh), but the G&Ts are huge, and the perfect wind-down after a day spent schlepping through the souks. There's no dress code as such, but a little effort would probably be appreciated by your fellow louche loungers.

Hivernage

In addition to the trio described below, all the neighbourhood's big hotels come complete with a couple or more bars – and that's probably as much as we need to say about them.

Cheek to cheek at **La Casa**.

La Casa

*Hotel El Andalous, avenue Président Kennedy
(044 44 82 26).* **Open** 8pm-2am daily. **Credit** MC,
V. **Map** p252 B4.

A bar that thinks it's a club, La Casa mixes food,
music and dance to great effect. It *is* primarily a
bar, dominated by a huge central serving area, surrounded on all sides by table-led seating. Above the
counter hangs a giant rig of multicoloured lights fit
for a Pink Floyd gig. Much flashing and strobing
occurs in accompaniment to a heavy Arab/Latin
beats soundtrack. There's no dancefloor, but then
there's none needed, as everyone just lets go where
they are – at least the curvy Marrakchi girls do; the
guys just sit and ogle. About the stroke of midnight
expect an 'impromptu' performance of dancing from
the chefs in the corner kitchen area. Berber columns
cloaked in purple drapes and charadters from the
Tifinagh alphabet highlit in ultraviolet add the
thinnest veneer of Moroccan theming.

Comptoir

avenue Echouada (044 43 77 02). **Open** 4pm-1am
Mon-Thur, Sun; noon-1am Fri, Sat. **Credit** MC, V.
Map p252 C4.

Been-there-dahling Marrakchi socialites will tell you
that Comptoir is *sooo* over, but on the right night it's
still the best night in town. From the outside it's a
well-behaved little villa on a quiet residential street,
but inside it's catsuit sexy, all sultry with spilt-wine
red walls and polished black furniture. The ceiling
is draped with billowing white cotton and the lighting is down low. The main room buzzes with
dressed-up diners (*see p113*), while on the first floor
is a spacious lounge bar. The real 'lounge' area
(where the word is an invitation not a noun) is the
garden courtyard with cat's-tongue pink walls, starry skies above and no seating other than plump
cushions for artfully posed limbs. Conditions of
licensing mean that drinks can't be served without
food, but it's amazing how long a small dish of nuts
can last. Drinks are pricey and wine mark-ups hefty,
but you were expecting that, weren't you?

El Menzah Piano Bar

avenue de France (044 43 85 95). **Open** 6pm-1am
daily. **No credit cards**. **Map** p252 A4.

A deep red carpet, darkwood panelling and proper
bar counter with real beer taps help make this the
closest thing in Marrakech to an old school British
pub. It's also authentically smoky and gloomily lit
(which does beg the question of why anyone would
come all the way to Marrakech, then spend time in
a faux-Brit boozer). The crowd that does gather here
is a mix of young*ish* Marrakchi chaps with a lady to
impress and jaded old expats. Either way, they must
all have eardrums of tin to endure the pitiful resident musician (keyboard and sax; typical toon: 'My
Way'). For clubbers, it makes a convenient meet-up
or stop-off before the Paradise Club (*see p158*).

Guéliz

The neighbourhood for vaguely-to-outright-
disreputable local bars, most of which are a
short falter from central place Abdel Moumen.
Relative newcomers Bodega and Montecristo
raise the tone a few notches.

Bar L'Escale

rue de Mauritanie (044 43 34 47). **Open** 11am-
10.30pm daily. **No credit cards**. **Map** p252 B2.

The menu claims L'Escale opened in 1927; the window says '47. Either way, most of the customers
look as if they've been settled in place since opening night. Most nurse slowly emptying bottles of
Flag Spéciale (13dh), half an eye on the big, boxy
wall-mounted TV, while engaging in sporadic chat
with the red-jacketed, grey-haired old gent who
patrols the big, bare paddock behind the high bar
counter. Though all male – or perhaps because it *is*
all male – Bar L'Escale is a totally non-threatening
environment (except maybe hygiene fetishists

might have a tough time). Beers can be taken out to the pavement tables and there's food in the form of grilled meats (*see p109*).

Bodega

23 rue de la Liberté (044 43 31 41). **Open** 7pm-1am daily. **Credit** MC, V. **Map** p252 B2.

Two defining characteristics of Bodega: very, very red and very, very loud. It's a modern bar (open a week when we visited) with stools up at the counter for boozers (local and imported beers, wine and cocktails), tables and benches for diners (tapas, tablas and boccadillos) and no space for dancing, which deters no one at all from trying, stomping on toes and elbowing earholes to the reckless encouragement of a DJ-mixed soundtrack of Latino vibes and urban R&B. Add flashing lights and video screen for a fine time had by all or a splitting headache,

depending on your age and outlook. There's a promising-looking courtyard out back, which should have been brought into play by now.

Café Atlas

place Abdel Moumen, avenue Mohammed V (044 44 88 88). **Open** 8am-10pm daily. **Credit** MC, V. **Map** p252 A2.

Along with Bar L'Escale (*see above*), this is one of only two places in town (at least, as far as we know) where alcohol can be drunk at streetside tables – ie in full public view – although seriously heavy Moroccan drinkers tend to hide their vice at the tables inside. A reputation as a rendezvous for foreign gents with local gigolos does the place few favours, but obvious uninterested parties are left well alone with the spectacle of the traffic free-for-all on place Abdel Moumen. A beer costs 13dh-20dh

Gay Marrakech

Moroccan law is clear when it comes to homosexuality – it's forbidden and the penalty for homosexual acts can be a prison sentence (for locals, that is; foreigners are left well alone). Despite this, sex among men is, and always has been, common, particularly given Moroccan society's strict separation of the sexes – no fraternising before marriage, the all-importance of a woman's virginity on the wedding night etc, etc. Things are getting ever more permissive, but male-on-male is still an expedient option. Besides, only the passive partner has ever been considered homosexual.

Since inheriting international favoured status, Marrakech has taken up the reins from Tangier as the most gay-friendly place in Morocco. Young colts are attracted here from all over the country, eager for the freedom playing away from home brings. There also remains the traditional heavy presence of old queens from Europe and America on tour in passionate pursuit of young delicacies, plus a newer, younger crowd of sophisticated weekend-away gays attracted by the glamour of Marrakech, staple of the fashion mags.

None of which amounts to any kind of gay community – yet – although there is a lot of action going on. So much so that a single man walking alone is likely to be approached at any time of day, and more especially at night. Male prostitutes are a slick and practised crowd (we wouldn't be surprised if they carry creditcard swipers), used to being spoiled by wealthy Europeans eager to spend on sex (often disappointing, so we hear, because of the Moroccans insistence on only

taking the 'active' role). Prime hangouts include the Café Atlas (*see p155*) in Guéliz, and several of the seedier nightclubs round place de la Liberté, notably Diamant Noir (*see p158*) – not every come-hither glance will be a rent boy but being poor here ain't going to make you many new friends.

Avenue Mohammed V between place de la Liberté and the Koutoubia Mosque doubles as a cruising area after midnight, but again, it's a search for money rather than love that propels (and beware the neighbouring Arset Abdelsalam garden where tourists have found themselves handing over wallets without even a grope in return). Romantic souls head for avenue El Yarmouk and a bench beneath the Old City walls, haunt of men looking for a bit of companionship or just a simple exchange of fluids, but not money. Biggest gay pick-up joint of all, though, is Jemaa El Fna. The majority of tourists pass through oblivious but among the circled audiences crowding the entertainers there are plenty of locking eyes. Likely prospects are approached from behind and a hardened 'expression of interest' none too discreetly pushed against them.

Pick-up by internet is increasingly popular and well facilitated by the proliferation of internet cafés. The local favourite is www.cybermen.com (Moroccan area code: mar). Cyber-contacts are quickly translated into mobile numbers and hence to meetings. Personal ads and responses also feature at www.kelma.org, which includes an online e-zine 'Kelmaghreb' focusing on gay issues in North Africa.

depending on the mood of the waiter, and patrons are also offered the chance to purchase anything from peanuts to lotto cards to carpets by itinerant salesmen. Leaving your cigs in view on the table invites a steady stream of supplicants, including those precisely groomed and scented boys in their snug-fitting white trousers.

Chesterfield Pub

Hotel Nassim, 1st floor, 115 avenue Mohammed V (044 44 64 01). **Open** 9am-1am daily. **Credit** MC, V (min 200dh). **Map** p252 B2.

Also known as the 'Bar Anglais', but don't be fooled as there's nothing particularly English about this vertically challenged little first-floor hotel bar. A tiny front lounge is cast in an eerie glow by a luminously underlit pool the other side of a glass wall; the larger back bar is an equally twilit gents' hangout, permanently heavy with a fug of cigarette smoke. Between is a polished mahogany counter area dispensing bottled and draught beers, spirits and cocktails at reasonable cost (*pression* Flag 30dh). Best of all is the open-air (poolside) patio with lots of garden-furniture-style seating, a languid air and friendly waiter service – a popular Friday night meet-up venue for expats on the razz.

El Moualamid Bar

Hotel El Moualamid, 6th floor, avenue Mohammed V (044 44 88 55). **Open** 5pm-2am daily. **No credit cards. Map** p252 A2.

It has all the charm of a Mongolian bus station waiting room – with added drunkenness – but the beer is cheap and there are great views from the outdoor terrace (six floors up) south down Mohammed V to the Koutoubia minaret. A resident band with a frightening way with a synth brings the elderly boozy males to their unsteady feet, while the hard-faced local 'ladies' patiently bide their time. On the right night it could pass for fun. To ascend to these tawdry heights, enter the uninviting corner bar just north of place Abdel Moumen and take the lift.

Montecristo

20 rue Ibn Aicha (044 43 90 31). **Open** 8pm-2am daily. **Credit** AmEx, MC, V. **Map** p252 A1.

Despite shameful beginnings (the developers tore down a fine 1930s villa to replace it with the present house-shaped pile of concrete), Montecristo hasn't turned out badly at all. Ignore the ground-floor restaurant (everybody else does) and head straight upstairs to join a smart set of foxy chiquitas and macho hombres (smell that aftershave! Check out those goatees!) slinking and strutting to samba and salsa. Off to the side of the dancefloor is a small area of non-ergonomic seating, made all the more uncomfortable by the inevitable crush of bodies. For elbow room and aural respite head up to the cushion-strewn rooftop terrace to sip by starlight. Bottled beers are supplemented by cocktails (70dh) and shots of tequila (also 70dh), delivered by waiters in blood-red sashes. Tapas dishes and single-wrapped cigars are available.

Musica Bar

boulevard Mohammed Zerktouni (no phone). **Open** 7pm-midnight daily. **No credit cards. Map** p252 B2.

Its gaping black hole of an entrance, signed with a desultory scrawl of neon, looks as if it belongs on the Reeperbahn or, at least the darkest corner of Soho. But the Musica Bar isn't as classy as that. Enter – if you dare – into a huge tiled hall of swimming pool acoustics that nightly reverberates to the mad cacophony of a five- or six-piece mini Arab orchestra. Fuelled by cheap bottled beer, punters are too far gone to dance but they bang their hands on the tabletops (and occasionally against each other) and wail along with the chorus. Downstairs is a nightclub of sorts that kicks off as the bar closes, but we've always declined to explore further.

Samovar

133 rue Mohammed El Bekal (no phone). **Open** 7pm-2am daily. **No credit cards. Map** p252 A2.

A small nursery's worth of potted plants fills the pavement outside, a vain stab at a camouflage of comformity for what is the most raucous saloon in town. Two rooms heave with a crush of cheap furniture, drunken wideboys, gnarled old soaks and steely women. Body contact is frequent, unavoidable and occasionally opportunistic. It's a place where 'too much to drink' is the natural state of being and the underlying threat of violence is periodically realised before being quickly smothered by laconic bar staff who calm the odd alarmed foreigner with a resigned shrug. You don't want to go to the toilets. Come, if you will, and take a walk on the Marrakech wild side, but don't come crying to us afterwards.

La Strada

90 rue Mohammed El Bekal (061 24 20 94). **Open** 7pm-2am daily. **No credit cards. Map** p252 A2.

By day this is a local take on a pizza restaurant, (which means at least the tabletops and floor get a wipe over every now and again), but by night the oven goes cold and place settings are pushed aside to accommodate steadily growing collections of empty bottles. Upstairs is a small air-conditioned lounge with cushioned seating, which is where the 'ladies' hang out. We feel safer staying down on the ground floor, watched over by a grimacing, bare-chested Anthony Quinn in a large, framed film poster of Fellini's *La Strada*.

Palmeraie & further afield

Karaoke Bar

Palmeraie Golf Palace, Palmeraie (044 30 10 10). **Open** 7.30pm-2am daily. **Credit** MC, V.

Part of the massive Golf Palace resort complex, the Karaoke is a pub-style hotel bar that does a good trade as a pre-club venue to the New Feeling (*see p158*) next door – although the drinks here are hardly any less expensive. Microphones and vocalless backing tracks do indeed constitute a major component of the house proceedings: locals take

Let's be **Avenue**, then.
See p158.

their karaoke very seriously indeed and give highly polished performances. Thankfully, there are usually enough willing and attrocious foreigners present to show how it really should be done.

KM9

Route de l'Ourika, km9 (044 37 63 73). **Open** 8pm-midnight daily. **No credit cards.**
Better known for its fine Italian cuisine (*see p114*), KM9 also has a reputation as a weekend party venue. Sofas and leather armchairs provide for lounging, with drinks delivered by waitservice. DJ decks and a small dancefloor aim to stir things up once the neighbouring diners are done. When summer nights really take off, guests spill out back into a garden hung with several hundred coloured lanterns. And if everybody is really good, the boys behind the venture open up their house, a palatial residence with room after room of kitsch and glamour (reclining golden Buddhas, carved tusks from Bali, Indian carved doors) plus disco lights, state-of-the-art sound system and glitter ball.

Clubs

The club scene is firmly stuck at disco – with nothing knowingly retro or ironic about it either. Expect a mix of jazzy Latino, Arab beats and the occasional descent into Britney. Tables are generally reserved for gents who slap down wadded cash for a bottle of spirits (800dh minimum). Unfinished bottles are labelled and stored for next time. Turn up before midnight and staff outnumber customers – most of whom will be 'working', if you know what we mean.

Avenue

Le Meridien N'Fis, avenue de France, Hivernage (044 43 11 51). **Open** 10pm-3am daily. **Credit** MC, V. **Map** p252 B5.
The newest of Marrakech clubs, Avenue's fronted by the most wonderful of entrances, in the form of a small rotunda filled with candles in pigeonholes. From here a grand staircase descends beneath glinting chandeliers to a fancy, under-lit, salsa-shaken disco lounge. Heaps of money have obviously gone into the place (check out the swirly metal inlaid tabletops), which is why punters are charged 80dh for a beer, 100dh for a cocktail – an attempt to recoup costs, possibly. No amount of mirrored walls can disguise what a mean space it is, but turn up on the right night and it packs plenty of grooves into its tight little party pants.

Diamant Noir

Hotel Marrakech, place de la Liberté, avenue Mohammed V, Guéliz (044 43 43 51). **Open** 10pm-4am daily. **Admission** 80dh Mon-Thur, Sun; 100dh Fri, Sat (incl 1 drink). **No credit cards.**
Map p252 C3.
Spurned by the smart set, Diamant Noir nevertheless remains popular with party boys and girls, and a smattering of expats, including the Euro queens.

It's a non-judgemental crowd, making it something of a refuge with the country-wide Moroccan gay community. Scout out the talent going in from the vantage of the neighbouring house pizzeria (it faces the club entrance; open until 4am) before descending down and down to the sub-basement dancefloor (passing a couple of bar levels and pool area en route). Music is a better-than-average mix of Arabesque and electrobeats spun by a roster of competent house DJs. Everybody is here searching for A Good Time – most people find it.

New Feeling

Palmeraie Golf Palace, Palmeraie (044 30 10 10). **Open** 11pm-3.30am daily. **Admission** 100dh Mon-Thur, Sun; 150dh Fri, Sat (incl 1 drink). **Credit** MC, V.
Rivalling the Paradise (*see below*) for the mantle of 'best club', New Feeling numbers local TV and movie stars among its habitués, and was once the haunt of the current king in his 'princely' days. A raised glass dance podium allows for maximum exhibitionism, while lesser stars twinkle on the polished steel dancefloor below. Weekends are so busy that it is virtually impossible to get a drink at the bar. Sit-outs are best spent on the smaller upper gallery, which is usually pleasantly empty. Be warned: taxis charge a minimum of 100dh each way to get out here from the city centre.

Paradise Club

Kempinski Mansour Eddahbi, avenue de France, Hivernage (044 33 91 00). **Open** 10.30pm-4am daily. **Admission** 150dh (incl 1 drink). **Credit** MC, V. **Map** p252 B4.
The largest club in town, the Paradise is the current in-place. It attracts a fairly sophisticated and mon-eyed crowd, which is predominantly Moroccan. A grand flight of luminous steps leads down to the main arena where spacious enclaves of seating encircle the comparatively small – and hence crowded – dancefloor. An upper level is equally as vast with added distractions of pool and table football, as well as prime viewing of the impressive light show playing over assembled little disco-poppets below.

Stars House

place de la Liberté, avenue Mohammed V, Guéliz (044 43 45 69). **Open** 10pm-4am daily. **Admission** 100dh (incl 1 drink). **Credit** MC, V. **Map** p252 C3.
The only nightclub not attached to a hotel, this club was hailed as the Studio 54 of Marrakech when it opened several years ago. It falls an abyss short of those ambitions, but that's not to say it isn't worth a visit. Flounce down the neon-striped tunnel to the upper-basement level where a jobbing Arabic orchestra saws away at Middle Eastern classics while local couples canoodle in the semi-gloom. Down again to the nightclub proper, with a circular dancefloor overhung by a sci-fi spider-like light rig. Equally alarming are the predatory, leather-clad local ladies, who between sultry demands of random men to 'light their cigarettes' (nervous males should not visit unaccompanied) shoot a mean game of pool.

Sport & Fitness

Football rules but Moroccan success remains firmly on the track.

If you want to strike up a conversation with any male in Marrakech – or in Morocco for that matter – just ask him what football team he supports. It's unlikely to be KAC, the local Marraekch outfit, struggling in the league as we go to press and finishing yet another season without silverware. Chances are the answer will be Manchester United or Liverpool or maybe Real Madrid, quickly followed by a run-down of the current line-up and pithy comments on home and away form. These guys are fiercely passionate about their footie – as was hammered home in posters plastered across the country not too long ago in an attempt to woo UEFA officials in the process of choosing a host nation for the World Cup 2006. The attempt failed but the Moroccans remain undaunted (*see p163* **2010: A football odyssey?**).

Look past soccer and there's little else to see, except maybe some lone figures in numbered singlets, single-mindedly pounding along an arcing stretch of pink gravel. The international success of athletes such as Said Aouita (former 1,500m, 2,000m, 3,000m and 5,000m record holder), Hicham El Guerrouj (five times 1,500m world champion and 2001 Athlete of the Year) and Nezha Bidouane (women's world champion 400m hurdler) has proved a national inspiration. Seriously sweat-stained runners are a common sight on the wide road that rings the age-old walls of Marrakech Medina. The success of Moroccans in these track events is remarkable considering the lack of facilities at grass roots level – which is also the reason why Moroccans have made little impact in the more technical (that is to say, expensive) disciplines.

Spectator sports

This is not a sporting city. Gates for league football games at El Harti Stadium are counted in the hundreds rather than thousands. Top local soccer team is **Kawkab** ('KAC': *see p163* **2010: A football odyssey?**). Second string to Kawkab are **Najm Sport Marrakech**, a second division semi-pro side in perpetual money trouble, whose players are forced to earn their keep elsewhere.

Marrakech also possesses **handball** and **basketball** teams, but interest is minimal at best, particularly since the local boys have dropped out of national competition.

The only other sport with any presence is athletics, with plenty of running clubs in town, whose members compete in local, regional and national competitions at all levels. However, the only real spectator sport element to this is the Marrakech Marathon held each January (next event: 18 Jan 2004). Now in its 15th year, the marathon starts and finishes on Jemaa El Fna and the route goes around the city walls and out through the Palmeraie. Last time round runners numbered around 5,000, though as yet, it attracts few foreign competitors other than the French. A half-marathon is also held on the same day over the same course. For details contact Monsieur Azizi of **Running Club Maroc** (+33 6 63 26 27 87/fax +33 3 88 29 64 16/www.runningclubmaroc.com).

Daoudiate Stadium
Route les Philistines, off avenue Palestine, Hay Mohammadi, Daoudiate (no phone).
An indoor stadium that's venue of choice for all non-footballing sports events of any significance.

El Harti Stadium
Jnane El Harti, Guéliz (044 42 06 66).
Map p252 B3.
Home to the Kawkab and Najm football teams. It seats just 15,000 and facilities are a little sparse. Tickets are usually bought on the day, but sometimes can be bought in advance for big games (against the top Casablanca teams for example).

Active sports

The development of the local sporting scene is led by foreign money – so few municipal swimming pools or five-a-side football courts for the Medina kids, but loads of moneyed-up activities like golf and quad bikes. The saving grace is the proximity of the mountains. A day trip tramping around the Ourika Valley or up to the ski resort of Oukaimeden makes for a popular locals' day out. It's the most incredible sight to see jellaba-clad Marrakchi families heating up their tajines while fully clad skiers in Day-Glo-coloured kit whoosh by. Unfortunately, the most accessible parts of the mountains have been well and truly over-developed by small-time entrepreneurs.

For contact details of local tour companies that organise trekking trips into the Atlas Mountains *see p89* **Around Marrakech.**

Thar' he blows: the
Marrakech Marathon.
See p159.

Climbing

Although Morocco has some incredible cliffs, there is little local enthusiasm for climbing as a sport. There are a handful of mountaineering clubs, but few people have the skills or equipment to participate. While the Todra Gorge on the southern side of the Atlas Mountains is the best known and most widely climbed bit of Morocco, there are also plenty of places to climb in the Marrakech region. Most of these sites are unknown and undeveloped.

High Country
31 Bab Amadel, Amizmiz (044 45 48 47/www. highcountry.co.uk/adventure@highcountry.co.uk). **Open** 8.30am-5pm Mon-Fri.
High Country is the only reputable locally based operator to offer rock climbing. It's a British- and American-run operation of over 12 years experience that sets up climbs for groups of four or more using sites deep in the Western High Atlas Mountains.

Golf

It's the most bizarre phenomenon – the push to market Marrakech as a golfers' paradise (*see p64* **Green tourism**). Several tour companies specialise in Moroccan golf packages, combining courses in several cities over the span of a week or two; typing 'golf' and 'Morocco' into a web search engine will provide names and phone numbers.

Golf D'Amelkis
Route de Ouarzazate, km12 (044 40 44 14/fax 044 40 44 15). **Open** *Summer* 8am-4pm daily. *Winter* 8am-2pm daily. **Rates** 18 holes 450dh; daily green fees 600dh; caddy fee 80dh for 18 holes. **Credit** AmEx, MC, V.
The newest course in town: 18-hole, 72 par, designed by American Cabell B Robinson. It's a ten-minute drive from the Medina, with the über-expensive Amanjena resort as a neighbour – slice your drive and you could take out a celeb. There's a kasbah-styled clubhouse fit to grace any first-class course in California with a well-stocked pro shop. Clubs etc are available for hire at 200dh.

Palmeraie Golf Palace
Palmeraie Golf Palace Hotel & Resort, Palmeraie (044 30 10 10/fax 044 30 63 66/www.pgp.co.ma/ golfpalace@pgp.ma). **Open** 7.30am-7pm daily. **Rates** 18 holes 450dh; daily green fees 600dh; caddy fee 80dh 18 holes. **Credit** AmEx, MC, V.
Part of a massive Palmeraie resort complex (complete with swimming pools, a kiddies' playground, tennis and squash courts, stables and paddocks, and various other activities), this is an 18-hole, par 72 course designed by Robert Trent Jones in classical US style with a Mauresque clubhouse, seven lakes and lots and lots of palms. Individual clubs to hire are 25dh, or 260dh for the full bag.

Royal Golf Club

Ancienne route de Ouarzazate, km2 (044 40 98 28).
Open *Summer* sunrise-sunset daily; *Winter* 9am-
2.30pm daily. **Rates** daily green fees 400dh; caddy
fee 80dh for 18 holes. **Credit** MC, V.
Built in the 1920s by the dreaded El Glaoui (*see p11*
The last despot), the Royal Golf is laid out around
a grove of cypress, eucalyptus and palms just south
of the city limits. It has a down at heel post-colonial
feel; fairways are tatty round the edges but some of
the holes offer stirring views of the Atlas Mountains
to the south. Winston Churchill and Dwight D
Eisenhower did the rounds here, and it remains a
favourite with members of the Moroccan royal family. Required handicap for men is 32; for women 35.
Caddies are mandatory. There's no clubhouse
(although a couple of old women do serve food and
drink out of a dark nook) and only a very limited
selection of equipment is available for rent.

Horse-riding

Marrakech has its horsey set, comprised of
expats and moneyed locals. For the latter group,
it's very much a status thing; the present king's
aunt, Amina El Alawi, is the president of the
Royal Association Equestre, and as such it
enjoys powerful royal patronage. For visitors, a
canter round the fields outside town makes
for a fine release from Medina madness.

Cavalier Ranch

*Route de Fès, km14 (062 61 22 51/cavalierranch@
menara.ma).* **Open** 8.30am-7pm Tue-Sun. **Rates**
100dh per hr; 600dh per day (incl food); 5,000dh per
wk. **No credit cards.**
Cavalier Ranch has only been established for a few
years and is relatively small, but a variety of horse-
riding trips are on offer, from an hour, to a day or a
week-long trip (with organised accommodation).

Club Equestre de la Palmeraie

*Palmeraie Golf Palace Hotel & Resort, Palmeraie
(044 36 87 93/www.pgp.co.ma).* **Open** *Winter* 8am-
noon, 3-6pm daily. *Summer* 8am-noon, 3-8pm daily
(Wed & Sat afternoon reserved for club members).
Rates *Horses* 150dh per hr; 800dh per day. *Ponies*
50dh per 15mins; 90dh per hr. **No credit cards.**
Part of the Golf Palace resort, the Club Equestre has
extensive stables with an adjacent training area for
beginners. Experienced riders are led out into the
groves of the Palmeraie to canter by local villages.

Jebel Atlas

*Golf Palmier Club, Club Boulahrir, route de Fès,
km8 (044 32 94 51/fax 044 32 94 54/
www.golfpalmier.ch).* **Open** 9am-6pm Tue-Sun.
Rates 150dh per hr. **Credit** MC, V.
This beautifully constructed, Swiss-run site has a
great atmosphere, and caters to all levels. After a
session in the saddle, there's a relaxing clubhouse.
Accommodation is available at the club, as well as
swimming, mini-golf and tennis facilities.

Royal Club Equestre de Marrakech

Route d'Amizmiz, km4 (044 38 18 49). **Open** 8am-
noon, 2-6pm Tue-Sun. **Rates** *Horses* 150dh per hr.
Ponies 15dh per 15mins. **No credit cards.**
Trainers are often well-known ex-national competitors and this well-run, state-owned establishment
has a wonderfully relaxed atmosphere. Longer
group trips don't have fixed prices or times, so it's
best to call beforehand. English is spoken by some
members of staff.

In-line skating

The Association l'Originalité et l'Continuité
Marrakech is devoted to the promotion of in-line
skating. So far, the main manifestation of its
efforts is an international competition that
debuted in Marrakech in January 2003. Place
du 16 Novembre and a large portion of avenue
Mohammed V in central Guéliz were closed to
traffic and adorned with ramps and bollards to
facilitate events like speed slaloming. For more
information contact the Assocation.

Association l'Originalité et l'Continuité Marrakech

Hay Inara, Targa Bloc 3, No.319 (061 92 90 75).
Open 9am-2pm, 4-9pm daily. **No credit cards.**

Karting & quads

Why Marrakech is such a magnet for karting
and quad operators is a mystery (too much silly
money floating around?) but their numbers
continue to grow steadily. Quad novices receive
a short training session prior to being taken on
a romp around the locale.

Atlas Karting

Route de Safi (064 19 05 37). **Open** 8am-7pm daily.
Rates *Karts* 100dh 10mins; 250dh 30mins; 300dh
40mins; 450dh 1hr. *Quads* 340dh as passenger, 500dh
as pilot 90mins. **No credit cards.**
Owned and run by a French karting pro, this is a
fully competitive course, challenging and fun to
drive. It's the venue for an annual 24-hour marathon
and is on the European Karting competitive circuit.
Quads have recently been added.

Mega Quad Excursions

Route d'Amizmiz, km6 (044 38 31 91). **Open**
8.30am-7pm Mon-Sat. **Rates** 800dh per quad (seats
2) for a half-day. **Credit** AmEx, MC, V.
Owned and run by a Belgian and European ex-
champion, it's a slickly run operation. Machines are
kept in tiptop order. You are expected to follow a set
route across country and along dirt tracks, with an
organised tea break midway en route.

Nakhil Quad

Route de Palmeraie (061 15 99 10). **Open** 9am-
noon, 2-5pm daily. **Rates** 500dh for 2hrs pilot,
340dh passenger. **No credit cards.**

Horses for courses at the **Club Equestre de la Palmeraie**. *See p161.*

Tucked away behind the Coralia Club hotel, Nakhil was the first with quads in Marrakech. However, it hasn't invested in updating and the machines are a little old and not as well maintained as they could be. Great location, though, allowing for fantastic rides through the Palmeraie and its villages.

Skiing

Oukaimeden, 70 kilometres (43 miles) outside Marrakech, boasts a number of chair lifts and ski runs. Ski hire is cheap (although equipment is old), the pass for the lifts is cheap – what would make it all perfect would be snow. However, in recent years drought has meant minimal precipitation and next to no snowfall. When it's wetter, the skiing season is usually from December through to the beginning of March. If it snows and if you don't have your own transport, you'll have to negotiate the hire of a taxi for the day, as it is almost impossible to find a return ride down from the resort; for an idea of daily taxi hire rates, *see* 'Getting Around' in the **Directory**.

Swimming

Most of the year Marrakech is hot, hot, hot, so you'd think there'd be swimming pools all over the place, right? Wrong. And those that there are have highly restricted access. All local pools are owned by the municipality and most are leased out to local clubs and hence closed to the public at large.

There are just three pools open to all-comers (Daoudiate, El Koutoubia and Sidi Youssef Ben Ali), although even these have associated training clubs that have exclusive use at certain times of the day. They're frequented wholly by

male adolescents (this is a Muslim country, remember), and women should stay well clear – the sight of a fair-skinned woman in a bikini would almost certainly result in mass staring, drooling, leching, possibly groping, certainly pant wetting.

Fewer hotels than might be expected have pools thanks to the space restrictions of the Medina. Those places that do, zealously enforce a guests-only policy. Exceptions are few; they include the **Palmeraie Golf Palace** (Palmeraie, 044 36 87 93, pool open 9am-7pm daily), which charges 100dh for day use, the **Sheraton** (avenue de la Menara, Hivernage, 044 44 89 98, 10am-6pm daily, 200dh) and the **Sofitel** (*see p52*), which charges 150dh (open 10am-6pm daily). In summer 2002 hotels **El Andalous** (avenue du Président Kennedy, 044 44 82 26) and **Les Jardins de la Koutoubia** (26 rue de la Koutoubia, 044 38 88 00) offered lunch and pool deals but at press time both were unsure whether this would be continued in summer 2003.

Piscine Daoudiate

Route les Philistines, off avenue Palestine, Hay Mohammedi, Daoudiate (044 31 04 28). **Open** 9am-noon, 2-5pm daily from 2nd wk June to 1st wk Sept only. **Admission** 5dh.

Piscine El Koutoubia

Rue Abou El Abbass Essebti, Medina (044 38 68 64). **Open** 9am-noon, 3-6pm Mon, Wed-Sun from 2nd wk June to 1st wk Sept only. **Admission** 5dh. **Map** p250 A5.

Piscine Sidi Youssef Ben Ali

Avenue El Mederisa, Quartier Sidi Youssef Ben Ali, (044 40 21 35). **Open** 9am-noon, 2-5pm daily July & Aug only. **Admission** 5dh. **Map** p251 F9.

2010: A football odyssey?

For young nations, flags, airlines and football shirts constitute a common banner, a shared identity. Many post-colonial African nations first applied to join world football's governing body, FIFA, well before completing the forms for entry to the United Nations.

Few African teams, however, had the pedigree and tradition of Morocco, footballing pioneer of post-independence Africa.

The Moroccans took to the game way back in the early 1900s, the Spanish having introduced it to Cueta and Ifni, and the French to Tangier, Casablanca and Fès. Much like South America, from that moment boys of every age could be seen kicking a ball about in communal games in the streets and on the beach. A local league was set up in 1916, won by CA Casablanca, where the league headquarters were based. Casablanca soon became the powerbase for the Moroccan game. Fierce competition bred world-class players, who exported their talents to the professional game in France. The prime example was Casablanca-born Larbi Ben Barek, a virtuoso talent who became a hero at Olympique Marseille and went on to play many times for the French national team. Ben Barek was a figurehead for the burgeoning game in pre-independence Morocco.

In this era of 16-team World Cup finals, the tournament was played almost exclusively by teams from Europe and South America. Morocco helped break this stranglehold in 1970. Having beaten major European teams in friendlies during the 1960s, the 'Lions of the Atlas' gave semi-finalists West Germany – Beckenbauer, Seeler, Muller and all – a huge fright, only falling to a late goal to lose 2-1. A creditable 1-1 draw with Bulgaria saw the Moroccan amateurs leave Mexico with pride.

Star of the side was Mohammedia striker Ahmed Faras, who would lead his country to their only African Nations Cup victory in 1976. By now, the local game had garnered enough state funds and sponsorship to keep the likes of Faras at home, and the leading players could turn professional. This allowed Moroccan teams to acquit themselves with credit in the major African club competitions. In 2002 the two major clubs from Casablanca, Raja and Wydad, each made the final of the two major continental tournaments, Wydad winning the African Cup Winners' Cup.

At home too Casablanca dominates, with Raja, Wydad or Olimpic winning the league title 12 times in the last 17 years. Although lagging behind the leading lights of Casablanca, modest Kawkab ('KAC') of Marrakech are a top league side. They were title winners in 1992 and have won the prestigious El Arch Cup (the Moroccan equivalent of England's FA Cup) five times. In 2002 they narrowly avoided relegation brought on by financial crisis, but have since brought in a well-known national trainer and bolstered the squad.

Both KAC and their more modest local rivals, Najm, play at the main El Harti Stadium in Guéliz. The rather sparse stadium is adequate for local needs, but such is the push to host a World Cup finals – Morocco has applied and failed twice, but still has high hopes to pip South Africa to stage the 2010 tournament promised to Africa – that a major new sports complex is being built on the outskirts of Marrakech. Still in the planning stage, the facility is to be built on the main road out to Casablanca, a fitting footballing goal to aim for.

Tennis

Most of the large hotels have tennis courts but, as with their swimming pools, use tends to be restricted to guests only. One exception is the Palmeraie Golf Palace (see the Golf section for details), where both squash and tennis courts are for hire to the general public at 100dh per person per hour.

Royal Tennis Club de Marrakech
rue Oued El Makhazine, Jnane El Harti, Guéliz (044 43 19 02). **Open** 7am-8pm daily. **Rates** 100dh per hr. **No credit cards. Map** p252 B3.

As much social club as sports centre, this is where Marrakech's well-heeled families meet to gossip and model all-whites. There are only six courts and the place is popular, so reservations are essential.

Health & fitness

Weightlifting and bodybuilding are beloved of Moroccan men across all income brackets and social groups (check the number of magazines on the newsstands devoted to ballooning musculature). Cheaper gyms and fitness centres tend to be dominated by men, and women will certainly not feel comfortable. Anyone who

Green tourism

In a region where average temperatures for most of the year are a grass-withering 25°C-38°C (77°F-100°F), where precipitation is minimal and water resources at a premium, covering great swathes of land with high-maintenance turf (ie fairways and greens) seems more than slightly mad. But it is madness with method.

Tourism is one of Morocco's few major industries and, after beaches, scenery and history, nothing attracts high-rolling, big-spending foreign visitors like golf.

Morocco's previous monarch, King Hassan II, also happened to be a golfing fanatic. He played as often as the royal schedule allowed and employed a squadron of caddies, one of whom was responsible for gripping the royal cigarette with a pair of silver tongs while the king swung.

Although not a natural player the king's scores were improved with help from American pro instructors (notably Claude Harmon, father of Claude Harmon Jr, teacher of Tiger Woods) and also by the fact that kings are not obliged to play from bad lies or out of sand traps.

Building golf courses became an important part of the royal vision for modernisation of the country. Prime showpiece is the Dar Es Salam Royal Golf Club in Rabat, which is also the venue each November for the annual King Hassan II Trophy, famous in sportswriting circles for its lavish junkets.

Marrakech benefits from any and all pro-am tournaments (including the Open du Maroc held every April) because although the comps tee off far to the north, plenty of the players also take the opportunity to indulge in a little golfing tourism down south. That's not to mention the jet-set European golfers who flit down to these balmy climes when winter rain puts a halt to their game at home.

The main course in Marrakech is the Amelkis, a rolling landscape of baize-like greenery, studded with palm groves – and real desert sandtraps – and fringed by sumptuous Moorish fantasy villas. For rich Marrakchis a house overlooking the greens is the ultimate in one-upmanship. Property options are soon to widen too, with a further 18 holes to be added at Amelkis and two completely new courses on the city fringes.

feels they can't cope without a workout should consider staying in a hotel with the requisite facilities – a list that includes all the big five-stars, plus riads Ifoulki, Kaiss and Mabrouka.

Gyms/fitness centres

There are probably over 100 small- to medium-sized gyms in Marrakech. Every area of the city has one. They all have equipment for weight training and possibly some of the following: boxing, judo, karate and taekwondo. Entry is typically by monthly subscription, which on average is around 150dh. Day rates are uncommon, but we wouldn't bet on not being able to get in on payment of a nominal fee.

Kawkab
Salle Couverte Ben Ron, Daoudiate (044 42 06 66). **Open** 8am-10pm daily. **Rates** 100dh-150dh per mth. **No credit cards.**

Kawkab Sportif du Marrakech
Battement Lahbess, Bab Doukkala, Medina (044 43 31 33). **Open** 6am-10pm daily. **Rates** 270dh-300dh per mth. **No credit cards. Map** p248 A3.

Nakhil Gym
75 rue Ibn Aicha, Guéliz (044 43 92 90). **Open** 8am-10pm daily. **Rates** 270dh-300dh per mth. **No credit cards. Map** p252 A2.
This place also offers aerobics classes for women three days a week.

Club Zitouna Sportif
60 Hay Mohammedi, Daoudiate (063 278 226). **Open** 8am-10pm Mon-Sat. **Rates** 270dh-300dh per mth. **No credit cards.**

Hammams

Anyone who's visited the famed bathhouses of Turkey or Syria is in for a big disappointment. The public hammams of Marrakech are a pedestrian lot. But if they're lacking in architectural finery, they are rich in social significance – and they get the job done of getting a body clean.

The advent of internal plumbing for all has meant that hammam-going is no longer the popular ritual it used to be, but many who live in the Medina will still go at least once a week to meet friends and gossip. For the uninitiated, entering a hammam for the first time can be a baffling experience. After paying (prices are set by the state at 7dh for men, 7.50dh for women), leave your clothes (and a little baksheesh) with the attendant. Men keep on their shorts, women go naked (all hammams are single sex). There are three rooms: one cool, one hot, one very hot (although for some of the poorer hammams read cold, cool, tepid). The idea is to spend as long as

you can in the hottest room then retreat to the less-hot place and douse yourself with water. In public hammams there's usually a 'trainer' who, for an additional fee, delivers a massage. Bring your own towels etc.

It's increasingly common for hotels to include a hammam as part of the facilities, and these are now some of the best in town (although without the social opportunities). Unfortunately, use tends to be restricted to guests only, but happy exceptions are La Maison Arabe, Riad Mehdi and Palais Rhoul, which is reckoned to offer the ultimate in hammam experiences (for all, *see p166*).

Hammam El Bacha
20 rue Fatima Zohra, Medina (no phone). **Open** *Men* 7am-1pm daily. *Women* 1-9pm daily. **Rates** 7dh men, 7.50dh women; massage 50dh. **No credit cards. Map** p248 B4.
Probably the best-known hammam in town, thanks to its past role as local soak for the servants and staff of the Dar El Bacha opposite. It boasts impressive dimensions and a 6m (20ft) high cupola, but it's very badly maintained – we wouldn't necessarily count on coming out any cleaner than you went in.

Hammam El Grmai
Bab Aylen, Medina (no phone). **Open** *Men* 7am-1pm daily. *Women* 1-9pm daily. **Rates** 7dh men; 7.50dh women; massage 50dh. **No credit cards. Map** p249 F5.
A traditional hammam, this place has the old-fashioned basin from which you collect water to wash in a bowl (modern hammams have taps). In the changing areas the floor is covered with *hsira* mats made of grass or palm leaves; interiors throughout are done out in tadelakt. Unlike modern hammams at which you pay on entry, here you pay as you leave.

Hammam El Mehdi
Belbcar, Daoudiate (no phone). **Open** *Men* 6am-9.30pm daily. *Women* 6am-9.30pm daily. **Rates** 7dh men; 7.50dh women; massage 50dh. **No credit cards.**
One of the newer public hammams, and therefore one of the cleaner, with a well-lit and fully tiled interior and separate men's and women's sections. It has no connection to the riad of the same name (*see p166*).

Hammam Menara
Quartier Essaada, Medina (no phone). **Open** *Men* 10am-9pm Tue, Thur, Sat. *Women* 10am-9pm Mon, Wed, Fri, Sun. **Rates** 60dh; massage 60dh. **No credit cards.**
The Menara is the first of a new breed of high-end 'luxury' hammams aimed at the local market. It's beautifully done with individual *vasques* with marble stools (so you don't have to sit on the floor), and the scrubdown with the *kissa* (loofah mitten) takes place on a slab. There's a pleasant salon in which to relax afterwards. It's located out beyond the Menara Gardens but most taxi drivers know how to find it.

Arts & Entertainment

Douche with panache at a **hammam**.

tiful setting in which most of us are ever likely to voluntarily sweat buckets. Best of all is the massage, administered MC Youssef, whose manipulation of joints is so vigorous that victims are reduced to jelly. Slither into the cool basin afterwards to be revived with fresh mint tea. It's the best pampering money can buy – but don't forget to factor in the cost of getting out to the Palmeraie and back.

Spas

Spas and associated treatments are becoming big news in Marrakech. Almost all riads offer massage on request, and an increasing number are making available extras such as aromatherapy. Riad Mehdi and the spa at Agafay had only just opened in spring 2003, and we've since heard of a great new Oriental Spa at the **Hotel Es Saadi** (*see p52*). Also in early 2003 the Marrakech Riads people (*see p45* **Dar Zelije**) were at work converting an old house in the Medina into a total holistic health and fitness retreat. More facilities of a similar nature are bound to follow. Watch this space.

Kasbah Agafay

Route de Guemassa (044 36 86 00/ www.kasbahagafay.com). **Rates** facials 500dh: hammam 400dh; massage from 400dh; pedicure & manicure 250dh. **Credit** MC, V.
Agafay's newly opened spa is accommodated in a tent-like structure in the grounds of the kasbah. It includes massage, aromatherapy, facials, hair treatment, manicures and pedicures, mud and algae baths, a fantastic yoga room hung with purple and scarlet chiffons and a central fountain infused with oils. Afterwards, herbal teas are served on the lawn. *See p58* for further details on the kasbah.

Riad Mehdi

2 Derb Sedra, Bab Agnaou, Medina (044 38 47 13). **Open** 8am-9pm daily. **Rates** facial 300dh; manicure 110dh; pedicure 140dh; hammam 60dh, massage 190dh-400dh; bath treatments 150dh. **Credit** MC, V. **Map** p250 B8.
Adjacent to the accommodation at Riad Mehdi (*see p48*) is an extensive spa complex occupying several rooms and a courtyard of an old Medina house. Treatments include all manner of baths – with essential oils, algae, refreshing mint and orange blossom milk – as well as various massages (Moroccan, Californian, relaxing, medical).

Sport et Bien

Résidence Dalia, avenue Yacoub El Mansour, Guéliz (044 44 30 39 23). **Open** 8am-9pm daily. **Rates** pool 75dh per day; gym 100dh per hr. **Credit** MC, V. **Map** p252 B2.
The best of its kind in Marrakech, Sport et Bien (formerly Beauty Line Space) offers a well-equipped gym and heated pool, as well as massage, hammam and general beauty treatments. Individual programmes can be tailored by a specialist.

Hammam Nakhil

Zohor 1, Ain Itti (no phone). **Open** *Men* 6am-9.30pm daily. *Women* 6am-9.30pm daily. **Rates** 7dh men; 7.50dh women; massage 50dh. **No credit cards.**
Another new hammam similar to the Mehdi (*see above*), but possibly easier to get to because of its location just outside the city walls. Beware the hot room, especially at weekends – the proprietor has a tendency to overheat it to discourage people from lingering. Unfortunately, people have been known to faint as a result. On your way out, when you're changing, collect a free cup of tea.

La Maison Arabe

1 Derb Assehbe, Bab Doukkala (044 38 70 10/ fax 044 38 72 21/www.lamaisonarabe.com/ maisonarabe@iam.net.ma). **Open** by appointment only. **Rates** see text. **Credit** MC, V. **Map** p248 A4.
The ultimate in self-indulgence – a hammam with rubdown (gommage) administered by a vicious pro, followed by an all-over body treatment (350dh). Another package includes the most thorough of massages (650dh).

Palais Rhoul

route de Fès, Palmeraie (044 32 94 94/ www.palaisrhoul.com). **Open** by appointment only. **Rates** 400dh. **Credit** MC, V.
The Palais Rhoul is one of those ridiculously opulent and exclusive Palmeraie villas, which exist outside the credit limit of most ordinary human beings. It is possible to breathe in its rarefied air, though, by booking a visit to the hammam. It's the most beau-

Best of Morocco

Getting Started

From pre-Saharan plains to cosmopolitan cities, Morocco packs it in.

Morocco is a country that, almost in sight of southern Spain, contains an area so ungovernable that huge tracts of land can be used for cannabis cultivation, despite all the efforts of the 'war on drugs'. This is a land poised between the medieval and the modern world, a place where you can catch a bus from a city of commuting white-collar workers to an oasis of camel jockeys in robes and turbans.

The motor (and inheritor) of Islam's Andalucian golden age and home to some of its most venerable cities, Morocco nevertheless retains different traditions from its Muslim next-door neighbours. Arabs have lived here since the seventh century but Morocco is also populated by Berbers, the ethnically distinct indigenous inhabitants whose name derives from the same root as 'barbarian'. Different Berber tribes are still scattered through the Rif and Atlas mountains, while the walled cities of the plains have engendered distinct urban cultures from a different kind of introspection. Stir in both French and Spanish colonial influences and the result is a country where no two cities or regions are very much alike.

With both Mediterranean and Atlantic coasts, four separate mountain ranges and a southern expanse of sand and Saharan scrub, Morocco offers a rich variety of landscapes, cultures and travel destinations. From Marrakech it's possible to head up into the wooded valleys of the High Atlas or down to the palm oases of the pre-Sahara, to chill out in the laid-back coastal resort of Essaouira or explore the modernist urban culture of Atlantic cities such as Casablanca, to follow ancient trade routes that connect with the medieval settlements of Fès or Meknes, or to strike out for the north, where Africa shades into Europe.

Rubbing shoulders with the locals – literally unavoidable in most public transport situations – you'll find most Moroccans to be friendly, hospitable and interested in who you are and where you come from. They'll be flattered if you ask questions in return, and enjoy curiosity about their culture as long as it stops short of being judgemental. To travel in Morocco is to realise that everyone has their spiel, from the excuses hustlers and touts will use to try and attach themselves to you prior to begging a few dirhams or steering you towards a carpet shop, to the sophisticated rationale supplied to justify a philosophy of hotel management or interior decor. It's sometimes hard to spot when an individual spiel is beginning to unfold, but one always appears sooner or later.

Morocco

0   100 miles
0   150 kms
© Copyright Time Out Group 2003

PORTUGAL

Seville ○

Cádiz ○

Strait of
Tangier ○

Larache ○

Souk el Arba du Rharb ○

ATLANTIC

Kenitra ○   Sidi Kacem

RABAT ○

Khemisset

Casablanca ○

OCEAN

Ben Slimane ○

El Jadida ○

Settat ○   **Khourihga** ○   Khenifra

Oued Zem ○

Safi ○

Beni
○ **Mellal**

Chemaia ○

El Kelaa
des Srarhna ○

MARRAKECH ○

Essaouira ○

M   O   R   O   M C

Taddert ○   Boumaine
Tizi n   ○ Telouet   du Dadès
Tichka
Tizi n Test   Ait Benhaddou ○   ○ Skoura

S   **Ouarzazate** ○

Agadir ○   ○ Taroudant

Tizi n   *Drâa*
Tinififft ○   *Valley*
Agdz ○
Zagora ○

A   T   L

A   A

Tiznit ○   ○ Tata   M'Hamid ○

○ Goulmine

○ Tan Tan

Best of Morocco

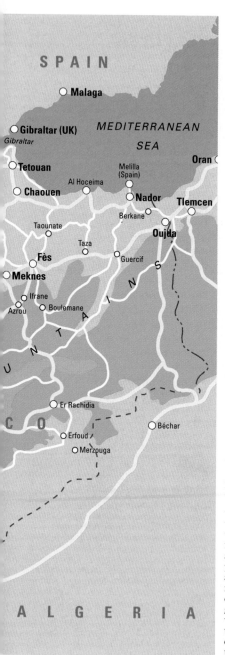

Though you will tire of the faux guides and hustlers at stations and medina gates, offering to show you around, sell you something or escort you to a Berber market, you'll soon develop your own strategies to deal with their persistent attentions. The best tactics involve remaining polite and friendly, while displaying no interest at all in whatever it is they are offering. Keep hold of your sense of humour, for this is an invaluable asset. Moroccans love to laugh and are quickly won over with jokes. While there are strict limits to what can be discussed with a serious face, humour can be pushed surprisingly far. Laughter lubricates the wheels of social exchange and one of the most enjoyable aspects of travelling within Morocco is how much can be negotiated with a smile. And in contrast to the occasional surliness or desperation of the touts and conmen, deep-rooted traditions of hospitality mean that, particularly in remote mountainous regions, you're as likely to be overwhelmed by generosity as taken for a ride.

The French colonial legacy has left most Moroccan cities divided between ancient medinas and 20th-century *nouvelles villes*. On the one hand this has admirably shielded the external forms of local culture froms the ravages of modernisation. On the other hand it has functioned as a kind of cultural segregation, first dividing 'natives' from colonials, and latterly the poor from the middle classes who moved into those economic, cultural and administrative spaces left behind by the departing French and Spanish. The city of Casablanca, almost entirely a French creation, is the biggest single monument to the colonial era. But the French also augmented an already developed gastronomic culture with pâtisseries and cafés that still stand next to their indigenous equivalents, and restaurants offering Gallic alternatives to excellent local dishes. (The traffic also went the other way – couscous is now as ubiquitous in France as Indian food is in the UK.)

The combination of colonial infrastructure with cultural and geographic diversity adds up to a country that's both easy and fascinating to explore. To travel around is not without its frustrations – the stubborn vagaries of Morocco at times seem expressly designed to test the patience of the infidel – but ultimately this is a country where a developed tourist industry manages to co-exist with a multifaceted local culture that doggedly bucks the trend of globalising homogeneity. The best of both worlds, then, from the southern edge of Europe to the fringes of the vast Sahara. This is a country to which travellers, once seduced, find themselves returning over and over again.

Best of Morocco

Travel around Morocco

By air

Domestic air travel is only really useful if you are travelling from or to Casablanca, as nearly all flights change there. **Royal Air Maroc** (090 00 08 00, www.royalairmaroc.com) has a good internal flight network between Casablanca and Essaouira, Fès, Marrakech, Ouarzazate, Rabat and Tangier. The Casablanca to Marrakech, and Casablanca to Essaouira routes are the most frequent.

If you hold a return international ticket (subject to certain conditions), you may be able to claim certain discounts on one-way internal flights. Rival airline **Regional Air Lines** (Casablanca, 022 53 80 80) flies from Casablanca to Agadir, Tangier and Laayoune, but is generally more expensive.

By bus

Buses run to all but the most remote of mountain or desert communities. The national – and probably the best – bus network is **CTM** (Compagnie de Transports Marocains) but there are numerous other private companies that compete. Shared grand taxis, usually Mercedes or Peugeots just about big enough for six passengers, offer an alternative means of hopping between villages and towns – just turn up at their starting point (usually close to the bus station), pay for *une place* in a taxi *collectif* and the car will set off once all the places have been filled.

By rail

An efficient rail network – the **ONCF** (www.oncf.org.ma) – connects Marrakech and the cities of the north. Though the trains can get crowded, a few dirhams extra will ensure a seat in comfortable first-class carriages.

Specialist tours

Independent travel in Morocco is manageable and inexpensive, but if time is short, or if you have a specific holiday interest, such as trekking, safari, cycling or cooking (for which also *see p114* **Kitchen breaks**), it can be worth enlisting the help of the experts.

Best of Morocco

Seend Park, Seend, Wiltshire SN12 6NZ (01380 828 533/www.morocco-travel.com).
A leading tour operator with over 30 years as a Morocco specialist, with all the in-depth knowledge that suggests. Tours are tailor-made to suit individual needs, including flights, transfers, hotels and travel, but must be a minimum of four nights. Activities on offer include cooking, trekking, skiing and camel trekking. Recommended.

The best...

Medina for getting hopelessly lost
Fès. *See p195.*

Chance to catch a camel to Timbuktu
Zagora. *See p180.*

Kasbah trail
Drâa Valley. *See p178.*

For bars
Casablanca. *See p193.*

For hatmakers
Fès. *See p200.*

Surfing beach
Sidi Kaouki. *See p188.*

For hassle-free souks
Rabat. *See p205.*

For a literary vibe
Tangier. *See p212.*

Thermal baths
Moulay Yacoub. *See p204.*

Roman ruins
Volubilis. *See p204.*

For celeb spotting
Ouarzarzate. *See p177.*

CLM Leisure

69 Knightsbridge, London SW1X 7RA (020 7235 0123/www.clmleisure.co.uk).
CLM (aka Morocco Made to Measure) is renowned for its flexibility – trips can be anything from a weekend to several months. Itineraries are individually tailored, but tend toward top-end accommodation.

Naturally Morocco

Hill House, Llansteffan, Carmarthen, South Wales (0709 234 3879/www.naturallymorocco.co.uk).
Ecologically leaning Moroccan holidays, with Taroudant in the south as a base. From here Naturally Morocco has a variety of activities on offer, including photography, art and crafts, cooking, swimming and music.

Tribes

12 The Business Centre, Earl Soham, Woodbridge, Suffolk IP13 7SA (012728 685971/www.tribes.co.uk).
Tribes organises trekking and activity tours in Morocco, taking a strong interest in ethically and environmentally sound travel.

High Atlas & the South

Wide-screen scenery from the Maghreb's loftiest peaks to the fringes of the vast Sahara.

The tallest mountain range in North Africa, the High Atlas is quite literally Morocco's biggest asset. Sweeping some 1,000 kilometres (622 miles) diagonally across the country north-east from Agadir, its imposing snow-capped peaks reach to over 4,000 metres (13,123 feet) in places. The northern foothills are an irresistibly pretty patchwork of emerald green terraced fields, rising to rugged, barren peaks sliced through by dramatic valleys and rugged escarpments, and eventually opening out on to the spectacular landscapes of the pre-Sahara.

Once across the High Atlas, southern Morocco packs in extraordinary scenic diversity into easily accessible areas, making it possible – at a pace – to glimpse stony desert, sand dunes, green mountains, arid mountains, canyons, gorges and palm-filled oases in the space of a few days.

WHERE TO GO

Two mountain passes give access from Marrakech to the south: the **Tizi n Test**, leading to Taroudant, and the higher **Tizi n Tichka** further east, which leads to Ouarzazate and eventually the Sahara. Of the two, the Tizi n Tichka (called the P31) is the quicker and safer road, providing the most direct access to areas of interest in the south, such as the Dadès Valley (*see p180*), the Drâa Valley (*see p178*) and the beginnings of the Sahara. The Tizi n Tichka pass is the one covered in this chapter, as it is the most suitable for a quick trip out of Marrakech.

Those with more time should note that the more remote, and sometimes difficult, Tizi n Test road offers particularly spectacular views and far greater trekking possibilites. With two decent hotels, the village of Ourigane is a good base on this route. And high up the valley, the beautiful

On the road

Hiring a car or renting a taxi on a daily basis is the best – if not the cheapest – way of travelling, giving you the freedom to stop off as and when. Buses cover most routes of interest in the south but can be irregular, slow and impractical – especially as you will want to stop off to see a kasbah or two en route.

For full details on car hire, see p221. Depending on the hire company and the destination, you may be able to return the car in a different city. It is worth thinking through your itinerary before departure – if you intend to venture off the main roads, you will need to hire a 4X4 for *piste* conditions because going off road in a standard vehicle will void the insurance cover. Note that the routes featured in this chapter are covered by decent paved roads, and do not require a 4X4 vehicle unless indicated.

Most major towns have a grand taxi rank in the centre, from where you can hire a taxi (either shared with others or for exclusive use). Prices are relatively stable for specific destinations but half-day and daily rates with stop-offs need to be negotiated with the driver.

Be warned that the mountain roads are narrow, contain hundreds of hairpin bends, and often verge on sheer and perilous drops – you are strongly advised not to cut corners. If hiring a grand taxi, check the condition of the car before departure and insist on slow driving. Avoid these roads on at night, as vehicle lights aren't mandatory. Winter months can be difficult for mountain driving, as roads are sometimes snow-

ruins of the 12th-century Tin Mal mosque marks all that is left of the city that spawned the Almohad dynasty. After Casablanca's landmark Hassan II Mosque, Tin Mal is the only Moroccan mosque open to non-visitors.

Back in the Tizi n Tichka, the P31 road leads to Ouarzazate, from which routes strike east towards the Dadès Valley, and south to Zagora and eventually M'hamid, the last outpost before the Sahara proper. Saharan treks for the more intrepid can be undertaken from the southern cities of Zagora or M'hamid.

Keeping time

Daytrippers...

...can make it to comfortably past the Tizi n Tichka pass to the **Telouet kasbah** in one day, returning before dark.

With three days...

...head to **Ouarzazate**, stopping en route at **Telouet** and **Ait Benhaddou** kasbahs, then out to **Skoura**.

With a week...

...it is possible – at a brisk pace – to visit all the places featured in this chapter. For a more relaxing pace, allow ten days.

When to go

Spring is the best time of year to head south, as temperatures can reach a blistering 50°C (122°F) in summer months. Spring temperatures are moderate and the flowers are in blossom. Note that winter conditions can make mountain driving impossible. *See above* **On the road.**

Tizi n Tichka route

It's only 196km (122 miles) to Ouarzazate but leave a good four hours (longer by bus) for the snakey mountain roads, built by the Foreign Legion in 1931. The journey is spine-tingling, each bend revealing a striking new panorama. Before the pass, the fertile slopes are shrouded in forest and Berber villages can be seen clinging to vertiginous gradients. The mountains here are full of fossils and semi-precious stones, and roadside sellers angle melon-sized geodes, broken in half, to show you the glittering light reflected by the red or green crystals within.

There are a few villages on the main road (P31) that make suitable stops for a breather. Of them, **Taddert**, about 15 kilometres (nine miles) before the Tichka summit, is probably the busiest. The small village is in two parts, the furthest part (if coming from Marrakech) has a better choice of cafés, some of which have terraces overlooking mountain streams.

At 2,260 metres (7,415 feet) above sea level, the **Tichka pass** is the highest in the Atlas. Despite its stature, expect no fanfare on arrival, just exposed and isolated expanses, some masts and a few stalls selling stones. The change to a more arid landscape happens quickly and dramatically beyond the watershed, leaving little doubt that the desert is where you're headed. **Telouet** – not far after the pass – is the first stop of interest.

Telouet

The crumbling Telouet kasbah is as dramatic historically as it is aesthetically. It was the powerbase and residence of the influential Glaoui tribe (*see p11* **The last despot**), who first rose to stature by helping the sultans of pre-colonial Morocco in the late 18th and early 19th centuries. After 1912 the Glaouis became allies of the French, turning themselves into repressive sub-rulers. This palatial residence was abandoned with Moroccan independence in 1956, and the 'lion of the Atlas', as its name means, lost its roar. Shunned as the historical remains of brutal collaborators, the kasbah is now in poor repair.

Telouet is definitely worth a visit, though, especially for the craftmanship on show: a fabulously ornate central hall, carved ceilings and delicate iron grille windows overlooking the village show fine attention to detail. Areas of the kasbah are out of bounds for safety reasons but the roof is open for views of the village. Beware crumbling walls and protruding poles.

Where to stay, eat & drink

There's not much bar the scenery and tranquility to keep you in in this tiny village. If you decide to kick back for a night, **Auberge Telouet** (Chez Ahmed, 044 89 07 17, double 100dh) is the best option, with a neat position overlooking the kasbah, plus clean and relatively modern facilites. There's an adjoining restaurant (meals 60dh), popular with passing tourists. The recently opened auberge-café **Lion d'Or** (044 88 85 07, single 50dh) is the nearest to the kasbah and is clean, but has no doubles.

There are further options in **Anmiter**, 11 kilometres (seven miles) from Telouet, where the bus will drop you.

If you have your own transport, by far the most pleasant place to stay (or eat) in this area is **I Rocha** (067 73 70 02, 250dh-300dh per person, lunch/dinner 100dh), a *maison d'hôtes* halfway between the Telouet turn-off and Ait Benhaddou. The rooms are beautifully simple and the food is of a high standard.

Getting there

Telouet is 21 kilometres (13 miles) off the main road between Marrakech and Ouarzazate. Look out for the left turn a few kilometres after the pass, where the road (6802) leading to Telouet is surfaced but narrow.

By bus, there's a daily service from Marrakech leaving from Bab Rhemat in the afternoon, stopping off at Telouet and then

Big sandy slopes near **M'hamid**. *See p80.*

Ouarzazate: a dusty desert outpost. *See p177.*

terminating at Anemiter (35dh single). It makes the return trip at 7am from Telouet. From Ouarzazate, a bus leaves at noon, returning at 7am (25dh-30dh single). Grands taxis are available from both Marrakech and Ouarzazate.

Note that there is an alternative, and very scenic, route southward from Telouet, but it requires a 4X4 vehicle. It will take you from Anmiter via Tamdaght to Ait Benhaddou, and makes an beautiful off-road trip.

Ait Benhaddou

If it's kasbahs you're after, you can't miss Ait Benhaddou. This is one of the most dramatic, easily accessible and – being a UNESCO-designated site – also one of the best preserved. If you have a sense of *déjà vu*, this is probably because around 20 films have used this place as a location, including David Lean's *Lawrence of Arabia*, Ridley Scott's *Gladiator*, Franco Zeffirelli's *Jesus of Nazareth* and Orson Welles's *Sodom and Gomorrah*. It's not hard to see why – palm-strewn Ait Benhaddou sits romantically on a shaft of rock towering over the shallow river Wadi Mellah, with snow-capped Atlas peaks looking on in one direction and hostile stony plains stretching out in the other as far as the eye can see.

Some of the Benhaddou *pisé* kasbahs are thought to date back as far as the 16th century, when it held a key strategic position on the trading route between Marrakech and ra. These days, Ait Benhaddou is really only strategic on the tourist trade route, the small population of villagers relying heavily on a steady flow of visitors.

Take the walk through the narrow dusty lanes to the summit to get a good view of compelling scenery and the crenellated towers that rise up from the reddish mud out of which they are made. The remains of a huge fortified granary perch on the top. Guides, easily picked up in the New Village, the cluster of buildings across the river from the kasbah, may be able to get you a glimpse inside one of the few occupied kasbahs, but otherwise aren't necessary.

Where to stay, eat & drink

There's a sprinkling of basic hotels, shops and cafés in the New Village, but none present any compelling reason to hang about. **Hotel La Kasbah** (044 89 03 02, doubles 180dh-280dh) is the most modern with air-conditioned rooms, a restaurant and a swimming pool (30dh for non-guests) overlooking the kasbahs. Budget travellers should head to roadside **Auberge La Baraka** (044 89 03 05, singles 50dh-80dh, doubles 80dh-100dh) for rock-bottom prices, clean rooms and a tented restaurant area serving trad Moroccan dishes.

Getting there

If you have your own wheels, arriving at Ait Benhaddou is a cynch – the left turn is 18 kilometres (11 miles) north of Ouarzazate on the

P31. After turning, drive four kilometres (2.5 miles) down the tarmac road. It comes to an end at the New Village on the west bank of the river. Otherwise, the best options are to share a grand taxi from Ouarzazate with others (15dh per person) or hire the whole thing yourself for a half-day (roughly 300dh). By bus, the only option is to descend at the turn-off and walk.

Ouarzazate

Ouarzazate (pronounced *war-za-zat*) occupies pole position on the main road between the High Atlas and the Sahara, just at the turn-off to the Dadès Valley.

A regional capital, Ouarzazate was built by the French in the 1920s as a garrison town to tame the south, and still has something of a functionalist air – the town is organised around a long line of modern concrete buildings known as avenue Mohammed V. Still, functionalism can come in handy – there's no shortage of banks, modern hotels, car rentals, internet cafés, travel agents and a supermarket which sells alcohol. What you won't find is much in the way of traditional sightseeing. Ouarzazate is good for an overnighter, or as a base, but not a lot else.

All that remains of the pre-French era, and the only thing worth seeing in central Ouarzazate, is the mid 18th-century **Kasbah Taourirt** (8am-6.30pm daily, admission 10dh) east of the centre along avenue Mohammed V. During the 1930s, when the Glaouis were at their prime in the south, this kasbah was one of the largest of its kind in the area, if not Morocco, housing numerous relatives of the dynasty and hundreds of workers and servants. These days much of it is ruined, some is being restored, and a substantial section is still inhabited. The section along the road has been maintained, and this is what gets shown to visitors – the principal courtyard, the harem and a few other rooms. Some of the poorest people in town live in the area behind it, and here you can wander freely if you don't mind being pestered for dirhams.

Directly opposite the entrance to the kasbah is the **Centre Artisinal** (open 8.30am-noon, 3-6.30pm Mon-Fri, 8.30am-noon Sat, 10am-noon Sun), a cluster of small shops selling good-quality, fixed-price arts and crafts, such as stone carvings, pottery, woollen carpets and jewellery.

Tiffoultoute (open 8am-7pm) is another kasbah built by the Glaouis and is seven kilometres out of town (take the westward road then turn right), dramatically placed between the Tifoultoute River and a palmeraie. These days it houses a restaurant aimed squarely at tour groups and offers accommodation.

The other string to Ouarzazate's bow, of some interest to the visitor, is the town's close links to the film industry since David Lean chose nearby Ait Benhaddou (*see p176*) as a setting for *Lawrence of Arabia* in 1962. Ouarzazate's very own film studios – the Atlas Coporation Studios – were born in 1983, accompanied by a flurry of modern hotels. The 1990s saw something of a boom in filmmaking at the studios, with credits including *The Sheltering Sky* (1990), *Kundun* (1996), *Cleopatra* (1998) and *Gladiator* (1998-9). Many commercial shoots also make use of the variety of desert landscapes in the surrounding area.

The **Atlas Coporation Studios** (044 88 71 71, www.atlasstudios.com, open 8am-8pm daily, admission 30dh, 15dh concessions, seven kilometres west of town, are open to the public except during filming, and can make an interesting stop-off for film buffs. You can take a look at the Tibetan monastery constructed for Martin Scorsese's *Kundun* (1996), the plane used in *Jewel of the Nile* and a film-set medina street. Then, of course, there's fun to be had lifting granite-looking boulders made of feather-light polystyrene. In recent years, there's been less foreign interest in filming in these parts and the studios have a run-down air, still clinging on to the sets of more prosperous times.

Where to eat & drink

La Date d'Or (044 88 71 17, menu fixe 100dh-110dh) is more like a café than a restaurant, but serves up a selection of reasonably priced set menus. **Restaurant Es Salam** (Chez Moulay, between boulevard Mohammed V & rue du Marché, 044 83 50 20, mains 50dh) offers excellent Moroccan standards and has a roof terrace. For bargain tajines, try **Snack El Hassanie Chez Omar** (near souk, mains 20dh).

Pizzeria Venezziano (avenue Moulay Richard, 044 88 76 76, mains 25dh-35dh) has decent pizzas and **Chez Dimitri** (22 boulevard Mohammed V, 044 88 73 46, mains 50dh-100dh) also caters to the homesick traveller with its Euro-Italian menu. It's pricey but mostly, if not always, hits the spot.

Where to stay

Ouarzazate has hotels for all budgets but is particularly heavy on soulless four- and five-stars geared to the package tourist (beware, Club Med is among them). There's none of the aesthetic riad culture of Marrakech here.

By far the best of the cheap options is **Hotel Royal** (24 avenue Mohammed, 044 88 22 58, single 35dh, doubles 50dh-92dh), with clean rooms, hot water and friendly staff. Another decent stand-by is **Hotel Atlas** (13 rue du Marché, 044 88 77 45, doubles 72dh-92dh).

Best of Morocco

Dar Daif (3km off Zagora road, 044 85 49 49, doubles 350dh-640dh, www.dardaif.ma) is one of few *maison d'hôtes* in Ouarzazate. Occupying a converted kasbah on the outskirts of town, three kilometres (two miles) down a stony track, Dar Daif has rustic charm. **Désert et Montagne**, a trekking and safari tour group, is run from here by owner Jean-Pierre Datcharry.

At the top end, **Kenzi Azghor** (avenue Prince Moulay Rachid, 044 88 65 01, double 800dh) is a decent choice with views and a large pool. Otherwise, 1980s-built **Riad Salam** (avenue Mohammed V, 044 88 33 35, riadsalamozte@ iam.net.ma, doubles 700dh) offers kasbah-style accommodation with a large swimming pool. Its three-star sister hotel **Tichka** (doubles 450dh) on the same site is a cheaper option.

Getting there

By bus

The CTM station (avenue Mohammed V, 044 88 24 27) is right in the middle of town near the post office and Cinéma Atlas. Buses leave for Marrakech, Casablanca, El Rachida and M'Hamid via Zagora. There are also private departures.

By car

There are Hertz and Budget offices, amongst others, in Ouarzazate. For more about car hire, *see 221*. The alternative is to hire a grand taxi from the rank next to the CTM bus station. To Marrakech, it is either 100dh per person in a shared grand taxi, or 400dh for exclusive use. You may have to pay more to stop off en route – this is negotiable with the driver. Communal petits taxis run up and down the avenue Mohammed V for 2.50dh per person.

By air

Taourirt airport (044 88 50 80) is 1km north of Ouarzazate. Royal Air Maroc (*see p220*) flies direct to Casablanca daily and to Paris twice a week. Air France flies to Paris once a week.

Resources

Internet

Ouarzazate Web *avenue Mohammed V*. **Rates** 8dh per hr. **Cyber Net** *near Hotel Amlal*. **Rates** 10dh per hr.

Police station

avenue Mohammed V (*emergency 190*).

Post office

avenue Mohammed V. **Open** 8.30am-noon, 2.30-6pm Mon-Sat.

Tourist office

Délégation Régionale de Tourisme *avenue Mohammed V* (044 88 24 85). **Open** 8.30am-noon, 2.30-6.30pm Mon-Fri.

Drâa Valley

The arid, stony plains south of Ouarzazate (still on the P31 road) are breathtakingly bleak – brown rubble flatlands stretch as far as the eye can see. Roughly 30 kilometres (19 miles) after Ouarzazate, the road begins to wind through extraordinarily dark, layered rock formations up to the 1,600-metre-high (5,250-feet) **Tizi n Tinififft** pass, plunging at points into deep, breathtaking canyons. The road is mostly wide and in good condition.

About 20 kilometres (12 miles) after the pass, the first strips of green appear on the horizon. In theory the Drâa runs all the way from the High Atlas to the Atlantic, but it hasn't reached the sea for over a decade, and then only during freak floods in 1989. Instead it seeps away into Saharan strands.

For 100 kilometres (62 miles) of the Drâa Valley, however, it runs strong and waters a heavily farmed palm oasis. Every last bit of fertile land is planted with dates, olives, almonds and citrus. The road runs along the oasis edge and fortified Berber villages, known as *ksours*, stand on its other side. The first extraordinary close-up views of this verdant valley carpet emerge just beyond the town of Agdz.

Agdz

Agdz (pronounced *ag-a-dez*) is an average town with a few carpet shops – but the scenery surrounding it is magnificent. It is on the edge of a palmeraie, over a mile wide at points, overlooked by Jebel Kissane, a spectacular terraced plateau rising 1,500 metres (4,921 feet).

After Agdz the valley widens and the river bed widens into one huge oasis that cuts its way through the parched desert terrain. The oasis is guarded by several *ksours* (fortified Berber villages), which are worth a look if you have your own transport. Ksar **Tamnougalt** is on the left roughly six kilometres (four miles) past Agdz, then three kilometres down a *piste*, and the more palatial Glaoui kasbah **Timiderte** is a further eight kilometres (five miles) south.

Where to stay

The **Kissane** (044 84 31 44, doubles 230dh) at the northern end of town is the most pleasant option, with rooms with balconies, a pool and a restaurant. **Hotel Drâa** (044 843 153, doubles 70dh) and **Hotel des Palmiers** (044 84 31 27, 80dh) are decent budget options on the Grande Place.

Zagora: only one street but plenty of palms. *See p180.*

Getting there

Buses and grands taxis both leave from the Grande Place. Passing buses are often full, but you have a better chance of getting on one in the morning.

Zagora

Zagora is Ouarzazate's little sister – a modern, French-built, one-street town with a few admin buildings (it is the administrative centre for the Drâa Valley) and some incongrously placed four- and five-star hotels. Zagora started out as a crossroads for trans-Saharan carvans on trade routes and, as the famous 'Timbuktou 52 jours' sign outside the Préfecture reminds, is still the last outpost of any size before the Sahara.

Though the large market on Wednesday and Sunday is interesting, there is little else to see in Zagora proper. But across the river in the hamlet of **Amazrou** there is a palmeraie and a mostly abandoned 17th-century Jewish kasbah, the **Kasbah des Juifs**. In one or two workshops, Berber craftsman still make moulded silver jewellery by traditional Jewish methods. There are also some 11th-century Almoravid ruins halfway up the Jebel Zagora, which rises spectacularly above the town.

Where to stay, eat & drink

Most of Zagora's higher-end restaurants are to be found inside hotels. Of them, the best are probably **Kasbah Asmâa** (044 84 75 99, doubles 250dh-300dh) and **Hotel La Fibule** (044 84 73 18, doubles 208dh-384dh), both good mid-range hotels. Along avenue Mohammed V there are several decent cheap eateries offering standard Moroccan fare: try **Restaurant Timbuctou** or **Restaurant Es Saada**.

For something a bit different, call **Mustapha El Mekki** (061 34 83 94): he lives with his family in the Kasbah des Juifs and, on request, serves up outstanding home-cooked food, either on the roof terrace on cushions or in the dining room. It's difficult to find so best ask him to meet you.

For a budget room, **Hotel Valée du Drâa** (044 84 72 10, doubles 65dh-85dh) is pretty reliable. Just outside the city gate, the **Hotel Riad Salam** (044 84 74 00, doubles 500dh) is the cheapest and nicest of the top-range options, with a courtyard centred on a pool.

Tamegroute

Tamegroute has been a key centre for religion and education since the 17th century. Its famous library still contains some early Koranic manuscripts printed on gazelle hide, and has other 12th- and 13th-century works on show. Visitors can enter the sanctuary and library from 8.30am-noon, then 3-6pm, by donation.

Tinfou Dunes

There can be no comparison between this handful of mini-dunes, covering an area the size of a few football pitches, and the more impressive sand dunes on the edge of the Sahara, but if you can't make it as far as Merzouga or M'hamid (*see below*), this modest line of shifting peaks provides a good sandy sampler, especially for first-timers.

Five kilometres south of Tamegroute, you'll see these golden dunes appear – rather surreally – out of the stony desert. There are a few low-key bivouacs and guys touting camel rides but in general this is a peaceful spot.

Should you wish to stay over, the characterful **Hotel Repos du Sable** (044 84 85 66, doubles 100dh) is a decent option, and serves up meals for around 60dh.

M'hamid

When you arrive at M'hamid, you know that you've come to the end of the road. This sandy outpost is just 15 kilometres (nine miles) from the Algerian border and the Sahara proper. There's very little to see or do in this small village, apart from a Monday souk, a few craft shops and some dunes about four kilometres (2.5 miles) away. But camel trips depart from here, with common destinations including Erg Lehoudi, Chigaga and Mesouria. **Sahara Services** (mobile 061 77 67 66, saharacamel@hotmail.com) organises camel trips for around 300dh per day.

If you're staying over, **Hotel Sahara** (044 84 80 09, doubles 80dh) and **Hotel Iraqui** (044 88 57 99, singles 300dh) are both good, central options.

Private and public buses leave from M'hamid to Zagora, Ouarzazate and Casablanca.

Dadès Valley

The Dadès Valley stretches east of Ouarzazate, sliced between the High Atlas and the jagged volcanic rock of the Jebal Sarhro to the south. The River Dadès runs along the bottom, providing moisture for lush vegetation. There are huge oases at Skoura (*see p181*) and Tinerhir, strikingly juxtaposed with their rugged surroundings. After the spectacular gorges of Dadès (*see p181*) and Todra, the road eventually leads to Er Rachidia.

The **Dadès Valley**. It rocks. *See p180.*

Skoura

After 30 kilometres (18 miles) of unforgivingly
arid terrain on the road east of Ouarzazate,
the appearance of the Skoura oasis comes as a
pleasant surprise. The 4,000-hectare oasis in
this area is well-stocked with kasbahs – it has,
after all, been dubbed the 'Route of a Thousand
Kasbahs'. Of the Skoura kasbahs, we recommend
17th-century **Amridil** (by donation), an old
Glaoui residence. Take any of the paths directly
behind **Ben Moro** (*see below*) and knock on the
door. It is proudly kept by the Nassar family,
who bring it alive in their tours (by donation).

Skoura is a small, dusty village best suited
to a stop-off en route to the Dadès and Todra
Gorges, but there are some decent places to
rest your head. **Ben Moro** (tel/fax 044 85 21 16,
hotelbenmoro@yahoo.fr, doubles 450dh), at
the western end of town, is a converted 17th-
century kasbah with simple but tasteful rooms.
Some of them are very dark, but that's kasbah
life for you. A short ride out of town, the **Gîte
Tiriguioute** (044 85 20 68, bouarif_elhachmi@
hotmail.com, 150dh per person) is a friendly,
family-run operation with hot showers, home-
cooked food and views of High Atlas peaks.

Dadès Gorge

The compelling rock formations and limestone
cliffs of the Dadès Gorge are most easily
accessed from the town of **Boumalne**, where
they begin. Follow the P32 from Ouarzazate
for 120 kilometres (75 miles) until Boumalne-
du-Dadès and the signpost to Msemrir.

Most visitors take transport from
Boumaine along the winding road through
the gorge, overlooked at points in the first
20 kilometres (12 miles) by various fortified
villages and kasbahs. The gorge is at its
most dramatic where it narrows just after
the village of **Ait Oudinar**, about 27
kilometres (17 miles) along, turning into
a spectacular reddish canyon. This is where
most tourists turn back, as the road becomes
more difficult toward Msemrir.

The Dadès Gorge has some excellent hiking
terrain, and, if you have the time, is a good
place to relax for a few days. Ask at your
hotel to recommend a hiking guide – they cost
roughly 100dh per day.

Accommodation options along the
Dadès Gorge are numerous and, in general,
reasonably priced, many of them with views.
One of the most pleasant hotels in the area,
and with excellent food, is **Chez Pierre**
(044 83 02 21, doubles 130dh-200dh), about
27 kilometres (17 miles) along the road to
Msemrir, before the canyon. For a cheaper
option try **Hotel la Gazelle du Dadès**
(044 83 17 31, doubles 80dh, mattress on floor
15dh-25dh), at 28 kilometres from Boumaine,
with a roof terrace and clean rooms. **Café
Mirguirne**, 14 kilometres along the road from
Boumalne, offers good cheap food and rooms.

Best of Morocco

Essaouira

The freshest fish, the wildest windsurfing and a laid-back '60s legacy add up to Morocco's most fashionable coastal resort.

From its eighth-century roots as a harbour for the exchange of ivory, gold and ostrich feathers to its 1960s renaissance as a hippie hangout and haunt of Jimi Hendrix, Essaouira has lured and captivated slaves, traders and independent travellers. It's now Morocco's most favoured coastal town. Out on a limb from the country's rail network and away from the well-heeled tourist track, it has managed to maintain a laid-back timelessness rarely seen on the bustling streets of modern Morocco. Inside the pink sandy ramparts is a blend of French-styled piazzas and whitewashed arches and avenues. Medina life revolves around the cafés and souks while donkeys, avocado carts and mopeds clog up the lime-washed streets.

Over the past ten years, Essaouira has gained worldwide recognition as a centre of arts, crafts and music, hosting an assortment of annual festivals and attracting visitors to its galleries and workshops. The fishing port, overlooked by grand fortifications, provides a constant source of supplies to local restaurants, while the wide, sandy beaches to the south, combined with high winds of up to 40 knots (46mph), have put 'Wind City Afrika' on the international windsurfing map.

Essaouira is probably the best place to be in Morocco during Ramadan. Cafés and most restaurants remain open during the day, unlike the bulk of towns in Morocco and the atmosphere in the evenings is crowded but calm

as the locals come out after the *iftar* (fast-breaking meal of soup and sweetmeats) to meet up in the streets and cafés. The town can also claim to be one of the cleanest in Morocco, with no vehicles in the Medina, the Alizées winds keeping the temperature to an equable average of 22°C (72°F), and regular street sweeping.

THE PERNICIOUS WEED

In 1878 British consul Charles Payton observed of the locals that 'they are a tough and hardy race these Moorish fishermen, bronzed and leathery of skin, sinewy of limb and yet not too fond of hard work… they would rather smoke the pernicious hasheesh in a foul and froway den of the back slums of the Moorish quarter than live out on the rippling sea.'

Today westerners come and envy the Souiris' ability to be comfortable doing nothing, even when not smoking the pernicious weed. This relaxed attitude is just as well: despite the town's recent popularity, all the renovations taking place (of 16,000 houses in the Medina more than 1,000 are owned by Europeans) and the fact that Essaouira has been named a World Heritage Site by UNESCO, there is high unemployment. Factories lie empty in the industrial quarter, and the town is still struggling to regain economic ground lost when the during the protectorate era the French developed Casablanca and Agadir to the detriment of Essaouira.

With the picturesque port no longer providing a living, the population knows that it is largely dependent on tourism. Their innate tolerance is only tested by insensitive tourists dressing and behaving in ways that are inappropriate for a Muslim country.

HISTORY

Essaouira has attracted travellers since the seventh century BC when the Phoenicians established their furthest outpost in Africa on one of Essaouira's offshore island. During the first century BC King Juba II extracted purple dye from Essaouira's murex shells for the Romans. The dyeworks were on the islands, which are still known as the Iles Purpuraires. In the 15th century, the Portuguese occupied Mogador, as it was then known, and built fortifications around the harbour. The town was one of their more important bases until they abandoned it in 1541. Sir Francis Drake is recorded as having stopped by in December 1577.

In 1765 the local ruler, Sultan Sidi Mohammed Ben Abdellah, captured a French vessel and hired one of its passengers – French architect Théodore Cournut – to redesign the place. The sultan wanted it to be an open city for foreign traders, but with walls and battlements that would deter marauders. A grid street layout was designed and the sultan

PLACE MOULAY HASSAN AND THE PORT

Connecting the Medina and the port, **place Moulay Hassan** is the town's social centre. With croissants from the **Pâtisserie Driss,** you can sit at any of the cafés and watch the theatre of Essaouira unfolding. Early in the morning fishermen pass by on their way to work, and the first wave of itinerant musicians and shoe-shine boys appear. (The latter can be quite insistent. Tempting as it is to become exasperated by the fact that they want to polish your sandals, bear in mind that these kids are often the sole money earners in their families.) By 10 or 11am the cafés begin their secondary function – as al fresco offices at which most Souiris conduct business at some time or another. Watch out for the town's eccentric personalities who enjoy bit parts on the stage.

Jack's Kiosque across the square sells newspapers, postcards and books. Purveyors of sunglasses, watches, carpets and a variety of chandeliers sweep from table to table, occasionally selling something. One can sometimes catch sight of a rare species: ageing (and not so ageing) hippies, who are as welcome today as they were in the heady days of Jimi Hendrix and the Living Theatre, for which the town and the outlying village of Diabat were famous. They used to congregate in what was then known as the Hippy Café, now the attractive hotel **Riad El Madina** (see p188). Today the cafés of place Moulay Hassan – still in a time warp of sorts – cater to hippie types with sounds from Bob Marley and Pink Floyd.

The **port** is worth a walk at any time of day, but is most interesting in the late afternoon when the fishing fleet rolls back into harbour. The catch is auctioned between 3 and 5pm at the market hall just outside the port gates, and fresh fish are fried and served up at tables on the promenade outside (see p187 **Where to eat & drink**). The ramparts of the **Scala de la Port** (open 8.30am-noon, 2.30-6pm, admission 10dh) offer fine views across to the islands and back over the town.

SCALA DE LA VILLE

Café Taros (see p188), on the corner of place Moulay Hassan, is a good spot to eat or drink, with a splendid roof terrace offering views over the port. From here, the rue de la Scala – which can also be reached by ducking through the tunnel-like alley leading off place Moulay Hassan – leads along the inside of the ramparts. **Galerie Aida** (2 rue Scala, 044 47 62 90) stocks fascinating objets d'art and a fine collection of books. A few doors along at No.5 the rugs and carpets of **Bazaar Mehdi** (044 47 59 81) will be unfurled, while Mustapha gives detailed

shipped in black slaves from the Sudanese empire to begin building what was to be the most important port on the north African coast. The gnawa brotherhood of mystic musicians (see p148) first set foot on Moroccan soil as part of the shackled workforce. With the work completed, Mogador became Essaouira, meaning 'the little ramparts'.

Wealthy families were invited to settle, and a sizeable Jewish community was welcomed, along with European merchants. Essaouira prospered until the French arrived and made Casablanca their centre of commerce. The town slipped into further decline with the departure of all but a handful of the Jewish community following independence in 1956.

Sightseeing

Arriving from Marrakech, you'll enter the Medina through the arch of **Bab Sbaâ**. The tourist information office is on the left, opposite the police station on avenue du Caire. Just before the second archway, marking the entrance to the Kasbah, this crosses avenue de l'Istiqlal, Essaouira's main drag. The bulk of the Medina, including the main souks and the Mellah, is off to the right of here. Straight ahead through the arch will bring you to the ramparts, while the **Kasbah** – the central Old Town – and **port** are to the left.

Place Moulay Hassan. *See p184.*

biographies of each one. His English is good and his knowledge of carpets excellent. Mustapha's brother has a smaller shop, the **Galerie Jama**, nearby at 22 rue Ibn Rochd. A little further on at No.10, **Dabili Art** specialises in jewellery, ceramics and textiles.

Continue following the ramparts until the **Scala de la Ville**. Locals gather up here on the sea wall to watch the sunset and lovers cuddle in the crenellations, where ancient cannons offer places to perch. You may recognise this place as one of the settings used in Orson Welles's *Othello* (1952). The town is proud of the association and has named a small square after the filmmaker. Welles stayed in the Beau Rivage (currently undergoing a facelift) and the Hôtel des Isles (unfortunately not undergoing a facelift but boasting an Orson Welles cocktail bar). After many pauses to find new funding, Welles eventually presented the film at Cannes under the Moroccan flag. Since then many films have been shot in and around Essaouira, including Bille August's *Jerusalem* and Claude Lelouch's *And Now Ladies and Gentlemen*.

Artisans sculpting thuya wood have their workshops in the arches below the sea wall and here you can find all manner of carvings and marquetry, as well as jewellery and (at No.34) camel bone framed mirrors.

From this stretch of the ramparts, Derb Laâlouj leads back into the heart of the Medina, past a variety of craft and antique shops and the **Musée des Arts et Traditions Populaires** (7 Derb Laâlouj, 044 47 23 00).

Essaouira was known as the Sanhedrin (Jewish cultural centre) of North Africa and there were 32 official synagogues in the 1950s, one of which remains further along Derb Laâlouj, founded by British merchants from Manchester. In this section of the Kasbah consulates, financial and administrative buildings were established and foreigners were invited to trade.

THE MELLAH

British merchants outnumbered other nationalities during the 19th century to the extent that sterling was the favoured currency. Arabs were not permitted to conduct financial transactions, so the sultan brought in Jews from all over the kingdom who by 1900 outnumbered the locals. All but the wealthiest lived in the **Mellah** district near the Bab Doukkala, an area that has been largely neglected since the majority of the Jewish population emigrated in the 1950s and '60s (*see p78* **Exodus**).

The Mellah can be reached by following the alleys just inside the ramparts beyond the Scala de la Ville – turn left off Derb Laâlouj – or by taking avenue Mohamed Ben Abdellah, which runs parallel to avenue de l'Istiqlal. At No.14 along here, the **Mini Kasbah** is run by the dapper Youssef who will show you his stock of antiques and textiles. Further down the street you can relax in the **Hamman Mounia**, in rue Oum Rabii (067 23 65 05).

Once the shops and businesses peter out, the Mellah begins. These days its grubby alleys are noticeably dilapidated and in decline; some houses look about ready to fall down. It was

Former Hendrix haunt
Riad El Medina. *See p188*.

always a gloomy quarter – until the end of the 19th century it was locked up at night. Maybe two dozen Jews remain in Essaouira, some still distilling fiery *eau de vie de figues*, but they don't necessarily live around here.

A little beyond Bab Doukkala, the **Christian cemetery** is a poignant reminder of the international importance of the town in its heyday. Next door, tombstones carved with symbols in the old Jewish cemetery, reputed to be five layers deep, are randomly but tightly packed together. A recent shrine housing the tomb of a celebrated rabbi mars an otherwise extraordinary windswept area.

AVENUE ZERKTOUNI AND THE SOUKS

Leading south from Bab Doukkala, **avenue Zerktouni** is a busy commercial street, bustling late into the evening. Coming back into the Medina, turn left towards the Chabanat district and explore the narrow lanes punctuated with tiny workshops. Cross Souk Ouaka to visit **Rafia Craft** at 82 rue d'Agadir (044 78 36 32). This is the original rafia shoe shop and although more expensive than its many imitators, the quality of its designs and workmanship make a trip worthwhile.

Back on avenue Zerktouni seek out the grain market where slaves were sold until the early 20th century – $75 was considered reasonable for the purchase of an able-bodied boy or girl, according to the British Consul at the time. Drop in to the **Poterie Berbère** at No.116 to buy some wonderful ceramics and argan oil from Aïcha.

The next cloistered square along, the **Joutiya**, comes to life between 4 and 5pm for the daily auction. If you can understand what is going on then this is the place to buy all manner of things. The auctioneers circle holding up second-hand alarm clocks, old fishing reels, worn leather slippers, ancient transistor radios – like a demented Moroccan variant of *The Generation Game*.

On the other side of the road the **fish and spice market** is lively and interesting, although beware of getting seduced into buying large quantities of spices. The stallholders here are experts at the hard sell; always check the price of 100 grams before committing yourself to a lifetime's worth of cumin. It is here that Souiri women come to buy chameleons, hedgehogs and many weird and wonderful plants for sorcery and magic.

From here, avenue Zerktouni turns into avenue de l'Istiqlal. The **jewellery souk** is on the left, a surprisingly quiet corner where it's possible to browse in peace before buying. A little further up avenue de l'Istiqlal, turn into rue Malek Ben Mourhal to find the

traditional pharmacy **Azurette** at No.12, which specialises in medicinal plants, natural perfumes and essential oils.

Beyond the arched Kasbah gate where you first approached the Medina, avenue de l'Istiqlal changes name yet again, becoming avenue Oqba Ibn Nafia. On this stretch is the **Galerie Damgaard** (044 78 44 46), where Danish gallerist Frederic Damgaard supports and helps develop the work of local artists. The naïve school of painting for which Essaouira has become famous began in the 1950s with the mystical painting and sculpture of Boujemaâ Lakhdar. During the 1960s hippies painted psychedelic murals wherever they found an available wall (none have survived) and this undoubtedly encouraged the Souiris to pick up their brushes and experiment with colour. Galerie Damgaard is the place to see the results.

WIND CITY AFRIKA

Known in surfing circles as 'Wind City Afrika', Essaouira brings windsurfers flocking to its coastline between March and September when the number of days of force four winds are at their highest.

Ocean Vagabond Fanatic Board Centre, which is on the beach, offers a ten-hour beginners' windsurfing course for £99. Those who have already learned the skill can hire a board for the week from £119. The wind discourages sunbathing, which leaves the beach free for football matches.

For hardcore surfing, head to **Sidi Kaouki**, 25 kilometres (15.5 miles) to the south of Essaouira, where a broad beach stretches for miles. The village is also popular with holidaymakers preferring a quieter environment than the town. There are now several hotels, including the **Auberge de la Plage** (044 47 66 00). The No.5 bus from Bab Doukkala goes there regularly, or you can get a shared or individual grand taxi.

Surfers also head for **Moulay Bouzerktoun**, a small coastal village 25 kilometres (15.5 miles) to the north.

Where to eat & drink

For the freshest food in town head down to the harbour where no time is wasted getting the sardines out of the boat and on to a wharfside barbecue. Make a selection from the iced catch displayed at one of the many stalls and the fish will be sprinkled with salt, grilled on the spot and served on a plastic plate with a slice of lemon and half a crispy baguette.

For more formal fish dinners head to the tip of the harbour and **Chez Sam** (044 47 65 13, main courses 80dh), which combines old-

Chalet de la Plage: the place for cats and fish. *See p188*

fashioned French styling with fresh seafood. It has a decent wine list too. Over on the beach, the **Chalet de la Plage** (mains 100dh) has a superb terrace overlooking the beach. Ask for the catch of the day. It's one of the oldest restaurants in town and the shuffling elderly waiter was a Welles extra in *Othello*.

Just off main avenue de l'Istiqlal is the hard to find **Restaurant Ferdous** (27 rue Abdesslam Lebadi, 044 47 36 55, main courses 60dh-80dh), which is well worth seeking out for excellent food at reasonable prices. The proprietor used to cook at the Villa Maroc.

Also superb value is **Les Alizées Mogador** (26 rue Scala, 044 47 68 19, menu 75dh), a small restaurant in the lee of the sea wall that offers traditional Moroccan cuisine in massive portions for very little money. Decent house wine is served by the glass or bottle.

For more drinks, hit **Taros** (place Moulay Hassan, 044 47 64 07), a literary café-cum-bar housed in a 200-year-old building with tiled floors and walls lined with bookcases. Non-bookish types can soak up the rays on the gorgeous roof terrace.

Where to stay

Essaouira is so small that there's no such thing as a badly located hotel; they're all just minutes' walk from the central place Moulay Hassan and the harbour. It's advisable to book rooms early, especially during festivals.

The standout is the legendary and beautiful **Villa Maroc** (10 rue Abdellah Ben Yassin, 044 47 61 47, www.villa-maroc.com, double 750dh-1,150dh), one of the first boutique hotels in Morocco and still one of the best. Equally famed is the **Riad El Medina** (9 rue Attarin, 044 47 59 07, www.riadalmedina.com, double 664dh), but, although the central courtyard remains attractive, rooms are grim and overpriced.

For cheap chic **Dar Loulema** (2 rue Souss, 044 47 53 46, www.darloulema.com, double 630dh-840dh) offers three doubles and three suites off a whitewashed colonnaded courtyard. It's run by a French world-class windsurfer and his artist wife. The **Palazzo Desdemona** (12-14 rue Youssef El Fassi, 044 78 57 35, double 700dh-900dh) is a big, rambling place overlooking main avenue de'Istiqlal; all rooms come with white linen-draped four-poster beds.

On a more intimate scale **Dar Adul** (63 rue Touahen, 061 24 52 41, www. daradul.com, double 550dh-660dh) is an old Jewish house lovingly maintained by a French couple. It has just five rooms and fine sea views from the rooftop terrace – as does **Dar El Bahar** (1 rue Touahen, 044 47 68 31, www.daralbahar.com, double 450dh), which is right up against the ramparts and whipped by sea spray.

The hippest place of all is **Casa Del Mar** (35 rue d'Oujda, 044 47 50 91, www.lacasa-delmar.com, double 600dh), run by a young couple from Mallorca. It offers four rooms and an attractive chillout space on the roof terrace.

Resources

Internet
Espace Internet Café *avenue de'Istiqlal, corner of rue Attarin (no phone).* **Open** 9am-10pm daily.

Police
avenue du Caire (emergencies 19).

Post office
Avenue el-Moukaouama. **Open** 8.30am-12.15pm, 2.30-6.30pm Mon-Thur; 8.30-11.30am, 3-6.30pmFri; 8.30-11.30am Sat.

Tourist information
Syndicat d'Initiative *10 rue du Caire (044 47 50 80).* **Open** 9am-noon, 3-6.30pm Mon-Fri.

Casablanca

Palm trees, art deco buildings, beaches, blue skies and a cosmopolitan club-loving local crowd – where'd you say we were again?

If all you know of Casablanca is the movie, then prepare for a surprise. Same if you're arriving from Marrakech or Fès. The only trace of Humphrey Bogart is the absurd Rick's Bar at the Hyatt Regency, where pricey drinks are delivered by waiters in trenchcoats and fedoras. Equally, anyone expecting another city of minarets and medieval street patterns will also be taken aback by the skyscrapers and broad boulevards of this thoroughly modernist metropolis. The streets are jammed with traffic. The men and women bustling along its downtown pavements are dressed in international styles. Blink and you could be in southern Europe. In many ways Casa, as everyone calls it, is more like Marseilles than the Maghreb.

This is the kingdom's economic hub: the principal port, the centre of finance, industry, commerce, media and manufacturing. Its imposing sprawl is home to just under four million inhabitants, and as the *bidonvilles* (shanty towns) on the outskirts attest, more are arriving every day. Casablanca is where

Moroccans come in search of fame and fortune, or at least a better standard of living. Not all of them make it, of course, and beggars and prostitutes also haunt the streets in stark contrast to the well-heeled habitués of downtown boulevard cafés. But Casa remains a magnet, its energy and verve unmatched anywhere in North Africa west of Cairo. The most remarkable thing of all is that, as recently as a century ago, almost nothing of this existed.

FROM PIRACY TO PROSPERITY

For most of history, settlement around here was restricted to what is now the well-to-do western suburb of Anfa. There was a Phoenician trading station here in the sixth century BC. Later it was the capital of a Berber confederacy, and fell in and out of Arab hands as successive dynasties tried to impose their rule. By the second half of the 15th century, the locals had seen off the Merenids and took to piracy, raiding the Portuguese coast with such efficiency that armadas were dispatched from Lisbon to put down the problem in 1468 and again in 1515. Sixty years later the Portuguese

Mosque of Hassan II: big, expensive and open to non-Muslims. *See p191.*

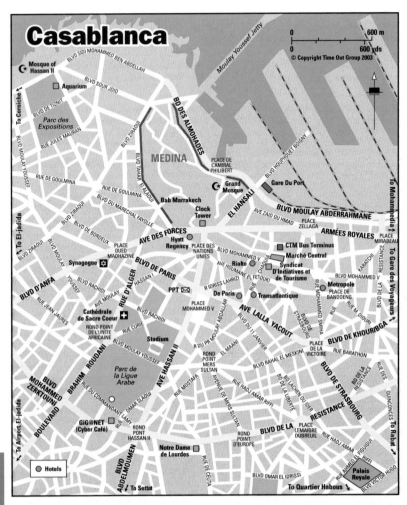

Casablanca

0   600 m
0   600 yds
© Copyright Time Out Group 2003

Mosque of Hassan II
Aquarium
BLVD SIDI MOHAMMED BEN ABDELLAH
BLVD SOUR JDID
To Corniche
BLVD DE TIZNIT
Parc des Expositions
RUE JULES MAURAN
BLVD MOULAY YOUSSEF
RUE DE GOULMINA
BLVD ZIRAOUI
BD DES ALMOHADES
MEDINA
BLVD TAHAR EL ALAOUI
Moulay Youssef Jetty
PLACE DE L'AMIRAL PHILIBERT
Grand Mosque
Gare Du Port
BLVD HOUPHOUET BOIGNY
RUE DE GOULMINA
Bab Marrakech
Clock Tower
EL HANSALI
AVE ZAID OU HMAD
BLVD MOULAY ABDERRAHMANE
PLACE ZELLAGA
ARMÉES ROYALES
PLACE MIRABEAU
To Mohammedia
BLVD DU MARECHAL FAYOLLE
AVE DES FORCES
PLACE OUED MADHAZINE
Hyatt Regency
PLACE DES NATIONS UNIES
BLVD MOHAMMED V
RUE CHAOUIA
CTM Bus Terminus
Marché Central
KARATCHI
To Gare des Voyageurs
BLVD ZIRAOUI
BLVD DE BORDEUX
BLVD DE PARIS
Riako
AVE HOUMANE EL FETOUKI
Syndicat D'Initiatives et de Tourisme
BLVD MOHAMMED V
To El-Jadida
BLVD ZIRAOUI
BLVD MOULAY YOUSSEF
BLVD RACHIDI
RUE D'ALGER
RUE MOULAY HASSAN I
Synagogue
R IDRISS LAHRIZI
De Paris
Transatlantique
Metropole
PLACE DE BANDOENG
RUE M. DIOURI
BLVD DE LA RESISTANCE
BLVD D'ANFA
RUE JEAN JAURES
PPT
PLACE MOHAMMED V
AVE LALLA YACOUT
RUE MOHAMMED SMIHA
RUE STRASBOURG
BLVD DE KHOURIBGA
Cathédrale de Sacre Coeur
BLVD RACHIDI
RUE CURIE
ROND POINT DE L'UNITE AFRICAINE
Stadium
BLVD DE L'Il JANVIER
PLACE DE LA VICTOIRE
RUE BARATHON
BD DE LA RESISTANCE
RUE DES
QUINCONCES
To Rabat
BRIAHIM ROUDANI
BLVD MOULAY YOUSSEF
R DU PR MOULAY ABDALLAH
EL MAANI
BLVD DE STRASBOURG
BLVD MOHAMMED ZERKTOUNI
AVE HASSAN II
Parc de la Ligue Arabe
RUE DU COMMANDANT LAMY
ROND POINT MERS SULTAN
AVENUE DE MERS SULTAN
RUE HADJ AMAR RIFFI
BD DE LA LIBERTE
BLVD RAHAL EL MESKINI
RESISTANCE
To Airport El-jadida
RUE OMAR SLAOUI
GiG@NET (Cyber Café)
ROND PONT HASSAN II
Notre Dame de Lourdes
RUE MOSTAFA
ROND POINT D'EUROPE
BLVD DE LA
PLACE LEMAIGRE DUBREUIL
RUE HADJ AMAR
RUE AHMED EL FIGUIGUI
BLVD
ABDELMOUMEN
To Settat
RUE DE CEUTA
BLVD OMAR EL IDRISSI
To Quartier Habous
Palais Royale
BLVD VICTOR HUGO

○ Hotels

Best of Morocco

arrived to stay, erecting fortifications and renaming the port Casa Branca – 'White House'.

The Portuguese stayed in town until 1755, when the earthquake that levelled Lisbon devastated Casa Branca too. Sultan Sidi Mohammed Ben Abdallah reclaimed the area in 1770 and built the Medina east of the ruined port – the surviving walls and grand mosque date from this period. Only the name of the Portuguese settlement survived, mutating into its Spanish version when European merchants in search of the hinterland's grain and wool began establishing themselves in the area after 1830. In 1907 the locals rioted against

increasing European influence and nine French port workers were killed. The French took this as a pretext to send in a gunboat, land some marines and depose the sultan. At this time, the population of Casablanca was still under 20,000.

In 1912 Lyautey became Morocco's Résident Général. He moved the political capital from Fès to Rabat, and decided that Casablanca should become the economic centre of what the French called 'Maroc utile', the 'useful bit of Morocco'. Detailed town planning, extensive port development and other large-scale infrastructure projects began to shape the Casablanca of today.

The old mercantile elite were quick to relocate from Fès to the coast and cash in on the corresponding property boom. Lyautey declared that while Rabat would be Morocco's Washington DC, Casablanca would become its New York.

The analogy holds to this day, although with its oceanside location, palm-lined boulevards and sprawling development based on land speculation and rapid population growth, Casablanca has more in common with Los Angeles than New York. It also has an almost Californian pot-pourri of architectural styles (*see p192* **Deco dreams**), plenty of citrus plantations in the hinterland, and a suburban beach culture that stretches west of the city centre along the Corniche of Ain Diab.

Casablanca might have been a French creation, but a generation after Lyautey it was in the vanguard of opposition to French colonial rule. With its concentration of urban poor, it stands as the heartland of Moroccan socialism and has remained a centre of political protest and the scene of periodic rioting – notably during the food strikes of 1982. But the stability and continued development of Casablanca are vital for the future of Morocco. The enormous Mosque of Hassan II, which has dominated the skyline since its completion in 1993, was perhaps in part intended to anchor Casa more firmly in the country's religious and monarchical traditions, but its waterfront site is also testimony to Casablanca's Atlanticist orientation. This is Morocco's most outward-looking city.

Sightseeing

Place des Nations Unies is an empty expanse, complete with concrete underpasses and dominated by the Hyatt Regency. But this is where the old Medina meets the new city, and from here Casa's main avenues reach out in all directions. **Boulevard Mohammed V** to the east was once the city's grandest shopping street, but is these days pleasingly down at heel. Reasons to walk this way include the Syndicate d'Initiatives de Tourisme, the main post office, an assortment of Mauresque and art deco buildings, and the bustle and fresh produce of the **Marché Central**.

More art deco (*see p192* **Deco dreams**) can also be found in the streets to the south, between Mohammed V and avenue Lalla Yacout. Delapidated arcades also cut through the quarter and the pedestrian area east of rue Chaouia offers a Westernised retail experience remote from any souk. This is the heart of the commercial downtown.

On the north side of place des Nations Unies is the entrance to the **Medina**. Disreputable touts and hawkers may accost you just inside, but after a few stalls of the usual tat, the alleyways are quieter and more broad than those of Fès or Marrakech. Although the oldest part of Casablanca, most of the Medina dates only from the 19th century, and is these days relatively depopulated. It's not geared up for tourism and you may find yourself the object of some attention, which is mostly welcoming, but still avoid this area at night.

Businesses are for the locals, such as the row of scribe shops north of Bab Marrakech on boulevard Tahar El Alaoui, where illiterates can dictate a letter or have a document explained. Wandering this way and weaving north and west takes you in the direction of the **Mosque of Hassan II**, which can otherwise be reached by a short petit taxi ride from the centre.

Perched oceanside at Islam's western extremity, and completed in 1993 after years of work by around 10,000 craftsmen, the mosque was the late king's most ambitious project. Remarkably, the whole thing was funded by public subscription. All $800 million dollars' worth. The proportions are totalitarian – the only mosque bigger is in Mecca – and its 200-metre (656-foot) minaret is the world's tallest, dizzying to gaze up at. The nine-hectare (22-acre) prayer hall, three times the size of St Paul's Cathedral, can hold 25,000 worshippers. A glass floor reveals the ocean below. 'The throne of God was built on the water,' notes a Koranic verse quoted by the king in 1980, when the project was announced.

This is the only working mosque in Morocco that can be entered by non-Muslims (one-hour tours 9am, 10am, 11am, 2pm; closed Friday). But even a walk around the outside reveals extraordinary detailing in mosaic, metalwork, masonry and woodwork – testament to a culture in which crafts still thrive. However, it is an odd building to serve as main landmark for worldly Casablanca, a city that's far from being any kind of spiritual centre.

The coastal road west from the mosque leads into the oceanside suburb of **Ain Daib**. There's a beach, but also beach clubs, with bars and pools more suited for swimming than the oily, rolling Atlantic. Most sell day or weekend tickets. This is also where Casa comes to play at night, with dance clubs clustering on the Corniche, all within a stroll of each other, many in chunks of concrete modernism that could have been airlifted from southern California. Further still to the west lies **Anfa**, site of the original settlement.

Deco dreams

Long before Niemeyer's Brasilia or Le Corbusier's orderly visions, Casablanca was supposed to be the world's most rational metropolis. When Lyautey decided to plant his new city here, the French colonial system rolled up to transform the existing small port into Morocco's economic powerhouse. Aerial views from bi-planes were consulted. Plan after rational plan was produced. A pattern of radial boulevards here, a tidy New Medina there. But the grand scheme failed to survive first contact with rampant land speculation and the housing pressures of rapid immigration. The result is an almost entirely 20th-century city, constructed at pace and during times of architectural experiment, with an eclectic mix defined as much by accident as design.

The bureaucratic centrepiece of place Mohammed V and the garden city-style medina of Quartier Habous are the main monuments to the Mauresque style – the French colonial version of neo-Moorish. But more interesting examples can be found along boulevard Mohammed V and among the streets to the south, where decorative façades collide with the art deco detailing of buildings such as the Hotel Transatlantique on rue Chaouia or the Rialto cinema around the corner on rue Salah Ben Bouchab. Much is in disrepair, but there are unpolished gems on every street and there's even talk of refurbishing this quarter into a historic district, in the manner of South Miami Beach.

The French colonial push died with the war, but in the decade before independence, a wave of cash, concrete and further rapid development washed up a new layer of modernism. Architects, mostly French, influenced by Le Corbusier and fully briefed on functional urbanism, laid out new housing in blocks and scattered the city with filling stations, schools, hospitals, beach clubs and cinemas. Most still stand today, their original gleaming white and crisp lines now grubbied and eroded by pollution. The avant-garde flag flies most proudly in the brutalist sculptural villas that sit on the palm-lined suburban streets of Anfa and Ain Diab.

If you don't mind your modernity a bit chewed up, there is plenty of fine work to be seen in Casablanca. The area around the strip of clubs along the boulevard de la Corniche offers a few good examples of the genre, but these days the influence is centred on America – McDonald's and its adjacent Ronaldland occupies the best seafront site and a fine retro villa was recently destroyed for the filming of Brad Pitt's Spy Game. But the current boss of greater Casablanca, Driss Benhima, has appointed an aesthetic committee to guard and guide the city's architectural heritage. Somewhere, somehow, Casa still dreams of becoming the burnished white Capital of Africa.

Before the Mosque of Hassan II, Casablanca's main landmark was what is now called **place Mohammed V**, a few blocks south of place des Nations Unies. A sign of different times, it's an ensemble of French colonial buildings in the Mauresque style (see p192 **Deco dreams**). To the east is the Palais de Justice or Tribunal, to the south is the Préfecture. In between is the French Consulate, fronted by a statue of Lyautey, protected by a fence. This is Casa's dry, bureaucratic heart, and the fountain only works on Fridays and weekends.

South of here is the **Parc de la Ligue Arabe**, with French layout and North African vegetation for shady strolling. On the western side is the striking, skeletal **Cathédrale de Sacre Coeur**, designed by Paul Tornon in 1930 but currently an abandoned off-white elephant. The Ecole des Beaux Arts is across the street.

The **Quartier Habous**, or New Medina, is a kilometre to the south and west – a short petit taxi ride from anywhere in town, and just beyond the inaccessible Palais Royale. Built by the French in the 1930s to attack a housing crisis, this is like a Western 'garden city' version of a Moorish quarter: neat and orderly, with a central green. Here is Morocco's most manageable souk, with a good variety of all local crafts and a couple of decent patisseries.

Cross the railway bridge south to find streets grubbier, busier and with more vitality. On some days the long market of **rue des Ait Yafalman**, dipping and rising, is packed to the horizon with shuffling humanity. Halfway down the hill and to the right is the **rue Taroudant**. Here are fortune-tellers reading from grubby cards, enchanters selling hedgehogs, crows, tortoises, owls and chameleons for black magic purposes. A reminder that Casa is no way as European as it seems.

Where to eat & drink

Is this the start of a gastronomic renaissance? Coming in summer 2003, Casa gets a new restaurant, bar and patisserie from Oliver Peyton, the formerly hard-boozing boy behind London's Atlantic Bar & Grill and a host of other one-time hip hangouts. The project is in collaboration with local partners and its location is the listed '50s Villa Zevaco on boulevard Franklin Roosevelt. Until then, the city has the range of eating possibilities you'd expect of a French-influenced city by the sea, and the drinking restrictions you'd expect of a Muslim metropolis. Only from mid-range upwards will you get a drink with your meal.

The French-run **Ma Bretagne** (boulevard Océan Atlantique, Sidi Abderrahmane, 022 39 79 79, closed Sun and Aug, main courses 120dh-250dh), specialising in seafood, is reckoned to be Morocco's finest restaurant. More centrally, **Retro 1900** (Centre 2000, Gare du Port, menus 160dh-220dh, closed Sun) serves a classic French splurge next to the more modest **Le Tajine** (main courses 75dh-170dh, closed Sun).

Modern, unfussy French dishes and classic desserts are served at the cool, upmarket **La Bavaroise** (133 rue Allal Ben Abdellah, 022 31 17 60, main courses 120dh-140dh, closed Sun). Two doors away, the tapas bar and restaurant **La Bodega** (129 rue Allal Ben Abdellah, 022 31 17 60, main courses 70dh-120dh) offers loud music (sometimes live) and relatively cheap alcohol for a mixed, well-heeled crowd. The relaxed and roomy **Positano** (12 rue El Farabi, 022 48 33 14, main courses 70dh-120dh) is quieter and less central, but just as fashionable. Thirty pasta specialities are its centrepiece.

Fresh ingredients from the adjacent Marché Central are served at the popular and women-friendly lunch spot **Snack Amine** (32 rue Chaouia, 022 54 13 31, main courses 20dh-40dh). The clean and comfortable **Snack le Marin** (9-11 avenue Lalla Yacout, 022 22 01 14, main courses 20dh-50dh) is another good lunch option with a variety of fish menus. Other Snack le Marin branches are at 69-71 rue Allal El Fassi and 268 boulevard Bas-Hammad.

Mogador (361 rue Mustapha El Moani, 022 20 07 50, main courses 40dh-100dh) offers everything from crêpes to steaks in pretty surrounds, bustling at lunch, quiet at dinner. The earthy **La Presse** (boulevard Brahmin Roudani, corner of rue Osama Ibn Zaid, 022 25 05 43, main courses 20dh-55dh), once a journalists' haunt, is an institution even older than its venerable waiters. Simple meals, paella on Sundays, friendly bustle, draught beer.

On the edge of the dockland, **Seaman's Club** (118 boulevard Moulay Abderrahmane, 022 30 99 50, main courses 30dh-70dh) is a useful venue for a drink or light meal and has a surprisingly pleasant garden out back. You can ignore the members-only signs if you treat the place with respect. **Vertigo** (110 rue Chaouia, 022 29 46 39) has a basement bar that serves until 1am daily and a small dancefloor with sounds ranging from Moroccan pop to Kylie.

Nightlife

Clubs coalesce on the Ain Diab Corniche in a limited but lively strip of popular joints featuring cover bands, drinks too pricey for anyone to get drunk, and jiving on every dancefloor, whatever the music. No entrance fees or cover charges.

Armstrong Legend (41 boulevard de la Corniche, Ain Diab, 022 79 76 56, closed Mon & Sun) has live local bands that more or less match its jazz-blues theme. Casablanca beer 90dh, shots 100dh. **Manhattan** (rue de la Mer Noir, Ain Diab, 022 79 86 30, closed Mon) has funkier cover bands and its own restaurant. The owner learnt his trade in New York, and the difference shows. Casablanca beer 75dh, shots 100dh. There's house music on the skinny dancefloor of **Fandango** (rue Mer Egee, Ain Diab, 022 79 85 08), with a quiet, candlelit conservatory out back and Italian restaurant upstairs. Casablanca beer 70dh, shots 80dh. **Le Balcon 33** (33 boulevard de la Corniche, Ain Diab, 022 79 72 05) is very full and very red, with restaurant tables and a disreputable air.

For cheaper drinks on the way out from town, **Le Petit Rocher** (boulevard de la Corniche, 022 36 32 77, closed Sun) on the promontory near the El Hank lighthouse, has a roomy lounge bar with plenty of alcoves and corners, plus DJs playing light house and chilled trance until 1am. Casablanca beer 45dh, shots 50dh, tapas and seafood served.

Where to stay

Where the Medina meets downtown, the **Hyatt Regency** (place des Nations Unies, 022 26 12 34, http://casablanca.regency. hyatt.com, doubles 1,700dh-2,600dh) is the pick of the top end, with a pool, pricey bars and international standards. The four-star **Hotel Transatlantique** (79 rue Chaouia, 022 29 45 51, doubles 550dh-700dh) occupies a restored 1922 building that's one of the highlights of the art deco district. The corner diagonal of the exterior is fashioned to resemble the prow of a ship; the grand interiors follow a French colonial theme,

Best of Morocco

Marché Central. *See p191.*

with almost too much attention to period detail. In the modern and unfussy mid-range, the **Metropole** (89 rue Mohammed Smiha, 022 30 12 13, doubles 400dh) is at the east end of the art deco district. The **Hotel de Paris** (2 rue Ech-Cherif Amziane, 022 27 42 75, doubles 250dh-300dh) has 36 light, quiet, small but tasteful rooms in the pedestrian district just off avenue Lalla Yacout. Go for those on the fifth and sixth floors, which have balconies.

Of the budget hotels on offer, the quiet and friendly **Rialto** (9 rue Salah Ben Bouchab, 022 27 51 22, doubles 140dh-160dh) is the pick, opposite the fine art deco cinema of the same name, with 21 rooms off a small, central courtyard.

Resources

Hospital
CHU Averroès Hospital, *8 rue Lahcen Laarjoun (022 48 20 20/022 22 41 09).* South of the city centre.

Internet
Gig@.Net, *140 boulevard Mohammed Zerktouni (022 48 48 10).* **Open** 24hrs daily. **No credit cards**.
Africa's largest cyber-café, with 350 places and high-speed connections for 10dh per hour. Café upstairs.

Post office
PPT, *Corner of boulevard de Paris & avenue Hassan II (160).* **Open** 8.30am-6.30pm Mon-Fri.

Police station
boulevard Brahim Roudani (022 26 93 93).

Tourist information
Syndicate d'Initiatives de Tourisme Casablanca, *98 boulevard Mohammed V (022 22 15 24).* **Open** 8.30am-noon, 3-6.30pm Mon-Fri; 8.30am-noon, 3-5pm Sat; 9am-noon Sun.

Getting around

Casa isn't difficult to navigate, and most things you might want to do are located in the same central area. Petits taxis are honest, cheap and easily hailed on the main avenues. It's hardly worth bothering with the complex and overcrowded bus system.

Watch out for street-name changes. Most notably, the two main central squares – now known as place des Nations Unies and place Mohammed V – which have only in recent years had their names swapped around by royal decree. Many old folks and taxi drivers have yet to register the change, some old maps are still on sale, and this is a source of enduring confusion. To make things worse, people sometimes refer to the place des Nations Unies (the square beside the Medina) as Houphouet Boigny, the name of the street that links it to Casa-Port station.

Getting there

From the Gare des Voyageurs, there are eight trains daily to Marrakech (journey time a little over three hours) and as many run in the opposite direction towards Fès, some continuing to Tangier. Trains to Rabat depart every halfhour from the Gare du Port, journey time one hour. Avoid the rush hour if possible as many commute between the two cities, just 97 kilometres (60 miles) apart. Train information can be found at www.oncf.org.ma.

Ten buses a day to Marrakech depart from the CTM gare routière on rue Léon l'Africain (behind the Hotel Farah). There are also ten services a day to Fès and five to Tangier, plus services to many other destinations. Grand taxis to all destinations also run from outside the CTM station.

Fès

So vast, medieval and labyrinthine, Fès is almost impossible to get to know –
but that shouldn't stop anyone from trying.

Author Paul Bowles described Fès as an
'enchanted labyrinth sheltered from time'.
No hyperbole there. It is said that there are over
9,000 alleys in the medina of Fès El Bali, the
world's largest living medieval city. For 1,000
years it dominated Morocco's religious, cultural,
commercial and political life. Even while
preserving its structure, the French did their
damnedest to dismantle its authority, moving
politics to Rabat, trade to Casablanca and local
administration to the nearby Nouvelle Ville.
But Fès remains Morocco's symbolic heart, a
deeply traditional centre of Islamic learning and
ancient craftsmanship. Despite electrification,
tourism and the ready availability of Coca-Cola,
the old city's 200,000 inhabitants still live and
work much as they have done for centuries.
To explore this warren of narrow passages,
teeming souks, huddled housing, archaic
industry and venerable mosques is to find
oneself in a space where the Middle Ages never
quite came to an end. Not even Marrakech is
much of a preparation for the experience. Fès
is, as they say, intense.

Modern Fès is actually three cities, each
quite separate from the others. Fès El Bali
('Old Fès') is the original town, founded at
the beginning of the ninth century and still
contained within 12th-century walls built by
the Almohads. To the west, Fès El Jedid ('New

Fès') is a 13th-century creation of the
Merenids, a royal city enclosed within a
separate set of fortifications. And, further
west and south, the avenues and boulevards
of the Nouvelle Ville were laid out by the
French at the beginning of the 20th century.
The latter is of little interest save for its hotels
and restaurants. Fès El Jedid, with its Royal
Palace and Mellah, is worth a walk through.
But the unique Fès El Bali is where you'll want
to spend most of your time.

HISTORY

According to legend, Fès was founded by
Moulay Idriss II, a great-great-grandson of the
Prophet Mohammed. Having inherited from his
father a kingdom centred on Christian Volubilis
and Jewish Sefrou, he searched for the right
place to build a new, specifically Muslim city
and found a broad, well-watered valley, fringed
with hills. Preliminary excavations unearthed
a golden pickaxe (*fas* in Arabic), and, thus, the
city earned its name. Many modern historians
believe that Fès was actually founded by
Moulay Idriss senior and only expanded by
his son but it is the shrine of Moulay Idriss II
that lies at the heart of the old city as a revered
sanctuary and place of pilgrimage.

Certainly, it was Idriss II who, in 808, allowed
refugees from Andalucia to settle on the right
bank of the river. They brought with them the

Borj Nord, keeping an eye
on the Medina. *See p198.*

Borj Nord, keeping an eye
on the Medina. *See p198.*

Best of Morocco

skills in mosaic and woodcarving that were to make Fès famous. Seven years later, he granted land on the left bank to refugees from Kairouan in Tunisia. The twin settlements of Fès El Andalous and Fès El Karaouiyine, as they're still known today, shared an Arab identity and a sophisticated urban culture quite distinct from that of the indigenous Berber tribes. The Andalous and Karaouiyine mosques were founded and the city gained a reputation as a seat of learning. Pope Sylvester II is said to have studied at the Karaouiyine University in the tenth century, and from here imported Arab mathematics into Europe.

Under the Almoravid and Almohad dynasties, the seat of government shifted south to Marrakech, but the city continued to prosper as the hub of an Islamic empire encompassing much of Spain and most of North Africa. It would become even more important after the Merenid conquest in 1248, when Fès El Jedid was built next door as a garrison town – both for the continuing campaign against Spain and to keep an eye on the unruly Fassis. In 1438 its barracks were converted into a quarter for the city's hitherto scattered Jewish population. One of their duties was to preserve in salt the heads of the executed, prior to their display on city gates. The word for salt, *mellah*, became the name for this and all future Jewish quarters.

The Merenids enlarged the Karaouiyine Mosque and developed its university, built the series of medersas that would accommodate its students, and added a network of fundouks to support the city's thriving commercial activity.

Expansion was fuelled by a new wave of Andalucian refugees fleeing Christian conquests in Spain, and Fès arrived at the pinnacle of its prosperity and importance. But the Fassis had never really taken to the Merenids and, after sporadic rebellions, the last sultan was dragged through the streets of Fès El Bali before having his throat cut in 1465.

The Portuguese took control over the Moroccan coast, an assortment of tribal dynasties squabbled over the rest and the next several centuries saw Fès slowly shrink in international stature. The Alaouite Sultan Moulay Ismail moved the capital to Meknes and actively encouraged the further decline of Fès. Later sultans were less hostile but decay was only checked in the late 19th-century reign of Sultan Moulay Hassan, who constructed avenue des Français (sometimes called avenue Moulay Hassan) and the Dar Batha Palace to link Fès El Bali and Fès El Jedid. Most of the bigger merchants' houses also date from this period.

But neither Moulay Hassan nor his sons were able to control the country's warring tribes and in 1912 a divided Morocco fell to the French. On 30 March, in what is now the Palais Mnebhi restaurant, Sultan Moulay Hafid signed the Treaty of Fès, which surrendered his rule and established the French Protectorate. On 17 April the Fassis protested by lynching the city's European population – over 80 bodies were piled up in front of the palace gates – and the sultan's army joined in the uprising. The next day a French force turned up from Meknes to shell and then occupy the city.

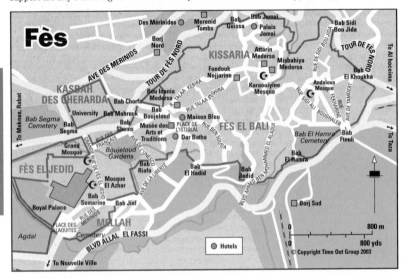

Bird's-eye view from the **Merenid Tombs**. *See p198.*

The French removed the sultan to Rabat and built the Nouvelle Ville to house the European population in safety. But Fès El Bali remained a centre of unrest. The Istiqlal (independence) Party was formed here in 1943 and Fès played a leading role in the events leading up to independence. As recently as December 1990, rioters set fire to the luxury Hotel des Merinides. Independence didn't bring back the seat of government and the Jewish population moved out in 1956. Their place has been taken by rural migrants, who have moved into the increasingly crowded Medina and into slums on the outskirts. A UNESCO Cultural Heritage Plan has assisted the city's physical preservation and many fine old houses have been restored. But though Fès proudly remains the centre of Islamic Morocco, a city that once rivalled Mecca and Medina in importance is now overly dependent on tourism and the handicrafts trade.

Sightseeing

Fès might well be the most confusing city you've ever visited. It's almost impossible to get a sense of the whole from ground level, but a

The **tanneries**: stinky but stunning. *See p200.*

circuit by taxi of the outer ramparts – a journey of around 15 kilometres (nine miles) – provides some kind of an overview.

From the kasbah of Borj Sud or the **Merenid Tombs** in the surrounding hills there are excellent views over Fès El Bali. **Borj Sud**, like its counterpart **Borj Nord** on the opposite side, was built in the late 16th century by the Saadian Sultan Ahmed El Mansour to watch over the rebellious medina. This is the best vantage in early morning. The site of the ruined Merenid Tombs, or the garden terrace of the nearby Hotel des Merinides, offers a splendid view over the whole medina and the

Karaouiyine quarter; the view from here is best towards sunset, as the dying light cascades down the slope of the valley.

Fès El Jedid

A walk through the easily navigated Fès El Jedid is a good warm-up exercise before entering the vast maze of the medina. Half of its total area is taken up by the inaccessible city within a city within a city that is the **Royal Palace**, also known as Dar El Makhzen. There are rumours that King Mohammed VI may open this complex of gardens, pavilions, palaces,

mosques and medersas to the public, but for now you only view the gleaming brass gates from the place des Alaouites.

From here the **Jewish cemetery and museum** (open 7am-sunset, closed Sat) are to the east, with the Mellah itself beyond. This is a warren of tiny alleys and covered passages, and houses with very un-Islamic grilled windows and balconies. Once Morocco's largest Jewish quarter, all save a handful of its 17,000 inhabitants emigrated after the end of the Protectorate. Five historic synagogues remain, mostly in alleys off the rue des Merinids, and mostly now private houses. Synagogue Rabbi Shlomo Ibn Danan has been restored as a historic monument and it is free to enter, but you'll need help to find its inconspicuous wooden door. Ask at the cemetery museum.

The jewellers' souk lies around Bab Semarine, through which the Grande Rue des Merinides leads north past a food market and two 13th-century mosques to the Petit Mechouar.

The avenue des Français leads east from here to Bab Boujeloud. This area was a no man's land until developed by Moulay Hassan in the 19th century. The peaceful **Boujeloud Gardens**, open to all, are cut through by ornamental watercourses and at the western end there's a café by an old waterwheel. Before straying into Fès El Bali proper, it's worth visiting the **Musée des Arts et Traditions** (open 9am-noon, 3-6pm, closed Tue, admission 10dh); the entrance is in the road off place de l'Istiqlal between the museum and the Hotel Dar Batha. Inside is a jumbled collection of artefacts from the tenth-20th centuries, demonstrating the timelessness of local crafts, and tranquil gardens that are alone worth the admission fee.

Fès El Bali

This is the heart of the matter. The Fès medina comprises 187 *quartiers*, each equipped with a mosque, a Koranic school, a fountain, a hammam and a communal bread oven. There are over 300 mosques in all. Even the widest streets are too narrow for cars and many of the narrowest are barely wide enough for two people to pass each other. Donkeys are the only form of transport and at the ubiquitous cry of 'Balak!' ('Attention') it's wise to duck to the side or risk a knock from a pannier full of brass ornaments or chairlegs.

As the city's prime source of income, tourists are subject to a lot of attention, from faux guides eager to show you around to single-product stallholders touting mirrors or nougat, rugs or remedies. The alleys and souks offer myriad sights, sounds and smells, and a simple stroll can be an almost overpowering

experience. Yet still most of the medina remains closed to the visitor, its inner life hidden behind unrevealing façades.

GETTING LOST AND GUIDES

It's easy to get lost. Even the best maps don't detail every last alley and more rudimentary plans are no use at all once you stray from the principal thoroughfares. On your very first visit it's wise to enlist the services of an official guide. These can be booked for the day or half-day (100dh-150dh) at the Syndicat d'Initiative in the Nouvelle Ville, at a booth by Bab Boujeloud or arranged through your hotel. Many have routines dulled by repetition and are principally interested in leading you to shops where they'll earn a kickback from your purchases. Research what you want to see and discuss it over a coffee before setting forth, but don't expect to avoid shops altogether. Sooner or later you'll find yourself gulled into entering a herbalist's stall or textile workshop and fending off the hard sell. On the other hand, not to purchase anything at all would be to miss out on the rituals of commerce, which are one of the city's central occupations.

Mosques and most other religious buildings are off-limits for non-Muslims. The four main sights accessible to the visitor – the Bou Inania Medersa, Fundouk Nejjarine, Attarin Medersa and the tanneries – can be done in half a day. It could take months to find all the lesser treasures.

BOU INANIA MEDERSA

Fès El Bali has 14 gates, but **Bab Boujeloud**, built in 1913, despite its more ancient appearance, is as good a place to start as any. Two main streets run from here to the central cluster of sights in the Karaouiyine quarter. Take rue Talaa Kebira, the one to the left of Kissariat Serrajine, a courtyard of stalls selling leatherwork and silverware, and 100 metres in you'll find the **Bou Inania Medersa**, the finest and largest medersa in Fès. The lofty, patterned interior demonstrates the sublime craftsmanship of 14th-century Fès. In recent years it has been closed for renovation but at the time of writing it was scheduled to reopen in late 2003. Scaffolding currently also hides the curious water-clock opposite: a row of brass bowls and water spouts positioned on 13 window sills, also dating from the 14th century. No one is really sure how it worked or even whether it was really a clock. It may have been some kind of musical instrument.

Talaa Kebira continues downhill past hammams and fountains, mosques and fundouks, stalls selling groceries or street snacks, and a row of blacksmiths. Just beyond the Gazleane Mosque on the corner of an alley

marked with a plaque as leading to the former house of historian Ibn Khaldoun, is the **M'Zara of Moulay Idriss**, a monument commemorating the spot where the founder supposedly sat to rest and ponder the shape of his future city.

FUNDOUK NEJJARINE

Further down on the left from the Moulay Idriss monument is the skinner's fundouk where animal hides are scraped clean. Cobblers dominate the next stretch and the Cherabliyn Mosque on the right is the slipper-makers'. By now the street has become the rue Ech Cherabliyn and there are stalls trading the gold-tooled leather bookbinding known everywhere as 'Moroccan'. From here it's not much further to the monuments and souks that are Fès El Bali's centrepiece. The Henna Souk can be found down a turning to the right. The next right turn leads past the spice sellers of the Souk Attarin, said to be the busiest in Fès, to a square containing a 17th-century fountain and dominated by the 18th-century **Fundouk Nejjarine** (open 9am-noon, 3-6pm, closed Tue, admission 10dh). This was recently restored and now houses a museum of wood that is way more interesting than it sounds. There's a small café on the roof for good views and a restorative mint tea. Nearby alleys contain the woodworkers of the Souk Nejjarine.

From here it's a short hop to the **Zaouia of Moulay Idriss II**, either via a dogleg from the east of place Nejjarine, or back along rue Ech Cherabliyn past the Dar Saada restaurant and right through the rows of stalls selling candles and nougat on the outskirts of the Kissaria. Wooden beams that must be ducked under mark the limits of the shrine's zone of sanctuary that infidels were once forbidden to enter.

Non-Muslims are still not allowed into the zaouia itself, but a glimpse of the legendary founder's tomb, draped in embroidered velvet and surrounded by candles, praying women and offerings of European clocks, can be had from the women's entrance.

At the end of the stalls opposite, by the south-east corner of the zaouia, is **Lamrani Frères** – an excellent hatter selling, among other headgear, the tassled cylindrical hat known elsewhere as a fez, but in this town called a Fassi tarbouche. If you want to buy one in its city of origin, this is the place. The rest of the Kissaria is a tight grid of alleys and one-man stalls – colourful and beautifully lit – catering to local needs with fine fabrics and threads, gleaming jewellery, slippers and robes. No tourist tat here.

ATTARIN MEDERSA

At the far end of the Kissaria is the **Attarin Medersa** (open 9am-noon, 2-6pm, closed Fri;

admission 10dh). Built in the early 14th century, it's not as grand as the Bou Inania, but has the same basic structure. Sixty cells for students are ranged on upper floors around a central courtyard with a fountain for ritual ablutions. The whole is finely decorated in tooled wood, stucco, mosaics and Italian marble.

On the other side of the crossroads is one corner of **Karaouiyine Mosque**, founded in the ninth century, improved and enlarged in the tenth, rebuilt in the 12th and still living and breathing in the 21st. It's typical of Fès that you can be right outside its biggest and culturally most important monument yet not necessarily even notice that it's there. Though large enough for 20,000 people to pray within and still leave room for one of the Islamic world's most significant libraries, it's so snugly embedded among shops and houses that its shape is impossible to discern from outside. Only occasional glimpses of the interior are afforded by whichever of its 14 doors happen to be open as you pass – ten of them if it's a Friday.

On the way clockwise around the Karaouiyine Mosque you will also pass the 14th-century **Misbahiya Medersa**, currently being renovated, and the well-preserved **Tetouani Fundouk** of the same period, now housing a carpet shop. On the far south-east corner of the Karaouiyine Mosque is place Seffarine, where coppersmiths hammer away producing kettles and cooking pots. The really, really huge ones, for weddings and festivals, are for rent rather than sale. The square has fig trees, a fountain and the entrance to the **Seffarine Medersa**, Morocco's first, founded in 1280. It's still in use by Islamic students, who can be persuaded to show you around.

DYERS AND TANNERS

The lane from the south-east of place Seffarine drops down to the Souk des Teinturiers, or **Dyers' Souk**. You'll see swatches of fabric stretched overhead to dry, brilliant in the sunshine, and grey-clad workers stirring ancient cauldrons, their arms often coloured to the elbow in the hue of the day. The colours are created by seeds and minerals crushed in a small riverside mill, and small gullies of water rush through the quarter, harnessed to various purposes in a living display of medieval technology.

Even more medieval are the **tanneries**, or Chaoura, downriver. Follow rue El Mechattine from the north-east corner of place Seffarine and the foul odour will soon confirm that you are heading in the right direction. From the Derb Chouara, a staircase leads up to the **Terrasse de Tannerie**, where a collective enterprise selling leather products opens on to

Babouches, babouches and more babouches at the local Slippers 'R' Us.

a terrace where you can view the work of the tanneries from a safe distance. Hides are dipped in and out of a honeycomb of vats below, some containing brilliant dyes, others solutions of chalk and salt or urine and pigeon shit. The barefoot dyers, wearing shorts whatever the weather, wade through it all – and as a result often become rheumatic in their 40s. At that point their sons are enlisted to help, ensuring the hereditary nature of the guilds. Around 50 families work here in what is the largest of the city's three tanneries.

FES EL ANDALOUS

Over the Bein El Moudoun bridge south of the tanneries or the El Aoud bridge close by the Souk des Teinturiers, it's possible to cross into Fès El Andalous. On this bank there are few shops, meaning that guides are reluctant to take you this way. The two main sights on this side are at the top of the hill: the Andalous Mosque and the Sahrija Medersa, both part of the same complex.

Little can be seen of the **Andalous Mosque**, founded at the same time as the Karaouiyine and even granted a library by the Merenids but never to develop into a separate university. The best view is from a side gate that looks across the courtyard toward the white minaret. The **Sahrija Medersa** (open 8am-6pm daily) is on the other side. Built in the early 14th century, it is slightly smaller than the Attarin and still

accommodates students. It's also been undergoing renovations and access may be difficult, especially outside term-time.

South of here, **rue Sidi Ali Boughaleb** brings you through a down-at-heel market to the *koubba* (tomb) of this particular saint, a patron of students and the mentally ill. Many gather here on Tuesday nights, waiting for the 12th-century mystic to appear in their dreams and suggest a cure for whatever ails them.

Getting around

Petit taxis in Fès are mostly honest and therefore cheap. They are useful not only for travelling between the Nouvelle Ville and Fès El Bali, but also from gate to gate around the ramparts, often the easiest way to get from one section of the medina to another.

Where to eat & drink

Fès El Bali is not blessed with many fine restaurants, but for a splurge **La Maison Bleue** (2 place de l'Istiqlal, 055 63 60 52, menu 500dh) is a good choice, for which you must book in advance, as are either of the two restaurants, one Moroccan (menu 430dh), one international menu (290dh), at the **Palais Jamai** (Bab Guissa, 055 63 43 31).

Otherwise, the medina offers mostly 'palace restaurants', housed in notable buildings but mostly serving set menus to prearranged tour groups. One such is the **Palais Mnebhi** (15 Soukiat Ben Safi, 055 63 38 93, menus 150dh-250dh), a splendid building where France and Morocco signed the Protectorate Treaty in 1912. In a palace at the north-west corner of the Kissaria, **Dar Saada** (21 Souk El Attarin, 055 63 73 70, menu 180dh) is a rare licensed restaurant at the very heart of the medina, open for lunch only.

North of the Dar Saada, up rue Hormis towards Bab Guissa, there's a convivial area of the medina full of tiny cafés and diners, many with room for no more than two. There's also a cluster of cheap places around Bab Boujeloud. Try the **Restaurant des Jeunes** (16 Serrajine Boujould, 062 01 33 54, main courses 30dh) for good, basic fare, followed by coffee or tea at one of the cafés around the corner, with pastries from the stalls opposite.

Street snacks such as chunks of pastilla, fried potato cakes, freshly made crisps and skewers of brochettes can also be found around here and along Talaa Kebira.

The pick of the Nouvelle Ville restaurants are the **Restaurant Zagora** (5 boulevard Mohammed V, 055 62 46 18, main courses 40dh-80dh), which has a long 'desert-style' menu and excellent salads, or the very popular **Restaurant Pizzeria Chez Victoria** (21 rue Brahim Roudani, 055 62 47 30, main courses 50dh-100dh), which serves Italian food with some French trimmings. Both are licensed.

The **New Peacock** (29 avenue Mohammed Siaoul, 055 94 11 87) has a fine selection of ice-creams, Moroccan pastries, fresh juices and shakes and a very mixed and relaxed clientele. It's open until mid-evening.

Where to stay

The **Palais Jamai** (Bab Guissa, 055 63 43 31, double 3,160dh) is the city's most famous and luxurious hotel, overlooking Fès El Bali from its vantage at the northern edge of the medina. Established in 1930 in an enclosed 19th-century palace, it has stunning Andalucían gardens, an enormous heated swimming pool, fantastic (and fantastically expensive) suites, and unsurpassable views of the city.

Just as convenient for the medina but much more moderately priced is the **Hotel Batha** (Dar Batha, 055 63 49 60, double 454dh), which has 61 pleasant, basic rooms, a variety of terraces and a pool.

Across the square is the entrance to **La Maison Bleue** (2 place de l'Istiqlal, 055 63 60 52, www.maisonbleue.com, double 2,800dh),

a family home turned luxurious guesthouse with six antique-furnished suites around a spectacular tiled atrium. It was built in 1915 by the grandfather of the current owner, Mehdi El Abbadi. He was a jurist and astrologer whose library can be found in the Fatima suite – named, like the others, after one of his wives. There are seven more suites at its sister establishment, **Riad Maison Bleue** (33 Derb El Mitter, Talaa El Kebira, 055 74 18 73, www.maisonbleue.com, double 1,900dh), near the Bab Ain Zleten, which also has a pool.

There are many other riad-style guesthouses in Fès and even more on the way. **Riad Fès** (5 Derb Ben Slimane, 055 74 10 12, www.riadfes.com, double 3,000dh) is serious and upmarket, themed on colonial-era trading connections between Fès and Europe, and imported influences on Moroccan culture. If the owner's around, every stick of furniture tells a story. There's a small pool, a hammam, a variety of suites and even a lift to the upper storeys. **Riad Al Bartal** (21 rue Sournas, 055 63 70 53, www.riadalbartal.com, double 900dh), owned by a friendly French couple, is more down to earth and better value, with a nice lounge full of books, seven very different rooms and an atrium full of lush greenery. **Riad Louna** (21 Derb Serraj, 055 74 19 85, www.riadlouna.com, double 450dh-950dh) is the family riad: good value, unpretentiously run by a Belgian couple, handily located near Bab Boujeloud, and with one room that can connect to a small adjoining room with two beds for children.

The rooms at **Pension Batha** (8 Sidi Lkhayat, 055 74 11 50, doubles 180dh-210dh) all have showers (not often the case at the cheaper end of the market), making this a good low-budget option near Dar Batha.

Pick of the mid-price options in the Nouvelle Ville are the recently renovated **Mounia Hotel** (60 rue Asila, 055 62 48 38, doubles 384dh), which has 83 spacious rooms, and the **Hotel Splendid** (9 rue Abdelkarim El Khattabi, 055 62 21 48, doubles 342dh), which has the advantage of a courtyard pool. The **Fès Inn** (47 rue No.2, Sidi Brahim, 055 64 00 89, www.fesinn.com, doubles 380dh) is friendly and welcoming with nice rooms, but is perhaps a little too far out of town to be anything but an emergency option in high season.

Getting there

There are eight trains daily to Casablanca, all of which stop at Rabat, plus five to Marrakech and four to Tangier. From the bus station outside Bab Mahrouk, there are eight buses daily to Rabat and Casablanca, six to Tangier and two to Marrakech. Grand taxis also make runs from

here to Casablanca or Rabat. From Fès airport there are daily flights to Casablanca and twice-weekly flights to Paris.

Resources

Internet
Gama Systems *34 boulevard Mohammed V, Dar Dbibegh (055 94 24 83)*. **Open** 9am-6.30pm daily.

Police
Comissariats: next to Post Office (*see below*) & off place de l'Istiqlal (emergency 19).

Post office
PTT *corner avenue Hassan II, New Town.* **Open** 8.30am-12.15pm, 2.30-6.30pm Mon-Thur; 8.30am-11.30pm, 3-6.30pm Fri; 8.30am-noon Sat.

Tourist information
Syndicate d'Initiative *place Mohammed V (no phone)*. **Open** 8.30am-noon, 2.30-6.30pm Mon-Fri, 8.30am-noon Sat.
This is the place to book an official guide.

Moulay Yacoub

This small spa resort in a valley of interlocking spurs is 20 kilometres (12 miles) north-west of Fès across gently rolling countryside. It's built on a precipitous series of hillside terraces, where natural sulphurous springs fill a series of hammams and pools, with separate sections for men and women (open 6am-10pm daily, admission 10dh). Bring trunks or swimsuits. Cars and taxis park at the top of the hill, leaving you to find your way down stairways equipped with small restaurants and cafès.

For mixed baths and cleaner water, the **Thermes de Moulay Yacoub** (055 69 40 64, open 6am-10pm daily, admission 90dh) is a modern facility at the bottom of the valley where you can either take a simple soak or sign up for one of their courses of treatment for rheumatic and dermatological complaints. The water comes up from 1,500 metres (4,921 feet) underground at a temperature of 54°C (129°F).

Getting there

Grand taxis run to Moulay Yacoub from the bus station outside Bab Mahrouk.

Meknes, Volubilis & Moulay Idriss

MEKNES
Meknes is the smallest and poorest of the former imperial cities and, after the experience of Fès, something of a disappointment.

La Maison Bleue. *See p201.*

Berber rather than Arab in origin and sited in a prime agricultural area, it grew from an eighth-century kasbah into the principal market town of the Meknassa tribe, from which it takes its name.

Its imperial status is almost entirely the result of one man, the Alaouite Sultan Moulay Ismail, who ruled 1672-1727 and intended Meknes to become Morocco's answer to Versailles. A true tyrant, his motto was: 'My subjects are like rats in a basket, and if I don't shake the basket, they will gnaw their way out'. He is said to have used some 2,500 Christian slaves to build the fortified palace that is the Imperial City complex – more comparable to Beijing's Forbidden City than anything in Morocco. He never finished his work, however, and the 1755 earthquake did great damage to what he had manage to erect. Many monuments were then stripped to provide building materials for projects elsewhere. Meknes fell into decline until the French revived it as their military headquarters.

Modern Meknes has a manageable medina equipped with the usual assortment of souks but lacking the magic and intensity of Fès El Bali. On the other side of the Mellah, the Imperial City is entered through the enormous Bab El Mansour. The most significant structure within is the Mausoleum of Moulay Ismail (open 9am-noon, 3-6pm, closed Fri), one of Morocco's few holy places that is open to non-Muslims. It was restored in 1959 by King Mohammed V. Behind it is the Dar El Kebira, completed as a complex of palaces in 1677 but totally destroyed 50 years later by Moulay Ismail's jealous son, Moulay Abdellah. Now it is just picturesque ruins. The true measure of Moulay Ismail's ambition can perhaps be best made by a taxi trip around the enormous ramparts – all 25 kilometres (16 miles) of them.

VOLUBILIS

Volubilis is about 30 kilometres (18 miles) north of Meknes. There were neolithic and Carthaginian settlements here long before the Romans arrived in the first century BC and built what was to become the southern-most city of Empire. It was a provincial capital and organised grain production and export in this fertile region. The Romans headed off home in the third century but the city was inhabited for another millennium and a half, only finally abandoned in the 18th century when Moulay Ismail began demolition to provide materials for his palaces in Meknes. If that hadn't happened, it could have become one of the best preserved Roman sites anywhere.

The remains (open sunrise-sunset, admission 20dh) are nevertheless impressive and you should allow at least a couple of hours to walk around it all. The town plan is clear and the remains of the Capitol, Basilica and Forum mark what was once the administrative centre. Little remains of the public baths but the Triumphal Arch has survived the ravages of history almost intact.

Its presence persuaded the French to begin the excavations that have unearthed the rest. Such work continues under the Volubilis Project collaboration between the Institute of Archaeology at University College London and INSAP, its Moroccan equivalent, with financial support from both governments. Most of the portable finds have been removed and put in the Musée Archéologique in Rabat (*see p208*), but many stunning mosaics – essentially decorated floors – remain in their original locations. The best are at the House of Ephebos next to the Triumphal Arch, the House of Orpheus near the olive oil presses, and the House of the Labours of Hercules on the Decumanus Maximus.

MOULAY IDRISS

The holy city of Moulay Idriss stands on a hill, cradled by mountains, just four kilometres (two miles) to the east of Volubilis – the view of the Roman ruins from here is fantastic. Built around the tomb and zaouia of Sultan Moulay Idriss I, it's a peaceful corner for most of the year but wakes up in August when thousands of pilgrims come to the *moussem* in honour of the founder not just of this town, but of Moroccan Islam. This is one of the most important religious festivals in the country, involving days of feasting and dancing, with tents scattered across the surrounding countryside.

Non-Muslim tourists can't enter the zaouia – a low wooden bar across the street marks the closest approach for infidels and beasts of burden – but are welcome to wander the narrow streets by day. You can look over the shrine from vantage points on the Khiber, taller of the two hills on either side. These are hard to find, however – ask a guide to take you to the Terrasse Sidi Abdellah El Hajjam. On the way up, souks sell votive candles and local nougat.

There are no hotels and non-Muslims are forbidden to stay here at night. The best day to visit is Saturday, when a market enlivens the town and makes it easier to get to.

Getting there

There are eight trains a day from Fès to Meknes, and the journey takes 45 minutes. Buses and grands taxis run from the bus station outside Bab Mahrouk.

From Meknes, buses and grands taxis make regular runs to Moulay Idriss from Bab El Khemis in the Medina or from near the Institut Français off avenue Hassan II in the Nouvelle Ville. You would need to charter a grand taxi to reach Volubilis but could visit Moulay Idriss on the same trip. Volubilis can also be reached by taking a bus for Ouezzane from Bab El Khemis and asking to be set down on the road nearest the site, from where it's a 500-metre (1,640-foot) walk downhill. Getting back, however, would involve hitching or walking to Moulay Idriss. Buses back to Meknes stop around 3pm.

At a pinch, it would be possible to charter a grand taxi in Fès and do Volubilis, Moulay Idriss and Meknes all in one day. But either Meknes or Volubilis and Moulay Idriss make a more manageable day trip.

Rabat

Twice an imperial capital, once a haunt of slave raiders but Rabat's quietened down a bit since then.

Doubling as both ancient imperial city and modern administrative capital, Rabat is the monarch's permanent residence, the seat of government, host to over 80 foreign embassies and home to some of Morocco's most important historical treasures. A clean and civilised sort of place, where 12th-century Almohad ramparts enclose one of Morocco's least hassly medinas and cut through with an elegant French colonial grid, this city of one million plays Washington DC to Casablanca's New York City. For the White House, Washington Monument and Lincoln Memorial, think the Royal Palace, Tour Hassan and Hassan II Mausoleum. Other similarities include one-way streets, a distinct lack of nightlife and lots of purposeful men with briefcases striding to important appointments.

According to mood, Rabat can feel either restful or downright dull. By day its tree-lined avenues are a sophisticated urban bustle, equipped with bookshops and newsagents, restaurants and cinemas. But when night falls, the city grows quiet. It can be hard to find so much as a café open after 10pm. Only during Ramadan does Rabat come alive after dark, with an all-night promenade along the boulevards of the Ville Nouvelle.

But while only a fool would come here looking for discos, Rabat's well-kept historical monuments are worth a day or two of anyone's time. It's an easy city to find your way around, you won't often be pestered by *faux guides*, and you might even meet a few people who don't depend on the tourist industry for a living.

HISTORY
During the last 2,500 years, the estuary of Bou Regreg has provided a safe harbour and Atlantic access for an assortment of civilisations.

The Phoenicians were here first, followed by the Carthaginians. Then came the Romans, who established the self-governing port of Sala Colonia at the southernmost extremity of the Empire. Its ruins are now enclosed within the Chellah (the most ancient part of the modern city). The Romans withdrew in the third century, but the town survived as a Berber trading post until the tenth century, when Arabs built a *ribat* – a combination of monastery and garrison – on the site of the current kasbah, and began tussling with the Berbers.

The Almohads arrived in the 12th century, replaced the *ribat* with a kasbah, and used the port as a base for seagoing campaigns against

Topless women at the **Chellah**. *See p208.*

Mausoleum of Mohammed V.
See p207.

the Reconquista (Christian Andalucíans). After a victory over the Spaniards at Alarcos in 1195, Sultan Yacoub El Mansour decided to transform his Ribat El Fatah ('Fortress of Victory') into an imperial capital. He built the extensive walls, added the Bab Oudaya to the kasbah, and started raising the grand Hassan Mosque. But work stopped at his death in 1199 and Rabat fell into centuries of neglect.

In the 14th century the Merenid sultans walled off the Roman ruins of Sala Colonia and used the site for their royal necropolis. Rabat was now a near empty town of a few hundred houses and even became second in importance to Salé across the river. Things perked up in the 17th century when the Saadian Sultan Zaidan gave the city to Muslims expelled from Andalucia by Philip II. They rebuilt or replaced many of the old Almohad structures and, because the area enclosed by the old walls was too large, erected the dividing wall that today still separates the Medina from the Ville Nouvelle.

Saadian rule collapsed in 1627 and the sister cities of Rabat and Salé established themselves as the independent republic of Bou Regreg. Its chief business was organised piracy. The 'Sallee Rovers', as the corsairs were known to the English, not only took out Christian ships that passed their way, but also raided as far afield as Iceland and the southern coast of England, where they made slave raids.

The independent republic came to an end when Sultan Moulay Rachid took Rabat in 1666. But even though the city briefly reattained imperial status at the end of the 18th century under Sultan Mohammed Ben Abdellah, unofficial piracy continued until 1829 when the Habsburg navy revenged the loss of a ship by shelling all of Morocco's coastal cities.

After a prosperous and mostly peaceful 19th century, Rabat was declared the administrative centre of the French Protectorate in 1912. As in other cities, the Medina was largely left alone while Lyautey planned the Ville Nouvelle around it, native traditions segregated from European quarters. In 1956 Rabat became the capital of independent Morocco.

Sightseeing

Dating only from the 17th century, when it was built by Muslim refugees from Andalucia, the compact and orderly Medina is less intriguing than those of Fès or Marrakech, but a cool contrast to the businesslike Ville Nouvelle. The main drag is **rue Souika**, which cuts north-west from the Medina continuation of avenue Mohammed V, just past the Marché Central. Rue Souika runs past both the mosque of Sultan Moulay Sliman, on the corner of rue Sidi Fatah, and the **Grand Mosque**, which, although founded by the Merenids, was rebuilt in the 19th century. The small fountain in the wall opposite, on the alley heading to the Bab Chellah, is the only remnant of the original.

Rue Souika continues as the covered rue Souk Sebbat, and then meets rue des Consuls. There's a tatty flea market between here and Bab El Bahr, and the Mellah, the old Jewish quarter and Rabat's poorest neighbourhood. There are over a dozen closed synagogues – some squatted, others locked and intact – in this quarter of dead-end alleys and downmarket street stalls, but you'd need a guide to find any of them.

Rue des Consuls, as the name suggests, was the diplomatic quarter before the French built the Ville Nouvelle. Several fine fundouks survive, notably the grand **Fundouk Ben Aicha** at No.109. Others are at Nos.31-2, 93 and 141. These days, covered by a shady trellis, rue des Consuls is the Medina's most upmarket shopping street. A stretch of silversmiths and jewellers gives way

to leather workers, antique shops and carpet sellers. If you're going to buy local crafts – particularly carpets, for which Rabat is renowned – this is one of Morocco's least aggressive bazaars. There are also auctions on Monday and Thursday mornings. Prior to bargaining, prices can be investigated at the (high) fixed-price **Ensemble Artisanal**. Turn right out of the northern end of rue des Consuls and it's on rue Tarik El Marsa, opposite the small **Musée National de l'Artisanat** (open 9am-noon, 3-6pm, closed Tue, admission 20dh).

Between the top of rue des Consuls and the entrance to the Kasbah des Oudayas, the Souk El Ghezel, now little more than a car park, was once both the city's slave market, where Christian captives were auctioned off, and the wool market for the Medina's carpet weavers, now relocated along boulevard El Alou. This is also an area of carpenters and wood carvers.

You'll be ambushed by young women offering henna 'tattoos' on the stepped approach to the **Bab Oudaya**. One of the masterpieces of Almohad architecture, the gate was added to existing walls (built by his father) around 1195 by Sultan Yacoub El Mansour. The Bab Oudaya originally led straight into the sultan's palace but its function was more ceremonial than defensive. The three chambers were where the town met the sultanate: here petitioners would wait, assemblies gather and justice be dispensed for all to see. These days it's used for occasional art exhibitions, and a smaller entrance to the Kasbah stands to its right.

The fortified **Kasbah** has been garrisoned throughout history both to repel European raiders and to boss the locals. These days it's a quiet, village-like, blue and white quarter reminiscent of the Andalucia from where its builders came. Ignore the guides, you don't need one. Rue Jemaa runs straight through the quarter. Halfway along on the left is the Kasbah mosque, the Jemaa El Atiq, founded in 1150 and the city's oldest. It was restored in the 18th century by an English defector, Ahmed El Inglizi, who worked for Sultan Sidi Mohammed.

Rue Jemaa continues to Le Platforme, as it's known – a broad promontory with fine views of the ocean, Salé across the river, and much of Rabat. Originally a semaphore station, from here the cannon of the pirate republic could shell merchant ships lured by the Sallee Rovers on to the submerged sandbank spanning the estuary mouth. Though a boon to pirates, the sandbank was later one reason why trade was diverted to Casablanca down the coast. From Le Platforme you can climb down to the uninviting beach.

Back through the Medina, either zigzagging southwards roughly in line with the walls on the riverside, or else retreating along rue Jemaa

and turning left down rue Bazzo, you will find the open-air **Café Maure**. With its warren of small terraces, tiled benches, cascading geraniums and river views, this is a prime spot for mint tea and almond pastries. Cheap too, used by Moroccans as well as tourists.

Beside the café is the entrance to the peaceful **Andalucían Garden**, which was actually laid out in the French colonial period, but follows Spanish principles, with sunken beds of hibiscus, datura, roses and poinsettia. Beyond the garden, the **Museum of Moroccan Arts** (open 9am-noon, 3pm-6pm, closed Tue, admission 20dh) is housed in a first-century palace built by Sultan Moulay Ismail and contains a large but slightly fusty collection of folk arts from Neolithic stone jewellery to contemporary carpets.

MOSQUES AND A MAUSOLEUM

On a rise at the eastern edge of the Ville Nouvelle, overlooking the bridge to Salé, **La Tour Hassan** has been Rabat's main landmark for over 800 years. Originally the minaret of Sultan Yacoub El Mansour's grand mosque, it was intended to be as tall as Koutoubia, but was only three-quarters finished when the Sultan died in 1199. It's an impressive structure with four different façades, and solid enough to have survived the 1755 earthquake, which destroyed what was left of the mosque. The paved expanse dotted with a grid of re-erected pillars gives some idea of its former dimensions. Twice the size of the Kairaouine mosque in Fès, which has space for 20,000 worshippers, it was the Almohad equivalent of Casablanca's Hassan II Mosque.

At the southern end of the mosque site, suggesting just such a historical continuity, are the **Mosque and Mausoleum of Mohammed V**. You can't enter the mosque, but the mausoleum, with its pyramidal, green-tiled roof, is open to all. Ascend the stairs, walk past the elaborately costumed royal guard, and enter to find yourself on an inner balcony overlooking a richly ornate interior and the sarcophagi of Kings Mohammed V (centre) and Hassan II (south-east corner), and Hassan's brother Prince Moulay Abdellah (south-west corner). A cleric often sits there too, reading aloud from the Koran. Completed in 1971 and one of the first prestige projects of independent Morocco, it was designed by a Vietnamese architect, Vo Toan.

THE CHELLAH

The main axis of the Ville Nouvelle is avenue Mohammed V, with its French-designed buildings in Mauresque style. The terracotta-coloured Chambre des Représentants, just north of the station, is the most prominent example. On avenue Mohammed V and the parallel avenue Allal Ben Abdellah, and in the smaller

roads in between, can be found the city's most interesting shops, restaurants and cafés.

Avenue Mohammed V runs all the way from the Medina to the northern gate of the Royal Palace grounds. The nearby **Musée Archéologique** (23 rue El Brihi, open 9-11.30am, 2.30-5.30pm, closed Tue, admission 20dh) contains relics dating back to the Stone Age, with an emphasis on Roman artefacts, many from the nearby Chellah. Its finest pieces are the bronze busts of Cato the Younger and Juba II.

The palace enclosure contains the monarch's residence and an assortment of working buildings including the Cabinet office, the Prime Minister's office, the Supreme Court, the Royal Library and various ministries. You can't enter any of these, but walking down the main avenue is no problem. On the eastern side, you'll also pass the El Fas Mosque, used for official Friday royal prayers. The ritual is rarely performed these days, but when it is, the king rides over from the palace in a carriage and returns to it on a horse, the royal brow shaded by a crimson parasol.

The southern gate opens into boulevard El Doustour, skirting the city walls. A left turn leads to Bab Zaers, from where avenue Yacoub El Mansour leads back into the Ville Nouvelle, and another road leads down to the turreted Merenid gate of the Chellah.

One of Morocco's most fascinating historical ruins, the walled **Chellah** (open 8.30am-6.30pm daily, admission 10dh) has a peaceful poignancy about it. There are freshwater springs in the hillside here and this patch was probably inhabited even before the Phoenicians set up shop, followed by the Romans – there was a city here for a 1,000 years before it fell into ruin. Centuries later, the first Merenid Sultan, Abou Youssef, chose the derelict site to build a *koubba* (tomb) for himself and his wife, taking his place there in 1286. Later sultans built the walls and added their own dead. Their koubbas are now also ruins.

From the gate, a stepped path descends through overgrown gardens of palm and bamboo, banana and fig. The Roman ruins are down to the left, occupying the northern half of the enclosure. The line of the main street is clear, flanked by the remnants of a triumphal arch, a bathhouse, a forum and a temple to Jupiter.

The adjacent **Merenid sanctuary** is a more intact cluster of roseate ruins, above which rise two minarets, both topped with storks' nests. The complex contained a mosque, a necropolis and a *zaouia* (religious school). There's not much left of the mosque, though the *mihrab* (prayer niche) is still identifiable. Behind it lies the **necropolis**, with several sultans' tombs, but far fewer than the 32 graves counted here

by Leo Africanus in 1500. The better-preserved zaouia is on the eastern side of the sanctuary, centred on a courtyard with a rectangular pool.

Below the zaouia is a slightly ragged formal garden, defined by a double line of orange trees. The view from the far end makes sense of the site: hidden from the sea by low hills and a bend in the Bou Regreg, surrounded by fertile lowlands, watered by fresh springs.

One such feeds the **Sacred Pool**, the Chellah's most intriguing feature. In the south-west corner of the enclosure, enfolded by a group of seven domed koubbas containing the remains of ancient saints, is a walled rectangular pool. This was built by the Romans and back then was probably fed by a hot spring. It now runs cold, for which the 1755 earthquake takes the rap. The pool is populated by dark eels. Someone will be sitting at its edge, selling candles and hard-boiled eggs. For women wishing to ward off sterility, here's the drill. Buy an egg, symbol of fertility, and peel it. Throw the white into the pool and watch as phallic eels writhe from the dark recesses to swallow it. (The crowd of expectant cats will be grateful for the yolk.) Some women also light a candle, just to be on the safe side.

Eggs and eels. Soundtracked by the clattering of storks, shadowed by ruined cities and holy tombs, the imagery is so archetypal and dreamlike that you might as well have stepped through a looking-glass.

Where to eat & drink

Rabat isn't renowned for its gastronomy, still less for its drinking culture, but there are sufficient options for a quick beer, a cheap bite or a slow dinner.

In a mood to splash out, you could do much worse than the excellent Moroccan kitchen and peaceful Medina courtyard of the **Riad Oudaya** (46 rue Sidi Fateh, 03 770 2392, menu 330dh). The menu has four irresistible courses and even vegetarians can dine in style (but warn them in advance). Booking vital.

From the photos of ZZ Top and the Stray Cats on the menu cover to the tapas, pizzas, pastas and steaks listed within, there's nothing at all German or pre-War about **Le Weimar Club Restaurant** (7 rue Sanaa, 03 773 2650, main courses 40dh-110dh) at the Goethe Institut. Cosmo, cool and spacious, you could be somewhere in Europe. Live music on Fridays, huge portions, shame about the art exhibitions.

Tucked in a small passage, **Café-Restaurant Saadi** (87 avenue Allal Ben Abdellah, 03 776 9903, main courses 35dh-120dh) is an old school contrast, with cork walls, deep red tablecloths and a French-Moroccan menu. This is one of the cheaper

Just hanging around at the **Bab Oudaya**. *See p207.*

places where it's possible to drink with your dinner. Excellent draught Spéciale. The well-regarded **Café Restaurant la Clef** (rue Hattim, 03 770 1972, main courses 45dh-85dh) is a decent first-floor lunch spot near the station. Downstairs there's a functional bar and terrace. The snack bar of the **Hotel Balima** (corner of avenue Mohammed & rue Jakarta, 03 770 8625, main courses 12dh-80dh) offers filling meals, but the café terrace is best for people-watching.

On a tight budget, head up avenue Mohammed V into the Medina. A block north of the Bab El Jedid is a selection of cheap and basic diners, packed at lunchtimes, where a tajine will cost no more than 20dh-30dh and a harisa can be had for a few coins.

There are cafés and pâtisseries all over the New Town, but **Café Maure** in the Kasbah des Oudayas (*see p207*) outshines them all. The **4 Saisons** (261 avenue Mohammed V, no phone) has the best Moroccan pastries and does a good breakfast.

Over the road, the **Café L'Alsace** (324 avenue Mohammed V, 03 772 3122) is a friendly bar in one of the avenue's oldest buildings. Bottled beer, no frills, no fuss and no local women, though female tourists are welcome. No music either, bar buskers. Down the avenue and opposite the station, the bustling **Harry's Bar** (corner of place du Gare and avenue Moulay Abdellah, no phone) is an even more male and functional stop for a beer. Both places close mid-evening.

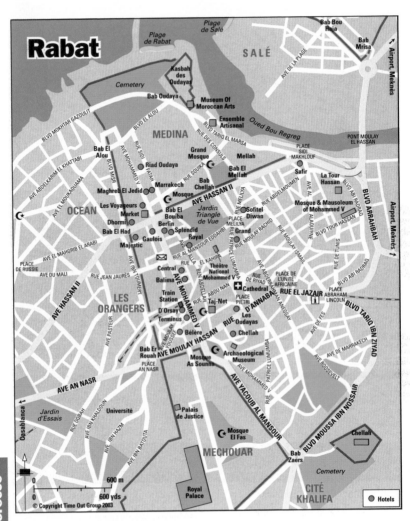

Rabat

SALÉ

Plage de Salé

Plage de Rabat

Kasbah des Oudayas

Cemetery

Bab Oudaya

Museum Of Moroccan Arts

Ensemble Artisanal

MEDINA

Grand Mosque

Mellah

Bab El Mellah

Safir

La Tour Hassan

Bab El Alou

Riad Oudaya

Bab Chellah

Maghreb El Jedid

Marrakech

Mosque

Sofitel Diwan

Mosque & Mausoleum of Mohammed V

OCEAN

Les Voyageurs

Market

Bab El Bouiba

Jardin Triangle de Vue

Dhormi

Berlin

Bab El Had

Splendid

Grand

Gaulois

Royal

Majestic

Central

Théâtre National Mohammed V

LES ORANGERS

Balima

Cathedral

Train Station

Taj-Net

D'Orsay

Les Oudayas

Terminus

Bélère

Chellah

Bab Er Rouah

Mosque As Sounna

Archaeological Museum

AVE AN NASR

Jardin d'Essais

Université

Palais de Justice

Mosque El Fas

MECHOUAR

Bab Zaers

Cemetery

Royal Palace

CITÉ KHALIFA

Chellah

● Hotels

0   600 m
0   600 yds
© Copyright Time Out Group 2003

PONT MOULAY EL HASSAN

Airport, Meknès

Bab Bou Haja

Bab Mrisa

PLACE SIDI MAKHLOUF

Where to stay

The recently built **Sofitel Diwan** (place de l'Unité Africaine, 03 726 2727, doubles 1,800dh) is the pick of the top end, with 94 unobtrusively tasteful rooms, plus restaurants, a bar and a hammam. Cheaper room rates are often offered. There's a different kind of luxury at the **Riad Oudaya** (46 rue Sidi Fateh, 03 770 2392, www.riadoudaya.com, doubles 1,300dh), a converted 19th-century house with two suites on the first floor (1,650dh), two doubles on the

second floor and a courtyard with fountain. It's spacious and, by Moroccan riad standards, unfussy in the decor department.

Opposite the Chambre des Représentants and built in 1940, the **Hotel Balima** (corner of avenue Mohammed & rue Jakarta, 03 770 8625, doubles 350dh-400dh) was once the grandest joint in town. Now it's fading nicely, but it still bustles and the bellboys wear dated blue uniforms with pillbox hats. The 71 rooms are basic but all have TV, phone and bathrooms.

Nearby **Hotel Orsay** (11 avenue Moulay Youssef, 03 770 1319, doubles 264dh) is handy for the station and offers 25 simple but colourful rooms. If it's full, there are two similarly priced establishments on the same short block. The **Hotel Splendid** (8 rue Ghazza, 03 772 3283, doubles 124dh-180dh) has 38 rooms around a pleasant courtyard, but only half have showers.

Just inside the Bab El Jedid and the pick of the Medina, **Hotel Dhormi** (313 avenue Mohammed V, 03 772 3898, double 130dh) is bare and basic but pleasant enough. A hot shower is an extra 10dh. A few hundred metres north, the **Hotel El Maghreb El Jedid** (2 rue Sebbahi, 03 773 2207, doubles 80dh) is cheaper. A few doors away, the **Marrakech** (10 rue Sebbahi, 03 772 7703, doubles 100dh) is another basic, budget alternative.

Resources

Internet
Cybercafé Taj-Net *53 avenue Allal Ben Abdellah (mobile 063 57 09 72).* **Open** 7am-9pm daily. Opposite the French Consulate.

Police
rue Soékarno (emergency 19).

Post office
Main Post Office *Corner of rue Soékarno & avenue Mohammed V.* **Open** 8.30am-noon, 3-6.45pm Mon-Fri.

Tourist information
Office National Marocain du Tourisme *31 avenue El Abtal (037 68 15 31).* **Open** 8.30am-6.30pm Mon-Fri.

Getting there

From Rabat Ville station there are half-hourly trains to Casablanca (journey time one hour), eight trains daily to Fès or Marrakech, and four to Tangier. Half of the Casa trains link with shuttle services (an extra 30mins) to Mohammed V airport. The Rabat-Salé airport, ten kilometres (six miles) north-east of town, has four daily flights to Paris but no internal connections.

Various bus companies run services from the cylindrical bus station, inconveniently located five kilometres out of town on the Casablanca road (take bus No.30 or a petit taxi). CTM runs half-a-dozen buses daily to Casa, Fès, Tangier and Marrakech.

Salé

For much of history, what's now Rabat's junior partner was the more important town. Salé was founded around the time Sala Colonia was abandoned. While the Merenids buried their

dead in the Chellah, over the river in Salé they were building the celebrated Medersa Abou El Hassan. Through the Middle Ages, while Rabat was little more than a village, Salé was a prosperous port. And the feared corsairs of the pirate republic were, of course, known as the Sallee Rovers, not the Rabat Raiders.

But Salé's supremacy began to erode when the Alaouites took power in the late 17th century and began building and living in Rabat. Once the French decided to make Rabat their capital and Casablanca the Protectorate's principal port, Salé was condemned to relative obscurity, literally bypassed by history – the French road to Meknes crossed a bridge way upriver, avoiding Salé completely. In fact, there was no proper bridge between the two towns until 1957.

No surprise, then, that Salé has a different personality from its neighbour: traditional where Rabat is modern, devout where the capital is secular. In some ways it has retained its medieval character. None of Lyautey's boulevards or mauresque buildings here. Salé is a town of quaint old houses, mazy alleys and ancient crafts still clustering together. In other ways, though, it's become that most un-medieval of things: a suburb.

Most of what's worth seeing is in the **Medina**. From the tree-shaded Souk El Kebir radiate streets variously full of blacksmiths, carpenters, leather workers and sculptors of stone. Near the small kissaria (a covered market for skilled artisans, here mostly concerned with textiles) is the 14th-century Fundouk Askour.

The main landmark is the **Grand Mosque**, which stands in an area full of merchants' mansions. You can't enter the 12th-century mosque, but it's worth looking around the fine 14th-century Medersa Abou El Hassan opposite. (If you can't find the attendant, ask at the nearby shops. Admission is 10dh.)

On the Medina's northern side, you can exit the Medina via the Bab Chafaa and follow clifftops and ocean shore to the **Koubba of Sidi Moussa El Doukkali** and the eroding **Kasbah of the Gnawa**. It's a walk of around three kilometres (two miles).

Getting there

Salé can be reached by buses Nos.6 or 10 from the bus station on boulevard Hassan II opposite Bab Chellah. Grands taxis depart from the same place. Both will drop you near Salé's Bab Fès, one of the main gates into the Medina. (Petits taxis are restricted to one side of the river or another.)

For about 5dh, you can also cross the river by rowing boat from the wharf below the Mellah in Rabat. From the wharf on the Salé side it's a steep climb up to the Bab Bou Haja.

Tangier

To Samuel Pepys it was the 'excrescence of the earth', to Joe Orton the 'Costa del Sodomy' – what more recommendation is needed?

If Morocco is in many ways caught between the north (Europe) and south (Africa), the West and the Middle East, then the same is true of Tangier, only more so. In the early 1950s, while this ancient port city was still a freebooting political conundrum under international administration, William Burroughs recast it as the 'interzone'. It was a contraction of 'International Zone', but the sense of a space somehow apart and between fitted a city full of exiles, refugees and adventurers, a place where nothing was true and everything was permitted.

Tangier lost its special status back in 1956 and these days, alas, is an interzone mostly in the sense of a place people pass through rather than linger. For many travellers Tangier is the first sight of Africa and the Islamic world, and this resort that once thronged with socialites, displaced aristocrats and literary luminaries now seems merely full of ghosts. Signs of the old days are as faded as the photos of Kerouac and Ginsberg in the Tanger Inn, or the words on a wall near the Petit Socco that advertise the long-vanished 'Bank of British West Africa Ltd'. There's an air of decay about the place, particularly palpable in many of the older cafés and restaurants.

For sure, Tangier doesn't present Morocco's best face. To disembark at the ferry port is to run an infuriating gauntlet of *faux guides* and persistent hustlers. The price of handicrafts is racked up way beyond what you'd pay in Fès or Marrakech, the better to fleece unwitting day-trippers. The town beach is cleaned only by the elements, the Medina's darker corners can be dangerous at night, and service personnel have a world-weary, slightly haughty attitude not often encountered elsewhere in the country.

But the seediness can also be interesting and there's more to Tangier than meets the eye. Though tourism from abroad may be in decline, many Moroccans now choose it for their holidays. And there's a Spanish and Mediterranean feel to the place that contrasts the Frenchified cities of the interior and Atlantic coast. It's also a centre for drug trafficking and migrants bound for the shores of Europe (a world hauntingly evoked in Mahi Binebine's 2002 novel *Welcome to Paradise*). Just as Tangier might be the Westerner's first taste of Africa, it's also the African's first hint of Europe. The old interzone isn't quite dead yet.

History

Perched at the continent's northern tip, in a commanding location where the Atlantic meets the Mediterranean, Tangier is probably North Africa's oldest settlement. Its origins are a matter of myth. Here Hercules slew the giant Antaeus and fathered a child by his widow Tinge, founding the city in her name. In reality it was probably founded by the Phoenicians, was later ruled by the Carthaginians, who called it Tingi, and had already been inhabited for over 1,000 years before the Romans showed up in the second century BC.

Under Roman rule it became Tingis and, before Volubilis (*see p203*), was capital of the province of Mauretania Tingitana. Later came Vandals, then Byzantines, and finally the Arab invaders who overran and settled Morocco in the eighth century. For all these invaders, Tangier's value was as a strategic commercial and military base. When pirates from here and Salé began to terrorise European shipping, the Portuguese took it as an excuse to attack and then occupy Tangier. It was a Portuguese colony from 1471 to 1661, at which point it was ceded to England as part of Catherine of Braganza's dowry on her marriage to Charles II.

Charles declared it 'a jewel of immense value in the royal diadem', but English rule was a disaster. Incompetent governors came and went, Sultan Moulay Ismail laid siege and launched guerrilla attacks, and after pouring around £1.5 million into this remote colony, the Crown finally gave it up as a bad job in 1684. Samuel Pepys, as a Secretary of the Admiralty, was there near the end, and hated a place he saw as nothing but 'swearing, cursing, drinking and whoring'. After evacuating the town, the final act of the English was to dynamite the Mole, a gigantic sea wall they had erected to protect the harbour. Pepys watched with evident satisfaction: 'The stones flew to a wonderful distance, endangering all the small vessels in the harbour.'

Repopulated by Berbers from the Rif Mountains, Tangier stayed under Moroccan control until the mid 19th century, when it became the object of intense rivalry between assorted European powers. The sultans essentially abandoned Tangier to the various

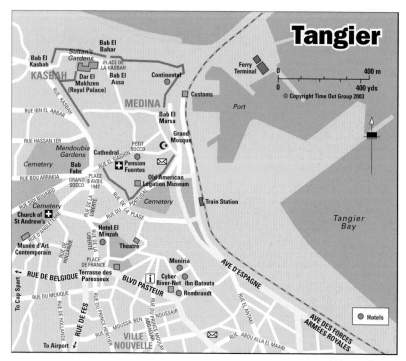

European consuls, a way to keep the Nazarenes at a safe distance from their court at Fès. The diplomatic corps amused themselves with pig-sticking expeditions into the nearby forests and the city slowly filled up with foreigners, mostly poor Spaniards who earned a living by selling alcohol and smuggling. It was already a heterogenous place of exile run by foreign powers before the 1906 Treaty of Algeciras bought off Britain with Egypt and Italy with Libya, leaving France and Spain to carve up Morocco. With the rest of the country partitioned, in 1923 Tangier was declared an 'International Zone', controlled by the resident agents of France, Spain, Britain, Portugal, Sweden, Holland, Belgium, Italy and the US.

Each of the controlling powers maintained its own currency, banks, police and postal service. In a climate of free market anarchy, fortunes were made through currency manipulation and Tangier became a haven for smuggling, political intrigue and espionage. During World War II, Allied spies hung out at the Hotel El Minzah, agents of the Axis at the Hotel Rif, while Franco took control of the town. It was in the International Zone, rather than Casablanca, where Sam should have played it again.

After the war, things returned to what passed for normal in the Interzone, and both writers and moneyed socialites were drawn to the city. The Woolworths heiress, Barbara Hutton, was mistress of ceremonies, Paul Bowles its mythmaker-in-chief (*see p217* **The dream life of Tangier**). With Moroccan independence in 1956 and the end of the French and Spanish Protectorates, Tangier also lost its special status. The banks and wealthy exiles hastened elsewhere, but the city retained a certain underground cachet, both for pot-smoking backpackers drawn by the Beats and as a gay tourist resort. Eventually, the authorities clamped down on both. In the 1970s and '80s, hotels sprang up along the seafront to cater for more mainstream foreign holidaymakers, but now this trade is also in decline, with tourists drawn to cleaner beaches, trendier resorts or Morocco's more exotic interior.

Sightseeing

Like all Moroccan cities, Tangier is divided between Medina and New Town. Both are interesting but neither contain anything that could properly be described as unmissable.

The **Grand Socco** lies between the two, a busy but amorphous open square that was supposedly the site of the Roman forum, and is Tangier's central point of reference.

Through the arch on the Grand Socco's northern side and to the right is the beginning of rue El Siaghin – 'street of the silversmiths', of which there are still a few. Past the old Spanish Cathedral (halfway down on the right) this leads to the plaza **Petit Socco** (also known as the Zoco Chico), heart of the Medina. Café Central was Burroughs' favourite hangout, while Bowles favoured the adjacent Café Tingis. No alcohol is served these days, but they are still good venues from which to watch the life of the town pass by.

Along rue de la Marine is the 17th-century **Grand Mosque**, though little of it can be seen save for the green and white minaret. It was built by Sultan Moulay Ismail to celebrate the departure of the English from Tangier. At the end of the road is the Bab El Moussa and a terrace with fine views of the port and bay.

Various alleys lead up through the Medina, past shops and bazaars selling everything from gold to goat's cheese, with occasional glimpses of the sea from between huddled houses. Keep going upwards and eventually you arrive at the **Kasbah**. The administrative quarter since Roman times, it is these days one of Tangier's most desirable residential areas. Richard Hughes, author of *A High Wind in Jamaica*, was the first European to take a house here. Barbara Hutton later outbid General Franco for the palace of Sidi Hosni, where she staged legendarily extravagant parties.

The main attraction here is the former royal palace of **Dar El Makzhen** (place de la Kasbah, 039 93 20 97, open 9am-1pm, 3-6pm, closed Tue, admission 10dh), built by Moulay Ismail and now housing a museum devoted to Moroccan crafts with a few mosaics and other finds from Volubilis. If you leave via the sultan's gardens, full of citrus trees, jacarandas and palms, you emerge near the stairs up to the **Café Detroi**t, once owned by Burroughs' cut-up collaborator Brion Gysin. Back then it served as a regular performance venue for the Master Musicians of Jajouka, who were to record an album with Brian Jones (*see p149* **Maroc 'n' roll**); there is nothing here now but an excellent view.

Leaving the Medina by the Kasbah Gate, rue Asad Ibn Farrat leads towards the **Marshan**, an upmarket quarter of diplomatic residences and posh clifftop villas. After the Italian Consulate on the left, a narrow lane to the right leads down to the **Café Haifa**, where mint tea and pastries are served among shrubbery on terraces overlooking the straits – a fine spot in the late afternoon and another old haunt of Bowles and the Beats.

Rue Asad Ibn Farrat morphs into rue Mohammed Tazi and leads to the **Palais Mendoub** (rue Shakespeare, 039 93 36 06, open 9am-5pm, closed Sat, Sun, admission free). The residence of the sultan's agent during the days of the International Zone, this was later owned by publisher Malcolm Forbes and is now a museum housing his collection of 115,000 toy soldiers, laid out in re-creation of battles from Waterloo to Dien Bien Phu.

Back down at the Grand Socco, rue de l'Angleterre leads west to the small 19th-century Anglican **Church of St Andrew**. Part of the Diocese of Gibraltar, it is still in use for Sunday morning worship by what's left of Tangier's British community. The overgrown graveyard contains the last resting place of Walter Harris, former *Times* correspondent and author of *Morocco That Was*. The amiable caretaker Mustapha Chergui can be found in the churchyard cottage and will let you into the church and show you around its faux-Moorish interior (open 9.30am-noon, 2.30-6pm daily). Rue de l'Angleterre continues to the former British Consulate General, now housing the **Musée d'Art Contemporain** (rue de l'Angleterre, open 9am-noon, 3-6pm, closed Tue, admission 10dh), devoted exclusively to Moroccan artists such as Chaibia Tallal, Fatimi Hassani, Abdellah Hariri and Farid Belkahia.

On the north-west side of the Grand Socco are the shady **Mendoubia Gardens** (closed Sun), which contain an extraordinary banyan tree, said to be 800 years old. On the other side, rue de la Plage and a left turn on rue du Portugal leads to the popular market, which was moved here from the Grand Socco in 1971. Just inside the Medina gate here is the **Old American Legation Museum** (8 Zankat America, 039 93 53 17, open 10am-1pm, 3-5pm, closed Tue, Fri, Sat, Sun, admission free), where an intriguing collection of old maps, furniture and paintings (including work by Delacroix and Oskar Kokoschka) is housed in a building gifted to the US in 1821 by Sultan Moulay Suleyman.

Rue du Portugal continues down to the port entrance, where a right turn leads to the beach. Broad and flat enough for football – there's always a game or two going on – it's not the best beach for bathing (women will feel particularly conspicuous sunning themselves here), though various beach clubs have changing facilities as well as cafés serving food and drink. Emma's BBC Bar serves English breakfasts, Joe Orton used to hang out at the Windmill, and Tennessee Williams wrote a first draft of *Cat on a Hot Tin Roof* at the Sun Beach. None of these places open in winter.

South from the Grand Socco, take rue de la Liberté past the Hotel El Minzah to the **place**

Grand Socco. *See p214.*

Old Bowles haunt the **Café Tingis**. *See p214.*

de France. The Café de Paris, opposite the French Consulate, is the main attraction here. Its outside tables were a legendary people-watching spot in the years of the International Zone. Boulevard Pasteur, main promenade of the New Town, leads east from here past a belvedere with old cannon, splendid views and lots of hustlers, into the commercial heart of Tangier. Tangier's venerable bookshop, the **Librairie des Colonnes** (54 boulevard Pasteur, 039 93 69 55, open 9am-1pm, 3-7.30pm, closed Sun), is one last reminder of Tangier's literary heritage.

Where to eat & drink

Up near the Kasbah, the **Restaurant Marhaba Palace** (67 rue Kasbah, 039 93 79 27, main courses 50dh-100dh) is an atmospheric, if somewhat cheesily decorated, old mansion with good Moroccan fare and live music. Call and they promise to collect you from your hotel.

In the New Town, **Romero** (12 avenue Prince Moulay Abdellah, 039 93 22 77, main courses 50dh-150dh) has a bar and offers a big selection of fish dishes, plus paella, lobster and a dozen non-fish options. If you're tiring of Moroccan fare or want more vegetarian options, **San Remo** (15 rue Ahmed Chaouki, 039 93 84 51, main courses 80dh-200dh) is a clean, old-school Italian off boulevard Pasteur.

For the big splurge, it has to be the **El Korsan** at the Hotel El Minzah (85 rue de la Liberté, 039 93 58 85, main courses 130dh), a seafood specialist of national repute. But if you want to eat without the 'folkloric show', try the less formal wine bar across the courtyard. There's also a piano bar.

At the other extreme, there are any number of cheap restaurants in and around the Petit Socco. Try **Restaurant Ahlan** (8 avenue Mokhtar Ahardan) or **Café Andalus** (7 rue Commerce).

Down on the seafront, when the beach clubs are closed, the **Hotel Marco Polo** (2 rue El Antaki, 039 32 24 51, main courses 40dh-80dh) has a restaurant serving simple food and a bar open to hard-drinking non-residents. The **Tanger Inn**, next to the Hotel Muniria, is a tiny pub, unchanged for decades, its Interzone roots marked by Ginsberg photos. It supposedly closes at 1am but will often stay open later.

Pick of the nightclubs is **Pasarela** (avenue des FAR), a complex with bars, a garden, an outdoor pool and disco dancing until 3am.

Where to stay

The **Hotel El Minzah** (85 rue de la Liberté, 039 93 58 85, www.elminzah.com, double 1,350dh-1,650dh) is Tangier's finest, with a 1930s ambience and a beautiful pool (featured in the Bond flick *Living Daylights*). The less pricey rooms have a street rather than sea view.

The **Mövenpick** (route de Malabata, 039 32 93 00, www.movenpick-tangier.com, double 1,000dh-2,400dh) is a tasteful new five-star around the bay, next to a big casino. A gorgeous pool makes up for a rather too rocky beach.

At the bottom of boulevard Pasteur, **Hotel Rembrandt** (boulevard Mohammed V, 039 93 78 70, double 500dh-600dh) is stylish and somewhat lackadaisical in an old-fashioned kind of way. Nice bar and cute garden. Overlooking the port from the edge of the Medina, the warrenous **Hotel Continental** (039 93 10 24, doubles 365dh) is full of character, with balconied rooms and two eccentric suites. Bertolucci used it as a location for *The Sheltering Sky*.

Burroughs wrote most of *The Naked Lunch* at the **Hotel Muniria** (1 rue Magellan, 039 93 53 37, double 150dh). Someone's now living in Burroughs' old room (No.11), but room seven is where Kerouac typed up much of the manuscript. Across the road, the **Hotel Ibn Batouta** (8 rue Magellan, 039 93 93 11, hotel.ibnbatouta@caramail.com, double 200dh) is a more upmarket alternative near the Beat haunt Tanger Inn.

If you want to hit rock bottom, **Pension Fuentes** (9 place Petit Socco, 039 93 46 69,

The dream life of Tangier

Once upon a time, customers of the Librairie des Colonnes at 54 boulevard Pasteur might have found themselves browsing next to any one of a number of literary lights. Paul and Jane Bowles were friends of the establishment; William Burroughs was a regular. Among others who would drop by were Truman Capote, Alan Sillitoe, Brion Gysin, Jack Kerouac, Allen Ginsberg, Samuel Beckett, Tennessee Williams and Jean Genet, who mostly used the place to cash cheques. Discerningly managed by sisters-in-law Isobelle and Yvonne Gerofi, the bookshop was owned by Genet's publisher Gallimard.

Drawn by the International Zone's sex, drugs and anomalous ambience – 'a wild west of the spirit,' as Brion Gysin put it – writers were a feature of post-war Tangier. Joe Orton only ever came to holiday on the Costa del Sodomy and Alfred Chester, a promising young contemporary of Susan Sontag's, was driven quite mad by the city, but others were productive here. Tennessee Williams mapped out an early draft of *Cat on a Hot Tin Roof* at the Sun Beach café and, in an apartment at 2 rue Pizzaro, wrote *Suddenly Last Summer*. At the Hotel Muniria, William Burroughs ground out the 'routines' that, after being typed up by Kerouac and edited by Ginsberg, were to form the manuscript of *The Naked Lunch*.

Burroughs' hallucinatory Interzone, a 'Composite City where all human potentials are spread out in a vast silent market', was to define the ragged edge of Tangier's literary image, but it was Paul Bowles who became the city's premier interpreter. First visiting in 1931 at the suggestion of Gertrude Stein, the 21-year-old Bowles formed an instant romantic attachment to a city he would finally set up house with in 1947. *The Sheltering Sky* established his reputation in 1949 and *Let It Come Down*, published three years later, was to link his name with Tangier's as firmly as Joyce's with Dublin or Isherwood's with Weimar Berlin. In translating Mohamed Choukri and transcribing the stories of Mohammed Mrabet and Larbi Layachi, he brought Tanjawi voices to an audience in the wider world. And in over 250 field recordings for the Library of Congress, he also catalogued the diversity of Morocco's musical traditions.

Both Burroughs and Bowles envisioned the Interzone as dreamscape – part magical gateway, part purgatorial limbo. Burroughs wrote to Ginsberg that 'it's like a dream, the other side, is always breaking through'. *Let It Come Down*'s Nelson Dyar peers around and realises that 'he was no one, and he was standing here in the middle of no country. The place was counterfeit, a waiting room between connections, a transition from one way of being to another...'

Burroughs moved on but Bowles was to linger until his death at 89 in 1999. 'Tangier is like a gong that rang years ago,' he said in 1990. 'I still hear the resonance.'

Best of Morocco

Slices of blue from the **Medina**. *See p214*.

doubles 100dh) – another Beat location – is above a noisy café and overlooks the Petit Socco.

Getting there

The airport, 15 kilometres (9.5 miles) south-west of town, has flights to Casablanca, as well as in some international destinations. Frequent ferries and hydrofoils run to Algeciras, Málaga, Cádiz and Gibraltar. By tickets in advance from any travel agent, or from the ferry terminal. The bus station is beside the port entrance, with five departures daily for Casablanca via Rabat, four for Fès and one for Marrakech. Grands taxis depart from here too. There are four trains daily to Rabat and Casablanca. The 11pm train continues to Marrakech, arriving at 8am. For Fès, change at Sidi Kacem. At press time, the old

station near the port was closed and trains were departing from Tangier Morara, about 6km (3.5 miles) out of town. A new station was scheduled to open in the Nouvelle Ville in late 2003.

Resources

Internet
Cyber River-Net *20 avenue Pasteur (no phone).* **Open** 8am-11pm daily.

Post Office
PPT *33 boulevard Mohammed V.* **Open** 8am-noon, 2.30-6pm Mon-Fri.

Tourist information
29 boulevard Pasteur (039 94 80 50). **Open** *June-Sept* 8.30am-7pm daily; *Oct-May* 8.30am-noon, 2.30-6.30pm Mon-Fri.

Directory

Directory

Getting Around

The following information is specific to Marrakech. For information on travelling around the country in general, *see p169* **Getting Started**.

By air

Marrakech's international airport (Aéroport Marrakech Menara) is located just six kilomentres (four miles) west of the city. From luggage carousel to city centre takes less than ten minutes by car. The airport information desk (9am-9pm daily) is in the check-in area. There are a couple of banks offering currency exchange in the arrivals hall, open 8am-6pm daily. For flight information, call 044 44 78 65.

Taxis wait outside the arrivals building. In a *petit taxi* (*see p221* **Taxis**) the fare to anywhere in the Medina or the New City is 50dh; to Semlalia it's 100dh; to the Palmeraie it's 120dh. Most taxi drivers picking up at the airport will accept dollars, euros or pounds at the equivalent dirham rate from passengers arriving outside banking hours.

Note that all the other airlines have their offices in Casablanca.

British Airways

avenue des FAR, Casablanca (022 47 30 23/025). **Open** 8.30am-12.30pm, 2.30-6.30pm Mon-Sat. **Credit** AmEx, DC, MC, V.

Casablanca is the main British Airways office in Morocco and you must call here to confirm all flights. The sales-only agent in Marrakech is **Menara Tours**: 41 rue de Yougoslavie, Guéliz (044 44 66 54, open 8.30am-12.30pm, 2.30-6.30pm Mon-Fri, map p252 A1).

Royal Air Maroc (RAM)

197 avenue Mohammed V, Guéliz (044 43 62 05). **Open** 8.30am-12.15pm, 2.30-7pm Mon-Fri. **Credit** AmEx, DC, MC, V. **Map** p252 B2.

There is a 24-hour call centre (090 00 08 00) for flight reconfirmation, flight information and reservations. RAM continually changes and cancels flights at short notice so reconfirming is a must.

By rail

Trains are operated by the national railway company **ONCF** (044 44 77 68, www.oncf.org.ma). The railway station is on the western edge of Guéliz, on avenue Hassan II. Marrakech is the southernmost terminus of two lines: the first north to Tangier via Casablanca and Rabat; the second north-east to Oujda on the Algerian border via Casablanca, Rabat, Meknes and Fès. A swarm of taxis meets each incoming train; make sure to get a petit taxi and not a more expensive big Mercedes. The fare this way into central Guéliz is 5dh-6dh; to the Medina 10dh. Alternatively, if you can be bothered with the wait, bus Nos.3 and 8 pass by the station en route to the place de Foucauld for Jemaa El Fna.

By bus

The *gare routière* is just outside the Medina walls at Bab Doukkala. Most long-distance buses terminate here, including those operated by national carrier **CTM** (after first stopping at the CTM main office on boulevard Mohammed Zerktouni in Guéliz near the Cinema Colisée). Both the central

Medina and Guéliz are walkable from the station; alternatively a petit taxi will cost 5dh-6dh, or catch local bus Nos.3 and 8 for place de Foucauld (Jemaa El Fna). The superior buses run by **Supratours** (to/from Essaouira, Agadir, Laayoune and Dakhla only) pull up at the forecourt of the company's own smart little terminus, which is next door to the railway station (*see above*). For **CTM** bus information, call 044 43 39 33; for **Supratours** information, call 044 43 55 25. Note that Essaouira is a popular destination and the Supratour buses fill up fast: it's wise to purchase your tickets at least a day in advance.

Marrakech has a limited city bus network radiating from the Medina out to the suburbs. Other than along avenue Mohammed V, no buses operate within the confines of the city walls – where streets are so narrow and tortuously twisted that donkey carts can barely pass in places. Few services are of any use to visitors. The exception perhaps is between the Medina and Guéliz, which is a fairly long walk, but it's much less hassle (and inexpensive) to take a taxi.

Buses

City buses (044 43 39 33) are regular coaches with no air-conditioning. They charge a flat fee of 3dh payable to the driver. Beware: the drivers never have any change. All of

these buses leave from place de Foucauld, opposite the Hotel de Foucauld:

No.1 to Guéliz along avenue Mohammed V
No.2 to Bab Doukkala for the gare routière
No.3 to Douar Laskar via avenue Mohammed V, avenue Hassan II and the train station
No.4 to Daoudiate (a northern suburb) by avenue Mohammed V
No.8 to Douar Laskar via avenue Mohammed V, avenue Moulay Hassan and the train station
No.10 to boulevard de Safi via Bab Doukkala and the gare routière
No.11 to the airport via avenue de la Menara and the Menara Gardens
No.14 to the train station

Taxis

Taxis are plentiful and there is rarely a problem finding one, whatever the time of day or night. They are also cheap enough that it makes little sense bothering with buses. The standard ride is known as a **petit taxi** (lettered on the side of the car as such) and is usually a little khaki-coloured four-door Fiat, Simca or similar. Drivers are reluctant to use the meter. Asking for them to switch it on sometimes works, otherwise it's just a question of knowing the right fare. From Jemaa El Fna to Guéliz costs 10dh; from Jemaa El Fna to Semlalia 20dh; from Jemaa El Fna to the Palmeraie 30dh. Expect to pay about 50 per cent more after about 8pm (9pm in summer).

Grand taxis (again, lettered as such) are bigger cars that can squeeze six people in and are normally more expensive. They loiter outside hotels and the railway station. Avoid them, unless you are a group of four or more (a petit taxi will only take three) or are travelling long distance: some grand taxis operate like minibuses running fixed routes to outlying suburbs, villages and towns, and even as far as Essaouira and Agadir. Specifics of these

services are given in the relevant 'Getting there' sections in the Around Marrakech and Best of Morocco chapters.

Driving

A car can be useful for venturing out of the city, especially for trips to the south, but unless you are a resident (making shopping trips, running the kids to school) is of limited use within Marrakech itself. For short-term visitors taxis are cheap and plentiful and easily hired by the day for 250dh (£15) in and around the city.

If you do drive, then traffic travels on the right. The French rule of giving priority to traffic from the right is observed at roundabouts and junctions, ie cars coming on to a roundabout have priority over those already on it. Speed limits are 40kmph (25mph) in urban areas, 100kmph (62mph) on main roads, 120kmph (74mph) on autoroutes. There are on-the-spot fines for speeding and other traffic offences. Seatbelts are not required within Marrakech itself but are mandatory and often controlled outside of city limits.

Be very wary when driving at night as cyclists and moped riders often have no lights. Neither do sheep, goats and pedestrians. In the case of an accident, report to the nearest *gendarmerie* to obtain a written report, otherwise insurance will be invalid.

Car hire

To hire a car, you must be over 21, have a full current driving licence and carry a passport or an identity card. There's nothing like EasyCar here and consequently rental isn't cheap; daily rates with a local agency start at about 400dh (around £25 at the time of

writing) for a Fiat Palio, Citroen Saxo or Peugeot 205 with unlimited mileage. A Peugeot 306 kicks in at about 700dh (£44) per day, a Peugeot 406 at 950dh (£60).

With the internationals like Avis, Budget or Hertz, expect to pay about 25 per cent more. The drawback with the local hire firms is the back-up service – cars may be unreliable, breakdown support may be lacking, replacement vehicles may not be forthcoming. Be aware that payments made in Morocco by credit card often incur an additional six per cent fee. This is one of several reasons why it works out cheaper to arrange your car rental in advance through the travel agent booking your flight or via the internet. The major companies allow you to rent a car in one city and return it in another. Rental cars in Morocco are delivered empty and returned empty. Almost all agencies will deliver cars to your hotel and arrange pick-up at no extra charge but this service must be booked in advance.

If you are heading south over the mountains, remember that you are responsible for any damage if you take a car off-road or along unsuitable tracks. (Four-wheel drives are available from most hire companies and start at around 1,200dh, or £75, per day.)

Avis
137 avenue Mohammed V, Guéliz (044 43 25 25/fax 044 43 12 65/ www.avis.com/avisrak@iam.net). **Open** 8am-7pm Mon-Sat; 8am-noon Sun. **Credit** AmEx, DC, MC, V. **Map** p252 B2.
Branches: Aéroport Marrakech Menara (044 43 12 65). **Open** 8am-noon, 2-11pm Mon-Sat; 8am-noon Sun.

Budget
Hotel Mamounia, avenue Bab Jedid, Medina (044 43 11 80/www.budget rentacar.com). **Open** 8am-noon, 2.30-7pm Mon-Sat. **Credit** AmEx, DC, MC, V. **Map** p250 A6.

Directory

Concorde Cars

*154 avenue Mohammed V, Guéliz
(044 43 11 16/fax 044 44 61 29/
concordecar@iam.ma).* **Open**
8.30am-7.30pm Mon-Sat. **Credit**
AmEx, DC, MC, V. **Map** p252 B2.

Europcar/InterRent

*63 boulevard Mohammed Zerktouni,
Guéliz (044 43 12 28/fax 044 31
02 30/www.europcar.com).* **Open**
8.30am-noon, 2-7.30pm Mon-Sat.
Credit AmEx, DC, MC, V.
Map p252 B2.
Branches: Aéroport Marrakech
Menara (044 43 77 18). **Open** to meet
incoming flights.

Fathi Cars

*183 avenue Mohammed V, Guéliz
(044 43 17 63).* **Open** 8.30am-
12.30pm, 2.30-7pm Mon-Sat. **Credit**
AmEx, DC, MC, V. **Map** p252 B2.

Hertz

*154 avenue Mohammed V, Guéliz
(044 43 13 94/www.hertz.com).*
Open 8.30am-12.30pm, 2-6.30pm
Mon-Sat. **Credit** AmEx, DC, MC, V.
Map p252 B2.
Branches: Aéroport Marrakech
Menara (044 44 72 30). **Open** 8.30am-
12.30pm, 2-6.30pm daily. Club Med
(061 36 75 37). **Open** 9-11.30am,
5-7.30pm Mon-Fri, Sun.

Majestic

*21 rue Tarek Ibn Ziad, Guéliz
(044 43 65 00/fax 044 43 43 92/
majesticloc@yahoo.fr).* **Open**
8.30am-12.30pm, 2.30-7pm Mon-Sat.
Credit MC, V. **Map** p252 B2.

National

*RAKC01, Marrakech (044 43 06
83/www.nationalcar.com).* **Open**
8.30am-noon Mon-Sat, 2.30-7pm;
8.30am-noon Sun. **Credit** AmEx,
DC, MC, V.
Branches: Aéroport Marrakech
Menara (044 43-78 46). **Open** 7.30am-
11pm daily.

Parking

Wherever there's space to park
vehicles you'll find a *gardien
de voitures*. They're licenced
by the local authority to look
after left vehicles and expect to
be tipped 10dh or so by way of
a parking fee (the local rate is
2dh during the day, 5dh at
night, but as a visitor you're
not going to get away with
paying that). Street-side
parking is easy enough in the
New City (look for the orange-
painted kerbs) but more

troublesome in the Medina:
the main parking spots are
opposite the Préfecture de la
Medina or on rue Ibn Rachid.
Red and white kerb markings
mean no parking.

Repairs & services

The agents below should be
able to help get you back on
the road.

Garage Ourika

*66 avenue Mohammed V, Guéliz
(044 44 82 66).* **Open** 8.30am-noon,
2.30-6.30pm Mon-Sat. **No credit
cards. Map** p252 A1.
BMW, Fiat, Honda and Toyota
specialist.

Garage Renault

*route de Casablanca, Semlalia
(044 30 10 08).* **Open** 8am-noon, 2-
6.30pm Mon-Sat. **No credit cards**.
Renault specialist.

Cycling

It's not quite China but
bicycles, mopeds and
motorbikes are a hugely
popular mode of local
transport – despite widespread
potholes, choking bus fumes
and the perils of having to
share the road with the
average lunatic Marrakchi
motorist.

If you fancy mixing it
yourself, try one of the listed
places for bike rentals, or there
are also a couple of hire outfits
at the northern end of rue Beni
Marine, the small street
running parallel and between
rue Bab Agnaou and rue
Moulay Ismail. Note that most
rental places do not offer
helmets or any kind of lock so
if you want to leave the bike or
scooter anywhere it'll have to
be with a gardien de voitures
(*see above* **Parking**). Before
taking a bike check the gears
and brakes as servicing is not
always high priority.

Guys with bikes for hire can
also be found on the central
grassy verge outside Hotel
Imperial Borj (5 avenue
Echouhada) in Hivernage and

Hotel de Foucauld (off place de
Foucauld) in the Medina,
though there is no affiliation to
the hotels in question. Prices
are roughly 20dh per hour with
negotiable daily rates.

Action Sports Loisirs

*1 boulevard Yacoub El
Mansour, apartment No.4
(tel/fax 044 43 09 31/mobile 061
240 145/actionsportsloisirs@
yahoo.fr).* **Open** 8am-7pm Tue-Sun.
Bicycle rental 40dh per hr; 100 per
half-day. **No credit cards.**
Map p252 A2.
Action Sports Loisirs has the best
bikes in town, both in terms of
quality of machines and attention to
maintenance. Owner Alain rents
bikes for all kinds of terrain, and also
organises excursions for 680dh
(including lunch and transport).

Adoul Abdellah

*14 avenue Abdelkarim El Khattabi,
Guéliz (044 43 22 38).* **Open** 9am-
noon, 3-6pm Mon-Sat. **Scooter
rental** 300dh per day.
Map p252 A2.

Hotel Ali

*rue Moulay Ismail, Medina (044
44 49 79).* **Open** 8am-4pm daily.
Bicycle rental 20dh-30dh per hr.
Map p250 B6.

Marrakech Motos

*31 avenue Abdelkarim El Khattabi,
Guéliz (044 44 83 59).* **Open** 9am-
10pm daily. **Scooter rental** 250dh-
300dh per day, depending on model.
Map p252 A2.

Walking

Walking is absolutely the only
way to get around the Medina,
which is where most visitors
spend the bulk of their time.
It's a compact area, perfect for
exploring on foot. Besides,
many of the streets and alleys
are too narrow for any thing
bigger than a motorcycle.

Make sure to pack a pair of
comfortable, flat-soled shoes
because the streets in the
Medina are rarely paved or
surfaced and as a result are
badly rutted by passing cars.
For visits any time from
November to April bring
something cheap and
waterproof because the
slightest bit of rain turns the
whole of the Medina to mud.

Directory

Resources A-Z

Addresses

In the newer quarters of the city streets are well signed in both French and Arabic. This is not the case in the Medina: major streets do have dual-script signs but the majority of smaller alleyways have signs in Arabic only – or more likely, no signs at all. Most of the time, when looking for a specific street or place the only option is to ask the locals. If the person questioned doesn't know, they'll usually put themselves out to find someone who does, and you'll probably end up with an escort.

When addressing an envelope, write the house number after the street name and place the postcode before the city, as in the following example:

Monsieur Ledoux
avenue Mohammed V
Marrakech-Medina
1050 Marrakech

Business

Casablanca is the country's economic centre, Rabat is the political capital and Marrakech is a modest-sized provincial city that trades largely in tourism. Big business is generally absent from the local scene, meaning facilities for the visiting powerbroker are few. If you are here doing business, don't expect deals to be closed in a single meeting, partly because of red tape, partly because haggling and hedging are standard practice, but also because getting to the point is often considered rude. Neither should you expect anyone to show up on time; why hurry when, as the local saying goes, 'A chance encounter is worth a thousand appointments'? Patience and flexibility will be rewarded. But not always.

Business centres

Marrakech's scant few business centres are all located in the large five-star hotels, including the Mamounia (044 44 44 09), Kempinski Mansour (044 33 91 00) and Le Meridien (044 33 94 00). However, such services as there are tend to be reserved for guests. Faxes may be sent from some *téléboutiques* (*see p230* **Telephones**) and most cybercafés will offer word-processing and printing.

Conferences

Marrakech has a fully equipped conference centre in the Palais de Congress, which is managed by the Hotel Kempinski Mansour (044 33 91 00). However, it's geared up primarily for major events not small-scale presentations. The hotels listed under 'Business Centres' (*see above*) all have more modest conference facilities.

Couriers

Within Marrakech businesses use petit taxis. Note the number of the taxi (painted on the door) so if there's any problem later the police can track down the cabbie through the drivers' register – although this is rarely ever necessary. Pay as you would as a passenger. The following international couriers have offices in Marrakech:

DHL
133 avenue Abdelkarim El Khattabi, Guéliz (044 43 76 47/www.dhl.com). **Open** 8am-12.30pm, 2.30-6.30pm Mon-Fri; 9am-1pm Sat. **Credit** MC, V. **Map** p252 A2.

FedEx
113 avenue Abdelkarim El Khattabi, Guéliz (044 44 82 57). **Open** 8.15am-12.30pm, 2.15-6.30pm Mon-Fri; 8.30am-1pm Sat. **No credit cards. Map** p252 A2.

Consumer

There are no such things as consumer rights. How could there be? You haggled for it and set your own price, in the course of which you examined the object in question to ascertain its value. If you feel cheated afterwards, you've only yourself to blame. However, if you do have a genuine grievance, take it to the tourist police, who are usually very good at settling matters promptly and usually in the favour of the visitor.

Customs

The following allowances apply to people bringing duty-free goods into Morocco: 400g of tobacco, 200 cigarettes or 50 cigars, 1 litre of spirits and unlimited foreign currency.

Moroccan customs officials can be funny about electronic and photographic equipment. If it's just one or two items, obviously for your own personal use, then you should be OK, but anyone with significant amounts of camera gear, for example, may have it written into their passports. Anything that can't be presented on leaving will be assumed to have been 'sold' and liable to a heavy duty tax. If the property has been stolen, you need police documentation to prove it. The best thing is to keep such items out of sight of customs officers.

Pets may be taken into Morocco as long as they have a medical certificate no more than ten days old and an anti-rabies certificate no more than six months old.

Disabled

Marrakech is tough on anyone with a mobility problem. Roads and pavements are

frequently uneven and pitted, occasionally rutted. Worse, routes through the Medina are invariably narrow and crowded and it's necessary to be nimble to avoid being run over by bicycles or donkeys. Outside of the bigger hotels (Les Jardins de la Medina, the Mamounia, the Sheraton and Sofitel all lay claim to disabled facilities), few buildings – if any – make concessions to the handicapped. In smaller hotels and riads, while facilities may be lacking, it's a given that people will try to make your stay as easy as possible but steps, if not stairs, are typically unavoidable. Problems may be compounded by the fact that banisters do not exist in traditional Moroccan homes and in most riads and small hotels.

Electricity

Marrakech and most of the rest of the country operates on 220V AC. Plugs are the French two-pin variety. Bring your own adapter, but if you forget they're available from most electrical shops for around 25dh (*see p136*). Visitors from the USA will also need to bring a transformer if they intend to use appliances from home.

Embassies & consulates

There's just the one diplomatic office in Marrakech, and that's the French, of course. As a reminder of colonial days past, it occupies the most prominent and significant site in the city, adjacent to the Koutoubia Mosque. Its high blank wall fringes the place de Foucauld. You'll find other embassies and consulates in Rabat and Casablanca.

British Consulate

17 boulevard de la Tour Hassan, Rabat (037 72 96 96/fax 037 70

45 31/www.britain.org.ma/consular/ services.html). **Open** 8.30am-12.30pm, 1.30-4pm Mon-Thur; 8.30am-12.30pm Fri.
Also handles Irish and New Zealand consular affairs. In the event of an emergency in Marrakech, contact **Residence Jaib** (55 boulevard Zerktouni, 044 43 60 78, mobile 061 14 84 44). Britain also has consulates in Casablanca and Tangier.

Canadian Consulate

13 rue Jaafar Es Sadiq, Agdal, Rabat (037 68 74 00/fax 037 67 21 87).
Also handles Australian consular affairs.

French Consulate

rue Ibn Khaldun, Medina, Marrakech (044 44 40 06). **Open** 8.30-11.45am Mon-Fri. **Map** p250 B6.

US Consulate

2 avenue de Marrakech, Rabat (037 76 22 65/fax 037 76 56 61/ www.usembassy.ma). **Open** 8.30am-5.30pm Mon-Fri.
The US also has a consulate in Casablanca.

Emergencies

Police 19
Fire service 15 or
044 43 04 15
Ambulance service 044 44 37 24

Health

Morocco doesn't have any reciprocal health care agreements with other countries, so taking out your own medical insurance is advisable. No vaccinations are required for Marrakech, although inoculation against hepatitis is a good idea. Travellers commonly complain of stomach upsets, but this is more often due to the change in diet than food poisoning. Make sure you bring along anti-diarrhoeal capsules, such as Imodium, and play safe by avoiding tap water: bottled water is inexpensive and available at all restaurants and cafés.

Should you get ill, then be warned that the Moroccan healthcare system is ropey. While good doctors can be

found and pharmacies are surprisingly well stocked and knowledgably staffed, for anyone afflicted with serious illness the best route to take is the one leading straight to the airport and home.

Contraception & abortion

You can purchase condoms as well as birth control pills over the counter at any pharmacy. If you aren't currently using birth control, bring an emergency morning-after pill kit with you as this is not available in Morocco.

Abortion is not an openly discussed subject. It is unavailable to unmarried women; any doctor practicing an abortion on an unmarried women can be arrested and disbarred. However, married women who already have children seem to be able to have abortions discreetly without any problems. For non-Moroccans the best bet is to contact an abortion clinic in Spain and fly to Barcelona.

Dentists

Dental care in Marrakech is of a reasonable standard – discounting the wizened old guys on Jemaa El Fna with the trays of pliers, wrenches and assorted loose false teeth (although an otherwise perfectly sensible English friend of ours swears one of them cured her abscess). Offices and equipment may not be state of the art, but the practitioners are usually highly competent. However, getting appointments with the best guys isn't always easy.

Docteur Youssef Dassouli

Résidence Asmae, apartment No.6, 1st floor (044 43 53 03, emergency contact 064 90 65 14). **Office hours** 9am-noon, 3.30-7pm Mon-Fri. **No credit cards**.
English spoken.

Directory

Doctors

There's no shortage of doctors and specialists in Marrakech, but the trick's finding a good one. We can recommend the following:

Doctor Béatrice Peiffer Lahrichi

10 rue Oued El Makhazine, 1st floor, Résidence Lafrasouk, Guéliz (044 43 53 29). **Office hours** 9am-12.30pm, 3.30-6.30pm Mon-Fri; 9am-12.30pm Sat. **No credit cards**. **Map** p252 B3. French doctor (speaks no English) working out of a very modern surgery with full lab facilities.

Doctor Frederic Reitzer

Above Café Zohra, rue de la Liberté, Guéliz (044 43 95 XX/emergency contact 061 17 38 03). **Office hours** 10am-noon, 4-6pm Mon-Fri; 10am-noon Sat. **No credit cards**. **Map** p252 B2. Speaks English.

Docteur Samir Bellmezouar

Polyclinic du Sud, rue de Yougoslavie, Guéliz (061 24 32 27). **Office hours** Emergency team 24hrs daily. **No credit cards**. **Map** p252 A2. Doesn't speak English but does make house calls.

Docteur El Oufir (gynaecologist)

125 avenue Mohammed V, Guéliz (044 43 18.28). **Office hours** 8.30am-1pm, 3.30-7pm Mon-Fri; 8.30am-1pm Sat. **No credit cards**. **Map** p252 B2. Speaks English.

Hospitals

The only place to go is the Polyclinic du Sud. This private clinic is frequented by almost all the expat community and is used by most insurance companies if any of their clients experience any problems. Avoid public hospitals at all costs, where the severe lack of personnel, equipment and funding is frighteningly apparent.

Polyclinic du Sud

rue de Yougoslavie, Guéliz (044 44 79 99). **Open** 24hr emergency service. **No credit cards**. **Map** p252 A2.

Pharmacies

Pharmacies in Morocco are clearly marked with a green cross and/or green crescent. They're plentiful and every neighbourhood has at least one. The drugs may have different names from those you are used to, but ask and you'll find staff are surprisingly well informed. Most pharmacies are open 9am to 6-7pm Monday to Friday. Some may also open on Saturday mornings or afternoons. When closed, each pharmacy should display a list of alternative pharmacies open after hours. For addresses, *see p136*.

Prescriptions

Next to anything can be bought over the counter at without a prescription; about the only thing that raises eyebrows are condoms.

STDs, HIV & AIDS

Sexually transmitted diseases, including HIV and AIDS, are here as everywhere else in the world. However, due to the cultural context these problems are not readily discussed. There has been talk of free AIDS tests but, as with all things sexual, the problem in Morocco is largely ignored.

The Association de Lutte Contre le Sida (ALCS, or in English, the Association for the Fight Against AIDS) was set up in 1988, the first of its kind in the Maghreb and Middle East. Its headquarters are in Casablanca but it is active in 11 Moroccan cities, including Marrakech. The ALCS can provide advice, prevention information and screening, as well as organising care for people living with HIV.

ALCS

17 avenue Massira El Khadra Maarif, Casablanca (022 99 42 42/43/www.alcsmaroc.org).

ID

You are meant to carry some ID with you at all times in Morocco. The Moroccans have identity cards but a passport is fine for foreign visitors, or better still, just photocopies of the information pages so you can leave the actual document safely stashed away back at the hotel. Valid ID is essential when checking into a hotel, hiring a car, changing or paying with travellers' cheques and collecting poste restante.

Insurance

All travellers should take out personal travel insurance to cover trip cancellation, emergency medical costs and loss or theft of baggage or money. If you're planning on taking part in horse-riding, skiing or mountaineering, for example, you should also consider additional 'dangerous sports' cover.

Keep a record of your policy number and the emergency telephone number with you.

Internet

Computers are expensive in Morocco, so most people resort to privately owned internet centres, which are becoming ever easier to find. In the Medina they're concentrated along rue Bab Agnaou, with at least half a dozen in a 200-metre stretch; in Guéliz the best are up around place Abdel Moumen. Prices are all roughly similar (about 10dh an hour, except Askmy, which is 12dh). ISPs tend to be oversubscribed and, with one or two notable exceptions, download times are painfully slow. You might want to take along a book. We're not kidding.

If you are lugging around your own laptop, then you can get connected in some of the better hotels by using an RJ-11 standard telephone connector.

However, few of the major ISPs have any sort of local access number for Morocco and you will have to call long distance to log on. Between the high cost of telephone calls and lengthy download times this can be a very costly venture.

Internet service providers (ISPs)

Ménara (Maroc Télécom's ISP, www.menara.ma) is available to those with a landline. To subscribe, visit the Maroc Télécom office (see *p230* **Telephones**). The other option is **Wanadoo** (081 00 63 63, www.wanadoo.ma) prepaid cards (10hrs for 50dh; 20hrs for 70dh). These cards don't include the telephone communications needed to access the server. Wanadoo cards can be purchased at Marjane (route de Casablanca, 044 31 37 24), Magawork (1 Résidence Maniss La Youne, boulevard Aila Fassi (044 33 13 92) or Buraliste Bouargan (168 avenue Mohammed V, Guéliz, 044 43 02 57).

Internet access

Askmy
6 Boulevard Mohammed Zerktouni, Guéliz (044 43 06 02). **Open** 8am-3am daily. **No credit cards.** **Map** p252 A2.
The best internet centre in Marrakech bar none, with 14 state-of-the-art computers hooked up with ultra-fast 128kbps connections.

Cyber Club
avenue Mohammed V (next to Café Koutoubia), Medina (no phone). **Open** 9.30am-1am, 3-10.30pm daily. **No credit cards.** **Map** p252 B5.
Right across from the Koutoubia a small sign points down a flight of steps to this basement room with a generous 11 online terminals.

Cyberland
61 rue de Yougoslavie, Passage Ghandouri, Guéliz (044 43 69 77). **Open** 9am-11pm daily. **Map** p252 A2.
A ramshackle place near the ONMT tourist office with around a dozen computers perched on battered old desks over two floors.

Left luggage

There are no left luggage facilities at Marrakech's international airport. Bags can be left at the railway station for 10dh per day, and staff insist that they are padlocked.

Legal help

Embassies and consulates (*see p225*) can assist nationals in emergencies and provide a list of English-speaking lawyers and interpreters.

Lost property

In general, if you've lost it, forget it. Recovering lost property depends on the good nature of the person who finds your belongings. If you've lost something on public transport, call the transport operator, who should, in principle, hang on to lost property – but don't hold your breath.

Maps

There is no commercially available map of Marrakech. A small city plan is inset on most of the Morocco maps but while these are good for overviews of the city they lack the detail required for navigating the Medina. At present, the maps in this book are as good as it gets.

The best overall map of the country is the Michelin sheet 959, on a scale of 1:1,000,000 with a 1:600,000 inset of the Marrakech area, useful for any one heading over the Atlas. Decent alternatives include Hildebrand's (1:900,000) and GeoCenter (1:800,000).

Media

Foreign publications

English-language publications are easy to come by. Expect to find the major dailies (usually just 24hrs old) including the *Guardian, Telegraph, Times, Daily Mail* and *Sun,* plus the Sundays and those weekly international digests put out by some of the broadsheets. There will also usually be the *International Herald Tribune, Time, Newsweek* and *The Economist* plus sundry fashion, style and interiors mags. A list of newsagents stocking foreign papers is given in the **Shops & Services** chapter.

Magazines

Most mags are in French, and anyone who can read French should look out for *Medina* and *Maison du Maroc*: the former is Morocco travel with places that will interest tourists, the latter is the local equivalent of *Homes & Gardens*.

Newspapers

The Moroccan press is published in French and Arabic. While there is increasing editorial freedom, the national dailies tend to restrict their coverage to the goings on of the royal family, sports and local events (sounds familiar, no?). There's little in the way of international events. If you read French, the best paper is the daily *Le Figaro*, printed in Casablanca.

Television

Most hotels and riads that offer TV have satellite with BBC World, CNN, French TV5 and occasionally Sky channels.

Money

Local currency is the Moroccan dirham, abbreviated dh (in this book) and sometimes MDH, or MAD. There are 100 centimes to a dirham. Coins come in denominations of 5, 10, 20 and 50 centimes (all useless) and 1, 5 and 10dh. Note that there are two different types of 5dh coin

in circulation: a large silver-coloured version and a smaller new bi-metal issue (which, in turn, is similar to the 10dh coin but smaller). It's confusing. Small change is useful for things like taxi fares and should be hoarded. Banknotes come in denominations of 20, 50, 100 and 200dh. (There is also a 10dh note but this is being phased out.)

Excess dirhams can be exchanged for euros or dollars (pounds sterling are often not available) at a bank. You may be asked to show the exchange receipts from when you converted your hard currency into dirhams – this is because banks will only allow you to change back half the amount of Moroccan currency originally purchased.

At the time of writing, conversion between currencies is easy, as 10dh = US$1 = €1.

ATMs

Cashpoints, or *guichets automatiques*, are common in most Moroccan towns and cities, and it's perfectly possible to travel on plastic – although it's always wise to carry at least a couple of days' 'survival money' in cash. Most are connected into the international banking systems and issue dirhams on most European and US debit and credit cards. If the ATM carries only a Visa symbol, don't go there; it will only process locally issued Visa cards and may well swallow the international variety (we've heard tales of this happening). Instead look for machines bearing the Cirrus, Link and Maestro symbols.

Most banks set a daily withdrawal limit of 2,000dh (currently around £125) per day on ATM withdrawals. If you need more, just go to an exchange bureau with your card and passport and get a cash advance.

ATMs are concentrated along rue Bab Agnaou in the Medina and around place Abdel Moumen in Guéliz. Avoid having to draw cash on Monday mornings when the machines are often empty.

Banks

The main local banks are Banque Commerciale du Maroc (BCM), Banque Marocaine du Commerce Extérieur (BMCE), Banque Marocaine du Commerce et de l'Industrie (BMCI) and Crédit du Maroc. All of these have agreements with major international banks. The heaviest concentration of bank branches is around place Abdel Moumen in Guéliz. For opening hours, *see p229*. Note that the BMCI on boulevard Mohammed Zerktouni (just round the corner from the Café Atlas) is open at weekends and on public holidays when most other banks are closed.

Bureaux de change

Almost all banks have a bureaux de change counter, as do most major hotels of three stars and up. The exchange rate is set by the Bank of Morocco and is uniform. No commission is charged. When changing money you will usually be asked to show your passport. There's a convenient exchange window on the north side of rue Bab Agnaou, 100 metres along from Jemaa El Fna; otherwise there are plenty of banks with currency exchange counters in the vicinity.

Credit cards

MasterCard and Visa are widely accepted at shops, restaurants and hotels; American Express less so. Places that accept AmEx often add five per cent to cover the high cost of processing the transaction. In shops and restaurants it's wise to carry cash back up because proprietors will often claim that the machine is 'broken' or that your card won't go through – they aren't keen on the delay in payment that processing a credit card entails for them. Most establishments can do a manual transaction ('au sabot') and phone for an authorisation. Be firm and insist this is your only means of payment and your card may suddenly work. Credit card fraud is also a problem in Morocco so keep all receipts to check against your statement.

BMCE banks will give cash advances on MasterCard and Visa up to around 5,000dh.

American Express is represented in Marrakech by Voyages Schwartz (044 43 33 21), whose offices are in the Immeuble Moutaouskil, 1 rue Mauritanie, Guéliz (map p252 B3). It won't give cash advances but it will issue a letter of credit that you can then use to get cash at any Crédit du Maroc bank.

Lost/stolen credit cards

All lines have English-speaking staff and are open 24hrs daily.
American Express *00 973 256 834*
Barclaycard *00 44 1604 230 230*
Diners Club *022 99 455/00 44 1252 513 500*
MasterCard *00 1636 722 7111*
Switch *00 870 000459*

Travellers' cheques

Travellers cheques are accepted by most banks, though you may be bounced around between counters or branches before finding someone to cash them. Stick to well-known brands like Thomas Cook and American Express. A commission is usually charged of around 20dh-25dh per transaction, irrespective of the number of cheques or amount cashed. The Banque El Maghreb is an

The brigade touristique

Hassle in a Marrakech? In a word: gone. While visitors to the city used to be plagued by the 'orrible aitches of hustlers, hassle and hard sell, all that's very much a thing of the past. Since the new king came on the scene in 1999 life has got so much easier for the visitor. Tourism is vitally important to the local economy and mindful of the damage aggressive touts and *faux* (unofficial) guides were doing to the city's reputation action had to be taken. Hence the formation of the 'brigade touristique', or tourist police.

Throughout the city plain clothes agents patrol the souks and alleys of the Medina benignly watching over all foreigners. They even haunt the alleyways by night, lurking in shadowy doorways around riads and guesthouses. Should any rash local make a approach foreign tourist with a view to waylay, cajole or entreat then wham, the brigade are in there like a shot and the miscreant is dragged off for a good talking to down at the station. It can seem a bit draconian, particularly when you're being accompanied by a local who is a genuine friend and some officious type halts them and demands to see their papers, but full marks for effort anyway.

exception in charging nothing. Some hotels and shops will also accept travellers cheques as payment.

Opening hours

The relaxed pace of life in Marrakech, and throughout Morocco, is reflected in a casual approach to opening hours. These should be taken more as guidelines than gospel. Many places close in the afternoon for a siesta, which is not always reflected in the opening times we give in this book. As a rule of thumb the working week is Monday to Friday, with a half-day on Saturday. Note that hours vary in summer (from around 15 June to the end of September) and during Ramadan (*see p233* **Public & religious holidays**), when banks, for example, will open 8am-2pm with no afternoon session.

Banks 8.30-11.30am, 2.30-4.30pm Mon-Fri.
Shops 9am-1pm, 3-7pm Mon-Sat.
Museums & tourist sights Usually closed Tue.

Police

Crime against visitors is low. Physical violence is almost unheard of. You do need to watch your pockets and bags, though, particularly around Jemaa El Fna. If you are robbed or have a complaint against an unscrupulous taxi driver or souk merchant, the place to go is the office of the Brigade Touristique.

Note, if you are the victim of theft or some other crime in Ouarzazate or elsewhere outside Marrakech, then you must make a report to the local police wherever the incident occurred – do not wait until your return to the city.

Police stations

The main police station (Hôtel de Police; map p252 B3) is on rue Oued El Makhazine in Guéliz near the Jnane El Harti park. There's also an office of the tourist police (Brigade Touristique; 044 38 46 01) on the north side of Jemaa El Fna.

Postal services

The main post office (PTT Centrale) is on place du 16 Novembre, Guéliz, halfway along avenue Mohammed V (across from the McDonald's). It's open 8am-2pm Mon-Sat. There is a second smaller PTT in the Medina on rue Moulay Ismail, between Jemaa El Fna and the Koutoubia Mosque, open 8am-noon and 3-6pm Mon-Fri in the winter and 8am-3pm in the summer. Stamps are bought at a dedicated *timbres* counter at the PTTs; they can also be bought at the *tabac* or at the reception desks of larger hotels.

Parcels should be taken along unwrapped for examination at the parcels counter. Paper, string and wrapping is supplied for a fee.

Mail delivery is painfully slow (it can take a week or more for a letter to reach Europe). Post offices provide an express mail service abbreviated to EMS, but also known as *post rapide*). If you have something urgent to send, it's probably safer to use one of the international courier companies, *see p224.*

Poste restante

Poste restante is not always reliable, but if you want to give it a go, have the letters addressed to 'Poste Restante, PTT Centrale, Marrakech', and make sure that the surname is clear. A passport will be needed to pick up any mail.

Religion

Morocco is an Islamic country in the same way that some-where like Spain, and particularly Andalucía, is Catholic. Religion underpins society, places of worship are prominent and religious festivals are a highlight of the annual calendar. Sex before marriage is taboo. Islam may

Directory

be tougher on alcohol, but the Moroccans have always been notably more liberal when it comes to drugs (*see p231* **Kif from the Rif**). Although every neighbourhood has its mosque, few Moroccans perform the required five daily cycles of prayer. Those who do attend the mosque are content to limit their visits to noon Friday, which is the main prayer session of the week, equivalent to Sunday morning mass. And like Sunday morning mass in most churches, the congregation tends to be quite elderly. Most Moroccans, however, do make an effort to observe Ramadan, at least for the first week, anyway; *see p233* **Public & religious holidays**.

Christian

Church of St Anne
rue El Imam Ali, Hivernage (044 43 05 85). **Map** p252 B3.
Catholic services are held in French, but there is an interdenominational service delivered in English at 10.30am Sunday (9.30am during July) with tea and coffee afterwards.

Smoking

Morocco is firmly in thrall to nicotine. Non-smokers are outcasts and few cafés and restaurants recognise the concept of a clean-air environment. So why buck the trend? If you don't smoke, then Marrakech is the perfect place to start. Foreign cigarette brands cost 28dh, or about £1.75, for 20, while the best of the domestic product goes for even less. Passive smoking or active, it's your choice, but you've got to inhale some time.

Study

The Institut Français de Marrakech offers a selection of reasonably priced classes in Arabic to foreigners and can recommend tutors for private study. An intensive 40-hour

summer course is available for 700dh. Marrakech also has the Cadi Ayyad University but this is of little interest to the average foreign visitor.

Institut Français de Marrakech
route de Targa, Jebel Guéliz (044 44 69 30/fax 044 44 74 97).

Cadi Ayyad University
avenue Prince Moulay Abdellah, BP 511, Guéliz (044 43 48 13/fax 044 43 44 94/www.ucam.ac.ma).

Telephones

Telephoning abroad from Marrakech is no problem. Either use the cardphones that are liberally dotted around town (cards are bought from post offices, tabacs or news vendors) or one of the numerous *téléboutiques*. The latter are identified by a large blue and white sign depicting a telephone receiver. They are small premises with anything from two to a dozen coin-operated phones in booths. The overseer supplies change. International calls require a minimum of three 5dh coins. In the Medina there's near enough a téléboutique on every main street.

Off-peak rates apply from midnight to 7am weekdays, from 12.30pm Saturday and all day Sunday.

Dialling & codes

Note that you need to dial the three-digit area code even if you are calling from the same area. For instance, if you are making a local call within Marrakech, you must still dial 044. To call abroad dial 00, then the country code followed by the telephone number. Mobiles have the prefix 06.

Area codes
Casablanca 02
Essaouira 04
Fès 05
Marrakech 04
Ouarzazte & the south 04
Rabat/Tangier 03

Faxes

Most, but not all, téléboutiques will send a fax for you. Prices for international destinations will cost around 70dh.

Mobile phones

There are two main mobile service providers offering a pay-as-you-go option: the national operator Maroc-Télécom and Méditel. Most European networks have arrangements with one of the two so that visitors can use their mobiles in Morocco (although bear in mind, it's expensive). Alternatively, mobile users can also buy a pre-paid SIM card from either of the Moroccan network operators. For a charge of around 200dh you are provided with a local number through which national and international calls can be made at more favourable rates.

Maroc-Télécom (Agence Guéliz Mobile)
avenue Mohammed V (opposite McDonald's), Guéliz (044 43 44 53/fax 044 43 10 23/www.iam.ma). **Open** 8.30am-7pm Mon-Fri; 8.30am-1pm Sat. **Credit** MC, V. **Map** p252 B2.

Méditel
279 avenue Mohammed V, Guéliz (044 42 74 44). **Open** 9am-9.30pm daily. **No credit cards.** Map p252 B2.

Aloha
15 avenue Mohammed V, Guéliz (044 42 00 34/fax 044 42 00 32). **Open** 9am-9pm Mon-Sat. **No credit cards.** Map p252 A1. Méditel franchise.

Ilaicom
117 avenue Houmann El Fetouaki, Medina (044 38 59 63). **Open** 10am-1pm, 3.30-7.30pm Mon-Sat. **Credit** MC, V. **Map** p250 C7. Méditel franchise.

Kent 2
40 avenue Abdelkarim El Khattabi, Guéliz (044 44 84 38/fax 044 42 00 32). **Open** 9.30am-9pm Mon-Sat. **No credit cards.** Map p252 A2. Méditel franchise.

Le Portable

8 rue Fatima Zohra, Medina (044 44 22 28). **Open** 9.30am-1pm, 3.30-8pm daily. **No credit cards.**
Map p248 B4.
Méditel franchise.

Operator services

The international operator can be accessed by dialling 120, and to make a reverse charge call say '*Je voudrais téléphoner en PCV*' but be prepared for a wait. To get the domestic operator dial 10.

For directory enquiries dial 16, but don't expect English to be spoken.

Time

Morocco follows GMT all year round, which means that it's on the same time as Britain and Ireland in winter but an hour behind during British Summer Time (late March to late October).

Tipping

Tipping is a must. It's expected in cafes and restaurants (round up the bill or add 10-15 per cent), by guides and porters, and by anyone else that renders you any sort of small service. It is not necessary to tip taxi drivers, who can just be content with overcharging. Five or ten dirhams is sufficient. Make sure you carry plenty of small change.

Toilets

Public toilets are a rarity – use the facilities when in bars, hotels and restaurants. They're usually decent enough (and occasionally stunning, as at Comptoir). It's a good idea to carry a packet of paper tissues as toilet paper is not always available – the traditional method here is to use the water hose to sluice yourself clean. A wastepaper basket beside the toilet is for used tissues,

Kif from the Rif

You won't be in Morocco long before someone tries to sell you some dope. However much you might fancy a toke, treat all such approaches with caution. It's not just that street dealers will supply poor quality at inflated prices. It's also that many double as police informers, angling not just for the cash you'll hand over, but also for a share of the *baksheesh* you'll later pay to buy yourself out of trouble.

Usage of marijuana filtered into the Maghreb from the Middle East sometime around the 12th century and has been a part of Moroccan life for hundreds of years. Discreet use is tolerated and a significant minority still consume the stuff: smoked as *kif* (grass) in a long pipe called a *sebsi*, eaten in the jam- or cake-like form of *majoun* or, in the bigger cities, as hash mixed with tobacco in European-style joints.

But Morocco is the world's largest cannabis producer and most is exported. In the area around Ketama in the Rif Mountains, up to 1,000 sq km are under cultivation. Techniques for producing resin were introduced in the early 1970s, enabling a compact and easily transportable product that is distributed throughout Europe and brings up to $3 billion a year back into the Moroccan economy.

That's one reason why the authorities pay little more than lip service to US and European pressure to stamp this trade out. But there are also practical problems. The Berber tribes of the Rif are fiercely independent and have successfully resisted assimilation for centuries. One mid-1990s attempt to burn the kif crop was met with armed resistance. The mountain valleys where it is grown are remote, many inaccessible by motor vehicle, and crop substitution is useless as nothing else of value will grow in this rocky landscape. And as there is already chronic unemployment in Morocco, the government is wary of measures that will increase the flood of unskilled migrants into the *bidonvilles* of Casablanca or Tangier. Meanwhile, the acreage under cultivation is, if anything, increasing.

Cultivation is still legal, but the government maintains stiff penalties for sale or consumption. Of the 600 or so Europeans in Moroccan jails, around 95 per cent have been banged up for cannabis-related convictions. To reduce the risk of joining them, follow these simple guidelines:
● Leave any transaction for a few days until you've got a feel for how things work.
● Avoid street dealers, especially in Tangier or Tetouan. The best bet are younger souk stallholders who might have a bit under the counter. Don't ask. Wait for their approach.
● Never buy more than a small amount for personal use, and don't travel with any in your possession.
● Don't buy the 'opium'. It may look, feel and taste like soft opium, but actually it's a kind of Berber hair shampoo.
● Avoid Ketama and surrounds. You'll be harangued by dealers waving breeze-block sized lumps of hash, and if stupid enough to buy any, will get into major trouble at the first police roadblock.

Islamic holidays

	Ramadan	Eid El Seghir	Eid El Kebir	Moharran	Mouloud
2003	25 Oct	24 Nov	12 Feb	4 Mar	12 May
2004	14 Oct	13 Nov	1 Feb	22 Feb	1 May
2005	3 Oct	2 Nov	21 Jan	10 Feb	19 April

Note these dates are approximate as the exact start of the celebrations depends on the sighting of the full moon.

which the plumbing generally isn't up to digesting resulting in blockages. At cafés the toilet attedant expects a few dirhams as a tip; it's bad form not to oblige.

Tourist information

The **ONMT** (Office National Marocain du Tourisme) has offices in most major cities in Morocco and some cities abroad (*see below*). Basic tourist information can be found at its website www.visitmorocco.com.

The two tourist offices in Marrakech offer much the same services, that is basic information and a handful of brochures. The ONMT is the marginally more useful.

Office National Marocain du Tourisme
ONMT, place Abdel Moumen, Guéliz (044 43 61 31). **Open** 8.30am-noon, 2.30-6.30pm Mon-Fri; 9am-noon, 3-6pm Sat. **Map** p252 A1.

Syndicat d'Initiative
170 avenue Mohammed V, Guéliz (044 43 08 86). **Open** 8.30am-12.30pm, 2.30-6.30pm Mon-Fri; 9am-noon Sat. **Map** p252 B2.

International offices

London *205 Regent Street, W1R 7DE (020 7437 0073/7734 8172).* **New York** *20 East 46th, suite 1201, 10017 (+1 212 55 72 520).* **Paris** *161 rue Saint Honoré, 75001 (+1 42 60 63 50).*

Visas & immigration

All visitors to Morocco need a passport to enter the country, which should be valid for at least six months beyond the date of entry. No visas are required for nationals of Australia, Britain, Canada, Ireland, New Zealand, the US and most EU countries. If in doubt check with your local Moroccan embassy; South Africans, for example, do require visas.

Travellers can stay in Morocco for three months from the time of entry. Extensions beyond this require applying for an official residence permit, which is a lengthy and tedious procedure. First it's necessary to open a bank account in Morocco for which you will need a minimum of 20,000dh (£1,250) deposited in your account and an *attestation de résidence* from your hotel or landlord. Then you need to go to the Bureau des Etrangers equipped with your passport, seven passport photos, two copies of the attestation, two copies of your bank statement, and a 60dh stamp (available from any tabac). Once all the requisite forms have been filled out in duplicate you should receive a residence permit a few weeks later

A simpler option may be to leave the country for a few days and re-enter, gaining a new three-month stamp. Spain is the obvious choice, or alternatively the enclave of Ceuta at the northernmost tip of the country.

Bureau des Etrangers
Comissariat Centrale, Guéliz. **Open** 8am-noon, 2-6pm Mon-Thur; 8am-noon Fri.

When to go

The tourist office claim that Marrakech receives 350 days of sunshine a year is stretching it a bit, but the weather is rarely a conversation point – it's hot, and there's little more to be said. December and January can be afflicted with overcast skies and rain showers, but Marrakech still makes for a good winter retreat with daily temperatures of around 15-20°C (59-68°F). Evenings can be chilly and you need to be in a hotel that has heating. By March to May is the perfect time to visited but beware high-season Easter price hikes. Summers can be oppressive; temperatures average 30-35°C (86-95°F), frequently pushing up toward 40°C (104°F). The heat is a drain on energy and pool-side lounging takes preference over sightseeing. It's not until September that things start to cool off again, with autumn being another climatically attractive season.

Public & religious holidays

Morocco's six secular holidays occupy a day each. Banks, offices and civil service institutions close, but many shops stay open and public transport runs as usual.

1 January New Year's Day
1 May Labour Day (Fête du Travail)
30 July Feast of the Throne (Fête du Trône), commemorating the present king's accession
14 August Allegiance Day
6 November Day of the Green March (Marche Vert), commemorating the retaking of Spanish-held Saharan territories
18 November Independence Day

Religious holidays occupy two or three days and if these happen to fall midweek then the government commonly extends the holiday to cover the whole working week.

Observance of **Ramadan**, the Muslim month of fasting and biggest event of the Islamic year is widespread. Many Moroccans abstain from food, drink and cigarettes between sunrise and sunset. This has some impact on visitors as quite a few cafes and restaurants will close during the day. It's also bad form to flaunt your non-participation by smoking or eating in the street. Ramadan nights are some of the busiest of the year as, come sundown, eateries are packed with large groups communally breaking their fast, a meal known as *iftar*. Jemaa El Fna is particularly wild.

The end of Ramadan is marked by the two-day feast of **Eid El Seghir** ('the small feast'). A few months later the feast of **Eid El Kebir** ('the big feast') commemorates Abraham's sacrifice of a ram instead of his son. It's not a good time for sheep as every family that can afford to emulates the Patriarch's deed by slaughtering an animal.

Three weeks after Eid El Kebir is **Moharram**, the Muslim New Year. The other big Muslim holiday is **Mouloud**, a celebration of the birthday of the Prophet Mohammed.

Islamic religious holidays are based on a lunar calendar, approximately 11 days shorter than the Gregorian (western) calendar. This means that Islamic holidays shift forward by 11 days each year. For the dates in 2003/4, *see p232* **Islamic holidays**.

Festivals

It was held for the first time only in 2001, but already the September **Marrakech International Film Festival** has established itself as the city's most prestigious and glitzy cultural event; *see p143*. The only other jamboree of note held in Marrakech is June's two-week **Festival of Folk Art and Music**. Now in its 40th year, the festival takes on a different theme each year, played out by dozens of troupes from around Morocco.

Outside of Marrakech, there's the annual **Essaouira Festival of Gnawa and World Music** (*see p150*), held each in the pretty little Atlantic port town. It attracts a host of international performers and is well worth heading out to the coast for if you happen to be in Morocco in June. Also in June is the **Festival of the World's Sacred Music** held in Fès, which is a celebration of international Islamic music.

Women

Though Marrakech is Islamic, few special rules apply. With some provisos, you needn't dress any differently here than at home. However, if you've a liking for minis and micros, leave those home. Shorts are out too. To avoid causing offence or being stared at, wear trousers or dresses and skirts that reach the knee or lower. Loose and baggy light cotton is the way to go. In more conservative areas such as the northern Medina, women should keep their shoulders covers (though a headscarf is *not* necessary).

In touristy areas such as around Jemaa El Fna and the main souks, you may get hit on. It's usually harmless and nothing more than you could expect to experience in Greece or Italy, but all the same it can be annoying. It's also generally easy to shrug off. Avoid direct eye contact. Don't beam wide smiles at men. Don't respond to invitations, come ons or obnoxious comments. If a man is persistant and in your face, raise your voice so others around know you're being bothered. Chances are someone will intervene on your behalf.

Work

Although Marrakech is welcoming of foreign residents, most of them are retired or living on incomes derived in their home countries. In such cases, as long as you can prove regular transfers of funds are being made into a Moroccan bank account, then it's a relatively easy matter to obtain a carte de séjour (residence permit). Earning your keep as a foreigner in Marrakech is harder. International companies setting up in Morocco (hotels, for instance) tend to do their hiring abroad.

Teachers with recognised qualifications (CELTS) could make inquiries at the American Language Center where English is taught to local students.

American Language Center (ALC)

3 Impasse des Moulins, boulevard Mohammed Zerktouni, Guéliz (044 44 72 59/http://marrakesh. aca.org.ma). **Open** 9am-noon, 3-7pm Mon-Fri; 9am-noon Sat.

Vocabulary: French

In French, as in other Latin languages, the second person singular (you) has two forms. Phrases here are given in the more polite *vous* form. The *tu* form is used with family, friends, young children and pets; you should be careful not to use it with people you do not know sufficiently well, as it is considered rude. You will also find that courtesies such as monsieur, madame and mademoiselle are used much more than often their English equivalents.

General expressions

good morning/hello *bonjour*
good evening *bonsoir*
goodbye *au revoir*
hi (familiar) *salut*
OK *d'accord*; **yes** *oui*; **no** *non*
How are you? *Comment allez vous?/vous allez bien?*
How's it going? *Comment ça va?/ça va?* (familiar)
Sir/Mr *monsieur* (M)
Madam/Mrs *madame* (Mme)
Miss *mademoiselle* (Mlle)
please *s'il vous plaît*; **thank you** *merci*; **thank you very much** *merci beaucoup*
sorry *pardon*; **excuse me** *excusez-moi*
Do you speak English? *Parlez-vous anglais?*
I don't speak French *Je ne parle pas français*
I don't understand *Je ne comprends pas*
Speak more slowly, please *Parlez plus lentement, s'il vous plaît*
how much?/how many? *combien?*
Have you got change? *Avez-vous de la monnaie?*
I would like… *Je voudrais…*
it is *c'est*; **it isn't** *ce n'est pas*
good *bon/bonne*; **bad** *mauvais/mauvaise*
small *petit/petite*; **big** *grand/grande*
beautiful *beau/belle*; **well** *bien*; **badly** *mal*
expensive *cher*; **cheap** *pas cher*

a bit *un peu*; **a lot** *beaucoup*; **very** *très*; **with** *avec*; **without** *sans*; **and** *et*; **or** *ou*; **because** *parce que*
who? *qui?*; **when?** *quand?*; **which?** *quel?*; **where?** *où?*; **why?** *pourquoi?*; **how?** *comment?*
at what time/when? *à quelle heure?*
forbidden *interdit/défendu*
out of order *hors service/en panne*
daily *tous les jours (tlj)*

Getting around

When is the next train for…? *C'est quand le prochain train pour…?*
ticket *un billet*; **station** *la gare*; **platform** *le quai*
bus/coach station *gare routière*
entrance *entrée*; **exit** *sortie*
left *gauche*; **right** *droite*; **interchange** *correspondence*
straight on *tout droit*; **far** *loin*; **near** *pas loin/près d'ici*
street *la rue*; **street map** *le plan*; **road map** *la carte*
bank *la banque*; **is there a bank near here?** *est-ce qu'il y a une banque près d'ici?*
post office *La Poste*; **a stamp** *un timbre*

Sightseeing

museum *un musée*;
church *une église*;
exhibition *une exposition*; **ticket** (for museum) *un billet*; (for theatre, concert) *une place*
open *ouvert*; **closed** *fermé*
free *gratuit*; **reduced price** *un tarif réduit*

Accommodation

Do you have a room (for this evening/for two people? *Avez-vous une chambre(pour ce soir/pour deux personnes)?*
full *complet*; **room** *une chambre*
bed *un lit*; **double bed** *un grand lit*; **(a room with) twin beds** *(une chambre) à deux lits*
with bath(room)/shower *avec (salle de) bain/douche*
breakfast *le petit déjeuner*
included *compris*
lift *un ascenseur*
air-conditioned *climatisé*

At the café or restaurant

I'd like to book a table (for three/at 8pm) *Je voudrais réserver une table (pour trois personnes/à vingt heures)*
lunch *le déjeuner*; **dinner** *le dîner*
coffee (espresso) *un café*;
white coffee *un café au lait/café crème*; **tea** *le thé*; **wine** *le vin*;
beer *la bière*
mineral water *eau minérale*;
fizzy *gazeuse*; **still** *plate*
tap water *eau du robinet/une carafe d'eau*
the bill, please *l'addition, s'il vous plaît*

Behind the wheel

no parking *stationnement interdit/stationnement gênant*;
speed limit 40 *rappel 40*
petrol *essence*; **unleaded** *sans plomb*

Numbers

0 *zéro*; 1 *un, une*; 2 *deux*; 3 *trois*; 4 *quatre*; 5 *cinq*; 6 *six*; 7 *sept*; 8 *huit*; 9 *neuf*; 10 *dix*; 11 *onze*; 12 *douze*; 13 *treize*; 14 *quatorze*; 15 *quinze*; 16 *seize*; 17 *dix-sept*; 18 *dix-huit*; 19 *dix-neuf*; 20 *vingt*; 21 *vingt-et-un*; 22 *vingt-deux*; 30 *trente*; 40 *quarante*; 50 *cinquante*; 60 *soixante*; 70 *soixante-dix*; 80 *quatre-vingts*; 90 *quatre-vingt-dix*; 100 *cent*; 1,000 *mille*; 1,000,000 *un million*.

Days, months & seasons

Monday *lundi*; **Tuesday** *mardi*; **Wednesday** *mercredi*; **Thursday** *jeudi*; **Friday** *vendredi*; **Saturday** *samedi*; **Sunday** *dimanche*.

January *janvier*; **February** *février*; **March** *mars*; **April** *avril*; **May** *mai*; **June** *juin*; **July** *juillet*; **August** *août*; **September** *septembre*; **October** *octobre*; **November** *novembre*; **December** *décembre*.

Spring *printemps*; **summer** *été*; **autumn** *automne*; **winter** *hiver*.

Vocabulary: Arabic

Within Marrakech (and other main towns and cities) you can get by in French, which is widely spoken by all educated Moroccans. However, a little effort with Arabic goes a long way, even if it is just a few stock phrases like 'hello' and 'goodbye'. Moroccan Arabic is a dialect of the standard Arabic language and is not the same as that spoken elsewhere in North Africa and the Middle East, although there are some words and phrases in common. We should point out that transliteration from Arabic into English is a highly inexact science and a wide variety of spellings are possible for any given word (for example Koran vs Quran). In this guide we've tended to plump for whatever seemed the most straight-forward. You are also likely to encounter Berber, which comes in three distinct dialects. Most Berber speakers will also be fluent in Arabic.

Arabic pronunciation

Arabic has numerous sounds that non-speakers have trouble in pronouncing but nobody is going to knock you for trying.

gh - like the French 'r', slightly rolled
kh - like the 'ch' in loch

Emergencies

leave me alone *esmahli la help!* *tekni!*
help me, please *awenni afak*
call the police *ayyet el bolice*
thief *sheffar*
I'm lost *tweddert*

General expressions

good morning/hello *sabah el kheir/salaam aleikum*
good evening *masr el kheir*
goodbye *masalaama*

please *min fadlak* (to a male); *min fadlik* (to a female)
yes *aywa/anam*; no *la*
How are you? *labas/kifhalak (to a male)/kifhalik (to a female)*
thank you *shukran*
no thanks *la shukran*
sorry/excuse me *esmahli*
Do you speak English? *Itkelim Ingleezi?*
I don't speak Arabic *Metkelimsh Arabi*
I don't understand *Mafayimtish*
who? *shkun?*; why? *lash?*; which? *ashmen?*; where? *feyn?*
today *el youm*; tomorrow *ghedda*; yesterday *imbara*
God willing *inshalah*
never mind/so it goes *malish*
tips *baksheesh*
let's go *yalla*
passport *passeport*

Shopping

how much?/how many? *bekam?*
Do you have...? *Wahesh andakum...?*
Have you got change? *Maak sarf?*
credit card *kart kredi*
travellers cheques *shek siyahi*
good *mleah*; bad *mish imleah*
small *seghir*; big *kebir*
beautiful *jameel*
that's expensive *ghali bezzaf*
enough *kafi*

Getting around

Where is...? *Feyn keyn...?*
Where is the hotel? *Feyn keyn el otel?*
airport *el mattar*
station *el mahatta*
bus/coach station *mahatta d'el ottobisat*
ticket office *maktab el werka*; ticket *werka*
train station *el gar*
bus stop *plasa d'el ottobisat*
museum *el mathaf*
embassy *el sifara*
pharmacy *farmasyan*
bank *el banka*
post office *el busta*; stamp *etnaber*
restaurant *el mattam*
mosque *jamaa*
left *yassar*; right *yemeen*
stop here *haten hinayer*
here *hina*; there *hinak*

Accommodation

Do you have a room? *Andak beit?*
key *srout*
room *beit*
sheet *eyzar*
shower *doush*
toilet *vaysay*
breakfast *iftar*

At the café or restaurant

table for... *tabla dyal...*
what's that? *shnu hada?*
I'm a vegetarian *makanakulsh elham*
I don't eat... *makanakuls...*
meat *ieham*
chicken *dzhazh*
fish *elhut*
bread *elkhobz*
coffee *qahwa*; tea *atay*
beer *birra*; wine *shshrab*
mineral water *sidi ali*
the bill, please *lahsab afak*

Numbers

0 *sifer*; 1 *wahid*; 2 *itnehn*; 3 *telata*; 4 *arbaa*; 5 *khamsa*; 6 *setta*; 7 *seba*; 8 *tamanya*; 9 *tesa*; 10 *ashra*; 11 *hadasha*; 12 *itnasha*; 13 *teltash*; 14 *arbatash*; 15 *khamstash*; 16 *settash*; 17 *sebatash*; 18 *tamantash*; 19 *tesatash*; 20 *eshreen*; 21 *wahid w'eshreen*; 22 *itnehn w'eshreen*; 30 *telateen*; 40 *arba'een*; 50 *khamseen*; 60 *setteen*; 70 *seba'een*; 80 *tameneen*; 90 *tesa'een*; 100 *mea*; 1,000 *alef*.

Days, months & seasons

Monday *el itnehn*; Tuesday *el teleta*; Wednesday *el arbaar*; Thursday *el khemis*; Friday *el jomaa*; Saturday *el sebt*; Sunday *el ahad*.

January *yanayir*; February *fibraiyir*; March *maris*; April *abril*; May *mayu*; June *yunyu*; July *yulyu*; August *aghustus*; September *sibtimber*; October *oktobir*; November *nufimbir*; December *disimbir*.

Glossary

Architecture

bab gate
dar house
fundouk medieval merchants' inn arranged around a central courtyard with stabling on the gound floor, sleeping quarters above
hammam traditional bathhouse
kasbah traditional Berber fortress/palace
koubba domed tomb
mashrabiya fretworked wooden screens traditionally used for windows
Mauresque French colonial version of neo-Moorish architecture
méchouar parade ground
medersa Koranic school for the teaching of Islamic law and scriptures
mihrab prayer niche facing towards Mecca in a mosque
minbar pulpit in a mosque for the reading of the Koran, usually free-standing
muqarna Moorish ceiling ornamentation resembling stalactites
pisé mud reinforced with straw and lime, and the primary building material of Marrakech
riad house with a central courtyard garden
tadelakt moisture-resistant polished plaster wall surface
zaouia shrine of a holy man, usually also doubling as a theology school
zelije coloured tilework typical of Moorish decoration

Around town

agdal walled garden
arset quarter
derb alley
caléche horse-drawn carriage
hôtel de ville city hall
jnane market garden
maison d'hôtes guest house
medina Arabic for 'city', often used to mean the 'old city'

marché market
mellah traditional Jewish quarter
place square
souk bazaar or market

Culture

babouche traditional leather slippers, typically yellow
baksheesh a tip or kickback
baraka blessings
ben son of (also spelled ibn)
Berber the indigenous tribes people of southern Morocco
bidonvilles unplanned slum dwellings on the outskirts of town
douar tribe
Fassi adjective for someone from Fès
gnawa semi-mystical brotherhood of muscians descended from black African slaves. Also the name of the music they play
haj pilgrimage to Mecca which observant Muslims are expected to perform at least once during their life time. Also the honorific title of someone who has made the pilgrimage
hijab headscarf warn by some Muslim women
imam priest of a mosque
jellaba traditional men's robe
jinn souls without bodies, usually malevolent (also spelled djinn)
kif the local marijuana, cultivated extensively in the Rif Mountains
leila all-night gnawa music performance (the word literally means night)
maalim master craftsman or master of any profession, including musician
majoun a cake or jam of marijuana
Marrakchi adjective for someone from Marrakech
muezzin the man who makes the call to prayer
oud musical instrument, like a lute

sidi saint
Souari adjective for someone from Essaouira
wali regional governor appointed by the king

Food

brouettes little envelopes of paper-thin *ouarka* (filo) pastry wrapped around ground meat, rice or cheese and deep fried, served as an hors d'ouevre
chakchouka dessert of light pastry filled with fruit
couscous coarse-ground semolina flour. Also the name of the cooked dish
harira Moroccan vegetable soup
pastilla ouarka (filo) pastry typically filled with a mixture of shredded pigeon, almonds and spices, served as an hors d'ouevre
tajine slow-cooked stew of meat (usually lamb or chicken) and/or vegetables. Also the name of the conically lidded dish it's cooked in
trid shredded pigeon wrapped in a crêpe soaked in broth

History

Almohads Berber dynasty (1147-1269) that ruled out of Marrakech before relocating to Rabat
Almoravids Berber dynasty (1062-1147) that founded Marrakech
Green March Action by which Morocco seized the Spanish colony of Rio del Oro in the western Sahara in 1975
Merenids Berber dynasty (1276-1554) that ruled from northern Morocco
Saadians Arab dynasty (1549-1668) that oversaw a brief rennaissance of imperial Marrakech
Treaty of Fés The act that formalised the imposition of French rule over Morocco in 1912

Further Reference

Some of these books, videos and CDs are out of print or deleted but try a websearch on bookfinder.com, ebay.com or similar.

Books

For more on Bowles and company, *see also p217* **The dream life of Tangier**. For books on Moroccan style and design, *see p29*.

Fiction

Benali, Abdelkader *Wedding by the Sea* (1999) Picaresque first novel by a young Dutch-Moroccan novelist concerning the retrieval of the groom from a brothel while his bride awaits.

Ben Jelloun, Tahar *The Sand Child* (1987) Gender exploration in which a father conceals the birth of an eighth girl by proclaiming the child a son, by Morocco's most acclaimed writer.

Binebine, Mahi *Welcome to Paradise* (2002) A ragtag group of the hopeful and the hopeless cower on a north Atlantic beach waiting for the boat that's to smuggle them into Europe. Highly moving.

Bowles, Paul *The Sheltering Sky* (1949) Of Bowles four novels, this is the best known thanks to a film adaptation by Bertolucci.

Brady, James *Paris One* (1977) The thud of a body toppled off a roof into a dirt alley in Marrakech triggers bitching, sex and bloodletting in the Parisian fashion world.

Burroughs, William *The Naked Lunch* (1959) Compiled in Tangier from hoarded scraps of stories and typed up in a hotel room by Kerouac, who suggested the title.

Eggers, Dave *You Shall Know Our Velocity* (2003) Two whiney naïve American dopes

set off round the world to give away $38,000, stopping in Marrakech to indulge in some 'reverse haggling'.

Freud, Esther *Hideous Kinky* (1992) A child's view of hippy life in the Marrakech of the early '70s; mum wants to be a Sufi, her two young girls just want to go home.

Goytisolo, Juan *Makbara* (1980) 'Spain's greatest living writer' is a long-standing resident of Marrakech and has a cavalier way with grammar and punctuation.

Grenier, Richard *Marrakech One-Two* (1983) Slight comedy about an international crew in Morocco to film a life of the Prophet. Includes obligatory hostage taking and sex-crazed female Arab radicals.

Maugham, Robin *The Wrong People* (1970) A tale of a repressed homosexual finding an 'outlet' in Tangier by a nephew of Somerset.

Taylor, Debbie *The Fourth Queen* (2003) Scots lass rises through the ranks of the harem in 18th-century Marrakech and has sex with a dwarf called Microphilius. Based on a true story, apparently.

Watkins, Paul *In the Blue Light of African Dreams* (1990) Lyrical tale of Foreign Legion flyers based in Mogador (Essaouira) who desert desert patrols to attempt the first aerial crossing of the Atlantic.

Non-fiction

Bowles, Paul *Their Heads Are Green* (1963) Non-fiction bits of travelogue in Mexico and Turkey but also in Morocco, up in the Rif and down in the Sahara.

Busi, Aldo *Sodomies in Eleven Point* (1988) Travels through Morocco and Tunisia in which museums and monuments take a back seat to gay sex.

Canetti, Elias *The Voices of Marrakech* (1967) A Nobel Prize winner's highly impressionistic tales and thumbnail sketches of the city.

Finlayson, Iain *Tangier: City of the Dream* (1993) Colourful evocation of the 1960s and '70s lit fest that went on in Tangier.

Green, Michelle *The Dream at the End of the World* (1991) Less 'literary' and more 'scene' than the Finlayson book and probably the single best read on the whole Tangier thing.

Harmetz, Aljean *Round Up the Usual Suspects* (1993) How a little-known play called *Everybody Comes to Rick's* became a legendary movie called *Casablanca*.

Harris, Walter *Morocco That Was* (1921) Correspondent of *The Times* who witnessed the downfall of the sultans and arrival of the French (1912) and documented all in a wickedly funny style.

Hopkins, John *The Tangier Diaries 1962-1979* (1997) 'Bill Willis calls my house "Scorpion Hall" there are so many. I keep viper serum and scorpion serum in the ice box in case someone gets bitten.' Magic stuff.

Maxwell, Gavin *Lords of the Atlas* (1966) The single best book on Marrakech – an account of the rise and fall of the depotic Glaoui clan.

Mayne, Peter *A Year in Marrakesh* (1953) Recently reprinted account by a loafing Englishman of local alley life with drugs, casual sex and garden picnics. A bit of a wheeze.

Film

See also p141-3 **Film**.

Casablanca *dir. Michael Curtiz (1942)* Depending on which poll you believe, the best film ever, with

iconic performances and misquoted dialogue that's passed into history.

Hideous Kinky
dir. Gillies Mackinnon (1998)
Solid adaptation of the novel with Kate Winslet romanced by Moroccan-born Said Tagmaoui and loads of gorgeous local scenery.

The Man Who Knew Too Much
dir. Alfred Hitchcock (1954)
Hitchcock's second take on the title begins with a slow 30-minute travelogue shot entirely on location in Marrakech.

Moroccan Chronicles
dir. Moumen Smihi (1999)
Haunting portmanteau of three fables: one shot in Marrakech, one in Essaouira and one in Tangier.

Morocco
dir. Josef von Sternberg (1930)
Marlene Dietrich vamps it up in Marrakech and elsewhere with legionnaire Gary Cooper. No plot to speak of.

A Night in Casablanca
dir. Archie L Mayo (1946)
The penultimate Marx Bros movie with a lot of plot about spies and hidden loot saved by ace sight gags and Groucho's one-liners.

Othello
dir. Orson Welles (1951)
Shot in fits and starts over four years, on a dozen locations including, notably, Essaouira, where the film crew's prolonged stay was a huge boost to the local economy.

The Road to Morocco
dir. David Butler (1942)
Like Webster's dictionary Bing (Crosby) and Bob (Hope) are Morocco bound, quipping and gagging as they vie for the hand of Dorothy Lamour.

The Sheltering Sky
dir. Bernardo Bertolucci (1990)
Adaptation of the Bowles' novel in which a travelling American couple go down the drain in the desert losing life/sanity against dramatic Moroccan backdrops.

Discography

See also p147-50 **Music**

Classical

Amina Alaoui *Alcaneara* (Auvidis Ethnic)
The great diva of Arab-Andalous music accompanied by three classical musicians. Ethereal and beautiful.

Moroccan Ensemble of Fes *Andalucian Music from Morocco* (Harmonia Mundi)
Good recordings of Moroccan classical music performed by one of Morocco's finest orchestras.

Berber & gnawa

B'net Marrakech *Chamaa* (Empreinte Digitale)
All-female ensemble from Marrakech who've been making a big impression on the European world music circuit.

Jil Jilala *Chamaa* (Blue Silver)
One of the most revered of all North African bands and this album illustrates why their sound remains so influential.

Lemchaheb *La Chanson Populaire Marocaine* (Club Du Disque Arabe)
A CD that captures the band raw before they went West.

Najat Aatabou *The Voice Of The Atlas* (Globestyle)
Outspoken female Berber vocalist who sings in Berber, Arabic and French and has risen to major star status.

Nass El Ghiwane *Le Disque d'Or* (Blue Silver)
Classic album from the early 1970s features Nass at their finest.

Various *Gnawa Music of Marrakech: Night Spirit Masters* (Axiom US)
Great recording of gnawa musicians in the Medina, featuring Brahim El Belkani.

Various *Maroc: Musique Populaire* (Club du Disque Arabe)

CD of *grika* (improvised) folk music. Spookily intense.

Various *Morocco: Jilala Confraternity* (Ocora)
An important recording of a small Jilala ensemble who perform rituals in rural Morocco on request.

Fusion

Aisha Kandisha's Jarring Effects *Shabeenisation* (Barbarit) This album comes with a high-tech Bill Laswell sheen and effectively marries hip-hop and electro influences to Moroccan music.

Gnawa Diffusion *Algeria* (7 Colours Music)
Reggae, ragga and funk fused courtesy of the hugely popular band from Grenoble in France.

Hassan Hakmoun *Trance* (Real World)
Produced by Afro-Celt leader Simon Emmerson, a jazz- and funk- influenced take on gnawa.

Horowitz, Richard & Deyhim, Sussan *Majoun* (EMI Classical)
Extraordinary collaboration between an Iranian vocalist, an American composer and a slew of Moroccan musicians.

Lemchaheb & Dissidenten *Sahara Elektrik* (Exile Music)
A collaboration between leading Moroccan *chaabi* (roots) and German experimentalists Dissidenten.

Master Musicians of Jajouka *Apocalypse Across the Sky* (Axiom US)
Bill Laswell captures all the elemental power of the Jajouka orchestra. Not to be filed under easy listening.

Momo *The Birth Of Dar* (Apartment 22)
Rockin' live but Momo's mixing of gnawa riffs over breakbeats falls a little flat in the studio.

Nass Marrakech *Boubera* (Harmonia Mundi)
A gifted gnawa group based in Barcelona. They are joined here by Latin jazz musicians Omar Sosa and Jorge Pardo.

Index

Note: page numbers in **bold** indicate section(s) giving key information on topic; *italics* indicate illustrations.

Advertisers' Index

Please refer to relevant sections for addresses and telephone numbers

Place of Interest and/or Entertainment . . . . ▢

Railway Station . . . . ▢

Park . . . . ▢

City Wall . . .. ━

Area Name . . . . GUÉLIZ

Mosque . . . . ☾

Church . . . . ✚

Post Office . . . . ✉

Hotels . . . . ●

Restaurants . . . . ●

Map

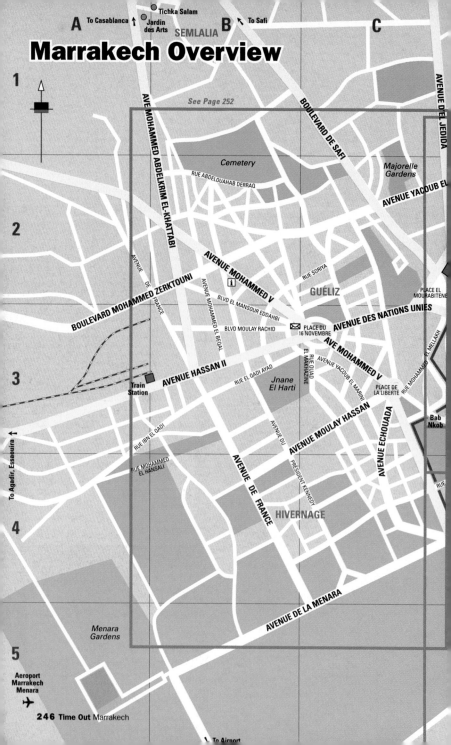

Marrakech Overview

To Casablanca ↑

Tichka Salam
Jardin des Arts

SEMLALIA

To Safi ↖

See Page 252

AVENUE MOHAMMED ABDELKRIM EL-KHATTABI

BOULEVARD DE SAFI

AVENUE DE JEDIDA

AVENUE YACOUB EL

Cemetery

RUE ABDELOUAHAB DERRAQ

Majorelle Gardens

AVENUE DE FRANCE

BOULEVARD MOHAMMED ZERKTOUNI

AVENUE MOHAMMED V

AVENUE MOHAMMED EL BEQAL

BLVD EL MANSOUR EDDAHBI

BLVD MOULAY RACHID

RUE SORIYA

GUÉLIZ

PLACE EL MOURABITENE

PLACE DU 16 NOVEMBRE

AVENUE DES NATIONS UNIES

AVE MOHAMMED V

RUE OUAD EL MAKHAZINE

RUE MOHAMMED EL MELLAKH

AVENUE HASSAN II

Train Station

RUE EL QADI AYAD

Jnane El Harti

AVENUE YACOUB EL MARINI

PLACE DE LA LIBERTÉ

Bab Nkob

To Agadir, Essaouira ↑

RUE IBN EL QADI

RUE MOHAMMED EL HANSALI

AVENUE DE FRANCE

AVENUE DU

AVENUE MOULAY HASSAN

AVENUE PRÉSIDENT KENNEDY

AVENUE ECHOUADA

RUE

HIVERNAGE

Menara Gardens

AVENUE DE LA MENARA

Aeroport Marrakech Menara ✈

To Airport

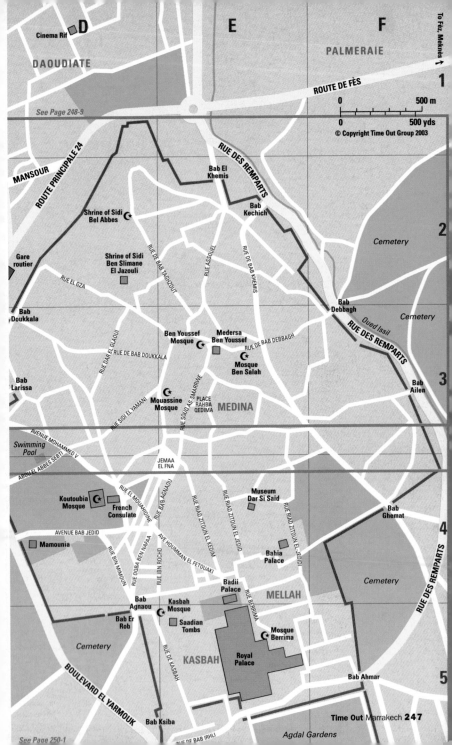

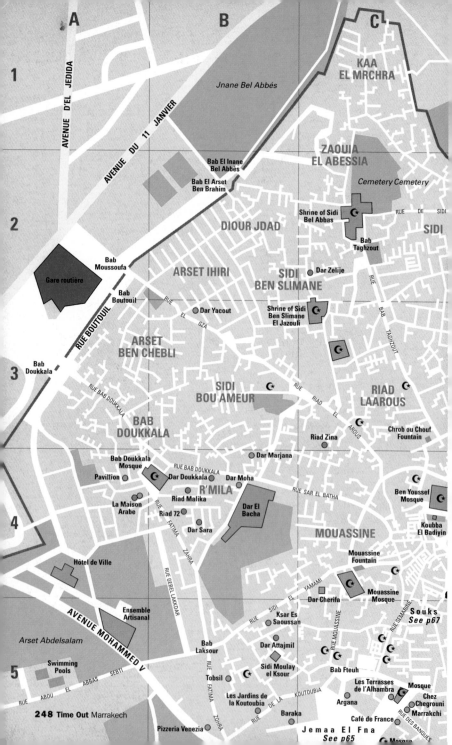

1

Jnane Bel Abbés

KAA
EL MRCHRA

AVENUE D'EL JEDIDA

AVENUE DU 11 JANVIER

Bab El Inane
Bel Abbes

Bab El Arset
Ben Brahim

ZAOUIA
EL ABESSIA

Cemetery Cemetery

Shrine of Sidi
Bel Abbas

RUE   DE   SIDI

2

DIOUR JDAD

Bab
Taghzout

SIDI

Bab
Moussoufa

ARSET IHIRI

SIDI
BEN SLIMANE

Dar Zelije

Bab
Boutouil

Dar Yacout

RUE   EL   GZA

Shrine of Sidi
Ben Slimane
El Jazouli

RUE BOUTOUIL

ARSET
BEN CHEBLI

RUE   BAB   TAGHZOUT

3

Bab
Doukkala

RUE BAB DOUKKALA

SIDI
BOU AMEUR

RUE   RIAD   EL   ARUS

RIAD
LAAROUS

BAB
DOUKKALA

Riad Zina

Chrob ou Chouf
Fountain

Dar Marjana

Bab Doukkala
Mosque

RUE BAB DOUKKALA

Dar Moha

Pavillon

Dar Doukkala

Ben Youssef
Mosque

R'MILA

RUE SAR EL BATHA

La Maison
Arabe

Riad Malika

Koubba
El Badiyin

Riad 72

Dar El
Bacha

4

RUE FATIMA

Dar Sara

MOUASSINE

Mouassine
Fountain

RUE GEBEL LAKHDAR

Hôtel de Ville

ZAHRA

Mouassine
Mosque

Ensemble
Artisanal

YAMAMI

Dar Cherifa

Souks
See p67

AVENUE MOHAMMED V

Arset Abdelsalam

RUE   SIDI   EL   YAMAMI

Ksar Es
Saoussan

RUE MOUASSINE

RUE SEMARINE

5

Swimming
Pools

Bab
Laksour

Dar Attajmil

RUE   ABOU   EL   ABBAS   SEBTI

Sidi Moulay
el Ksour

Bab Fteuh

Mosque

Tobsil

Les Terrasses
de l'Alhambra

Chez
Chegrouni
Marrakchi

RUE   FATIMA   ZOHRA

Les Jardins de
la Koutoubia

Argana

Café de France

RUE DES BANQUES

RUE DE LA KOUTOUBIA

Baraka

Pizzeria Venezia

Jemaa El Fna
See p65

Mosque

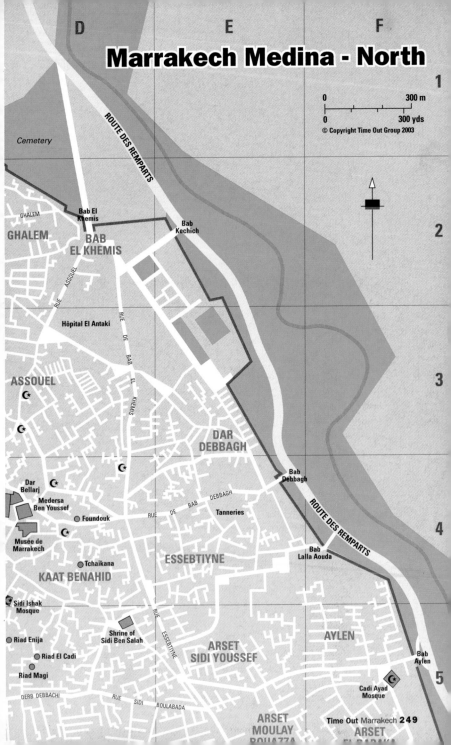

Marrakech Medina - North

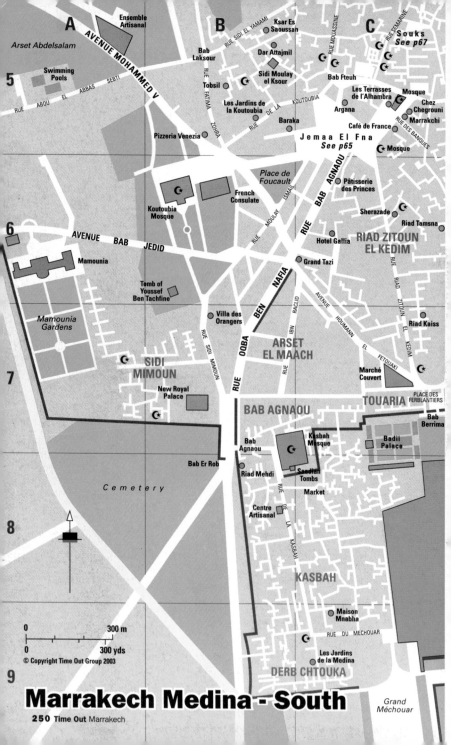